TWO CATS

AARON KITE

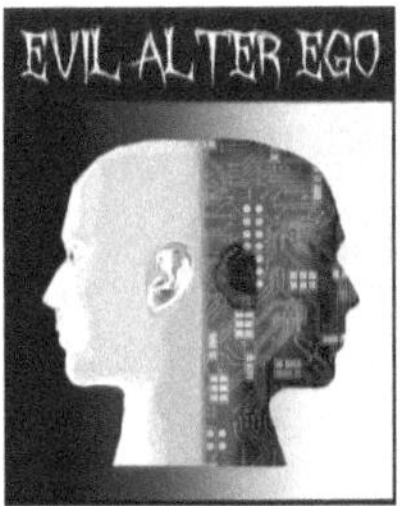

EVIL ALTER EGO PRESS

www.evilalteregopress.com

Evil Alter Ego Press

www.evilalteregopress.com

Published by Evil Alter Ego Press, 869 Citadel Drive NW, Calgary, AB T3G 4B8, Canada

Two Cats Copyright © 2019 by Aaron Kite.

Edited by Jeffrey Hite & Barbara Jacobson

Cover by Jeff Minkevics, copyright © 2019 by Jeff Minkevics.

Interior design and layout by Michell Plested.

Print version set in Cambria; titles in Cambria, byline in Cambria.

Published in Canada

Library and Archives Canada Cataloguing in Publication

Kite, Aaron, 1972-, author

Two Cats / Aaron Kite.

Electronic monograph issued in EPUB and print format.

ISBN 978-1-988361-16-1 (pbk.).
ISBN 978-1-988361-17-8 (epub).

To Mom and Dad,

who never got tired of hearing about it.

I'm blessed.

Prologue

SCARS. I SHALL talk about scars.

Well...*write* about scars, I suppose. Not "talk", as such.

Damn. I've made a mess of the first page already. This is quite a bit harder than I thought.

Whenever my father wished to "rough up a page" as he called it, he'd leap upon the very first thing he felt like talking about, moving from that subject to the story that he wished to tell. While waiting for the drying sand to mix with his freshly inked page to heat up and etch the words onto the fireproof pages of his journal, he would often attempt to teach me some small tidbit of his own writing process before beginning work on his next page.

Sometimes I listened in rapt attention. Other times, I found myself too enthralled by the wisps of gray smoke curling up from the page to hear a single word he spoke. I do recall him talking about first starting, however - that moment when you first set out to put marks on a page, when you realize you have to get over the idea of a large, white sheet of nothing just sitting there, mocking you.

I didn't quite understand what the big deal was at the time, the simple act of beginning to write. Sitting here now, in his chair, at his desk, I very quickly found myself in perfect understanding of what he tried to tell me that day. I've spent the past few hours sitting here, several candles lit to keep me energized and awake, hand poised over the first page of parchment as if about to write something, yet dramatically failing to do so.

This is the first journal I've ever undertaken to write myself, and I find so many things need to be considered. If there's one thing I've learned from reading my father's eighteen journals, as well as the multitude of others tucked away in my library, it's that you cannot assume the person who picks up your tome knows everything that you do. You need to give details, provide context for the story you're trying to tell.

Where might this book end up, after all? How much do I need to explain? Does it sit on a shelf beside dozens of other tales written by other lords, or does it stand alone? Does the person reading it have the context of the other books I've written to lean on? Or has this, the first of my memoirs, been parted from its cousins lining the bookshelves of our family library?

Is it even being read by a fellow resident of my native city, Harael, someone already familiar with our way of life and our customs? Or has it fallen into the hands of a lord from a faraway land, someone unfamiliar with Thieves' Rule or the nuances of our style of government?

As I'd stared at these once-empty pages, all of these questions seemed to pile up all at once... a hundred starving guests clamoring at the entrance to a great feast, all leaping forward at once and, in so doing, preventing anyone at all from getting in.

Rather clever metaphor, that.

The only thing I can know for certain is that this book will never be cradled in the arms of a son or daughter of my own. Sterility is one of the long-term consequences of rose blight, in addition to the patches of white scar tissue. Mine shall be the last books ever to bear the proud mark of two cats, one blue and one white, sitting protectively back to back. Vincent Tucat, the very last lord to wear the crest of my family's name, the many scars littering my body mutely testifying to that fact.

And so I begin with scars. I'm something of an expert, after all.

I read once that scars are "a violent echo of the past firmly etched upon our skin - permanent reminders of who we are and where we've been." They remind us of our shortcomings and our mistakes, of moments when the only thing that saved us was a bit of luck and some quick thinking. Like how the almost invisible white line on my left wrist reminds me to be careful when sneaking about on roof tiles, for not all roofers are expert with nail and hammer.

As such, I can seldom look at any of my blight scars without thinking back to when I was fourteen years old and rose blight was taking its toll on my young body, along with my father's, my mother's, and my sister's. Of my dozens of plague scars, there are two that stand out in my mind - the one on the back of my hand, and the one that rests upon the left side of my nose, beginning at the bridge and fanning out toward the cheek.

The blossom of blight on my nose showed up the first day signs of the disease began appearing on the four of us. I suppose the timing of it was rather fortunate, in a way. All of the servants of Tucat Keep had been given leave to attend the Harvest Festival just prior to the appearance of the disease, and were mercifully spared from infection.

In those first few days I'd catch myself staring at it in the polished metal mirror in our dining hall, attempting to assess the damage as best as I could in the dull grey reflection. I distinctly remember wishing I could buy a better mirror to see it in, like the glass ones that could be purchased just down the street from us. However, the two-year quarantine the prince himself had levied upon Tucat Keep prevented any of us from stepping foot outside our doors.

What I remember most about this particular blight sore was the maddening itch. As a family we'd spent hours in the dining hall engaged in conversation, retelling stories, or any one of a dozen things to take our minds off the physical discomfort our diseased flesh was causing us. On many occasions I'd see their fingers curled in frustration, twitching, as if trying to simulate the act of scratching. None of the others in my family suffered sores on their faces, though they all had similar blossoms in other places, and the looks of sympathy I caught from them whenever they looked at my face spoke volumes regarding just how well they understood my own pain.

In its own way, the scar that was left behind reminds me of a time when I had a family.

The scar on the back of my hand is also from rose blight, but has very different associations.

I remember I was halfway through burying my father, who had himself buried both Jillian and my mother in the weeks previous. I had shifted about half of the garden dirt back into the freshly dug hole, atop his body, and was leaning heavily against my shovel trying to catch my breath, weak and dizzy, and numb in a way that only those who suddenly find themselves orphans can truly understand or appreciate.

And I remember looking up and seeing my hand resting gently atop the pommel of the shovel, and I noticed the festering sore with its black fringed edges, tendrils of infection and dead skin lazily winding up toward my knuckles...just like the wisps of grey smoke that would snake up from the pages of my father's book as he wrote, dancing with the air currents until nothing of them remained.

It was at that moment I truly understood I'd never again see my father swish his quill across the page in his easy, looping gestures, a satisfied half smirk on his face as he recounted some aspect of his story that amused him. I'd never again see his face break into a grin as I asked him some infantile question about how to be a proper thief, or how to govern territory. He was gone. Forever. Like my mother, I realized, and my sister.

And I died inside.

Violently pierced by that simple realization the numbness had protected me from until that very moment, I simply stared at the frighteningly large sore on my hand and wept for my family that was no more.

For the sake of brevity, I'll spare you the heart-wrenching details of my recovery during the remainder of my quarantine - a total of nineteen months after the day I became an orphan, two years of complete isolation in all.

The one thing I will say about it is this - I had a lot of time to read.

Unencumbered by social interaction or any other activities befitting a child of my years, I read the entire Tucat family library. Several times. Fourteen hundred and seven books in all.

Some were written by lords who were more accountant or business manager than proper thief, others penned by lords who were legendary for things like subtle strategy, cunning wit, and master thievery. There are stories in those tomes that make me howl with laughter at the audacity of the author's plans. Other stories give advice so useful and profound that it seems a miracle that such lessons are not common knowledge. All those with ambition to become a member of the aristocracy of thieves governing the city of Harael would benefit from such study.

I read, and I learned. I had nobody to distract me, after all.

The library has since grown and, as of this writing, the collection stands at sixteen hundred and twenty-two books in total. Some books I've found more useful than others, although I've discovered that every book has its own unique value, and can sometimes be useful in quite unexpected ways.

The immaculate journals of Lord Redgraves, for instance. Each is stamped with identical glyphs of three crimson tombstones receding into a snowy background, twenty-seven books in total, and every page of every volume contains specific and detailed accounts of what Lord Redgraves had to eat that day for breakfast, lunch, and dinner, and naught else.

I had thought the entire collection without value or merit, until the keep's cook, Mosond, discovered that I was in possession of these particular books and was planning to divest myself of them. After stomping his way down to my exercise hall (and nearly dying in the process...even for all his yelling, I barely had time to disarm the booby traps in the hallway), he threatened to quit that very day if I sold them, something his indignant and disbelieving voice suggested was sheer lunacy.

Eventually, and after much thought, I informed Mosond that the entire set would remain in my library and was at his disposal, and that he or his heirs would inherit all twenty-seven books, provided that the cause of my death was not poisoning. Should I succumb to poison, I added, there were instructions for the entire collection to be destroyed.

I don't think there's a lord currently living who fears murder by poison less than I do.

Other books can be useful in much more straightforward ways. Domestic manuals, lessons on mixing this compound with that liquid to create a gooey tar, the best way to climb a wall - all manner of "how-to" documents such as these litter my collection. They're useful, and I'm glad the information they contain was written down, so that the knowledge will not be lost to the ravages of time. I'm grateful to be in possession of such knowledge, because it helps me tremendously in both operation and reputation as a thief-lord of Harael.

However, I've always found anecdotal learning to be more satisfying in many ways. More valuable somehow.

And so, as my father before me, I shall endeavor to document my knowledge through story, providing insight into how I do things through examples of what I've done. The law states that all lords must keep a journal beginning at the age of thirty so that their knowledge is not lost forever when they pass away, but simply pouring the collective sum of my technical expertise regarding governance, thievery, subtlety and political intrigue into a book and stamping the cover with my name and family crest...well, it holds no appeal for me.

No, I shall write as my father did, sitting in his chair, at his desk, accomplishing more through tales and fanciful storytelling than a dozen or more lords could accomplish with page after page of raw, uninflected facts and recipes.

It's tradition, after all, and tradition is all that remains of my family. I can sense a tenuous connection to them, feel their presence extend across the curtain of death and into the realm of the living, simply by knowing that what I do attempts to honor their memories, and that my actions follow the lessons that they were able to teach me in life.

And traditionally, as I was saying before this sudden flurry of writerly activity found my hand struggling to keep up with my thoughts, father would begin "roughing up" an empty page by leaping upon the first thing he wanted to talk about.

Scars.

Specifically, I believe I shall relate how I acquired a couple of particularly nasty *new* scars. Just recently, as a matter of fact . . .

Chapter 1

THERE'S SOMETHING POWERFULLY amusing about looking someone in the eye and making them uncomfortably aware that they're staring when they shouldn't be.

Try as they might, people can't quite help but stare at the scar bridging my nose, a drape of pale white arcing over my cheek like skeletal fingers reaching out to grab my left ear. There's nothing romantic or dashing about it - not like a sword cut stretching over one eye, or some other testimony to epic heroics. I've seen scars like that, and they're infinitely more interesting.

Mine's just...there. Big, ugly, not the slightest bit romantic. People notice it, and then they try not to.

And I notice people trying not to notice it.

Sometimes while they're staring I'll grin or cough, politely waiting for them to realize that either I've stopped talking or they have. Eventually, they snap out of their daze with a shake of their head, apologetic and begging forgiveness while looking anywhere but my face. Oft times they're so concerned about not causing offense, they actually drive themselves to distraction just to avoid...well, becoming distracted. Ironic, really.

Clearly, this was one of those special cases.

I cleared my throat gently, blinking a questioning look at the shopkeeper, who was staring at my face in rapt fascination.

He had the typical reaction, stammering his apologies instantly, eyes hurriedly trying to find something interesting about a nearby wall.

"S-sorry Milord, I was just – I don't know where my head is this morning. It's been a rough week and all, what with- . . ." He trailed off, tossing his head sharply toward the back of the shop, where several boxes of merchandise lay spilled on the floor. A large portion of his storage area there was conspicuously empty.

I didn't recognize the fellow, and he probably had never had an opportunity to meet me, his lord, either. His hair was shorn to the point where he almost had none, and those frayed bits that remained were half dark grey and half white, in a fascinatingly splotchy manner.

"Think nothing of it," I said with a dismissive wave. "You've quite obviously had your hands full, dealing with this problem. Which, of course, brings us to the whole purpose of this visit."

"Yes, Milord. I...to be honest, I hadn't thought this would go any further than a couple of your knights. 'Twas the furthest thought from my head to be bothering ye with the likes of this, and I'll confess to being truly surprised seeing you comin' in through the door, like you was taking a personal interest in my business and all, and-"

"Oh, but I do! You are, in fact, one of my favorite shopkeepers, no word of a lie!" I smiled in what I hoped was a winning manner, for I could sense the unease coming off of him like the fumes from the aromatic candles he kept lit throughout the store. The sign in his shop window claimed they were lovingly crafted by hand, a fact that also explained a great deal about his awkward demeanor.

Candlemakers were a twitchy bunch, and for good reason. When I thought about the stimulation and energy the herbs in my morning candle provided me, and then stopped to consider that candlemakers routinely inhaled a hundred times that amount over the course of a single day, I couldn't help but feel a little sorry for them.

"F-favorite, Milord?"

"Of course! I mean, let's have a look at the facts. It's been five years since you opened up shop in my territory, correct?"

"Five years, two months. Milord."

"Well done, then. So, in those five years and two months, I have yet to hear of a single case where my knights failed to secure from you the monthly tribute. We come in, first of the month, and beside the register are a ledger and a purse of coins, just waiting for my men. In truth, I wish I had a hundred more like you."

"Why, th-thank you, Milord!" he beamed, looking slightly relieved.

"'Tis the truth, and I'm more than happy to share it. Likewise, in all of that time, not once have I heard a complaint from you regarding stolen merchandise, or a request for an extension, or any of the other numerous problems that I am regaled with on a daily basis."

"I do try my best not to bother you, Milord, and the tithes I must pay ye seem very reasonable indeed. I've no cause for complaint, not at all."

"And that's exactly what I like to hear. Then, this morning I received word that you had encountered a...problem of sorts? Some merchandise going missing, some circumstances that were particularly unusual? I think to myself, 'Now, here's a good chap. He works hard, behaves himself, runs a good business and has gained a well-deserved reputation as the best candlemaker on Finnay Street. He's run into a spot of trouble, and that's unusual. I should see what I can do to help him out!' And so," I shrugged lightly and smiled casually at the shopkeeper, trying to remember his name, "I thought I might investigate these circumstances personally. You being one of my favorites, as I mentioned."

He was tense. I sighed inwardly, continuing to project peace and understanding outwardly at the slight figure. He was probably expecting some sort of setup, I realized, possibly due to some cruel arrangement with his previous lord that had firmly prejudiced him against all lords. Unfortunate, really - I hated dealing with tenants who behaved with the wariness of spooked horses.

"So, you reported to my knights regarding the stolen merchandise in question - your monthly delivery of herbs, berries, and plant essences you use for your candles and such. And furthermore, you mentioned that these materials were-"

"Unmarked, Milord. Aye, I feel so foolish admitting it, as it's not something that I'm prone to do. Usually the instant new product comes in I'm up until the wee hours of the morning, marking every piece that comes through the door, I swear. I just, it's that-" He sighed, appearing downcast and distraught, his hand disappearing into his tunic and pulling out his Tucat merchant seal. He concentrated briefly, causing the seal to glow softly in his hand, as though he wished to prove he hadn't forgotten how such things worked. "I've not been feeling all that well lately, and could hardly manage to remain upright even as they were hauling the stuff inside my shop. I don't think I could have managed branding the entire stock in one evening, Milord."

While it isn't exactly difficult to magically mark merchandise with a merchant's seal like the one I'd given him, it does require concentration and tends to eat up time. That combination of factors had likely caused this shopkeeper to put the whole exercise off until the following morning, much to his detriment. Doubtless everything had already been marked with some other shopkeeper's merchant seal by now, which made tracking down and identifying the stolen merchandise all but impossible. What's more, the thieves appeared to know exactly *when* it would be best to break in and steal what they were after, which was troubling.

The candlemaker confessing that he wasn't feeling well was troubling as well, considering the means at a candlemaker's disposal for...well, feeling better. If a candlemaker started to feel unwell when handling herbs needed for certain types of candles, they often simply switched to making candles meant to induce the opposite feeling until everything balanced out, mood-wise.

I cringed when I thought about how unhealthy that must be.

"So, if I'm understanding things correctly, you failed to mark this stolen merchandise, meaning that its theft falls outside of my responsibilities as lord of this property?" I asked.

"Yes, Milord," he said morosely, as though the words I uttered were extinguishing the last spark of hope left within him.

"This shipment of raw materials...how much did it cost, precisely?"

"Ninety-four gold and four grey marks, Milord," he answered, voice glum and ashamed. "It would have been less, but my stock of greyberries had become low."

"So, almost ninety-five gold marks then. And you'd like to be reimbursed for the money you lost on unmarked product, compensated for the cost of materials that I can scarcely hope to recover now that they are 'in the wild', so to speak?"

He barely nodded, not meeting my eye. Ninety-five gold marks was a lot of money for a shopkeeper, even one in a lucrative line of work such as candle making.

"Done," I said simply, with a carefree shrug. Then I took a few seconds to just stand there and enjoy the moment.

Gods, I love those moments.

On a regular day, ninety-five gold marks couldn't buy me the kind of comically surprised, stunned look I had produced on his face. Sometimes, such a look is worth more than all the gold marks in Prince Tenarreau's back pocket.

It soon became clear that I was going to have to be the one to resume our dialogue.

"Now then, you can't possibly have thought that I was going to come all this way down here just to disappoint you, can you? Why, as I believe I've stated, you're one of my best tenants - my *favorite* tenants - and I can hardly let something like this cause you to entertain the notion of going elsewhere, now can I?"

"M-Milord, I would never dream of going...that is, I-" he stammered.

"Quite right, quite right. And, between you and me, I couldn't bear the thought of a skilled candlemaker such as yourself no longer being available to me, either. Why, hardly a morning goes by that I don't rouse myself to wakefulness in the presence of one of your candles, no word of a lie...may I be struck down where I'm standing if I do not speak truly!"

That last bit was always a little bit dangerous, because you never knew what god might be lurking within audible range.

"I...I'm flattered, Milord. Truly, I had no idea that...I don't know what to say! I had been hoping for a temporary loan of some sort, or perhaps a discount from one of your tenants who dealt in the herb trade, but . . ." He stood there, at a loss for something to say.

"Well, I shall be asking for a favor. It is a small one, which need not concern you unduly," I said, and leaned close as if to impart a secret. I waited until he leaned in solemnly and turned his ear toward me before continuing. "Promise that we'll keep this a secret, this particular oversight. Why," I stepped backwards slightly, no longer speaking in a conspiratorial whisper, "I could hardly run my territory properly if others suspected that I didn't treat every tenant equally. Reimbursing a merchant for property he did not mark? I would be undone!"

I winked slyly at him as he nodded in agreement, still looking bewildered and amazed, likely thinking that things were going far too well.

He was right, of course. According to the law I had no obligation to him whatsoever. There were other factors influencing my decisions at that moment.

"Of course, Milord! I shall not tell another living soul!" he sputtered in grateful disbelief.

"Splendid! Now, if you would care to show me where the vandals broke in to your shop here, I shall make a few notes and see what I can make of it. I might even be able to track the scoundrels down, hey?"

"Indeed! Right this way, Milord!"

And so it went for ten minutes or so. I didn't pay that much attention, since I'd already formed a couple of theories of my own, and the stolen merchandise had likely been marked with some other lord's seal and delivered to some other candlemaker or herbalist elsewhere in the city. My main job here was to look interested and nod thoughtfully.

In the end, I handed over a small purse of coins containing enough to cover his loss and repair the damage done to his door. I spoke of the value of taking on an apprentice, and even offered to send a few potential candidates to him.

I stood and listened to his stammering thanks for a suitable amount of time, then gently reminded him of our bargain, to keep secret this great exception to the rules that I was granting him.

He'd pressed a box of his very best foxmallow tapers into my hands, insisting that I take them with me as a token of his appreciation. I inspected them. They actually weren't bad at all, mixed with greyberry to give the flame a green cast when lit. A nice touch, if green was your thing.

I put them in the sling pack I carried on my shoulder, right next to the three packets of blended pumice-kelp soap I had idly stolen off the shelves when he'd had his back to me, which I could have simply asked for, and which I needed not at all. Really though, a thief's got to stay in practice.

As I left the small, battered shop I began to whistle a random tune, cheered by how that had all gone. While it had felt quite good to give that particular shopkeeper a bit of much-needed help just then, that wasn't the sole reason I'd done it.

I'd been working hard on my reputation in the preceding months, and saw this sort of thing more and more as an opportunity, rather than a trivial annoyance to be dismissed out of hand. The plan was to bolster my tenants' opinion of me directly at the street level in the hopes of attracting more businesses to my territory, tighten things up.

It hadn't cost me all that much to help the poor fellow out, either...less than a hundred gold, all told. I also suspected that a story like the one I'd just provided the twitchy and absent-minded shopkeeper wouldn't be staying a secret for very long, promise or no. And if word of my generosity just happened to reach the ears of other merchants who were looking for a new location for their shop, well, I certainly wouldn't complain. At the very least, some of the gossip being whispered in my territory might now feature Lord Vincent Tucat swooping in and saving the day for some luckless candlemaker. Possibly they might even use descriptive adjectives like 'benevolent', or 'charming', or-

Out of the corner of my eye I noticed two adolescent males to my left stop in the middle of the street, heads turning to watch me as I passed. Though I wasn't looking at them directly, I could feel them staring at the blight scar on my face as I walked by.

I managed to keep my cheerful expression in place, though I did allow my whistle to fall into a minor key, the otherwise cheerful tune becoming a touch sad and melancholic as a result. Half a dozen steps later, the two young men disappeared from my periphery, and I allowed myself an inward sigh.

Yeah, maybe it would be nice for there to be a bit of gossip that didn't involve my scars, or speculation as to how I got them. That would certainly be a nice change.

A short while later, the next building I was due to visit came into view, and I forced a scowl onto my face. Then I bowed my head and began muttering to myself, loud enough for any passers-by to hear.

"-perfectly good space, and for what?" I snarled, taking several angry strides to the building's front door, above which hung a battered sign displaying a poorly painted bird next to a yellow circle. "Freeloading orphans! Scruffy little vagabonds with nothing better to do than sit around draining gold from my pocket, when they could be out making an honest living? Why, if it weren't for Prince Tenarreau I'd have the whole lot of them thrown into the street!"

I scowled mightily for the duration of my short walk over, and upon arriving at the entrance to the building I reached forward and pushed down on the handle. Then I pulled the wooden door wide open, giving the entire street and everyone in it a dark look before storming inside.

"All right then, *headmistress* Robinson," I announced brusquely, giving the door a gentle tug so it would begin to close. "What's the bloody matter this time, hmm? I swear, if you've dragged me all the way down here for nothing, I've-"

The door clicked itself shut behind me, and I regarded the room's only other occupant. The grin I'd been suppressing up to that point somehow managed to take over my face.

"Why, hello Abigail," I said cheerfully, giving the grey-haired woman a quick bow as I removed my gloves. "I hope the morning finds you well."

The woman was giggling silently, breathlessly, exactly the same way as she had countless times before.

"Oh, Milord Tucat," she said once she'd gotten the better of her mirth. "Sometimes I think the only reason you come down here at all is so you can put on that famous scowl of yours and play the rogue."

"Now, we both know that isn't true," I said, waggling a finger warningly at her. "I only put on performances like that one because charitable donations come much more readily if people think your lord is giving you a hard time. We both know the real reason I come down here." I sniffed, testing the air, then put on a disappointed frown. "Wait...can it be? No soup today?"

She shook her head. "Kids get bread and cheese today. Ol' Gadwall raised the price of his onions again. More 'n double! I swear, there are days where I think he waits until he sees me coming, 'cause he knows I need 'em. Charging an arm and a leg just so people can put together good, honest fare. Doesn't seem right."

"No," I said, giving her a slow, thoughtful nod. "No, it doesn't."

Indeed...I'd have to look into that later. Depriving Abigail of onions, thus preventing her from turning them into her mouth-watering soup, well, that was bad enough. However, Gadwall operated on my territory, and if this latest dramatic price increase of his wasn't reflected anywhere in his books he turned in for the month, he and I would be having a little talk soon. Shopkeepers tinkering with their bookkeeping was a common enough thing, but if they got too bold it was sometimes necessary to step in and give their attitudes a bit of an adjustment.

Speaking of attitude adjustments . . .

"So what else is new, Abigail? How are the children doing?" I asked. "Staying warm?"

"Indeed, Milord, the children should be plenty ready come winter." Her eyes twinkled a tiny bit. "And you'll never guess the reason for it. Not in a score of years!"

"Oh?" I asked, mildly. "What is it?"

"Guess!"

"Abigail, you yourself just informed me it would take a score of years to guess correctly, and I'm afraid I haven't that sort of time this morning." I gave her a patiently amused smile.

"Well, a whole bunch of thick wool blankets came in this week - enough new bedding for all the kids, and a half dozen more!" Her eyes got a bit more twinkly. "An' you'll never guess who donated them."

"Yes, we've established that. Me, guessing, 'score of years', all that." I waved for her to continue.

Looking like she were suppressing something that was half amusing, half scandalous, she held her hands up to her face briefly, and grinned.

"Shopkeeper Forvine!" she half-whispered.

I affected a look of shocked amazement.

"Forvine?" I asked, trying to sound surprised and bewildered.

The older woman nodded excitedly. "He came in the other day, pointed out that it was going to be getting colder soon, and asked if the children might find some new blankets useful. And then he brought them over himself, early yesterday morning. Warm ones. Took him several trips, too...and he said he didn't want anything for them. I could hardly believe it!" She tilted her head while shaking it. "Perhaps he's not the heartless old gaffer I pegged him for."

Actually, he kind of was. Forvine was a skinflint the likes of which I'd scarcely encountered in all my years as lord, the sort of fellow they probably had in mind when they'd invented the word 'crotchety'. I'd recently become aware of the fact that he was running a secretive off-book gambling enterprise out of the back of his store, and had suggested to him that offering blankets free of charge to the orphanage down the street would go a long way toward convincing me his momentary lapse in judgment had never happened.

His expression at the time suggested that the mere idea of helping needy children caused him considerable physical pain, which meant I'd probably have to make a point of spreading word of his generosity. There's probably nothing more annoying to a miserly shopkeeper than everyone suddenly thinking they've developed an altruistic streak.

"Well, how delightfully unexpected," I said, beaming at her. "I shall have to drop by Forvine's place later, commend him on his excellent character." I brought my gloves together in a satisfied dusting-off motion. "Well then, is there anything you need from your lord this fine morning?"

"Oh goodness, no Milord," she said, shaking her head in exactly the same way as she had the dozens of times I'd asked her before. "Things are going quite well, and I promise you we'll be caught up with the rent no later than month's end."

I drew my eyebrows together and gave her a puzzled look. "Sorry, caught up?"

"Twelve gold? From last month, Milord."

"No, that was stamped paid last week. Saw the papers myself," I said, attempting to shift my expression to one of wary suspicion without accidentally smiling. "That wasn't you?"

"It-...no Milord!" she practically gasped. "Twelve gold? I certainly would have remembered if it was me."

I shook my head and gave a low whistle. "Well, it seems your secret admirer has struck again, from the sounds of it.

And it appears he's even stepped up his game a little. You're certain you have no idea who it might be?"

"None whatsoever," she said, her cheeks coloring slightly.

"Well, I'll ask my knights again, see if any of them can remember anything about the fellow. Unfortunately for me, since I don't know who it was who actually *paid* your debt, I can't exactly give the money back. Which in turn means I can't in good conscience accept *your* money." I looked up at the ceiling and gave a long-suffering sigh. "You're certain you don't know who it is?"

She shook her head, and I did likewise before heaving one last sigh.

"Fie, I hate mysteries like these. We'll figure out who it is though, never fear," I said, idly reaching for my gloves, a gesture usually meant to indicate I was preparing to leave and considered the conversation over. Midway through donning them I paused, and frowned as if contemplating something. Then I reached into my purse with an ungloved hand and pulled out five grey marks, putting them on the kitchen counter and sliding them in Abigail's direction.

"Milord?" she asked, her confusion evident.

"Well, if a cheapskate like Forvine can see his way to donate some blankets, seems only right that I contribute something, hey?" I gestured with my chin at the coins. "Get yourself some onions. Next time I come down here I want to be greeted by the delicious aroma of your onion soup. Why, as it is, this morning's lack of it has left me feeling positively cheated!"

I gave her an easy smile and a quick wink, then turned and made my way to the door. My hand was practically on the handle when I froze in place, holding myself like that for a good five-count before turning my head slowly to the left.

A bedraggled young boy with black tousled hair had appeared at the bottom of the stairs, and was sitting on the bottommost step, elbows on his knees, cheeks resting atop his palms. We locked stares for a moment, neither of us moving.

"Say, aren't you one of those ghastly little street urchins I've been hearing about lately?" I asked.

"Who wants to know?" the boy replied in a brazenly impudent tone.

I favored him with an arrogant sneer. "Do you not recognize me?"

The boy's head came up out of his hands, and his eyes narrowed.

"Hey, are you Lord Tucat?"

I nodded, bowing slightly. "And you are?"

He opened his mouth to say something, then appeared to think better of it. He frowned, looked slightly panicked, and after a moment's hesitation he asked, "What are you doing here?"

"Am I not free to wander about my territory as I please?"

"Are you?"

"What do you think?"

He paused briefly. "So this place kind of belongs to you?"

"Exactly right."

There was a pause, and the boy's face practically lit up.

"Ha...statement!" he announced, pointing at me excitedly.

I gave a loud groan and made a face as I reached into my purse for a second time, pulling out a single grey mark and inspecting it briefly before tossing it into the space between us. The soft ringing sound lasted for a mere half second before the coin was snatched out of the air by a small, eager hand.

"Damn. How is it I can never seem to win a simple game of questions against you, Tad?" I muttered. "How many wins in a row does that make?"

"Nine, Milord!" he beamed.

Grinning, I gave him a look nearly identical to the one he'd given me a moment ago, and I held out my hand expectantly, palm-up between us.

"Statement," I said brightly.

The boy's smile fell away, quickly replaced by an expression of panic. He considered me for a moment or two, and then, barely able to keep the cheeky grin off his face, he turned and bolted up the stairs, screaming *"Aaaaaaaaaaah!"* in the manner of small children everywhere.

"What the-...I've been robbed!" I cried up the stairs after him, stifling a laugh. "That's my money! I won it back fair and square! Get back here, you tiny scoundrel!"

The fading high-pitched cry transformed itself into something resembling laughter, and a door somewhere above me slammed shut. I smiled, and turned around to face the beaming headmistress.

"He'll share with the others?" I asked.

"Always does," she agreed. "Even with the new ones. He's a good kid, that one." She gave me a warm, appraising look. "You know, you'd make a wonderful father, Milord."

Her words seemed to reach inside of my chest and pull all of the air out.

My smile got a touch larger out of reflex, despite the fact that I felt a little like I'd just been punched in the gut.

She didn't remember. Or, maybe I'd never actually told her and she simply hadn't known. It wasn't like I brought up my scars and subsequent inability to have a family in everyday conversation, after all.

Or perhaps she was simply doing what she did best - advocating for the children, doing her level best to find situations for them. Likely she might consider me a potential candidate, and had no idea what sort of chum-filled shark pool she'd be tossing some poor luckless orphan into as a result. Either way, it wasn't her fault.

My head knew this. My heart's always been a little slower on the uptake . . .

I put all my upset, prickly feelings aside and took a slow, calming breath before beaming at her.

"Why, I'm flattered that you might think so, Abigail. And believe me, if the problems surrounding adoption and lordship weren't so Baal-be-damned complex, and if it didn't practically *ensure* a miserable childhood, I'd have snatched up young master Tad many months ago." I sent her a quick nod and a smile, tipped the brim of an imaginary hat in her direction as I walked over to the front entrance, suddenly keen to be somewhere else. "Must be off...I just wanted to stop by to ensure you didn't need for anything. See you next week, headmistress Robinson? With some soup at the ready, I hope?"

"Until then, Milord," she said, beaming happily.

Resting my hand on the door handle, I looked over at Abigail and put on a ferocious scowl, then pulled it the door wide open.

"-or so help me, you and all of these unwashed little miscreants will have to find a new home by month's end!" I practically shouted, giving the headmistress a quick wink before stepping outside and closing the door shut behind me. I knew from experience that if I dawdled long enough to hear her begin to giggle I wouldn't be able to hold on to my annoyed expression.

I walked out into the street and turned right. Once I figured it was safe to do so, I abandoned my scowl. Most of it, anyway.

Hmm. It seemed that lately I'd become unusually sensitive to things like people bringing up family, or even my scars. That, or perhaps people were bringing up things like that more often around me and I'd just now noticed. Definitely worth pondering later, I decided. I dislike it when my emotional state leaves me open to things like manipulation.

My stomach growled, which made me realize I should start to head back to my keep if I was going to make it in time for whatever extraordinary lunch Mosond had prepared for me that day. I dared not miss a single one of his creations, or arrive at the table without sufficient hunger. His sulks were legendary, and could last for weeks.

I adjusted my route slightly and reviewed the things I'd taken care of so far. The morning had gone tolerably well, and I'd already accomplished most of what I'd set out to do. I'd even managed to drop another hint to Abigail regarding the existence of her secret admirer, though it had been me who had forgiven the twelve gold marks she owed rather than the soft-spoken shopkeeper next door who wished to court her.

Perhaps she'd begin picking up some of the shy, tentative signals her neighbor had been sending her as of late.

"Tucat!" I heard a boisterous, familiar, and unfriendly voice boom across the street at me.

Speaking of neighbors...

"Haundsing," I remarked dryly, watching as the large and imposing figure crossed the street toward me, his huge strides making short work of the journey. The two house knights on either side of him, scarlet cloaks adorned with the glyph of a howling wolf over the left shoulder, found themselves running awkwardly just to keep up. I quickly stifled a grin at his exasperated expression, and waited until the assorted fellows were close enough to see me rolling my eyes before doing so.

He stopped and stood in silence not two feet away. Lord Theodore Haundsing had a well-trimmed beard and a very prominent chin, a combination that made me think of horse brushes for whatever reason just then. He bristled.

Both knights, earnest looking young men, took their cues from their lord and tried to bristle as well. They were pretty good, too. I swear, one of them actually seethed at me.

When enough time had passed that everyone involved had begun to feel awkward, I broke the silent stalemate.

"Uhm...Yeess?" I have this way of making the word "yes" about five times longer than it ought to be. I find that it annoys people.

Theodore certainly appeared to be annoyed.

"You know perfectly well why I'm vexed with you, Lord Tucat," he spat, becoming...bristlier? "And yet, here I find you, walking down the street just as...as-" he stopped mid-sentence, trying to think of the appropriate thing to say.

"Natural as you please? Bold as a courtier in the kitchen? Cursed words, they can be so difficult sometimes, neh? Hang on, I might be able to help," I said, innocently pretending to consider the matter.

He growled at me, gleaming white teeth hard to ignore. I smiled back at him.

"Wait, I think I may have it!" I said, snapping my fingers as though struck by sudden realization. "You meant 'walking down the street' just as your *mother* does, right? Or...no, wait!" I affected a look of surprised dismay. "This street is nowhere near a brothel."

One of the young knights made a motion as if he was about to draw his sword, managing to stop himself just in time. His eyes looked to his lord, then to me, then narrowed with anger.

It appeared that Haundsing's knights were particularly sensitive today. I smiled cheerfully at the young fellow, wondering if he would actually draw on me. It would serve him right if he did. Of the two of us, I probably had the more accurate picture of what would happen.

"I would take steps to hold my tongue in the presence of your betters, if I were you," Theodore said menacingly, "lest a sword blade split it down the middle. I've made it abundantly clear that I do not wish to see you cavorting around my subjects. And yet here I find you, in full view of their businesses, walking down the street just as carefree as...as-"

"Two things, if I may," I gently interrupted. "First of all, if we could take note of whose side of the street we're presently on? I could hardly be considered 'cavorting' with your businesses if I were unable to make out the sign at their door, could I? And secondly . . ." I pursed my lips and looked thoughtful, as if attempting to broach a difficult subject.

"Yes?" the larger man growled, impatience evident.

"Well, I've noticed in passing that whenever we meet, you use expressions like 'if I were you' time and time again. Now, I don't want to make a big deal of it, and I'd hate to cause you embarrassment, but," I pointed at my chest elegantly, "I'm beginning to sense that perhaps you wish you could actually *be* me. No shame in that, I suppose, but to be perfectly frank you'll need to work at it quite a lot. I've got to tell you that I'd never in a thousand years wear those pants you have on. Tragic, really. I know this tailor, an excellent fellow named Roderick, whose shop is right down-"

He interrupted my monologue with bared teeth, as if unable to contain his rage, stepping toward me menacingly.

"You go too far, Tucat!"

"Really?" I smiled innocently at him, "You're wearing *those* pants, and *I'm* the one going too far? Seriously, are those things even pants? Or perhaps did two peacocks simultaneously find your legs irresistibly attractive and throw themselves"-

"A word of caution, you malodorous imbecile," he interrupted. "Stop roaming about my estate! It's bad enough that fate has located your territory next to mine in the first place, but proper lords, such as myself, should not have to tolerate your scar-ridden, plague-eaten face poking around their places of business. It will stop, one way or another. Am I understood? I'll not be repeating these words to you in the future!"

"As to the last, your news comes as something of a relief, for I readily admit I was becoming rather tired of hearing those same words from you, again and again. No doubt you can use this opportunity to learn some exciting new words. Here's a new and interesting phrase," I said, idly moving my hand to belt level, palm resting against my sword pommel. I tilted my head slightly and half-squinted up at him. "It goes something like this - get the *hell* off my side of the street, or I'll provide you with an opportunity to learn what the words 'cleft in two' mean."

There was a perfect moment of stillness between all of us as he and I stared at each other. Both of his knights were close, a half-pace behind their lord, hands on their swords, practically snarling.

Just then, a small boy clutching an old gray wooden sword, presumably running from imaginary foes, spoiled the dramatic scene completely by appearing out of nowhere and barreling headfirst into the legs of Lord Haundsing.

"Oops!" the young urchin began, looking up. "Sorry mister, I...*holy geeze!*"

Awed by the unexpected presence of his towering lord, the boy quickly turned and fled the way he had come.

My experience is that you cannot maintain dramatic tension after something like that. You can try, but you just end up wanting to giggle.

"Boys," Theodore said, voice clinging to whatever shreds of menace were still possible. "Back to the Keep. I've said my piece, and I trust Lord Tucat understands me. Let's go."

I watched the three men cross the street and disappear down a side road a few moments later, the two young knights turning back to level angry glances at me periodically as they walked. I waved, smiling cheerfully.

Interesting.

I tossed the rather fancy dagger I'd lifted from the shorter of the two knights into my bag, then hurriedly walked back to my keep, taking a quicker route than I'd planned and arriving earlier than I'd expected. I did remember to nod briefly to both guards at the gate, and a dozen steps later I'd crossed the threshold and entered my home.

Talia heard me arrive, head turning toward me in a motion that seemed unconsciously designed to maximize the impact of her thick golden curls. My keepmistress was one of those women who seemed to do everything in a manner capable of catching an appreciative eye and holding it. "Lovely" didn't even begin to describe her.

She smiled upon seeing me. It was the kind of smile that could make you forget what you were about to say or what day it was, stun you mid-sentence and leave you looking like a buffoon. Gods know that if I could properly capture that smile with paint and canvas, I'd be lauded a genius among artists.

Her eyes seemed to light up a little whenever she greeted me lately, though I'm pretty certain that was just my imagination. Or wishful thinking. Or both . . .

"Talia?" I said, rolling the sling sack off my shoulder and lowering it to the lovingly tiled marble floor, pausing only to retrieve the dagger I'd stolen from Haundsing's knight. "I know I said I'd take lunch in the dining hall, but could you please send my apologies and tell Mosond that I'll be taking lunch in the exercise hall again?"

"Aye, Milord," she said grudgingly, making a face that suggested she'd rather have been given the task of pounding one of her fingers wafer thin with a steak mallet.

Hey, if it were easy, *I* would have done it.

"Thank you, Talia," I said, dropping my gloves and cloak on a nearby chair, confident they would be looked after in short order. "How's Cyrus?"

"Your Knight-captain is currently looking into that trash fire that damaged that shop by Two-flag and Panag street, Milord," she said.

"When he gets back could you please pass along a small message for me? Tell him that I suspect that the candlemaker he brought to my attention may have been robbed by his suppliers, or whoever made the delivery. He works alone, and opportunistic thieves would probably consider him a fairly soft target. Maybe suggest that a couple of his knights look into who made the delivery."

"I will inform him as soon as I next see him, Milord."

"Very good. And how are you today, Talia?"

"Things about the keep have gone smoothly all morning, Milord."

I tried not to sigh. No matter how often I tried to put Talia at ease around me, it seemed I was always 'Milord'.

"I see. Any meetings scheduled for the next few hours?"

"Two, Milord. Shopkeeper Woodrain indicated he'd be dropping by at precisely two bells this afternoon."

"Likely he wants to whine about the condition of the street in front of his shop again. I've told him twice now that that much recobbling will have to wait until spring. The man's got a hearing problem - if you would be so kind as to blow him off for me, I would appreciate it. The second?"

"That one tenant of Lord Bloodmane's is here, Milord. He's the shoe cobbler, the one who wishes to move to Yellow Shoal."

"Well, since Cyrus isn't here, tell Janviel to meet with him...he's been getting good at handling those," I said, quickly shuffling through the collection of letters and papers sitting on the nearby writing table, inspecting each. There were a few petitions, requests for extensions, and a formal invitation to what promised to be a devastatingly boring banquet scheduled for that evening.

What caught my attention, however, was the slightly oversized envelope near the bottom of the pile. It bore no color or decoration, its only feature of note being the blob of crimson wax on the reverse side that bore no family crest or impression of any sort.

I held the unmarked envelope up for Talia to see. "And this is from-?"

"I do not know, Milord," Talia said, pursing her lips slightly. "It was delivered shortly after you'd left this morning, and the courier would not provide me with any details." She looked slightly troubled before continuing. "He wore a mask, Milord."

I gave her a skeptical look. "Seriously? I mean, I know some lords have taken to that sort of thing lately, but a masked *courier?*"

"Yes, Milord."

"Well, that's certainly different." I turned the envelope over and inspected it further. "The courier left no message with it? Nothing at all?"

"No, Milord."

I frowned slightly, then gave her a quick nod of thanks and a smile. Talia bobbed her head in return before turning in place and proceeding toward the hallway leading to the kitchen. Likely she'd be informing Mosond of my wishes regarding lunch, which would probably result in him yelling for at least a few minutes.

Holding the unmarked letter in one hand, I idly flipped the dagger I'd recently stolen in my other and walked briskly through the well-lit foyer, past the painted mural of the family crest, down the hallways I usually used to get to the main hall, past the doors leading to the stairway, and all the way to the rear of the keep, near the garden entrance. There, I saw a familiar crouched figure tending to a rose bush.

"Hello Danica. How fares the garden today?" I asked.

"Milord," the figure said noncommittally, not bothering to look up from her work or acknowledge me in any way.

"Did the new bushes bloom to your satisfaction?"

She shrugged.

"Hmm. Looks like we've got some lovely weather in store for us this afternoon. What do you think?"

"Milord," she replied, her tone indicating reluctant agreement.

"Excellent. Well, carry on," I said, grinning to myself as I walked past her toward the shadowy hallway on my right.

'Milord' was the only word Danica had ever spoken aloud to me since joining my employ some two years ago. It had annoyed me a bit at first, but I've since come to regard the whole situation as a bit of a challenge. Honestly, I was beginning to suspect that if one of these days she *did* say something besides 'Milord' to me, I wouldn't have the faintest clue how to respond.

Once at the end of the narrow hallway, I turned and went down the stairs to the wine cellar, then down an inconspicuous hallway. After a few hops over the pressure plates and other cleverly hidden booby-traps I'd installed in this passageway, I arrived at the large wooden door guarding my exercise hall.

Unlocking the bolts required both the twist of a special key and the presence of my family seal pressed up against an engraved spot near the center of the door. Once that was done, I pressed my thumb against a light grey square near one of the hinges and waited. I felt the tiniest of buzzing vibrations across my skin, followed by a second clicking noise, which came from the truly impressive-looking lock on the front of the door. This was followed by a click-clack sound, which was in turn followed by the door swinging itself slowly open.

I tucked the envelope I held inside my vest and walked in, noting that the lamps and torches were still glowing softly, the familiar heady scent of vimroot and the slightly musty smell of rock welcoming me. It is the largest room in my keep, having originally been intended as a banquet hall.

Lacking the finery that once adorned them, the walls were simply a vast expanse of grey rock and wooden partitions - large climbing frames and scaffolds that held up planks and formed small ledges. The wall to the right contained all of my fencing gear and sword apparel, fencing gloves, practice coat and the like. A long, narrow fencing run occupied the center of the room, and a larger dueling circle was set into the stone floor, encompassing it. To my left was a plain wall, which was bare and uninteresting most of the time.

At the present moment, however, it harbored countless dark shadows, and a particularly large inky void off in the corner, away from the torches. It was from this dark corner that I first spied movement.

A tall, familiar figure strode into the light of the torches. Extremely familiar, this figure. After all, it's hard to forget someone you've only just been accosted by in the streets.

Lord Theodore Haundsing now stood before me, alone, torchlight catching the bejeweled pommels of the twin longswords that hung from his belt, an easy and confident look upon his face.

The door clicked closed behind me, and I heard the numerous bolts lock themselves into place, the heavy clacks bouncing off the walls with a musty sort of echoing quality.

"Well now. I'll bet you thought I was joking," he chuckled, his short beard unable to hide his expression of amused contempt, "didn't you, Vincent?"

Chapter 2

"JOKING, THEO? ABOUT what, exactly?" I furrowed my brow at him in a puzzled manner, and then gestured behind me. "Wine?"

"Please," he nodded, stepping lightly across the stone and wood floor nearly as swiftly as he had crossed the street earlier, but much more calmly.

I retrieved a bottle of red wine and two glasses from the small table that was recessed into the wall beside the door, extracting the cork from the bottle's neck and pouring two half-full glasses of the room-temperature liquid. Upon finishing, I re-corked the bottle and placed it back upon the table, holding one of the glasses out to my visitor.

Theo inspected his glass and raised an eyebrow. "Red? Really?"

"It's a nice *Tapiche* that's been growing on me lately. So - joking?"

"I beat you; back to my own keep and down through the tunnels faster than you could walk straight here. I told you I would, last week, and you said I was crazy." He grinned, rubbing his chin. "I swear, I should have put money on it."

"Oh, had there been money involved, I can guarantee there would have been a different outcome," I smiled. "You might have found the hidden door a little more difficult to open. Good work, though. Are you still running?"

He nodded. "Lost nearly eight pounds, too. I still have my doubts about my ability to 'cat burgle' as you call it, but I'll give it an honest shot. Any resulting failure will not be because of how much I weigh, I guarantee you that much."

"Trust me, my friend," I said, "you'll see. I don't maintain this toothpick-like build for the sake of fashion, you know."

"One thing I've always wondered is how you're able to maintain that weight while employing one of the greatest cooks in all of Harael."

"Bah, I can't be telling you all my secrets, can I? Oh, and by the way...one of your boys must have dropped this," I casually tossed him the dagger I held.

He snatched it out of the air with practiced ease, inspecting it briefly before rolling his eyes.

"Show-off. I was watching, too. When did you manage to grab it?"

"About the same time that adorable little child with the sword pretended to accidentally plow into you so he could steal this," I said, tossing Theo's purse of coins back to him as casually as I had the dagger. "I managed to nick it from the rascal as he was bolting away."

Theo muttered several dark curses under his breath, shaking his head slightly as he caught his money pouch and tucked it away. I chuckled.

"So, our encounter in the streets...you mentioned my scars, you insensitive brute!" I chuckled. "You've caught wind of something that requires my attention, I take it?"

"As to that," he said, frowning in a manner I recognized. "Is it really necessary that we keep doing this sort of thing?"

"You know how useful it can be, Theo. If our hostility toward each other is well known, it loosens the lips of fellow lords who might be plotting against one of us, give us a leg up on them."

"Yeah, but do we really need to use your plague scars as part of our 'secret code'? I feel like a complete horse's ass every time the words come out of my mouth. It's not something I'd ever intentionally comment on in public."

"Well, we must appear to truly hate each other for the subterfuge to work. In fact, it becomes even more credible when the statements are out of character for you."

"Yes, I can understand that, but"-

"Theo, we are almost brothers. Acting like we hate each other will obviously have moments of awkwardness. Do you think that it's any easier for me to speak disparagingly about your mother - the woman who took me in to your family's house as if I were her own?" I said, gently. "We both know the truth, and that's what matters...not these terrible things we say."

"I suppose. Speaking of terrible...are my pants truly as awful as you said?"

In truth, they fascinated me to no end, as I'd never been simultaneously blinded and horrified before.

"Well, Theo...we've known each other fourteen years, and I'm not going to lie to you."

I took a sip of my wine, watching as he waited expectantly for me to continue.

"Yes? And?"

I pressed my lips into a smile, saying nothing. Soon he was grinning back at me.

"Ass," he chuckled. "Still, I know more than most about what you went through, and I do hate having to say those things."

Despite my best friend's gruff appearance, impressive physical stature, and ferocious reputation as a duelist, he is actually one of the most sensitive souls I've ever known. Evidently, he couldn't even remark upon my disfigurement in jest without feeling like a louse.

"Hmm. A point," I conceded. "Maybe we'll revisit the code one of these days, neh? Come up with some other signal that we need to talk. Perhaps you can make fun of my hair, or some such thing instead. So, what have you heard? I'm assuming it's important."

He walked with his goblet over to a nearby leather chair and sat down heavily. I followed him after retrieving the wine bottle from the bar, setting it down on the table between us and taking my usual seat.

"You," he said, pausing for another small sip from his cup, "have upset someone."

Several seconds passed in silence.

"Wow," I said sarcastically.

He nodded gravely.

"Uh, would it be impolite to mention that I've heard soothsayers give advice that was less vague?"

He chuckled. "Shall I elaborate, then?"

"Please do."

Theodore gave a grand and expressive sigh as he sat back on the couch, looking up as though attempting to remember something. There were times, like now, when it was obvious that my friend took a great deal of pleasure in knowing something that I had yet to learn.

"Yesterday evening I received a letter requesting that I make myself available the second hour after dusk, in order that I might engage in conversation. Once there, I met a rather theatrical fellow in a mask who . . ." he paused artfully and ensured he had my full attention, "tactfully suggested that it would be most helpful if I were to avoid, for the next three days, anything that might cause you concern or otherwise lead you to boost the defenses inside your keep."

Mask.

My thoughts went to the unopened letter I'd brought down with me.

"That's...actually quite interesting," I said.

"Exactly. So, being the master of subtleness and diplomacy that I am," he said, his voice becoming ironic, "I bluntly told him that he was crazy, and warned that if he presumed to declare formal war against you before I had a chance to, he'd have to climb over my lifeless corpse. I think I may have threatened to cut out his liver at some point."

"Subtle."

"Yeah, I thought it was quite tactful and clever, myself," he said cheerily.

Hmm. Theo's news, the nonsense with the masks, and the many gentle, testing thefts in my territory I'd noticed lately, seemed to suggest the same thing - one of my neighbors wished to steal from me, likely in order to initiate a territory war.

My stomach went a little icy to consider it. The two minor territory skirmishes I'd been involved in so far had both played out favorably for me, but I had instigated both of those myself, and had chosen times when it was advantageous to do so.

I'd lost a lot of sleep during those months, though. I groaned inwardly.

There was something in Theo's half-smile that told me he wasn't quite done yet, and still knew something that I didn't.

"You don't think it's the start of a war, though," I ventured, voicing the question as a statement.

"No, they just want to steal from you and make you look silly, I'm guessing. From what I was able to gather, the lord who wants me to kick my feet up by the fire for a few days does not actually border your territory, and thus is quite incapable of starting a legal war. In fact, I was encouraged by this fellow to begin thinking about my own territory war against you, considering the opportunity that might be coming up."

I nodded. "So – a masked stranger working for an unidentified lord told you to rest assured that he was not planning on starting a war with your neighbor? Why, that doesn't sound suspicious at all . . ."

"Come on, Vince! If one of the other lords on your border wanted to start a formal war, they surely wouldn't come to me for permission, or do something silly like warn me first. They'd simply do it. This has all of the markings of something smaller, I would think."

I had a sudden thought, and felt a stab of concern.

"Theo, what if the target is actually you? What if the whole point of this is not to keep my schedule exactly the same, but to change your schedule instead?"

He sat still, momentarily taken aback, and then appeared to consider. After a few moments, he smiled and shook his head, turning back to me with a grin.

"Nope!" he said. "There are three reasons why I don't believe I'm the target."

"And they are?"

"First, I was invited to attend a banquet this Son's Day, the sole purpose of which is to bear witness to your abject humiliation."

"Somewhat irrelevant, since the victim of token embarrassing thefts is always invited to such gatherings."

"Right. Errr...okay, then, there are two reasons. Although," he considered thoughtfully, "the fellow I was speaking to seemed quite excited at the prospect of embarrassing you, so I think my first is still valid. Anyway, next we talked about some of my properties – they wanted me to stamp a permit they could bring to some of the shops facing your territory, nearest your keep. They all seemed like pretty good staging areas if they planned to pay you a visit."

"You didn't give them a permit, did you?"

"Hmm, let's see. Did I give a permit bearing my personal seal to a man who wore a mask and failed to identify the lord he was working for?" Theodore snorted, draining the remainder of his goblet and holding it out for me to fill. "I'm not a complete moron, you know."

"I never thought it for a moment, my friend," I said, quietly relieved. I focused on pouring another half-glass of wine into his cup.

"I told him that he could bloody well tell me which buildings he wanted to use, at which point I would take it up with the tenant personally. I figured that was more in character for me anyway, plus I could find out where, roughly when, stuff like that. They already said the time will be the day after tomorrow, from sunset until two hours past midnight, and they're supposed to tell me once they've scoped out the place, confirmed that it'll suit their purposes."

"You got the time from them, to within a few hours? This is unbelievable! Are they complete amateurs?"

"Could be, could be...although I'd like to think that my insightful prying and astounding interrogation techniques may have played a role in recovering this information. Still, Vince, you and I both know that amateurs can be just as dangerous, especially since they don't know the rules they're supposed to play by."

"Agreed. Well, I suppose you've got a point, Theo. Now, you said this lord you met with wore a mask?"

"I did."

"This can't be coincidence," I said, reaching inside my vest to pull out the letter I'd retrieved from the writing table earlier. I held it up briefly for Theo to see. "This arrived just this morning. Reportedly, the courier who delivered it was wearing a mask as well."

"I've seen a few lords wandering around wearing them lately. Still, a courier?" Theo snorted. "Well, I'd say this is either a tremendous coincidence, or that letter definitely has something to do with the matter at hand." He frowned, then shrugged one shoulder. "Or, perhaps we're witnessing the birth of a rather unfortunate new fashion trend."

I chuckled, cracking the envelope's wax seal in half and then opening it. After a small amount of effort and some tearing, I discovered that the envelope held a single piece of cream-colored parchment that had been folded inexpertly in half. The paper itself was of good enough quality that the carelessness with which it had been folded seemed wrong somehow. Perhaps it was a calculated effect, like when a lord bought frightfully expensive boots for the sole purpose of mucking around in them.

The folded parchment slid free of its envelope with very little effort, and unfolding it revealed a collection of words written in a hand that was unfamiliar to me. Holding the paper about chest height, I began to read.

By the time I finished reading the contents of the note I was very angry...angrier than I'd been in a long, long time. I quickly re-read the note to confirm exactly what it was I was looking at, just to be sure. Then I got even angrier.

My heart was thumping hard enough for me to notice.

"Vince?" Theo asked, his voice full of wary concern. I realized that this wasn't the first time he'd spoken my name since I'd opened the note.

Looking up from the parchment I held, I locked eyes with Theo, who had leaned forward in his seat and was now wearing a look of concern that matched his voice. I looked back down at the paper and felt the left side of my upper lip curl.

"Theo," I said with a shake of my head, leaning forward and tossing the note face-up onto the table between us. I sat back in my chair, tented my fingers, and exhaled through my nose before continuing. "I believe it is safe to say that I am extremely pissed off right at this moment."

Looking puzzled, Theo reached out and retrieved the note from the table, holding it carefully in front of him as he read it out loud.

"Day forty-six, Year seven Tenarreau. Quarantine continues to hold, four souls in total. I've arranged temporary billeting for servants, with property concerns being forwarded to magistrate Lasche. Additional anecdotal evidence now suggests deliberate infection was not merely possible, but likely. I can hand this off to South, but will continue work here in the meantime. Please advise." He frowned at the letter, turning it over once before staring at the words, peering closer at the note. "Well, this does look pretty old, and it's not signed except for this letter 'A', but...hold on-"

"Aleksandra," I said, nodding grimly. "I believe that was the first name of Preceptor Cheyne, the former West Preceptor of Harael."

"The one who...and this is dated-" Theo began.

"A few days after I and my family became sick, yes."

Theo ran the fingers of his free hand through his short beard and stared hard at the note before speaking again. I used the opportunity to practice breathing, and calmed myself marginally.

"Am I reading this right, Vince?" he asked.

"Well, I suppose that would depend entirely on what you think it means."

"Deliberate infection," he said, pointing to the topmost portion of the letter. "If this is about you, it's essentially saying you and your family were targeted...that the rose blight outbreak at your keep was-"

"A calculated act of murder. That's definitely what it's implying, so yes...I believe you are reading that correctly."

There was a goodly amount of silence. Theo considered me gravely.

"Are you okay, Vincent?"

"Oh, no." I smiled. "No, not at all. Did I not mention how unbelievably pissed off I am at the moment?"

"So...you think this is real?" he asked, indicating the letter with a bob of his head.

I snorted. "Of *course* it's not real, Theo. You're asked to a meet with a masked lord who has a keen interest in me the *very same day* that an anonymous masked courier drops off an unmarked envelope with something like this inside? The timing is utterly *ridiculous.* That letter is just part of whatever it is we've stumbled onto, meant to occupy my thoughts or otherwise distract me from what is really going on."

My friend gave me a puzzled frown. "Well then, why-"

"Why am I so pissed off?" I asked, my voice both catching slightly and increasing in volume. "Oh, I don't know...perhaps because someone thought *this* was a *good idea?* Somebody out there figured that bringing up my family like this, all for the sake of *distracting* me for a time, was the perfect plan!" I struck the padded leather armrest of my chair with a snarl. "Hey, this guy's family died when he was a boy...you know what'd be fun? Let's make him wonder if they were *murdered* for a while, just so we can keep him preoccupied!"

"Hmm," said Theo after a while. "I suppose someone wanted to make it personal."

"Yeah," I agreed, reaching out and picking up my glass of wine from the table. "And I'd say they succeeded admirably. Whether or not they will still consider it a *good* idea once I find out who this bastard actually is, remains to be seen. However, you've definitely convinced me - it does look like I'm the target of this presumed robbery. Fie," I muttered, cursing under my breath. "At least I have some idea when they'll be attempting it, so I can try to be prepared and catch them in the act. If they're as amateurish as they sound, it may not be too terribly difficult to do, but still, not the best news I've heard. My whole week is ruined. And I was just beginning to catch up on my sleep, too."

I glanced at Theodore. He was wearing that smug *there's-something-you-don't-know-yet* look again.

"There's more?" I asked, incredulous.

He nodded, seeming very satisfied with himself. "Saved the best for last, I did. Wanted to hear you whine about losing sleep before sharing it. Third reason I had for not thinking it's me being set up. Or, uh, second. Whatever. Anyway, I managed to discover precisely what they might be up to, and I don't think they meant to let me know."

"Oh?" I said, waiting for him to continue.

"Well, yes. I was going on and on with this fellow about how difficult this was going to make my life, you being my sworn enemy and all. I began ranting about how you'd probably increase security afterwards making it harder to spy on you, saying he'd better not be after certain things you already knew I wanted to steal from you because you'd blame me for it, and-" He took a deep breath and let it all out at once. "Well, you get the idea. Eventually, perhaps just to shut me up, he told me the thing they were after didn't actually belong to you. And he implied I could forget my concerns about your security because you were likely to find yourself extremely busy with other things soon."

"What they're after doesn't belong to me?"

"That's what he said. I realize that's not the greatest clue regarding what they *are* after, but I figure if we look at all of the things you've stolen in the past little while, or...hey, could he have been talking about one of your books? I didn't think so at first, but then I started- "

"I think I know exactly what they're after," I said.

"You...oh. Okay." Theo leaned back into the couch. "Care to shed some light on the matter for those of us in the cheap seats?"

I put my glass of wine down, stood up from my comfortable chair and gestured for him to do likewise. Groaning slightly, he stood and followed me over to the nearest corner of the exercise studio, which had a tiny half-room recessed into it.

Smelling heavily of oils and other fragrances, it contained a simple easel, two large tables covered with paints and wooden stretchers, and a chair. Beside the easel was a plinth elegantly draped in cloth, and atop the cloth sat a metal goblet, a wine bottle, and a large bowl containing various fruits as well as a pear in the latter stages of decay. On the easel was an unfinished painting that represented the objects in the bowl, back when things had been going far, far better for the pear.

"Nice," Theo said upon viewing the painting. "Is it new?"

"Well, 'new' in the sense that it's my most recent work, but not 'new' in the whole sense that it's been sitting here for, well . . ." I shrugged and gestured at the pear.

"I see. It's good, though. I'm liking it so far."

"As am I." I pointed directly at the goblet. "Know what that is?"

"A still life model? A wine glass? Some opportunity for you to dramatically bring up the point you're about to make?"

"It is," I said, grinning at his wit despite myself, "one of two wine glasses that once belonged to Prince Galli Copperfen over two hundred years ago."

Theodore let out an appreciative whistle. "Wow. Hey, you mean that is-"

"Yes," I said, "one of the famous 'poisoned goblets' from the story. I'd been dying to paint something with historical significance, and I figured the Copperfen goblets would satisfy that craving nicely. I have this cup on loan for a time, a small miracle that required over a year of practically begging Lord Greybridge."

"Oh. Geeze," Theo said, putting the pieces together.

In Harael, there is no better way to point out the shortcomings in another lord or lady's ability to govern than to steal from them, or otherwise cause them to become embarrassed. It's expected...encouraged, even. The whole point is to demonstrate your ability to come up with an elegant plan and execute it without flaw, utilizing all of your talents and skills as a schemer, a manager of people, and a thief. Prince Tenarreau often took contests such as these into consideration when redrawing city boundaries, ultimately deciding who lost territory, and who gained it. His decisions were announced at the yearly ceremony all lords were required to attend, which was barely one week away.

Someone wanted to use me to improve their position in life and at court, and was planning to steal something from me that would disrupt my life a great deal.

My untimely, violent death at the hands of Lord Greybridge, for instance, would almost certainly ruin all of my plans.

"Theodore, my friend," I said, "I'm beginning to suspect that I've upset someone."

Chapter 3

"MILORD, I'VE GOT the most recent of the plans you requested. Where would you like me to put them?"

I looked up at Cyrus, who was holding several rolled up sheets of vellum in his arms. Some were older than others, making the white of the newer ones stand out even more against his black jerkin and black slacks.

The only color my captain ever seemed to wear was contained in the blue and white Tucat crest on the high left shoulder of his three-quarter cloak, and even that would disappear in a swirl of black if he tossed the front-most piece behind his shoulder, a move I'd seen him make whenever he was about to draw his sword.

I gestured with my quill toward the table I was working on, which was bare except for the two vimroot candles I had lit earlier, and the papers and other items that I was concentrating on.

"Be a good man and move those candles first, will you? I'd not want to get any wax on those drawings, after all."

"Quite, Milord," he said, putting the floor plans I'd requested down on the chair beside the couch, freeing his hands so that he could move the candles closer to where I sat.

"Made any headway tracking down the origin of that forged note I gave you?" I asked.

"Not yet, Milord. Knight Brandon remembers the masked courier passing him at the gate, but could offer no helpful details. I shall look into it further, later this evening."

I gave a grunt of acknowledgment. Upon inspection, the note had turned out to be quite an accomplished forgery, and had even possessed a passable likeness of the former West Preceptor's glowing seal when I'd held it to the light of a greyberry candle. Cyrus was a better hand at spotting forgeries than I was, so perhaps he'd eventually glean some useful details from the note, such as its origination.

My attention fell back down upon the piece of parchment before me, and the hastily sketched lines I had drawn there. I stared at the drawing and attempted to picture the location it represented.

There was an apologetic clearing of the throat. I looked up.

"Ah, Cyrus, thank you. That will be all," I said, smiling at him before turning back to the floor plans I labored over.

"Milord," he nodded, not making any move to leave.

After a few moments, I realized that he wanted something. I stopped what I was doing, sighing softly, and rested my quill upon the table. Then, cursing myself for an idiot, I picked it up and put it back properly in the ink well, looking for some sort of handkerchief to clean up the ink I'd just gotten on my table.

I'm prone to get a wee bit careless about things like that when I'm deeply engrossed. In fact, sometimes my staff has to remind me to do things like eat, or sleep.

"Yes? Was there something else?" I asked, carefully wiping ink from the dark wood of the table.

"Yes, Milord. I did have a question that I was hoping to ask you."

"Well, I suppose that I might be due for a small break," I said, stretching and rolling my shoulders. "Speaking of...what time is it?"

"I believe it's just after five bells."

"Really?" I kept the surprise off my face. "Errr, did I have lunch?"

Cyrus gestured with his head at the empty plate that I had moved onto the stone floor, several crumbs covering its surface.

I believe I already mentioned what happens when I get too focused.

"Ah. Well then, ask away."

"Yes, Milord. Please don't take this amiss, but...are we preparing to move against Lord Greybridge?"

I stared until I could sense him becoming uncomfortable.

"And how, pray, did you arrive at this notion, Cyrus?"

"Begging Milord's pardon, but you did send me out earlier to retrieve the most current floor plans for eight Lords about the town. I noticed Lord Greybridge's name on the list, and when I delivered the remaining plans just now I noticed you poring over a drawing of what would appear to be Lord Greybridge's estate."

"And what is your reason for asking, exactly?"

"I . . ." he paused and looked thoughtful, as if wondering how to say something without causing offense. "I wanted to know if perhaps I should get my affairs in order, Milord."

"Well," I said blandly, "and if we were?"

"Two things I would take this opportunity to point out to you, Milord. The first is that from a tactical standpoint, considering the resources I suspect he has and comparing them against your own, I would have to say that our life expectancy does not compare favorably to that of, shall we say, a lamb that has wandered into a kebab shop."

I chuckled. "And the second?"

"Well, Milord, as head of your security, the second thing would be to point out that I'm not being paid nearly enough for this opportunity to be violently slaughtered on your behalf."

"Cyrus, you are absolutely right. If ever I ask you to die for me, I shall endeavor to provide you with a large salary increase just prior to doing so. Can't have you going to the afterlife all disgruntled about your personal worth, neh?"

"Indeed. Very considerate, Milord," he said.

"Well, fear not Captain," I said, tenting my fingers and looking at him knowingly, "we are not, in fact, making a move against Lord Greybridge."

"Thank you, Milord. I hadn't meant to intrude upon your time, but-"

"At least, not really . . ."

He paused and looked at me, waiting expectantly for me to explain what I meant. I pursed my lips and thought for a moment.

Often, I have found myself wondering if I should share more of my plans with Cyrus, given that he plays such an important part in keeping my territory running smoothly. Just as often, however, I find myself thinking of how catastrophically bad things could potentially get during one of my carefully laid plans, should someone accidentally let something slip, or share a tidbit of information they ought not to. Not every caper I'd ever put together went as planned, true...but I'd never had a plan of mine go pear-shaped because somebody else wasn't able to keep it a secret.

That's the nice thing about keeping everything to yourself - if things don't go according to plan, you know exactly who's to blame. Even if that does mean you end up blaming yourself.

"Well Cyrus," I said, "this particular endeavor I'm planning is unusual, and as such I haven't gotten all of the details worked out yet. What I can tell you is that I hope what I'm planning does not antagonize Lord Greybridge, or otherwise bring chaos and doom and metaphors involving lamb kebabs down upon us. If things go according to plan we should actually be much safer, in fact. Once everything has played out and I've achieved what I hope to, I'll share the details concerning exactly what happened with you, if you wish. Fair enough?"

"I...yes, Milord." He frowned slightly as he clicked his heels together and gave a slight bow with his head before turning to exit the room. I heard the door click closed behind him, and the familiar sound of his boots hopping over the pressure plates and trip-wires in the hallway leading away from my exercise hall.

It's not like I *didn't* trust him, after all. Aside from me, he was the only one who even knew how to get into this room. Didn't that indicate some level of trust?

There was a familiar scraping sound followed by a click that echoed from the other end of the room. A moment later Theo appeared at the secret entrance.

Well, okay...Cyrus was the only other person to know the *proper* way to get into this room.

"Theo! Just in time to help me move some of the climbing apparatus to resemble a ledge that I wish to practice climbing on. You overheard most of that, I take it?"

"Well, I did hear something about lamb kebabs. Care to share a couple?"

"Terribly sorry to disappoint you my friend, I have no idea what might be for dinner this evening. Say," I said, my voice tinged with suspicion, "how is it that you always seem to arrive at the dinner hour, or just before? I'm starting to suspect it's more than mere coincidence."

"Bah. You're crazy," he said, gesturing dismissively. "Speaking of crazy, would you care to tell me why you're combing through the building plans for Greybridge Keep? Clearly there's some sane explanation that eludes me."

"Care to take a stab at it?" I asked.

"What?"

"Come now, let's see if you can figure it out. I want to see if I'm being as subtle as I think I am. I have Lord Greybridge's keep drawn out in front of me, and it would appear as though I mean to pay him a visit. What do you suppose my plan is? Take a guess."

Theodore considered me, and then turned his attention to the piece of paper that was stretched out on the table in front of me, and the rolls of vellum on the side table.

I got up and went to the bar, pulled a dark glass bottle from the icy water of the cooler, and poured two half-glasses of the *Ak'rheus* eighty-seven I had opened earlier that afternoon. I brought the glasses back to the table and offered

Theo one, which he gladly accepted before turning his eyes back to the drawing I had made.

Odd as it may sound, I've come to rely on Theodore's talent for seeing the extremely obvious. It's actually a very useful skill, especially if your plans gets so convoluted and full of twists and turns that you're not even certain what you're trying to accomplish anymore.

I recall one time where I had laid my entire grandiose plan before him, and spent an entire hour going over it in detail. When I had finally finished describing this masterpiece of subtle cunning to him he crinkled his forehead at me and said, "Yes, but why don't you just do this instead?" He then provided me with a one sentence summary of a simple action I could take that accomplished everything my plan had been designed to do, and with none of the drawbacks.

It took me less than half an hour to pull off what he'd suggested, and it worked perfectly. None of my spectacularly complex, cunning plan ended up being used at all. I'd been absolutely deflated.

"Any ideas?" I asked eventually, sitting down in my chair and watching him study the marks before him.

"Gimme a minute," he said, taking a sip of wine. Then, he looked at the wine glass suddenly as if it surprised him. "Vince, why do you do that?"

"Hmm?" I asked, mid-drink.

"Pour just enough wine to fill the glass halfway like that. Are you afraid I'm going to spill or something?"

"Why, I thought you knew!" I said innocently. "I've always thought of myself as an optimist."

There was silence. Then, more silence. Theo closed his eyes and groaned disgustedly.

"Glass half full - you've been waiting months for me to ask that, haven't you?"

"Years, actually," I said cheerfully.

"Some days, I wonder why I even hang out with you. Okay, here's what I'm guessing you're planning to do. Are you ready?"

"Ready. Tell me what you suspect."

"Okay. You, being one of the most devious and truly strange fellows I know-" he raised his glass to me in mock salute, "are going to do the unthinkable, something no lord has ever done that I can recall, and break in to the home of Lord Greybridge . . ." he paused melodramatically, "in order to return the goblet to its rightful place before it gets stolen."

I burst out laughing, and immediately tried to rein it in so I could explain that it wasn't to mock him.

"No, no...that was excellent. Seriously, I hadn't even thought of that possibility. Oh, gods, wouldn't that be a hoot? People would think me crazy! However, I can already see a couple of snags with that plan . . ."

"Oh? Such as?" Theodore asked good-naturedly.

"Well, how would I explain its sudden reappearance to Greybridge? Given that it's one of his most prized possessions, I doubt I'd be able to convince him that his memory was playing tricks on him. Messing with him like that would probably just get me on his bad side."

"I suppose that's true, yes," he agreed.

"Additionally, there would be a much easier way to accomplish the same thing, something that you yourself would probably point out. Why not simply return the goblet to him before it gets stolen?"

"I *was* going to point that out to you, as a matter of fact. Sneaking into someone's keep to return something you've borrowed legitimately may be funny as hell, but it's not really practical for anything other than showing off your skills. Not exactly something you want to do against that fellow, in my mind."

"Indeed, and it also still leaves us with a rather troubling concern."

"And that is?"

"Well, have you forgotten that I've suddenly acquired an unknown enemy? One who is going out of their way to bring me grief? If I return the goblet before they have a chance to steal it, I've bought myself time, nothing more. I would have no idea who my enemy is, or where the next attack on my honor is likely to come from, and I couldn't count on being lucky enough for you to be engaged a second time by the same plotters. Plus," I said, smoothing my shirt sleeve with one hand while giving him a tight-lipped smile, "after that crap they pulled sending me that note earlier, I find that my primary interest is in learning the identity of this would-be thief, not simply preventing the theft from happening."

"Ah, very true. So," he shrugged, "I give up. If you're not doing that, what exactly are you doing?"

"Why, I'll be doing the very opposite. I'm breaking into Greybridge Keep so that I can steal the other goblet, obviously."

There was a very long stretch of silence.

"Obviously," Theodore said, dubiously.

"Quite."

"And you're doing this because, uh," he scratched his jaw and gave me a sideways look, "you've gone loopy?"

"Not at all."

"Well, could you perhaps explain it to me a little, then? Right now you're making about as much sense as a guy who's been drinking ash water."

"All right. Here's what I'm proposing." I put the wine glass on the table next to the sketch of Greybridge Keep that I had been working on, focusing my attention on Theodore, who did likewise. "We've identified the most likely target for my humiliation - the Copperfen goblet. Everything you've told me of your meeting yesterday evening would seem to support this conclusion. Would you agree?"

"With you so far."

"Right," I continued. "So, while we do not yet know who's behind this, we do have the advantage of knowing what they're after, and when they plan on stealing it. So, let's pretend a moment that they were successful in their plan."

"Uhm, okay." Theo held out his hand to me. "It's been nice knowing you."

"Okay, okay, the long-term impacts of such a thing aside, what happens immediately after the theft?"

"You mean, what do the thieves do? Well," he narrowed his eyes and looked upwards to think, "I'm assuming that the banquet this Son's Day is where they'd share the news, with several other lords and ladies as witnesses, myself and Lord Greybridge included, and that they'd attempt to spring the news on you without warning."

"Right, and also without antagonizing Lord Greybridge. Perhaps they'll say that an attempt to steal finery from me netted them the goblet by chance, and they only learned of its true ownership once the marks were studied after the theft had taken place. Publicly returning the goblet to its rightful owner serves to chastise me for allowing it to be taken in the first place, at which point not only have I been made to look careless and foolish, but I will have also vexed Lord Greybridge. That last bit is something I probably want to avoid."

"That last bit - can I just say that I've always admired your gift for understatement?"

"Heh. Okay, so is that how you see the thing being played out, were I to allow everything to happen?"

"I would have to say that sounds about right, yes."

"So, since I know when and I know what, it's near certain that I could prevent this theft from happening . . ."

"A most sensible idea, I would have to agree," Theo said.

"...or, I could break into Lord Greybridge's estate, steal his *other* goblet, bring it back to Tucat Keep and leave it in a suitable place, allowing *that* one to get stolen instead."

I could almost see the various puzzle pieces falling into place inside Theodore's head as I spoke.

"You see, this way I can find out who is behind it all. I allow the second goblet to be stolen, and simply wait for the banquet. The thieves will launch into their speech regarding the artifact, at which point I affect surprise . . ."

"And pull out the goblet you've been keeping safe the entire time!" Theo said excitedly.

"Precisely. Why pass up an opportunity to enhance my own reputation at the expense of the very person who sought to discredit me? I could profess that I was so nervous about being responsible for such an important artifact that I could hardly let it out of my sight for any length of time, explaining why I was carrying it around with me. Nobody will believe that, of course."

"No, of course not. But they'll know you still have the goblet that was originally given to you, which puts your antagonist in rather an unfortunate spot."

"Of course. Everyone attending will recognize that this attempt to dishonor me has gone terribly wrong, humiliating the host and leaving me looking," I allowed myself a smug smile, "quite spiffy."

"You're right, this plan just seems to have your name tattooed all over it. I can't-...hold on a second. What about Lord Greybridge?"

"What about him?" I asked.

"Vincent, you can't possibly expect him to believe that someone accidentally broke into the wrong *keep*, can you?"

"Oh, of course not. No, everyone in the room will know it was me who risked my own neck in order to set the perfect counter trap. Of course, I'll deny having ever set foot inside Greybridge Keep. The proof that I have been stolen from will all but disappear, and the only certainty will be that my adversary is now in possession of a priceless relic believed to be in Lord Greybridge's possession, most notably by Greybridge himself."

"But won't he be somewhat annoyed with you?"

"Somewhat, but I think he's savvy enough to recognize that this was an attempt to use him as well, and that will annoy him more. If things play out the way I expect, there should be no damage to his reputation, and any desire to exact revenge should be directed at the thief for involving him in the first place. After all, none of this was my idea. If necessary, I'll find a way to make amends somehow, but I suspect that I will not be the one carrying the brunt of his anger."

"Quite right. It is, in fact, quite brilliant. Good thing I got to hear the details now...it would be quite out of character for me to be grinning madly as you spring your trap upon this mystery lord, what with people believing us enemies and all. As it is, I think I shall have to practice my scowl, just to be on the safe side," said Theo, picking up his wine glass and raising it in an unspoken toast.

I returned the gesture with a nod of thanks. "So, all that I must do now is figure out how to break into Lord Greybridge's estate and steal his second prized goblet without falling victim to his security or otherwise being found out."

"Ah, yes. As to that." He held out his hand to me a second time, grinning. "It's been nice knowing you."

"Pfah...are you saying I can't do it?"

"*Two days*, Vincent! You have less than two days to pull this off if you are to get the cup in time. I don't know anybody who can move on a completely unknown mark that quickly! Why not have a copy of the cup crafted instead? Why not go directly to Lord Greybridge, tell him of your suspicions and *ask* him for the thing instead of suicidally risking your own neck trying to steal it?"

"Theodore," I shook my head in mock sadness, "where would be the fun in that?"

Chapter 4

I LET THE air slowly emerge from my lungs as I watched one of Greybridge's guards slowly walk away from me, and took a carefully silent breath of new air in celebration.

He'd been literally right beside me a few moments before, causing me to go still and hold my breath for an uncomfortably long period of time. Thanks to the thoughtcloth cloak I was wearing, I had just done a fine impression of the cream colored hallway, apparently blending in with the wall behind me well enough to satisfy the bored looking fellow, who clearly didn't wish to be awake at this late hour. Even so, I'd been fairly lucky. If the large potted plant hadn't been sitting in that corner to provide partial cover, I would have stood out rather obviously.

Truly, that had been a little closer than I liked, and I willed myself to take a few slow, deep breaths in order to calm down a bit. I was on the third floor near the central hallway deep inside of Greybridge Keep, and my heart was pounding so loudly that it seemed as if anyone would be able to hear it thumping in my chest at thirty paces.

It had taken me over an hour and a half to get to where I was. My approach was slightly different than usual, mostly because of the relative lack of setup time and preparation. Under these particular circumstances, it was a much better idea to wait an extra minute or two than to take unnecessary risks for the sake of expediency. And even then, you could always be surprised by things such as a slightly early guard patrol, like I'd almost been just now.

So, all things considered, I was doing pretty well at an hour and a half. The patrols up to now had been fairly regular, every ten minutes or so, and were mostly on the ground floor where I had started, thinning out once I got to the second floor. I hadn't yet used any of my specialty tools or climbing gear whatsoever, preferring to rely on simple elbow grease to climb up the West side of the keep where the stables met a nice sheet of wall about twenty feet high, which . . .

Well, I suppose those sorts of details are fairly unnecessary. Suffice it to say that I was now on the third floor, and my progress thus far had been slow, methodical and, with the exception of the encounter I'd had with the guard moments ago, boring.

It was almost time for the uncertain, exciting bit.

I remained in my spot behind the plant, and watched the guard disappear around the corner at the far end of the hallway. Once he was gone from view, I checked for signs of patrols in either direction. Hearing and seeing none, I got up and bounded lightly toward the large door the guard had walked past moments before.

I wasted no time in shoving two skinny pieces of grey metal into the two bolt-lock chambers and sending a mental burst of energy down their length. The metal twitched slightly as it expanded, taking the shape of the space between tumblers inside the lock, forming itself into a passable key.

I pulled them out while they were still soft and put them aside to harden and dry, a process that would take three minutes or so.

Two obstacles down, an unknown quantity to go.

I inspected the door further, looking for some of the telltale signs belonging to the traps and alarms that were surely protecting it. I noticed there was no thumb-plate lock on the door, which was good. Those were always a pain to disable without breaking them completely, something I wished to avoid tonight.

Reaching into a pocket located behind my cloak, I pulled out my augur - a small teak rod with a selection of gems set into it. I waved it carefully over the door, watching the gemstones for any flashes of light.

The blue gem pulsed twice - once at the handle, once at the bolt. Two movement-based alarms then, located fairly close together. Standard protection, really - any sort of motion near the handle or lock would trip an alarm of some sort. I had ways of dealing with-

What the hell was that?

It seemed as though there had been a brief flash of green, almost too quick to see. I stared at the emerald gem on the rod I held.

There it was again.

Tricky. It appeared that the Lord Greybridge was fond of some cutting edge stuff. I timed the flashes, which appeared every five seconds. One of those new "pulse monitor" contraptions that periodically tested a circuit of metal surrounding a room to check for breaks, probably hooked up to an alarm. Probably a very loud one.

In all likelihood I would find something inside that was designed to trip me up unless I could open, enter, and close the door all within five seconds. I didn't think much of my chances. What's more, I hated being hurried. Better to eliminate the need for rushing in altogether.

I marked the approximate center of the magical alarms around the bolt and door handle with a small pin-sized grey dot for later. Then, I focused my attention on the pulse alarm.

Green flashes meant silver. I reached into my left leg pocket and pulled out my compasses - small glass cubes filled with water and several specks of free-floating metal. It took a moment of sifting through the collection before I found the silver-tuned one, at which point I picked it out and returned the rest to my pocket.

I put the small glass cube up near the top of the door and slowly slid it down, making a note of when I saw the metal flakes twitch and leap toward the door. I did a couple of checks in a couple of different spots to ensure there was no other silver on the door or near the walls that might contaminate my reading. There didn't appear to be any. It also seemed as though the silver was located approximately three inches below the top of the door, and four inches behind the door frame.

Tricky, but not impossible.

I chalked the spot I wanted as best as I could, put my augur and compass away, then reached into my sling pouch and pulled out two six-inch long strips of silver, as well as a small bottle of metallic adhesive. I also pulled a small hammer from my sling-pouch and held it momentarily in my teeth.

Opening the bottle awkwardly in one hand, I held the two strips of silver together with the other, and poured adhesive on either side of them. That done, I held the strips up to where I'd marked, and used the hammer to gently tap them into the crack between the door and the frame until they were flush with the surface, barely noticeable. A quick test indicated that both silver strips were now wedged between the silver behind the door, and were pulsing with them as though part of the circuit.

I briefly inspected the area around the floor for any sort of additional signs of things to be concerned about, just to be cautious. There didn't appear to be any, so I gathered up my two key-shaped metal strips from the floor next to my boot and retreated to the camouflaged safety of the wall corner, located behind the spiny plant. The whole thing had taken maybe six minutes.

Four and a half minutes later I found myself holding my breath, attempting to make no sound as the bored-looking guard once more walked within several feet of me. He did not appear to see anything unusual regarding the door as he walked past it and further down the hall, stopping only to scratch himself in a way he might not have, had he realized he was being watched. Soon he disappeared around the corner.

Okay, I had maybe ten minutes and one shot to do this. A familiar excitement crept up into my arms and shoulders.

I walked quickly toward the door, reaching into my sling pack and pulling out a very sinister looking steel bar and a small loop of wire that had been fashioned into a loose coil, like a spring. It was maybe four inches long, at least for the moment.

Locating my silver strips, I very carefully wedged the steel bar below it and pried the door away from the wall, widening the crack ever so slightly. The small sliver of metal split into two before my eyes, and I pinched the claw-like clips of the coil onto each of the two ends before relaxing the pressure I was applying against the door.

Pulling two small glass vials from another pocket, I held the first up to the doorknob in my gloved hand and applied enough pressure to crack it, causing a fine mist of gas to appear. I repeated the process for the second spot I'd marked, dropping the empty vials into a pocket after.

So far, so good. I twisted the bolt-locks open with my preformed keys, took a breath, turned the handle and pushed against the door very gently.

The silver coil stretched its way between the door and the wall, remaining connected to the two strips of silver I had wedged there, maintaining the circuit.

My eyes quickly scouted the interior of the room.

"Oh, damn," I muttered.

I leapt toward the door, and stepped onto the metal handle while my fingers found some portion of door to cling to while it swung open. No part of me touched the floor, which was covered by a rug with a pattern I recognized.

Anything touching that thing, no matter how gently, would result in a screech that could wake the dead.

The two small foot-high copper pillars, one in each of the furthermost corners of the room, were another security measure I recognized. Double-damn.

I leapt from my perch atop the door handle and into the room, arms reaching out for a ceiling beam, and I clicked my boots together as I did so. My fingers found enough of a groove to grab on to, and I used my forward momentum to swing my legs up toward that same wooden beam, slamming the insides of my feet forcefully against it. The small, sharp spikes that now lined the instep of my boots tore into the wood with a thunk, securing themselves firmly to the beam.

My hands released their grip and let the upper half of my body fall, my right hand immediately reaching my inside vest pocket to retrieve a small marble-sized piece of sling ammunition as I swung backwards, suspended by my boots.

At the apex of my swing I loaded the sphere into my wrist sling and took aim at one of the copper pillars, releasing it during that terribly brief moment when everything was still. As I swung back, already reaching into my pocket for a second sphere, I heard the *'pffffffssssht'* noise of the marble exploding into a fine, mossy powder that would be sucked into the pillar, preventing it from monitoring movements in the air currents like it was supposed to.

On my second swing I repeated the process for the second pillar, then allowed myself a moment to inspect my work.

First try for both pillars. Not bad. It would have taken several seconds for the air from the door to hit them, so I probably could have taken a bit more time, but I wouldn't have had more than a couple of chances at disarming them either.

Still swinging upside-down, it took me a good minute or so to pull out my collapsible metal baton and use it to close the open door I'd come through. I had to be careful while doing so, ensuring that my silver coil remained inside the room once the door was closed so it wouldn't be seen by the passing guard.

As the door clicked shut I allowed myself a sigh of relief, taking my first good appreciative look at the inside of the room itself, albeit an inverted one.

Whatever else he was, ruthless, calculating, vengeful, a tad belligerent, Lord Greybridge was certainly not without taste. The silver pulse alarm had been worked into the filigree along the ceiling trim, and matched the dark green walls and light warm wood paneling nicely. Some nicely elegant furniture that also matched the room had been placed here and there as well.

And, of course, there was also that spiffy rug.

My legs were beginning to complain about the work I was making them do, so I scouted around the room for the large box I knew the rug would be attached to. There didn't appear to be one. Grunting, I craned my neck and pulled my hair back out of my face, studying the rug's pattern for some clue as to where the pressure sensitive fibers went.

They all led to the center of the rug, where there was nothing. He'd buried the alarm box in the floor. Cute.

Pulling a different marble from my pocket, I took careful aim and launched it directly .at the center of the pattern. It exploded into a shower of white foam, dousing most of the rug there almost instantly. I counted down from five before bending at the waist and yanking my feet away from the wood, falling soundlessly onto the carpet below. Continued silence greeted my ears.

After scanning the dozens of other treasures in the room I spied the second goblet, the twin of the priceless chalice that had been entrusted into my care, sitting on a finely crafted wooden stand against the far wall.

I had hoped that the cup would not be in a position of relative prominence. There had been no time for a copy of the goblet to be crafted, which meant leaving an empty wooden stand behind. To make matters worse, there was definitely a pressure plate underneath the cup itself.

Well triple-damn. You'd think this fellow didn't want to be robbed or something.

I spent several minutes attaching four small pressure clamps made of a light cheeni wood on each corner of the plate, then slowly twisted the levers to apply pressure, watching the gems at the top turn from blue to green as I tightened. Once all gems were a uniform shade of green, I held my breath and gently removed the cup from the metal plate that served as its resting place.

Nothing happened.

Wrapping the cup up in two pieces of cloth from my pack, I put the bundle into the small box that I had hauled with me for the occasion, then put the box back in my pack alongside my other tools.

I breathed a quick sigh of relief. Compared to how long it had taken me to get upstairs and into this room, leaving would be a breeze, though not nearly as interesting. It is ridiculously more difficult to get from the ground floor to the third than it is to get from the third to the ground, provided you're not too fussy about the method of descent. Or the landing.

It had been about ten minutes since I'd originally entered the room, and so I waited another two minutes for the guard to have enough time to turn the corner and out of sight of the door. Then, I waited for an additional two minutes before opening the door and reentering the empty hallway, yanking the silver wire from the door once it was closed.

I pulled out my break-rope and quickly walked down the way I had first come. I followed it to another hallway, which was connected to a stairway, which itself connected to a balcony overlooking the yard.

The ground below was not completely clear, but was littered with thorny bushes beside the walls of the keep, which I'd have to be careful of if I wanted to avoid getting pricked. You can't have everything go your way, I suppose.

Tying the looped end of the break-rope around a stone support on the balcony itself, I wasted no time in attaching the clip to the harness I was wearing under my tunic and stepping carefully off of the ledge, turning to face the walls of the keep. After several seconds of violent yanks pulling at my chest, and numerous thin threads snapping one after the other, I fell just to the right of a small, dangerous-looking bush, and was safely on the ground.

The used strands were already beginning to burn where they had broken. After cutting the remaining ropes in half, I unhooked the clasp from my harness and tossed the collection of leftover string behind the nearby bush.

The stringy fibers were smoldering and burning away, now that the chemical buried deep in the middle of each string had been exposed. Soon the only traces of the rope would be a negligible amount of ash and the musty smell of flitleaf hanging in the air, a smell you might assume belonged to an employee or some other servant who had come outside for a smoke.

Taking a moment to inspect my surroundings, I concentrated briefly on turning my thoughtcloth cloak a dark green color so I might blend in with the grass. Then I sprinted lightly to the nearest edge of the estate.

Once there, I paused long enough to take a few quick breaths, turning to look at the keep behind me. All was quiet.

"Damn, I'm good," I whispered aloud.

A few seconds later I switched my clothing to a light gray stone color and vaulted over the seven-foot wall with my prize.

Chapter 5

I LIKE TO rethink my actions after the fact, make certain I haven't missed anything.

Well, perhaps 'like' is too strong a word.

I *take comfort* in the fact that my brain is constantly working away after committing a burglary, reconsidering my decisions that led to the act of thievery, wondering if anything I did was out of the ordinary.

You know...worrying.

And I suppose I don't really "take comfort" so much as convince myself that being sick with worry is a good sign, because it means that I'm not relaxed or complacent about-

Okay, I hate it.

Dozens of questions had gnawed at me, managing to keep me awake and pensive for most of the evening, and I found myself asking the same questions over and over. Who was trying to steal the goblet from me in the first place? Why were they trying to foster ill will between me and Greybridge? Were they any good? Did they lack the skill to penetrate my keep's defenses? I'm no pushover when it comes to security, and some of my surprises can be lethal to an unskilled intruder.

Were they even really after the goblet? What if my assumptions were wrong? Or, conversely, what if they were actually after *both* goblets?

That last thought gave me a small heart attack, and I allowed my eyes to flick over to my dresser and reassure myself that the box containing the original goblet - the one I didn't wish to be stolen - was still there.

It was. I gave it a quick frown before getting comfortable and trying once more to relax, secretly hoping that I might even get an hour or two of sleep, despite being so keyed up. It was a very unlikely and insanely optimistic hope, but it was hope nonetheless.

I found myself periodically wondering if the thief had struck yet, or if the burglary was happening even now as I lay there in bed. There is something inherently troubling about the idea of someone breaking into your keep, even if you're expecting such a thing to happen. It's disturbing, and creates a feeling of vulnerability. Nobody really enjoys being robbed from, after all, and many lords wished nothing to do with these sorts of games, making a point of discouraging them in the strongest manner possible.

Getting that particular message across to other lords wasn't that difficult to do, either. After all, any lord who felt that he had sufficient reason, could petition the prince to give a dueling challenge between houses his blessing, and once so blessed that challenge could not be declined. This could be expensive, since you either had to fight the duel yourself or hire a duelist to fight on your behalf, and those guys weren't exactly cheap.

Not many duels were fatal, but they could get extremely nasty or humiliating from time to time. If a lord made it a habit of hiring duelists with a reputation for cruelty, the price other duelists charged to fight in your stead rose sharply.

Lord Greybridge was one of those lords who valued being left alone, and he employed some very nasty duelists indeed. His last officially sanctioned duel was three years ago, where he'd challenged some luckless young lord who had stupidly stolen some small thing or another, and who did not have the resources to pay the fee that even the most inexperienced and desperate of swordsmen were demanding for the privilege of representing him.

The day of the duel it was rumored that Lord Greybridge's duelist would get an extra thousand gold marks for shaving the young lord's head and leaving him beaten in the middle of the ring without a single scrap of clothing. The rumor was confirmed within the first minute of the bout, once the first yield the lord offered had been declined. The spectacle had lasted for an hour, with hundreds turning out to watch.

Perhaps something similar was in store for me, if things didn't happen as I'd planned. Greybridge had no reason to love me, and though it wasn't really me who had dragged him into all of this, he might decide to hold me responsible regardless. What if he opted to challenge me to a duel instead of my unknown antagonist? Exactly how well would I fare against the caliber of swordsman Greybridge was able to afford? And of course, though they were generally frowned upon, there were other less savory means of letting a lord know you weren't happy with them. What if he resorted to something like that?

I realized that such thoughts were not helping me relax . . .

Sighing, I closed my eyes and once more attempted to get some rest, an activity that had eluded me ever since I'd arrived back at my keep. Surprisingly, I may have actually achieved some measure of success, as the next thing I can recall was being jolted to full wakefulness by a sudden urgent cry.

"Milord!" Cyrus called out from somewhere beyond my thick bedroom door. "It's Cyrus! Please open the door, Milord, we have a situation!"

Startled, I sat up and did a brief check of the lines on the oil reservoir of the lamp beside my bed to get a sense of the time. It appeared to be early morning, which meant that the thieves' window of opportunity to steal the goblet had passed.

Finally.

Ignoring the sounds of my knight-captain, who had now taken to rapping his knuckles against my door in addition to urgently calling my name, I stood up and stretched a bit before heading over to the box containing the Copperfen goblet. I knew it held the original goblet - breaking into my bedchamber is no small feat, even when I'm not occupying it - but I spent a few moments turning it over and inspecting it to ensure that it wasn't a fake or substitute, just to pacify my nagging sense of unease and paranoia.

The din in the hallway continued, and Cyrus began pounding at my door even harder in an effort to wake me from my presumed slumber.

Likely he was here to inform me that someone had found their way past my defenses and burgled something from Tucat Keep at some point in the night. If the banquet meant to humiliate me was being held today like Theo had been told, then I'd be sure to receive an invitation to it sometime this morning, which would allow me to discover the identity of my mystery thief. All I had to do at this point was sit back and wait.

Except...

I considered. Whoever was behind this wanted me extremely wound up and agitated, that much was obvious. What's more, they wanted to create ill will between me and Greybridge. Why, exactly? Was the plan to get me angry enough to do something stupid if challenged or provoked by Greybridge?

If so, I would probably do well to try to find out all I could about my unknown antagonist as quickly as possible, as that might influence my plans for later in the evening, when I attended whatever banquet I'd been invited to.

The urgent thumping sounds coming from the door were beginning to get tiresome.

"Coming!" I called out, presumably loud enough to be heard in the hallway. This was evidently the case, as the pounding on my door ceased. I straightened out my clothing, tugging at the long shirtsleeves to ensure they both fell evenly, and went to the door.

It took a half minute or so for me to disarm all the locks and open the door. Cyrus looked positively dreadful, his pale and stricken face showing signs of perspiration. Every feature, from his wide eyes to his mouth hanging slightly agape, conveyed shock and panic.

"Milord," he said in his calmest yet characteristically urgent there's-something-rather-the-matter voice, "It's-"

"Cyrus, before I forget, have you gotten anywhere with that forged note I gave you?" I interrupted.

He paused mid-word, his mouth half-opened as though to speak.

"It-...some progress, Milord," he said haltingly. "I spent a portion of the evening at the palace looking into it. However, there's-"

"But you've confirmed that it's a forgery, I take it?"

"I...not precisely, Milord. So called 'field notes' sent to Prince Tenarreau by preceptors are fairly rare, but apparently Preceptor Cheyne avoided visits to the palace whenever possible. I've determined that the paper's stock appears to be the same age, color, and wear as others stamped around that same date, but have not yet been able to inspect anything with Cheyne's handwriting on it as of yet. I-...Milord, there's something much more urgent I must-"

"Please do make that note a priority, would you? I'm most keen to learn everything you can find out about it, and as quickly as possible." I waved an apologetic gesture to him. "Sorry for interrupting just now. You were saying?"

"Yes." Cyrus collected himself and took a quick breath. "I know not how else I can say this, Milord. We've been burgled."

"Indeed," I remarked, inspecting my fingernails. "Do we know what they've stolen?"

"Not as of yet, Milord," he said apologetically. "The knights are still going over the inventory in the vault and are looking for any sort of clues that were left behind. It seems that they came up through-"

"Yes, yes, I'm sure there will be a full report. Have you been to the vault yourself? Seen it with your own eyes?"

He nodded that he had.

"Well," I said, walking back to the box that contained the goblet and closing the lid, "there was a rather plain stand that had been put there recently. Did you see one of the Copperfen goblets on it?"

"The Copperfen- why, it's in your exercise studio, is it not? I glimpsed it there not a day ago!"

"Indeed. I had reason to move it yesterday afternoon. Was it there?" I asked calmly, hefting the box under one arm.

"No," he gulped, his eyes becoming even wider. "It wasn't Milord. I would have noticed it had it been there, and do recall an empty stand that I did not recognize. If you've put the goblet there, I fear that-"

"Excellent," I said, beaming at him. "Tell the men to clean up and reset all of the security measures, and report to me any alarms that have been permanently disabled or require replacing. Also, let them know that I'm extremely happy with my security, as always. I would hate for any of them to feel as though they were responsible in some way."

"M-milord?" Cyrus appeared to be on the verge of complete collapse.

"Oh, and also there's one last thing. I anticipate that I'll be receiving an invitation to a dinner gathering tonight, arriving by messenger sometime early this morning. Could you please look after it yourself, and then bring the invitation directly to me once you've received it? Show no one if you can help it. If you don't recognize the messenger try to give him a look of astonished confusion or bewilderment," I favored him with a thoughtful expression. "Yes, much like the one you're wearing right now, actually. That would be perfect!"

Moments passed, and the expression he wore gave me the impression that he was on the verge of saying something, but could not find the words. Then, his face changed, and he looked at me with a sort of wary recognition.

"Copperfen, from Lord Greybridge. You...you had me find his floor plans the other day, and," he said, haltingly. "You've been...expecting this? This was anticipated?"

"Quite, and all appears to be going as planned. I shall share the details with you later, as I've said, but for now please ensure that all of the follow-up details are taken care of, would you?" I smiled in a relaxed manner.

He stood there before me, mute for several moments, before meeting my eyes and sketching a brief and unhappy salute. His eyes registered a certain amount of hurt just as he turned away to walk down the hallway, presumably to do what I had just bid him.

I sighed. Considering how spectacularly well things were going, that was a bit of a downer.

I made a note to take him into my confidence later, and describe some of the intricacies that led to decisions where he was kept in the dark. Had Cyrus known about the impending theft, even one that I was allowing to happen, he may have given his knights different instructions and potentially tipped my hand. Surely he would see that the precautions I routinely employed were necessary.

I opened the box and snuck a look at the goblet again, just to be sure, before tucking it under my arm and leaving my bedchamber, to head down the stairs leading to the main dining hall, already looking forward to the prospect of a leisurely breakfast. I felt well rested and full of vigor, despite my apparent lack of sleep. There's something about the feeling you get when things are going just as you've planned that does remarkable things for your energy levels.

Halfway there I encountered Talia, who was coming up the stairs. She gave me a look that was at once surprised and puzzled, likely due to the fact that I actually appeared to be awake and moving about at this early hour.

I'm not exactly what you'd call a 'morning person' . . .

"Ah, Talia," I said, smiling. "I'm glad that-"

My voice failed me entirely when I finally noticed what she was wearing on her feet. I stared down at her slippers, and after a few seconds or so Talia did likewise, flushing slightly.

The word 'adorable' came to mind, as did the words 'big' and 'fluffy'. Though I couldn't identify precisely which woodland creature her slippers were designed to emulate, I assumed that freezing to death during the winter months wasn't one of their primary concerns.

"I am *so* sorry Milord," said Talia quickly, sounding aghast, her cheeks quickly deepening in color. "I know these aren't exactly livery standard but, you see, they're much *quieter* than sandals, and my morning duties see me walking past many bedchambers, and since hardly anyone is awake, and I'm not answering the door at this hour, I figured it would be fine to-"

"To disguise your feet as small woodland creatures?" I asked in a playful, mocking tone.

"I promise it will not happen again, Milord. I-"

"Don't worry yourself about it, Talia...how you choose to disguise your feet this early in the morning is up to you. I'm just glad I caught you." I gave her a quick smile. "I'm about to be invited to a banquet, I'm afraid, and so I'll be requiring some rather dashing formal wear for this evening."

"Of course, Milord," she said, visibly relaxing.

"So then, could you please set out a few things for me to try on, possibly hang around later to give your opinion on what might look good? I can't afford to look anything less than devastatingly handsome this evening."

"You'd hardly need clothes to...uh-" she began, and then suddenly looked shocked, and colored slightly for the second time in as many minutes. "That is to say...I meant that...y-yes, Milord."

"Excellent. Thank you, Talia," I smiled, politely ignoring the fact she'd misspoken, continuing past her toward the hall and descending the stairs two steps at a time. Perhaps it was time I gave up trying to put her at ease entirely. She'd been in my employ for nearly nine years and yet, despite being one of the most senior of my employees, she always seemed to become flummoxed and nervous when in my presence, like she were caught in the act of doing something wrong. Some people were just like that around lords, I supposed.

Reaching the bottom of the stairs, I headed to the dining area to see if any tea had been made up. I ceased my cheerful whistling once I realized I was doing it, just in case Cyrus was still within earshot.

The grin, however, remained firmly planted on my face.

Chapter 6

"LORD VINCENT TUCAT, here by invitation of the Lord Teuring," I said, handing the formal invitation bearing the symbol of two circles interlocked and side by side to the butler, or doorman, or whoever the guy at the front of the doors to the Teuring estate was attempting to be.

He had tried to dress the part, but looked a fright with the wisps of white hair hanging about his face from his sideburns and his temples, the hair atop his head having abandoned him long ago. He gave the impression of a man who was held together by sheer act of will. Excruciatingly old, and solemn. Possibly even dead...I didn't want to look too closely.

"Thank you, Milord," he said in a wavering voice, taking the invitation and holding out his arm as an offer to take my cloak, which I waved away. I was holding a rectangular box under my three-quarter cloak at the moment, and didn't feel like drawing attention to the fact.

My stomach was still a little twitchy with worry, as it always is during these sorts of situations. I smiled at the aged gentleman and nodded my head for him to proceed. He gave a quick nod in return, as was proper given his advanced age. I feared that if he were to try a formal bow, he'd all but fall apart right there in front of me.

We walked down a modest hall containing sparse decorations, past the coatroom and on to the main dining hall, where my slow-moving, ancient escort introduced me to all in attendance.

I very nearly jumped out of my skin.

"The Honorable Lord Tucat!" his voice boomed out to the crowd of people before us, to my complete and utter surprise. I swear, I also saw several other nearby lords twitch at the sheer volume being projected by this seemingly fragile old man. There may have been echoes.

Nodding at me, he turned back toward the door and left me, and what remained of my shattered nerves, standing at the entranceway to the keep's great hall.

Well, maybe 'great' is a bit generous.

My first opinion of the hall and its contents wasn't a very charitable one. Everything gave a clear impression of a host putting out their best finery, and hoping it will be enough.

A large tapestry at the back did its level best to try to cover some rather major cracks and damage to the wall behind and next to it. Most of the lords were to my right, socializing around the stunted, irregular looking tables that had been hastily set up for cheeses and wines, all draped with cloths that did not even attempt to match the place settings set up at the main table.

And then there was Lord Teuring himself - a mere boy by my estimation. The paleness of his face was offset by dark black curls, which were trimmed short above the ears and at the nape of the neck. His outfit was gray and burgundy, with an embroidered pair of interlocking circles upon the breast of his tunic. Despite looking relatively clean and new, the outfit he wore did not quite seem to fit him properly, leaving you with the impression it was borrowed.

This inexperienced stripling of a lord had thought he was clever enough to make me enemies with the infamous Lord Greybridge, who I could see had also been invited and was currently standing by the cheese table, wearing a bored expression. Well, either this boy didn't know what he'd been doing, or he'd not known exactly who he was trifling with, either with respect to myself or Greybridge, take your pick.

Doubtless this attempt to flex his muscle at my expense would be a learning experience for him.

Exactly what he learned might well depend on Lord Greybridge's disposition this evening.

I smiled and nodded at Teuring as he caught my eye. He waved an appreciative gesture of thanks, eyes half-lidded, trying to act as though my presence was nothing special. I waved back with a smile, attempting to hide the fact that I knew what *he* knew, in addition to knowing he was completely unaware of what *I* knew, which was that he himself didn't know that-

Well, let's not try to put it into words.

"Asshole," I muttered under my breath, looking around the room for someone with which to mingle, or perhaps fluster a tad. After all, that's what you did at such things. They'd be an unbearably bothersome affair otherwise.

As luck would have it, I happened to spy Lord Marcsun, a belligerent ass whose territory bordered my own, attempting to entertain a couple of lords I didn't recognize with a story of some sort. I say "attempting" because I've heard his stories before. Judging from the expression on the faces of the lords he was speaking to, he was doing about his usual best.

I walked over.

"-dazed from the fall from my second story window, when I looked down upon him and I scowled, saying-"

"Hello Lord Marcsun!" I said in what might be considered an overly cheerful manner. "Why, isn't it about that time where you start reciting that *dreadful* story about the poor fellow who was attempting to steal his wedding necklace back from you? The one whom you bankrupted and forced into your employ as a gardener as punishment for falling on your roses?"

He'd stopped speaking, his mouth open mid-word for several frozen seconds, and after an exasperated sigh looked up at the ceiling in frustration while gritting his teeth, momentarily nonplussed. The part of the tale I'd mentioned was, of course, what he considered to be the dramatic ending for the story he was telling, one that he had told over and over.

It's true, I can be an inconsiderate bastard when it comes right down to it...but then again it wasn't much of a story.

I kept the fiercely innocent grin on my face as I waited for him to begin his inevitable tirade about courtly manners, which I would also interrupt rudely.

And then, contrary to every expectation I had, something rather unusual happened.

He smiled.

"Lord Tucat," he nodded. Then, turning to nod to the two men he'd trapped in conversation, he turned his back to me and walked toward the wine table.

Interesting. Unprecedented, even. I would have to ponder what it meant, exactly.

I gave the two lords he'd been talking to a quick nod of acknowledgment before turning and looking about the room, pocketing the cloak broach I'd just stolen from Lord Marcsun as I did so.

A few dozen lords and ladies stood in the room with me, most of them chatting idly and sipping at their wine glasses. I noticed that the vast majority of those who had been invited to this affair either didn't care much for me or actively disliked me, which made sense. Unfortunately, that meant there were very few people here who would wish to engage me in small talk as we waited. In fact, given *some* of the people I could see were in attendance, I might have to watch my step a little. I began to mentally prepare myself to 'accidentally' overhear some barbed comments about skin care, or scars, or anything else some lord or lady might wish me to overhear. I've often found it surprising how uncreative people can be when their only intention is to be cruel.

Casting a glance about the room in search of a friendly face, I soon spied Lord Cleaver, one of my neighbors to the North, and who I was on fairly good terms with. Once I could see I'd gotten his attention I gave him a solemn nod, and he returned my look with a slight bow of the head. More or less, this was banquet shorthand for 'Shall we talk?' and 'Yes, let`s.'

We made our way over to one another, and I took the opportunity to visit the refreshment table and grab my own glass of wine, a slightly cheeky green with just a slight oak finish.

"Vincent," he said.

"Matthew. How are things?"

"Oh, they're well. You know, the usual stuff." He indicated Lord Marcsun with a gesture of his glass. "Still doing what you can to annoy bubble-britches, I see."

I chuckled. "Well, it's not like it requires a lot of effort. Not that being polite would make any difference really - I don't think he's ever going to forgive me for stealing his own bed from his keep."

"Right," he laughed, face splitting into a grin, "Maybe that's because he was trying to sleep in it at the time, and had a rather nasty start as a result of waking up in the street. Some people can be so sensitive about those sorts of things."

"True, but only fair considering what he had tried to pull before. I hate that heavy-handed nonsense," I said, taking a small sip of wine. "He seemed to take my interrupting his story with some small grace however. Who knows, maybe he's mellowed out."

"Ah," he said. "As to that...I think I can explain his reaction."

"Oh?"

"You," he said, casting his jovial countenance aside in favor of a more serious, somber one, "have made someone upset, it would seem."

Deja-vu.

"Really? Upset someone? Me?"

"Truly, a remarkable thing, I know," he said, rolling his eyes. "However, in all fairness I figure I should warn you that this evening's entertainment may in fact be directed at you. Of course, one never truly knows who the target of such gatherings is until the trap's sprung but, if I had to guess, I would say that you're the unfortunate fellow who will be hung out to dry tonight."

"Ah. And you presume that Marcsun's reaction to me is indication that he's become aware of this fact?"

"Or involved, yes." His voice dropped to a near whisper, and he moved closer to me. "Just last evening, I received word from a source that you were going to be targeted for a small token theft of some sort, with the perpetrators requesting permission to stage it from Marcsun's territory where it borders yours."

Just like Theodore had been approached, it seemed. That was rather odd. Perhaps the overly ambitious Lord Teuring had foreseen some trouble getting cooperation from my neighbors and scouted out several possible staging areas.

"Last evening? Surely you could have warned me in time?"

"Fah, it was too late to try to arrange a meeting, and time was of the essence. What I *did* do was escort a few of my knights in suitable attire out into your territory where it bordered Marcsun's, hoping to catch the thieves as they were making off with whatever had been stolen from you, so that I could return it to you with a minimum of fuss or embarrassment. I'm not above having the infamous Lord Tucat owe me a few favors."

"Or, you could have mugged the thieves and decided you wanted to keep whatever they'd stolen to use for yourself, of course," I said, smiling.

"Heh. There was that possibility as well," he chuckled, shrugging lightly. "Alas, we saw nothing. In fact, it was so quiet last night that I had my doubts as to whether the burglary had taken place at all. However, judging from where we find ourselves this evening . . ." He let his voice trail off.

"Yes, something was in fact stolen last night," I said, answering the unspoken question.

He nodded to himself, and then he looked at me, his eyes narrowing in suspicion. "You don't seem particularly bothered by this news."

"Really? That's odd. I guess I must be doing a good job of hiding the soul-crushing anxiety I'm feeling," I mused, taking another unconcerned sip of my wine.

"Ha!" he said, an eager smile lighting up his face. "You're up to something! I've always said that someone'd have to be snorting candle-ash to think they could get the better of you. What have you got planned?"

"Oh, let's not spoil the big surprise, shall we? I'm sure that our honored host will not want to keep us all waiting for his announcement, now that the dinner hour is almost upon us."

"Indeed. I'm sure it lives up to your usual standards," he laughed, nodding a quick goodbye before wandering off to mingle with some of the other guests, chuckling as he did.

From there, I simply did as was natural at these sorts of events; I wandered around and greeted the various lords and ladies who had been invited. After a while, my box began to press uncomfortably against my ribs from holding it under my cloak.

The mingling lasted perhaps half an hour, all told, at which point we progressed to the second portion of the evening.

"My honored lords and ladies!" boomed the incredibly old gentleman who had shown me in, looking as though his very voice was threatening to shake him apart. "Dinner is served!"

And away we went.

We were seated at the long table slowly, greeted by a very striking female hostess who was standing at the head of the procession. I was momentarily taken aback when I realized that this beautiful woman must be Lady Teuring.

She wore the same burgundy and gray being worn by Lord Teuring, only she wore it far, far better than he. She stood at the head of the line of advancing dinner guests, thanking them with a smile for coming, or making small curtseys at some compliment or another.

There were several things about her that could be complimented. Whatever poor judgment this boy Lord Teuring might have, it certainly didn't extend to his taste in women, or simple aesthetic beauty.

The line progressed forward, and soon it was my turn to greet the hostess. She smiled brightly when she saw me.

"Lord Tucat," she said demurely, once my section of the line had made its way to the table. The smile she gave me seemed quite genuine. "If you could please follow me?"

That is ordinarily the moment that a lord or lady discovered that perhaps the evening was not going to turn out particularly well for them. Some lords prefer to storm off and let the evening proceed without them at this point. That sort of reaction seems childish to me, so I tend to avoid it. Plus, with all my planning it wasn't exactly like I was about to storm off in a huff.

Besides, this beautiful woman had her arm extended to me in invitation, and wished to escort me to my seat. How could any man whose heart still beat in his chest refuse something like that?

Putting on a rueful smile, I took her arm and allowed myself to be led to the far end of the long dining table.

"I...thank you, Lord Tucat," she said after a moment, smiling up at me uncertainly as we walked. "I have neither hosted nor attended many of these, but I understand that many lords in your situation are far less pleasant to accompany to their seat."

"My dear lady, had I known that I would be seen arm-in-arm with someone as breathtakingly lovely as yourself, I would have arranged for your husband to attempt to steal something from me ages ago."

She colored slightly and acknowledged the statement with a grateful smile. Then, after a moment's pause, she turned to me with her brows knitted together.

"Attempt?"

Oh, damn it.

"You misheard me, surely," I said with an easy smile. "Why, I will admit to being rather surprised that I am guest of honor here tonight, but it is not impossible for me to be robbed from. I do not believe that anything of great import belonging to me has gone missing recently, and if I am mistaken then the honor is his. I am not, as you may have heard, an easy man to steal from."

"Indeed, Lord Tucat. For weeks my husband prepared, and it...oh, I should not speak of such things. I am near hopeless when it comes to the fine nuances of dealings between lords, though Angelo claims that it is a skill that no-one should have cause to brag about. I do sometimes find myself talking without considering the consequences my words may have. I wouldn't want to let something important slip."

"True!" I laughed lightly. "You wouldn't want that."

Very true. Weeks, was it? A theft that took weeks to plan, requiring little more than an errant word and two days for me to ferret out, neutralize, and turn upon the very man who hatched the scheme in the first place. Several weeks versus two days.

Damn, I'm clever sometimes.

"Your chair, my lord."

I was barely clever enough to avoid tripping on an irregular floor cobble and fall tumbling to the floor. Pretending not to notice this evidence of shoddy workmanship, I smiled my thanks at Lady Teuring and allowed myself to be seated at the table's end, directly opposite of Lord Teuring, who was standing behind his chair and slightly to the left as he watched his guests being seated.

I was very nearly the last to sit, and did not have to wait long before Teuring stepped forward and sideways, taking his place in front of his chair and stretching his arms to the gathered lords in welcome. It was time for me to pay attention, for proper timing could mean everything at a moment like this.

"My honored lords," he said in a voice that didn't crack, but was clearly capable of the feat. "I welcome you to my table this night. It is my humblest wish that I be allowed to honor you all with food, drink, and a modest tale of cunning theft that transpired recently, which I thought I might bring up with our guest of honor this evening, Lord Vincent Tucat."

He smiled in my direction and reached for his glass as the dozens of heads along both sides of the table turned away from him and toward me.

I wondered if I turned my head as predictably when I attended such functions, looking toward the victim once cued by my host. I made a note to watch myself for it the next time that I was at such a dinner.

Sitting lazily to one side, I waved cheerfully at the assorted faces, which they took as their cue to look back to their host.

"I had cause to recently visit the estate of the honorable Lord Tucat," he began loftily, "a thief of some small reputation."

There was a smattering of chuckling at the understatement, I noted proudly. I chuckled and nodded to him from thirty feet away, as well as made a special effort to locate Lord Marcsun from among the faces assembled at the table so that I might point and wink knowingly at him. He saw my gesture and scowled.

Hey, I have to amuse myself somehow, don't I?

"And so, as preparation for my visit to his keep I confess to you all that I prepared for all manner of possible traps for the unwary. I studied his methods, his habits, and all manner of things I might have to contend with. And yet, what I discovered upon actually setting foot upon his estate surprised me more than any clever trap possibly could have. My fellow lords, I found myself to be, I must confess, embarrassed for our poor Lord Tucat."

Indeed? That's how he was playing it? I raised an eyebrow at him from across the table.

"For all of his vaunted cunning," he continued, smirking slightly at the reaction that his newest words had received from the collected lords, "Tucat Keep, of proud bearing and mighty reputation, was unprepared for my visit in every way possible. Sleeping guards, unlocked doors...I was scarcely able to believe that I was able to wander about so freely, practically bumping into riches and relics that my own humble house would have bankrupted itself to try to protect."

Okay, this was already starting to get a little ugly. I felt any misgivings I may have had about devastating this audacious adolescent evaporate, and gave him the kind of cheerful smile that suggests that death by evisceration is imminent.

"And thus, with the entirety of Tucat Keep practically at my disposal, I was tempted to take pity on Lord Tucat and simply leave, when I happened upon a thing of...of utter beauty. I recognized this object through my studies of history, though I was scarcely able to believe the place of relative dishonor it had been assigned – a mere table ornament for the Lord Tucat's own amusement.

"I saw on the table before me...one of the Copperfen goblets."

He paused to allow the assorted lords and ladies to 'oooh' and 'ahhh' in an appropriate fashion, somehow looking grave and smug at the same time.

"I felt as though I had been struck, no word of a lie my lords and ladies," he continued. "To see this artifact, this tribute to a momentous and historical event that has shaped our past, treated in such a slipshod and contemptuous manner...well, I admit that it made my blood boil. I had no choice but to rescue it from the ignorant lord who doubtless had no inkling as to its true historical value."

The words this boy had chosen seemed to be deliberate – this was a very serious attempt to breed ill will between myself and Lord Greybridge, an insulting sort of attack that was directed specifically at my reputation, and how little regard I placed on property I'd been entrusted with.

I also realized just in what manner this speech was going to backfire on him. I stifled a grin, covering it with a yawn. This poor, poor bastard.

"When I returned to my keep to inspect the chalice, I became amazed. To rescue such an object from ignominy is one thing, but to discover that it does not even belong to the lord who possesses it? I can hardly put such horror into words."

One of the lanky youths came forward with a fairly sizable box, not entirely unlike the one half-hidden under my cloak, placing it on the table. The youth then turned away from the table, accepting the greyberry candle and flint-box being offered by an even younger servant. After the momentary shower of sparks had subsided, he turned back to the table, large candle in hand, a violet-blue flame shining brightly at its tip.

Lord Teuring opened the box with exaggerated slowness as he took the brightly burning candle from the subservient young man, allowing the contents of the box to be displayed down the table to the collected lords. There was another round of slight gasps and appreciative 'Oooh's once he brought the candle near enough that its light illuminated the lord's mark that had magically been set upon it.

I couldn't see well enough to make it out, but I knew what must be visible. A gently arching gray footbridge, outlined with lines of fine white, glowing wavy blue lines representing water running underneath it. It was the symbol of property belonging to Lord Greybridge.

"And so," he added triumphantly, "I now take this opportunity to return this priceless artifact back to you, Lord Greybridge, having rescued it on your behalf. It is saved from the unworthy fate of languishing in an inadequately kept keep, the guest of an unappreciative house, managed by a complacent and undeserving lord."

I'd have to remember to buy Theo something nice for his birthday. This might have hurt, had I not acted to thwart it.

He'd had his fun. It was my turn now.

I waited until he had begun to pick up the goblet before coughing loud enough to get everyone's attention, and then coughing as if I was covering a laugh, followed by a kind of throat-clearing cough to indicate that I had gotten the best of my laughter and was attempting to speak. Teuring froze in place, holding the goblet gently by the stem, which was perfect.

Sitting back slightly, I raised a skeptical eyebrow across the table at him and spoke loudly enough for all to hear.

"My Lord Teuring, there are many things for which you should be congratulated, and I would like to take this opportunity to do so. First, for this fine meal that we...no, wait, we haven't been served dinner yet." I rubbed my chin, looking thoughtful. "Well then, for an opportunity to glimpse these glorious surroundings, which...uh. Hmm."

I continued to look troubled, as if trying to find something appropriately nice to say. He smiled condescendingly at me, probably assuming that this was my best shot, the only way I figured I'd be able to defend my family name. I abandoned my troubled look for a bright smile, and continued.

"Ah, well then I suppose I should congratulate you for the theft of a...sorry, was it a cup? Well, for stealing whatever it is you've got down there. I'm afraid I can't see it that well, I've got some dust from this ancient, cracking ceiling stuck in my eye. Possibly mold, I'm not sure. Still, you seem happy with it, and so, well done!"

I applauded gently, but stood as I did, making it clear with my body language that I was not finished with my sarcastic tirade just yet.

"However, most important of all, I would like to thank you for inviting Lord Greybridge to this affair, for it seems I have two things I need to present him with this evening, one of which," I nodded gravely in his direction, making a note of the furious expression on his face, "is a most sincere apology."

There were new murmurs, and an even bigger, arrogant sneer of a smile leapt onto the face of young Lord Teuring.

"And so, Lord Greybridge, I must ask for your forgiveness," I said, lifting my box gently with one hand and placing it upon the table so that I could open it, "for until this very evening I had no idea my keep so closely resembled your own in appearance. Apparently they're near identical, for I can think of no better reason how our bewildered young host could have possibly gone and robbed the wrong keep by mistake.

"As for the second thing, Lord Greybridge, I wish to return this priceless Copperfen goblet you entrusted to my care some months ago, which I have not allowed out of my sight since the moment-"

I stopped talking, since there was no point in trying to be heard over the scandalized murmurs once I opened the wooden box to reveal the second Copperfen goblet. Over the din of noise I recognized the sound of Lord Cleaver's booming laughter.

Lord Greybridge looked furious, glaring balefully down the table at me, and then at Lord Teuring.

Lord Marcsun was clenching his jaw and looking down the table at me, his mood having drastically changed after seeing that I would not be the one being humiliated that evening after all.

Lady Teuring was wide-eyed and looking up at her husband, an undisguised look of anxious concern on her face.

Lord Teuring looked as though he'd just fallen into a nest of live asps, standing there in mute astonishment, eyes the size of dinner plates.

Myself? I figure I looked rather clever.

Chapter 7

IT'S MOMENTS LIKE that which remind me why I take such great care to plan things down to the last detail.

Suddenly, nobody knew what to do. In fact, we might have all gone home hungry had it not been for a lad from the kitchen darting up to the immobile Lord Teuring and hurriedly whispering something in his ear. Since the moment I'd made my announcement to the rest of the room the young lord had merely stood there, unmoving, staring across the table at the object that he probably believed spelled his ruin.

As beliefs went, it was a good one.

"Dinner," he said, his manner suggesting that the slightest breeze might be sufficient to knock him to the floor, "will be brought out for your enjoyment in...a few moments."

"Hang on!" I practically yelled, sounding scandalized. "We've got wine in front of us, but nobody's performed the toast! You can't just begin dinner without a toast!"

Jaw working, eyes clouded with failure, he leveled a look of hatred down the table at me. Setting the Copperfen Goblet down in front of him, he reached for his dinner wine glass, raising it out before him with a perfunctory nod to all assembled and bringing it to his lips without a word.

"To Lord Teuring!" I bellowed, holding my own glass out as dramatically as I could, "May his success this evening be indicative of the kind of success he may achieve in all of his future endeavors."

I took a gentle sip from the glass I held. The green wine it contained was now only slightly below room temperature, but tasted sweet.

Very sweet indeed.

Sitting back down, I pretended to take no notice of the various looks being sent my way. It wasn't too terribly often that something like this happened, where a dramatic shifting of circumstances disrupted all plans and expectations for the evening. I enjoyed it all the more for its rarity, as I'm sure many of the other lords and ladies present did, regardless of what they thought of me, personally.

I attempted to exchange some minor pleasantries with the fellow sitting beside me, discussing the vintage of the wine we were enjoying, idle speculation regarding what kind of meal the wine's characteristics might suggest we were going to be served. Every now and again I glanced down the table at Teuring, whose demeanor now possessed all of the qualities of a broken, stricken man. Shoulders slumped, complexion pale and waxy in the insufficient light, he sat looking forlornly at the table, eyes still wide.

"Tucat," a solemn voice said, nearby and to my left.

"Lord Greybridge," I said, standing up and sending him a quick bow from the waist. He'd made his way from the host's end of the table to mine, presumably to inspect the goblet I had brought. The evening was not entirely over, I reminded myself, and the outcome still needed attending to.

The rotund, elegantly draped man held his hands out expectantly toward the goblet in front of me. I retrieved the boxed item and delivered it gently into his outstretched arms.

He drew the goblet from its case and inspected it, and I saw him nod slightly to himself as he turned the metal chalice by its stem. I don't know what he might have seen – I'd had both goblets together for a time and could not spot a single difference between them.

A few seconds later he put the goblet into the wooden box, closed it, and waved for me to lean closer so that we might talk.

I gestured away from the table, suggesting that we should remove ourselves from earshot first. He nodded his acquiescence and, once we'd put a few feet between us and the table, he spoke quietly to me.

"Our keeps look nothing alike," he said blandly.

"Very true. I can only dream of my own humble home someday achieving a mere fraction of the prominence and majesty of your own."

"Yes. Well," he scowled, "I don't know who I'm more annoyed with at the moment."

"Understandable, although I would point out that it was hardly my idea to bring you into this in the first place. I know how much value you place on your privacy."

"Indeed? The cup you brought with you is the one that I had given to you originally, meaning that our young friend over there," he gestured with a backwards toss of his head to indicate the table behind us, "had either stolen the other goblet from my keep, or he was set up. Given his reaction, and yours, I suspect the latter. The very fact that you were able to retain my property suggests that you could have thwarted these plans without somehow getting me involved."

He was right, and it couldn't really be helped. I nodded solemnly in agreement.

"It is true, my lord, that I could have arranged things differently, and I apologize. However, consider what our audacious host was attempting with this evening's entertainment. He sought to involve you regardless, to perhaps use you as a tool against me. How would you have reacted had the goblet actually been stolen in the manner suggested by Lord Teuring, and returned to you in the manner he had planned, with the toast he'd just proposed?"

"So instead of being used by him to cause you grief, I find myself being used by you instead. As well, there's the lingering notion that I may have played a part in setting up our young host. My reputation suffers regardless. Also," he added, giving me a meaningful look, "being robbed from rather pisses me off."

"Of course, I apologize for the inconvenience of being brought into this intrigue...a situation that, I should again wish to point out, was not my idea. The individual planning the theft of the goblet was unknown to me when details of this plot first came to my attention. I had thought you might prefer that the culprit reveal himself, so that he could understand the full measure of what it means to trouble a Greybridge."

"There is that," he nodded, considering. "I'm certainly not happy with young Teuring either, and will take steps to ensure he understands that shortly. In the end though, I believe you owe me. I will most certainly be requiring something from you - something more substantial than a mere apology."

"Of course. I would not have allowed this evening to conclude without some sort of an understanding in that regard," I offered quickly, relieved. He appeared to be accepting my words at face value, and the last little detail was working itself out. "I will be more than happy to make things right in whatever manner you may require."

He continued to look at me, considering, and then looked away toward the hall doors that led to the main foyer.

"I've dispatched one of my knights with a message for the prince, requesting a duel," he said, simply. "I should receive word back before this evening is out."

A duel then. Yes, Greybridge was quite annoyed by this evening's entertainment, I could see.

"I, of course, would be delighted to take over all responsibilities for the duel on your behalf. It would be ridiculously unfair if your involvement in this fiasco cost you even a single copper mark."

"That would be adequate," he murmured. "You are something of a swordsman yourself, I understand?"

"I cannot deny that I have some small reputation," I said, affecting a small bow.

"Well then," he said, turning back toward the table, "I shall make my announcement to all assembled once I have received word from the prince. I expect you will want to announce your plan to represent me shortly after."

"Certainly." It was exactly how I would do it as well. By offering my services spontaneously, I could preserve the notion that he wished no part in this, as well as repay him for the presumed embarrassment of having it be known that he could be robbed from. In truth, I was more than happy to offer my services, given how I suddenly felt about young Lord Teuring.

We walked back to our seats at the table, and I noted that the meal was in the process of being served, despite Teuring looking as though he no longer had any appetite whatsoever.

I was starved. I could feel some of the anxiety leaving my body, leaving in its wake a glorious kind of famished hunger, the kind that you get after a good amount of exercise. Life was good.

I passed the ring of my left hand over the appetizer inconspicuously before sampling it, not really expecting the jewel adorning it to glow even as I did so. Poisoning a guest at your table while in the company of your peers would result in ostracism, or worse. I do, however, believe in being prudent around those who may no longer think they have anything left to lose.

Risking a quick look down the table, I saw Teuring, shoulders slumped and staring down at the tablecloth just beyond his plate with a forlorn expression on his face, much the same as he'd been a few minutes before.

I brushed off any feelings of sympathy I was tempted to feel for him and focused on the meal, tearing off a piece of the small dinner roll in front of me and using it to pick up one of the lightly fried shallots.

While the others at the table were being presented with food courses and chatting idly with one another, I continued to take notice of Lord Teuring and what he was doing. He was sitting at the head of the table, all but ignoring the feast he had been responsible for putting together, and was instead looking down at the table with a desperate kind of bleakness.

His wife sat awkwardly to his left, head turned away from him, looking hurt. The body language they exhibited suggested trouble, like he'd said something out of character to her, perhaps in the heat of the moment. Easy enough thing to understand, really - it's difficult to maintain a cheerful disposition when your plans have very publicly blown up in your face.

I spent the majority of dinner ignoring the meal being served, choosing instead to spend my time staring down the table at my host, a cheerful expression of relaxed contentment on my face. Once it became apparent to Teuring that I was doing so he straightened in his chair and began to stare back at me, returning the favor.

And we stared . . .

It was hard to say just how much time we spent in this manner. I'd sit there, staring and smiling at him, and he'd stare back, attempting to appear unconcerned, or angry, or whichever expression he felt would best mask how he was actually feeling. We'd each occasionally glance left or right, blink away from each other's gaze for a few moments as if we were scouting some feature of the room that held some interest, or acting as though some sudden move had grabbed our attention. Staring can be quite exhausting sometimes.

Eventually the meal came to an end, and just as the dessert glasses were being ushered away, I noticed an out-of-breath young man in a gray uniform half-stumble through the door. He looked around the room in wide-eyed exhaustion until his eyes found Lord Greybridge, at which point he began to stride over to him. Then, remembering who was assembled and what was going on, he began to walk at a much slower, measured pace.

Once he was close enough to have been noticed by his lord, Greybridge stood and stepped away from the table, whispering to his liveried servant before accepting a piece of paper that was being offered him.

He inspected the note briefly, and then waved the young man away.

"My honored lords and ladies!" Greybridge said loudly, turning to address the room once his messenger had scurried out of sight, "I beg you all attend my words for a moment."

I glanced at Teuring. He looked as though he wished he could be anywhere else right at that moment, his features showing every inch of his inexperience.

"I will be brief. It would seem that Lord Teuring had made plans that involved antagonizing myself and the honorable Lord Tucat. In so doing, he has dishonored my name, inconvenienced me, absconded with my property, and caused me offense. I have secured permission from Prince Tenarreau to issue a challenge, and I believe that I shall exercise that privilege now.

"Lord Teuring, I hereby challenge you to a duel, and require the presence of either you or your representative in three days time, at the dueling hour, at the Circles." He looked from Teuring to the collection of faces seated at the table with him. "I thank you all for your polite indulgence."

Greybridge sat back down upon his chair, not looking the least bit annoyed or worried. In fact, he'd made the whole thing sound as if he were giving instructions to a servant regarding what to do with his laundry.

"Lord Greybridge, I cannot allow this!" I said indignantly, standing up and placing my hands forcefully upon the table as I did so. "It simply will not do. I feel awful about this entire misunderstanding. Why, it's not your fault that our two keeps resemble each other so strongly – it's a mistake any of us here at this table could have made!"

I allowed my smirk to be seen for a brief moment before continuing.

"In truth, I would not be able to live with myself if I allowed you to spend a single copper mark on this duel. Please, my lord, grant me the opportunity to defend your good name. Allow me to take full responsibility for this duel, and you will find no cause for complaint, I assure you."

"Indeed." Lord Greybridge stood and nodded to me in acknowledgment. "I do graciously accept your offer Lord Tucat. In three days time, if-"

"No!" a voice half-shrieked desperately. "Lord Greybridge, this wasn't...my intention was not to cause offense! This was not supposed to happen like this! Not at all!"

"Now, now, young Teuring," I said, shaking my head in mock sorrow, "It is over. Accept it with-"

"My lord?" he said to Greybridge, plaintively, "surely you must know that I meant no disrespect! That I was only . . ."

His voice trailed off once he saw Lord Greybridge had once again taken his seat, affecting not to notice Teuring was speaking. The young lord slumped, his shoulders sliding forward in his ill-fitting garment.

"Boy," I said quietly, not bothering to disguise the fact that I had become annoyed. "Take your medicine. Compounding your humiliation by engaging in behavior suited a small child will simply make you look more foolish."

"I...*fine!*" Teuring said petulantly and with hesitating uncertainty. "Duel? Fine! That's absolutely wonderful! I welcome the opportunity, you insipid weasel-faced...*cretin!*"

"Thank you for making my point," I muttered. A few lords close enough to hear me chuckled softly at that.

"If Lord Tucat wishes to duel me, then I shall oblige him," he continued, his disconsolate appearance replaced by a blusteringly overaggressive pose. "Three days hence, at the Circles!"

"Delighted, though if I may make one small suggestion? Please do try to eat something between now and then, would you? I noticed that you hardly touched your food this evening, and a growing young man like yourself needs to keep his strength up. We can't have you fainting from fatigue, can we? Made to look foolish in front of dozens of your peers, why...how embarrassing would *that* be?"

He scowled. I smirked. We stared at each other a few moments more before I realized that it was a perfect time for me to exit.

"My honored lords and ladies, I regret that I will be taking my leave of you now. I am pleased to say that this evening's entertainment has lived up to my expectations entirely," I said, stepping away from the table before turning and bowing extravagantly with a hand flourish and slightly bent knee. "I wish you all a pleasant evening, and look forward to seeing many of you in three days time."

Leaving the keep amid nods and bows, I walked toward the exit where the carriages were stabled, still smiling and in high spirits. I even paused long enough to give Marcsun's cloak broach to one of Teuring's servants, claiming to have found it on the floor. That done, I made my way outside and headed to the area I'd last seen my coachman, Tarryl.

"If you would be so kind as to take me home, Tarryl," I said once I'd located him, stepping onto the small footrest and ducking my head slightly as I entered the coach.

"Aye Milord," he replied.

The carriage ride home was quiet and smooth, spent in silence as I watched silhouettes of buildings and other city structures flit past the window, a smile on my lips.

Chapter 8

"BULLY," THEODORE SMIRKED, beads of sweat standing out on his brow. "That poor, poor kid."

"Trust me, the vile little prig deserves worse, what with the stuff he said about me. Even a kid like him should have known better." I took off the fencing mask, quickly moving to wipe my sopping forehead with my left arm...

Bam! Ow.

I remembered too late that I was still holding my tonfa in that hand. I hate forgetting things like that, not just because it makes me look absent-minded, but also because...well, it hurts.

Theo was right there, laughing at me as I began to rub my now-tender forehead.

"You amaze me sometimes, Vincent. Here we are in the safest room in your keep, wrapped up in practice gear, but I guess that you're just such a sneaky, vicious bastard that you actually waited until your mask was off before catching yourself off guard, mounting a surprise offensive against your forehead. You're your own worst enemy sometimes, I swear."

"Oh shush," I chuckled. "I was simply distracted by my own superb storytelling, bringing you up to speed on all that you had missed. By the way, what happened to you last night? I thought you said you'd received an invite."

"Ah, yes. Something came up, I'm afraid. It was probably for the best, all things considered. I don't think I would have had an easy time maintaining an angry scowl, based on your description of the evening."

"True. Still, this 'something' that came up wouldn't have been a woman, perchance? A dalliance that went on for a little longer than you expected?"

"Vincent," said Theo with the barest trace of indignation, "not everything that holds sway over my day to day activities must possess cleavage, you know. I have a large keep – one over three times the size of your own – and my own territorial dealings to handle. I'm a busy, busy man!"

"Very well, I apologize for assuming it was a girl," I said contritely. "What was her name?"

"Wynnifer," he sighed, ghost of a smile on his face. "Ah, but you should have seen her. Gorgeous length of red hair, eyes so green I thought I was swimming in the ocean. Ah, me. You really should come out in disguise with me one of these nights, wigs and all that. Sometimes it's nice to just let loose and pretend to be someone else, forget your troubles for a while."

"Pass," I said, tossing down the remainder of my shoulder gear and beginning to unbuckle the chest-piece I was sweating uncomfortably in. "I'm sure it's fun, all that, but I'll leave it to you and your knights. No doubt someone would recognize me out with the Haundsing boys, neh?" I pointed at the bridge of my nose to emphasize the point.

"Bah! We'll dress you up in a knight's outfit, tell everyone you got those scars from being hit in the face by a torch-wielding brigand who was trying to run off with a baby, whom you saved heroically. The ladies will fawn over you for hours with a story like that, even if...yeah, yeah," he said, noticing my look. "You're too busy with other stuff, and I keep forgetting that you have this unexplainable aversion to fun."

"We going to go down this vole tunnel again? We've talked about it before."

"Vince, there's no good reason why you can't have a relationship with someone, or connect with someone in a way that doesn't involve you being a lord, or they your tenant. I mean, gods, man! Do you have any company aside from me who comes to the keep? Someone not here on business? Anyone at all?"

"It's not quite that simple. I can't just go and-"

"And I'll be taking that as a no. You work yourself to the bone, trying to do everything yourself. You never have any fun, Vince! You have to learn to let go a bit, delegate. How many people besides me can you say you even trust?"

I opened my mouth as I thought of Cyrus, and then closed it again when I recalled how his shoulders had slumped after dropping off the floor plans, the momentary look of hurt outside of my bedchamber as he realized I hadn't shared the fact that I'd been counting on being robbed that night.

"I'll tell you this much," he continued, "if we didn't know each other – if you and I shared a border and the only thing I knew about you was what I'd heard - you'd have me twitchier than a candlemaker with insomnia."

"You can't be serious! I'm not like that at all, and you of all people should-"

"I know better, Vincent, but *they*," he gestured sharply with his hand toward the door, "don't know any of that, do they? You're like this maniac when it comes to artful thefts and intrigue, and that's all anybody ever gets to see. None of them see you cut loose, or relax...and that makes them nervous! Hades, it even makes me nervous, watching you work as hard as you do, and I'm actually able to come and talk to you about it! Nobody really knows what kind of a guy you are, aside from me, and even that we have to keep a secret!

"So what...I should take up falconing? Visit the bordello? Get roaring drunk in public and wake up in the middle of a street with my trousers down and my face painted green?"

"Nothing like that, but you've got to find balance. Ease up and relax a little every now and then. I mean, just look at you – even this conversation is making you tense, isn't it?"

"No," I said, trying to relax my shoulders without him noticing.

"Liar. You've got to allow for some fun in your life...some living! Did your father shut himself in his keep, or did he take the odd moment or two to actually enjoy being a lord?"

I frowned. He had a point.

"Okay, okay...you can stop badgering me. Next opportunity that comes up where we can don a disguise and go forth into the street, I promise that I'll accompany you-"

"Tonight! Wynnifer has this adorable friend, a tiny little blond thing with the cutest little cleft chin, who-"

"...just as soon as the duel is over and done with."

"Oh, right. Well," he sighed and gave me a sly sideways look, "I suppose I could hold off on seeing her for a couple of days, give her a chance to get her breath back. You know what they say, 'Absence in the heart makes growing...' uh, something, something."

"Theo, your fondness for well tooled phrases tugs at my heart like a...something-or-other."

"Couldn't have said it better," he chuckled, reaching for his foil. "You want me to use something other than rapier and tonfa this time?"

Theo's grounding in weapons and swordplay far, far exceeds my own. To put it in perspective, I am rather smugly told that now, at the age of thirty, I'm approximately the same level of fencer that he was at the age of eighteen. Sometimes when he's sounding particularly smug about it, I'll challenge him to a game of cards just to remind him there are some skills he could stand to improve on as well.

The point is, I've seen Theo fight in serious duels, and I'll be the first to admit that I don't understand half of what he's doing at times. The duelists who don't outright worship him still give him a wide berth and noticeable respect.

Not a bad guy to have as your teacher, really.

"No, rapier and tonfa will be fine." I waved a hand at the dueling circle etched into the floor in front of us. "Shall we continue?"

"Bah, it wasn't me who needed a breather in the first place."

"Well, I could have sworn you needed a break there near the end, what with you hanging your guard so low that your sword was practically scraping the floor," I said in a friendly, mocking tone.

He smiled a special Theo smile. "Want to see what would happen if you tried to get through that?"

"Sure...your funeral. I was trying to be nice and pretend it wasn't there," I shrugged, standing up from the bench and reapplying my protective fencing gear before putting my mask back on.

"You ready?" he asked, opting to put on his mask for this round. Usually he went without when we were practicing, probably just to give me the heebie-jeebies.

"I'm more ready than you, apparently. Up, up!" I said, parodying his own habit of getting me to raise the point of my sword higher if I were letting it drop.

"Indeed. My guard is far, far too low. I look like a rank amateur. Am I?"

"Uh, no. An emphatic 'no' even."

"Well then, you see this...what's your move? How would you take advantage?" he asked.

"Straight lunge through the center, left arm at shoulder height to parry if you attempted to sweep at me as I did so."

"Very good, solid approach. Go ahead."

I did so. I steadied myself for a lunge, and...well, how can I describe it? There was the hiss-sliding of metal, a feeling of panic, the realization that I was taking an additional step forward when I should be stepping back, and then the sound of me hitting the floor with a 'whump'.

When I looked up, Theo was standing on my sword, which was pinned with the flat against the floor, and I was nowhere near it...lying on my side about three feet away from him.

He looked smug. Very smug.

"Don't make me challenge you to a game of cards," I muttered feebly.

His brow furrowed. "Pardon?"

"Never mind. Okay, so that was fun. What exactly happened?" I asked, pulling myself up with the help of the hand he offered me.

"You're getting good enough that you're entering one of the more interesting stages of swordsmanship, where the rules become complex and change ever so slightly. Your defense is near perfect, you maintain your guard well, and you think in terms of how you might leave yourself open to attack even as you yourself attack. So now, when I give you an opening," he said, performing a guard stance and positioning his sword too low, as he had before, "I expect you to take it, and I'm prepared for it. Knowing that you'll be lunging, I begin to block a lunge the instant I see you move, which results in a slightly heavier upwards parry because my sword started so low." He motioned as if performing the act of deflecting my lunge. "Once overextended, even though you weren't off-balance you found that your arm had been diverted upwards, and your instinct was to recover guard position as quickly as possible. Your sword being so high," he took his tonfa and brought it over his head, where my imaginary sword would have been, "all I had to do was help your sword on the way down so that the blade would hit the ground, and once there, step, step, swing to push you over . . ."

He moved with exaggerated slowness so that I could see every detail of what he had done much, much faster when he'd disarmed me. It looked pretty slick.

"Well, so I guess I've learned something today," I said, picking up my practice foil, "And that would be 'Never believe for a second that Theo is getting sloppy or tired.' A question though – Why is it that I don't see people doing things like that more often in duels?"

"Ah, but if you know the person you're fighting is good, you see right through that trick. So, you keep a perfect guard up at all times so that when he sees you with a lower guard and thinks you don't mean to do it, he'll jump at the chance, which you've prepared for...but if they know that you've prepared for it and they only let you think that they're going to take...errr, you know what? First things first. Like I said, the strategy gets pretty complex, and you're in the very beginning stages of learning it."

"So, what you more or less did was open yourself up to a certain type of attack, because you knew that that's how I would have taken advantage of it?" I asked.

Something about how that sounded bothered me.

"Exactly. Now, one of the reasons it's so tricky at this stage is because you might be fighting people who are legitimately worse than you, and you'll begin to wonder if the opportunities you see are...hey, are you okay? You hurt something on the way down?"

"No, I . . ." I said, taking my mask off once more, lost in thought. "Theo, this duel with Teuring, what do you make of it?"

"Well, from all accounts he lacks the funds to even pay a tenth of what a duelist would ask for the prospect of fighting you, in turn meaning that he shall have to fight it himself. I suppose this means that all of us in attendance will be made to laugh, occasionally saying something like 'that poor, poor bastard' to one another as you run him around the dueling circle a few times and leave him utterly exhausted, even if you lack the sadistic temperament to actually make him bleed in unfortunate places. Likely you'll only need to seriously wound him if he goes berserk on you and just starts flailing away with his sword. Inferior swordsmen can sometimes get through even the best defensive guard if they're lucky enough, or simply erratic enough."

"Yes, but . . ." I fought to put my uncertainty into words. "What if he's actually good? Being humbled in a duel against a young lout like him, that would be just as damaging to my reputation as being stolen from, would it not? We knew little enough about him yesterday, even after I went to his keep to spring my surprise on him. I don't recall seeing anything on the information I got from Cyrus regarding Teuring's swordsmanship."

"Then he likely has none," Theo shrugged.

"Yes, but I can't know that, can I?"

"My friend, the two of us have been practicing our fencing together every week since we were both sixteen years old. As lords go, I don't think there's a single one who doesn't come from a line of professional duelists that would give you trouble. In truth you could probably take at least half of the so called 'duelists' I've been introduced to lately. I'll even go so far as to give your ego a boost and claim that you're downright dangerous. You know, except against me," Theo smiled. "Then you're weak and timid, like a little boy whom I might scoff at. 'Ha!' I'd say, scoffingly, and-"

"Okay, let's grab a deck of cards, play some low-stakes lords and deuces later, and I'll take your money one copper at a time until your humility returns. I'm not even certain that 'scoffingly' is a real word. However, I'm very serious, Theo. You've told me that I'm about as good as you were when you were eighteen or so, and he's at least twenty-three. I know next to nothing about this kid. What if he's better than me?"

"Vince, relax," he said, obviously meaning it. "You got like this the last time you had a duel, remember? Even if Teuring hired a trainer as a teenager and practiced every other day...you'd still have next to nothing to worry about. You're actually fencing around the level where I was when I was dueling professionals. And winning, if you'll recall. This kid is a lord, remember...one who barely has enough native talent and smarts to manage his own affairs correctly, and who was stupid enough to want to make his first move against you, of all people. He certainly doesn't sound rich enough to be able to afford proper sword training, or smart enough to feel he needs it."

"No, no I suppose not. No point in borrowing worries, which I suspect is half of my problem. Say, you know what might be interesting?"

"Do tell."

"Well," I said, "he may have gone down to the Circles today in order to solicit the services of a duelist, or has become worried enough about the possibility of having to represent himself that he wanted to flash some steel down there. I think I'll make an afternoon of it, drop by the stables and say hello to a few of the boys. Getting some information on what this kid's been doing or who he's been talking to might be enough to calm my nerves somewhat."

"You know what also might calm your nerves?"

"What?"

"Another lunge, or three," he said with an eager grin, putting his mask back on. "C'mon Vince! I've been waiting years for you to get good enough to use this move against you. You gotta let me have at least a couple more . . ."

"Bully," I laughed, quickly putting my mask back on. "You just watch my fingers...and if any floorboards knock the teeth out of my head, you'll be the one picking them up."

"Sounds fair to me," he chuckled, assuming the same guard position I'd seen minutes before.

I tried getting past Theo's guard five more times. The results? Well, let's just say that I expected to see a few unlikely bruises on my hip the next morning, and that I was very much looking forward to the next time Theo and I found ourselves at a card table.

Chapter 9

EVERY HARAELIAN POSSESSING eyes has seen the architectural marvel known as the Circles. If you have not, I cannot do it justice with these humble words. Poets have tried, some deciding to make describing it their life's work.

Quickly, it is an arena. *The* arena, if you will.

Built against the back entrance of the palace, it's shaped like an enormous bowl that has been tipped toward you and half-buried beneath the sandy ground. It has a multitude of sculpted stone benches for those who are there as spectators, as well as almost a dozen large dueling circles set into the dirt at the heart of the arena floor for those who are there to cross swords. Smaller buildings line the inside of the structure as well, each providing things like food, drink, weaponry, or a better vantage point to watch the action from.

While I'm certainly no stranger to any of these buildings, I usually end up spending most of my time in the large practice area affectionately referred to by duelists as 'the stables'.

"Gentlemen," I called out to three familiar figures sitting at a table not ten feet away from one of the nearby practice circles. Three heads turned to face me, and were almost simultaneous with their smiles of recognition.

"Vincent!" the nearest fellow, a shorter dark-haired fellow named Mouser, answered back happily. "I haven't seen you in a dog's age!"

"Mouser? You're still alive?" I chuckled at the familiar joke, extending my hand to him in greeting. He beamed at me, and stood up to shake it vigorously, as he always did.

"Coming off of six wins in a row, actually. As a matter of fact," Mouser looked briefly to Ashkin and Ismir, both of whom remained seated beside him at the table, "can I tell him?"

"Mouser," Ashkin said patiently, the blond giant of a man grinning sideways at his friend, "you can tell whom you like. I keep telling you, you're not going to hurt my feelings. You've earned it."

"Gods...Vince!" Mouser said excitedly, "You will hardly be able to believe it yourself!"

"Believe what?" I asked.

"I was on run number four this morning with foils, practicing against Ashkin. He...I've got a move! It's like...when you go around – okay, let's say that I'm you, and you're attacking me. No, wait," he said, bubbling with excitement, "if I'm me and you're you that'll make things less confusing. Only, you're Ashkin. Okay, wait. Uh . . ." Mouser paused mid-thought, brow furrowing as he pondered how he might be able to explain it.

I was fairly used to this sort of thing from him by now. I raised an amused eyebrow at Ashkin and shrugged one shoulder in a 'care to explain?' gesture.

"What our comrade is trying to say is that he nicked me. Bad. With practice foils, no less...using a move that Ismir and I figure was half accident, half brilliant. Got me early this morning, he did," the large man said, lifting an already elevated leg onto the bench he was half-reclined on so that I could see the mass of bloody bandages that had been tied around it.

"That, from practice foils?" I asked incredulously, staring at the red stained linen. Then I peered closer and added, "*Calf?!* You got him on the *calf* that badly with a *practice foil?*"

I spun to face Mouser, who was beaming with immodest pride.

"It was the damnedest thing, too," Ashkin said in an amused, rueful tone, gesturing toward his slight companion. "I was doing an overhand crescent, angled to my left because we were trading parries back and forth...and the little bugger decides to do a shoulder roll over to my right to avoid me entirely so I'd overextend a little and turn. Except he muffs it up and his sword gets stretched out behind him because he forgot where to hold it when he does a roll, and he's half on his back and facing the wrong way suddenly, so he spins on his knees with his arm behind him to turn at me and his hand just kind of naturally-"

He made a sideways chopping gesture with his hand. I winced.

"I felt so bad at first!" Mouser grinned, obviously not feeling at all bad now. "He was bleeding pretty heavily, and I yelled for some other trainers, and when they got there they could hardly believe it themselves."

"We had him try it again so we could figure out exactly what happened, and it turns out he can make the exact same silly mistake every time he tries. It's deadly. Ismir just barely managed to hop out of the way in time, and he was watching for it."

"Sneaky, it is," Ismir agreed, nodding to his injured companion. "Had I not known to look, same for me, I think."

"We were just sitting here having a drink and discussing its merits," Ashkin said, gesturing invitingly toward an empty wooden stool at the table. "It's not something that we'd want to practice daily or allow to get well known, but it could be useful under the right circumstances. We were thinking of ways it could be blocked safely."

I took the proffered seat with a nod of thanks, grabbing one of the stoneware mugs that rested on the table beside the pitcher of warmed Iskanian pale ale they were in the process of enjoying. It's vile stuff, brewed with more hops than any sane brewmaster would ever consider using, and always makes my cheekbones seem to hurt when I first taste it...sometimes even when just recalling the taste. It was, however, what most everyone drank at the Stables, and it had a knack for taking the edge off tired, aching muscles. I think they also use it to remove rust from swords, to be honest.

"Well, I'm assuming that thrusting the point of your sword in the ground would do it," I said, bringing the cup toward my lips and bracing myself for a mouthful of the sour, bitter-tasting beverage. "It would stop him in mid-spin, I would guess."

"Bah, you're always trying to be too dramatic, Lord Tucat," Ashkin snorted, "Sticking your sword in the ground is a terribly awkward position to put yourself in, something I'd never do. For one thing, when-"

And we were off. I was at ease and enjoying myself, talking shop with the boys. I found myself listening, talking, arguing, laughing...an hour eaten away by conversation. Ashkin, with his deep booming voice, would describe some strategic situation in terms of cause and effect, and quiet Ismir with his heavy Vereetian accent would interject from time to time to point out some exception to a rule Ashkin was quoting.

Mouser, still in the throes of excitement, demonstrated his move a few times for me. It looked silly and awkward, like a completely inept shoulder roll...right up to the point where his sword was forced to whip around with enough force to cut the legs out from under you. I was impressed despite myself.

It was interesting, if not surprising, that Mouser had come up with something new completely by accident. The other two larger swordsmen were quite expert - you knew what to expect. They practiced form, perfected lunges, and critiqued each other's footwork. When Ismir was focusing on practicing western-style fencing routines alongside Ashkin you could watch the two figures move in almost perfect unison.

Mouser was not like that at all. Erratic is simply not a strong enough word to describe it. Practicing would be a waste of time for him, had it not the added benefit of a workout. However, he had a bafflingly strong defense, and the effect that his terribly executed and seemingly haphazard moves had on his opponents was remarkable - it threw their timing off completely.

The four of us discussed Mouser's newest discovery for a good long time before the conversation began to meander, which is what usually happened when the four of us sat together for any length of time there. In truth, I might have forgotten my reason for being there entirely and instead spent an evening discussing the finer points of palace politics, or attempting to explain my theories on why the price of silver goes up whenever Norsh has a particularly bad winter, had our conversation not been interrupted.

"Ashkin," a confident-sounding voice called out from somewhere behind me.

The blonde man's eyes fixed on a spot over my left shoulder, presumably to focus on the owner of the voice.

"Lord Foxglove," he said, nodding.

What followed was an expectant, uncomfortable silence. Eventually Ashkin seemed to realize something, gave a soft grunt of dismay, then grabbed the edge of table nearest him and propped himself up into a standing position.

"Milord Foxglove," he said once he'd transferred enough weight to his good leg to offer the lord an unsteady bow.

"You've been injured, I understand."

"I'm afraid so," said Ashkin, somehow managing to sound both jovial and glum at the same time. He gestured to his raised and bloodied leg while awkwardly balancing all his weight on his uninjured one. "Probably have to stay off it for at least a couple of weeks."

"I see. Well, that's a bit of luck, at least."

"Milord?"

"Why, the timing! Had this injury occurred prior to your performance yesterday, I might have been rather put out...having to find another duelist and all," Foxglove said, and with the hint of a chortle.

Ashkin gave the comment a patient half-smile as he hopped in place a couple of times. "Aye, Milord."

"He'll be fine, by the way," I announced brightly, turning in my seat so I could smile up at Lord Foxglove, then gestured apologetically toward him. "Sorry to butt in like that...very sorry. It's just I was *certain* your very next question would be about Ashkin's health, so I figured I should answer it before you died from worry."

With exaggerated slowness, Foxglove twisted his neck to look down at me, an expression of distaste upon his face. He blinked slowly, as though processing something, then shifted his attention back to Ashkin.

"I was just reminded - do go and see a healer about your leg right away if you haven't already. If it's attended to quickly enough perhaps you won't be left with a grotesque, unsightly scar."

The comment didn't really bother me - I'd received dozens of similar comments from him in the past, and so was usually prepared for at least one or two of them when he was around. I allowed the awkward, uncomfortable silence to linger for a few seconds before speaking.

"Hang on," I said, snapping my fingers. "I saw what you did there. Did you see that, guys? He noticed Ash's injury, then he saw my face, and *then* he spontaneously ad-libbed a connection between the two! Right there, on the spot...unrehearsed! Truly, as much as I dislike the tired cliché of likening someone's wit to a rapier, I fear that in *this* case-"

"In addition, Ashkin, since you appear to have some time off your feet to reflect, you may wish to spend some time considering the company you keep," Foxglove continued, turning as though about to leave. "I fear your choice of companions may have a negative impact on your employment prospects once you've recovered."

"See," I said, speaking behind my hand in an excessively loud whisper, "I've decoded a few of his subtle clues over the years, and it turns out he doesn't care for me much. I can't for the life of me understand why."

"You don't? Well that's easily remedied - I don't care for your face!" Foxglove said sharply, addressing me for the first time. "Does that help at all?

"Really?" I gave him a light shrug. "Well that's okay, I suppose. I don't care for your trousers, so it all balances out."

"Hardly," he said, not quite sneering at me. "Tonight you'll still be a blighted, disfigured creature with *that* to look forward to every time you glimpse a mirror." He waved a hand at my face and gave me a smug smile. "I, on the other hand, can always change my trousers."

"True," I said, giving him a winning grin wide enough to show off just about every tooth in my head. I grabbed the handle of my sword with my right hand and rattled it gently in its scabbard. "Would you like me to provide you with an excuse to change your trousers *now*, Lord Foxglove?"

His expression barely changed, but it was now contained a trace of uncertainty. I continued grinning maniacally at him.

This time the uncomfortable silence contained the barest hint of electricity.

"I wish you a speedy recovery," he mumbled to Ashkin under his breath, then spun on his heel and brusquely walked away from our table. I waited until he was out of earshot before chuckling softly.

Ashkin sent me a contrite look. "My apologies for that, Lord Tucat."

"Gods, why? That wasn't your fault, was it? And sit back down, for Baal's sake . . . you're not doing your injured leg any favors right now." I gave him a quick grin. "You fight duels for him, it's not like you're one of his knights and have to actually defend him, or his behavior. I imagine his lack of tact is the reason why he's forced to hire duelists as often as he does."

"That sort of thing happen to you often?" asked Mouser as he gingerly helped the much bigger swordsman ease back down into his seat. "I thought lords were all formalities and politeness when dealing with one another."

"Oh, I see rudeness often enough," I said, shrugging one shoulder. "To keep a long story short, my illness has left me unable to have children, and thus aligning myself through marriage with a lady or daughter of a lord isn't really a possibility. Some believe that means they're no longer required to use things like tact around me, since I'm so inconsequential, politically." I gestured at the retreating form of Lord Foxglove. "I've noticed that it's easier to glean someone's true character when you aren't in possession of something they want, or if they don't consider you a threat."

"And they *forget* you're a threat, too...until you challenge them to a duel," said Ashkin with a smirk, nodding to himself.

"Oh, speaking of," I said, attempting to move to a different subject, "I suppose by now you've all heard the details concerning my upcoming altercation? Duel," I added for Ismir's benefit once I noticed his brow wrinkle at the unfamiliar word.

"You mean besides the fact that you're fighting a duel against some kid for Lord Greybridge for free," Ashkin asked blandly, "presumably robbing an honest swordsman of the opportunity to earn a half year's wages in a single bout?"

"Well...as to that, there were some mitigating circumstances I can't really get into at the moment. Long story short, if I hadn't agreed to fight the duel for him, he'd be paying one of you chaps for the opportunity to duel me instead."

"I'm fine with that." Ashkin smiled. "I'm pretty sure I could still take you...and you'd probably net me a tidy chunk of change. Asking price for you was getting steep there for a while, if I recall."

"Well, sorry to have quashed your financial plans like that. Perhaps we could spar for a bit, five gold marks a touch? Oh wait." I feigned disappointment, gesturing at his leg. "I forgot about your injury. Perhaps another time . . ."

"Like I said," said Ashkin, who stretched his mighty arms behind him and grinned good-naturedly at me, "I'm pretty sure I could still take you. As a matter of fact, the injury might make me feel better about collecting my winnings."

"What winnings? I'd just start jogging whenever you got within ten feet of me." I smirked. "Still, this kid wouldn't be much sport for you from what I'm given to understand, unless you've suddenly gone in for stuff of the nasty variety. You know, scars on the arms and face, humiliation, other whatnot?"

"No," he said, seriously, "and you're right, to be honest. I've turned down contracts like that because they're just not my style, and I would have turned this one down if it had been offered with that sort of 'teach him a lesson' caveat. I'm not a butcher, or a bully. Humiliation, putting a scar on a man...lords don't get over stuff like that very easily. You of all people probably know that."

"Yeah," I nodded, ignoring the brief looks of concern both of Ashkin's mates gave him. One of the things I liked about this place, and Ashkin in particular, was the ability to discuss anything frankly and openly. Ashkin made no apologies for referring to my scars, nor did he shy away from the topic when it came up. To him it was a cosmetic part of a person, like the color of their hair.

"No," said Ashkin, "much better that someone like you gently let the kid down, no lasting harm or any nonsense like that. Unless you *want* to, of course...entirely your right, according to the code." He shifted in his seat so that he might adjust how his leg was propped up.

Mouser looked uncomfortable for a second and anxiously offered assistance, which was waved away. Ismir grabbed the now empty pitcher of beer, stood up with a nod and headed toward the nearby vendor's booth, presumably to acquire more.

"Yeah, I'll let him off easy, I figure," I said, shrugging lightly. "No point in making an enemy for life, neh? Young kid, just getting into the game, doesn't really know what he's doing yet. Something like this might just smarten him up. As it is, with what he tried to pull, there's going to be some talk of my restraint if I don't end up giving the young Lord Teuring a scar or permanent reminder of some sort."

Ashkin spluttered beer over his cup mid-sip, and began coughing as if choking. I sat up suddenly and looked to the burly man with concern.

"Oh, gods!" Mouser cried from my left as he doubled over and fell to the ground, disappearing from view. Ashkin began to turn red, breathing coming in labored rasps and short, barking coughs.

I was half convinced the beer we were all drinking had been poisoned, until I realized that they were both laughing.

"Vincent," Ashkin said in a now raspy voice, hand wiping away the lone tear that had formed in the corner of his eye, "you really must warn me when you do that."

"Do what?" I asked, half annoyed, half alarmed.

Instead of answering, the large blond-haired man leaned back on his stool and tilted his head far to the side so he could observe Mouser, who had collapsed on the floor.

"You okay, buddy?" he asked.

The only response I could make out was an awkward, breathless laugh that reminded me of chicken clucks. Ashkin smiled and sat back up in his seat.

"Yeah, he'll be a minute or two," he chuckled.

"Okay, could you please explain what in the name of Hades is so damned funny?"

"My apologies, Lord Tucat. I heard you had a duel, but I didn't hear it was against Lord Teuring. He was here this morning, practicing on one of the wooden crosses. If you could call it practice."

I blinked. "Bad?"

"Hmm, let's see," he mused, chuckling. He leaned back in order to address his friend on the floor. "Hey, Mouser. What did you think of that kid's self-riposte? Or that lunge he tried?"

The laughter from the floor increased in intensity, stretches of silence doubling in length, and punctuated by the occasional explosive gasp for breath.

Mouser was laughing hysterically at the fencing moves he'd seen earlier that morning.

I mean...*Mouser!*

The very man who instructors occasionally used as their "how not to parry" prime example, whose form was so legendarily bad that it was doubtful he could perform a proper forward extension even if he was offered a thousand gold marks and all the girls his tongue could cope with...*he* was laughing at how bad Teuring was!

Oh my.

I had originally supposed that Teuring wasn't an experienced swordsman, it was true...but to be so bad that even the most erratic of swordsmen fell to the floor amid peals of laughter just because you'd mentioned his name...ye gods!

Theo was right...this kid wasn't going to be any problem for me to handle. I felt a small smile find its way to my lips, and my shoulders began to relax marginally, releasing tension I hadn't even been aware I'd been holding there.

Hell, I even started to enjoy my sips of beer a little. Either that or my taste buds were starting to go numb.

"Ismir!" Ashkin yelled, attracting the notice of the darker-skinned man who was standing at the counter with the empty pitcher. "Hey, remember that kid who got disarmed by the wooden practice dummy? He's dueling Vincent!"

And yes, even the quiet, cool and unexcitable Ismir was not immune. Eyes wide with sudden understanding, he grinned uncharacteristically. A second later I could see his massive shoulders shaking in silent mirth.

Wow.

"Oh, this is going to be good," Ashkin laughed. "If only I had known, we could have booked a private arena, arranged to sell tickets...made some money!"

A very red-faced Mouser slowly clawed his way back up into his seat, still laughing as he clutched the edge of the table for balance, eyes awash with the remnants of laughter-inspired tears.

"All right," I said, "so, through my keen powers of observation, I have managed to glean the impression from you fellows that my opponent is less skilled than myself. Astonishing deductive feat, I know. Did he spend any time trying to find some swordsman willing to work for him, asking prices and whatnot?"

"Not from what I was able to see...and I was here all morning, too. He stalked in here just as I was doing my warm-up stretches, scowling and looking blue murder at everyone until his fencing partner arrived. Didn't seem too happy to see him either – dressed him down for being late, wasting time. While waiting, though, he'd pulled out a practice foil and, well . . ." he chuckled.

"How bad?"

"Take the worst swordsman you can imagine, and blindfold him. I'd bet even money on him against Lord Teuring."

"You can't be serious!" I laughed.

Mouser, still flushed and teary-eyed but having recovered his composure, was once more able to contribute to the conversation.

"Oh Vincent, it was so funny. He...he *disarmed* himself! Tried this terrible half-thrust with his sword edge, and it caught on the wooden dummy as he was pulling his hand away. His grip was too light, and it bounced and-" Mouser said, trying to keep his voice even as he spoke, "it almost pinned his foot to the floor! Point came down and missed his boot by a fingers-breadth!"

"Practicing against a wooden dummy? You're joking!"

"No word of a lie, gods steal my voice," he swore, giving a quick throat-slashing gesture with his thumb. "I couldn't stop laughing. Even some of the fellows who felt sorry for him were having difficulties keeping a straight face after a while."

"Well then," I said, sliding my stool back and putting my boots up on the table, "I guess I may just be able to relax a little for this one. Take a day off or something. Still, disarmed by a wooden dummy...the skeptical side of me wonders if you aren't pulling my leg."

"Believe it, you should," said Ismir, who gently set down the full pitcher of beer in front of us with a clunk. He beckoned toward me with his now empty hands, an eager smile on his face. "But see it, you must. Come, this way!"

"What?" I said, perplexed. Then I felt my features go slack with understanding. "He's still here? He's still around, practicing?"

Ismir was nodding as I bolted to my feet in childish glee, already heading in the direction he was pointing.

Mouser rose to his feet as well, while Ashkin shifted forward in his seat as if to stand, groaning slightly and wincing with a pained look of realization, having momentarily forgotten he was too badly hurt to stand.

"Good idea! You stay here and guard the beer, Ash," Mouser said with an impish grin, dancing out of Ashkin's reach a moment later.

I grinned a look back at Ashkin and then hurried to follow Ismir, who was walking quickly and purposefully to the last fencing run at the very edge of the building.

The soft clinking of swords coming over the rise of the last wall contained awkward pauses between strokes, making it sound as though the world had slowed to one tenth its normal speed. A quiet, gentle voice said, "Good! Other side," during one of the longer pauses, and the soft, timid sword-on-sword sounds began anew at the same slow pace. We turned the corner of the last wall then, the three of us, and looked down the narrow strip at the two figures occupying it.

The instructor facing us was about fifteen feet away and near the center of the run, attention absorbed by the movements of his fencing partner. The sweaty, bedraggled, curly-haired figure who had his back to us was wearing a familiar ill-fitting garment embroidered with two linked circles, the crest of Teuring.

"Good! And one last time," said the instructor, encouragingly, beginning an extremely slow attack-block routine that covered the four primary zones that you could perform a basic cut and basic block if fighting one-handed. You attacked while your opponent blocked, and then reversed, a string of eight moves in total, designed to get you comfortable with the notion of stopping and striking a sword blade with your own.

I learned it when I was nine.

Halfway through the routine, as we all stood there watching, young Teuring attempted a clumsy cut at the second position, producing a louder clang than the others he'd made. Then, unbelievably, he reacted to the sudden sound and unexpected vibration of metal on metal with alarm, pulling his arm gingerly to his chest.

Without the fencing blade.

It hung there in the air for a split second and, with sudden realization of what he'd done, he reached desperately for it as it fell to the ground, his dark curls springing frantically about his face as he lurched forward to catch his weapon.

Catch it he did. By the blade, just above the hilt.

"Gahh! *Damn!*" he yelped, flinging the foil to the ground with a clang and pulling his injured hand to his body, arms and elbows all but disappearing from sight as he curled himself protectively around his injury.

There was no helping it. We all laughed simultaneously. Poor Mouser sounded like a marsh-cat keening for a mate.

Teuring spun to face us, his face a twisted mask of pain and rage. His eyes widened as he recognized me, and yet his face barely changed with the acknowledgment. As a matter of fact, he managed to look even more enraged and murderous.

"You!" he spat, clutching his hand even tighter, as though attempting to hide his injury from me. "What right do you have poking your blighted nose into my private affairs like this?"

My hackles, already up a little from my encounter with Lord Foxglove, bristled further at his slight regarding my nose. I considered him a moment, then gave him a beatific smile.

"Terribly sorry. Please forgive the intrusion, but I'd heard so much about your proficiency that I had to come and see for myself." I shook my head in mock solemnity. "Now that I have, I fear I must seek out a priest, for I am now flooded with thoughts of my own mortality."

Ismir chuckled, while Mouser appeared to be well into the throes of another spasmodic laughing fit, face frozen in the most remarkable sort of expression.

"A priest? Capital plan," said Teuring, an arrogant sneer now replacing the incensed look of pain and fury as he clutched his hand to his chest. "Why don't you run along and do that now. The next time I see your disfigured, scar-streaked face, it had better be in the arena!"

There was silence, and even the fencing instructor seemed taken aback by the comment. I smiled a little tight-lipped smile at him, quelling the momentary flash of anger I felt.

It looked like the responsibility of being the reasonable, mature one in all of this was going to fall to me.

I sighed, and waved a 'let me handle this' sort of gesture at Mouser and Ismir before taking a few steps over to where Teuring was standing. Judging from his expression, he appeared torn between the idea of hurling epithets at me and that of running away in fright.

"Hey," I said, and in a voice quiet enough that he'd be the only one to hear it. "Let's talk a moment."

"We have nothing to discuss," he snapped, taking a step back and pulling his hand slightly closer to his chest, wincing slightly.

"On the contrary, I-"

"There is nothing I would *willingly* choose to discuss with you, nor do I wish to subject myself to the unpleasant experience of being forced to stare at your unsettling, plague-eaten horror of a face for any length of time. Say," he murmured, cocking his head slightly, "there *is* something, now that I think on it. I have this theory that the gods are merciful. Proof of it just occurred to me, this very moment. Would you care to hear my thoughts on it?"

A tight anger filled my chest, and I fought to keep it hidden, willing my features to relax and attempting to look as placid and calm as possible. I gave him a half-smile and a patient nod.

"Well, the very sight of *that* plague-eaten, utter travesty of a face looming over them," he said, waving a backhanded gesture at me, "would scare any newborn witless, causing them to shriek and cry, day and night. And thus the gods, in their boundless wisdom and infinite mercy, keep those stricken with rose blight from having children. You know, for the benefit of the rest of us." He smiled nastily. "So that we all might be allowed some sleep."

He took a step backward before giving me a satisfied look, eyes roaming over my features as though attempting to appraise the effect his words had. It was for that very reason I kept my face as impassive as I was able, attempting to betray nothing of my thoughts or feelings just then.

About ten angry heartbeats later I felt it was safe to speak. I took a slow breath.

Perhaps this crass young lordling believed simply being a lord afforded him immunity to the consequences of unspeakably rude and tactless behavior. It could be that he was also under the impression he might actually win this upcoming duel between us.

I decided I would disabuse him of both notions simultaneously.

"Such courageous words, young Teuring. Such *confidence!* Why, no one would talk like that unless they were *certain* of victory." I strode forward so that my foot was next to his fallen foil, watching with amusement as Teuring took an involuntary step backwards at my approach. "No doubt the dropping of your blade was part of a well-timed, well-practiced move designed to give me a false sense of hope as we dueled. Fie, young men can be so cruel."

"Make jokes while you can, Tucat," he sneered, a flicker of embarrassment crossing his features.

"Oh, I make no joke about it. Doubtless you wanted it to be a dramatic moment, us in the arena, your sword on the ground before you, when...may I?" I gestured at his foil on the ground.

He glared murder at me and ground his teeth, still clutching his bleeding hand to his chest. I decided to interpret that as a 'yes'.

"Why thank you. Where was I? Oh yes...the dramatic moment. I come rushing forward, and you-" I slid my foot underneath the blade where it met the guard and lifted the foil upwards with a quick kick. The sudden scrape against the ground caused the blade to sing as it leapt up into my outstretched hand.

Pausing long enough to cast a meaningful look at the bewildered instructor, I swung with exaggerated slowness toward him. He came out of his momentary stupor to make the obvious block.

"At this point, with the element of surprise, you would simply have to back-cut," I said, performing the move as I called it out, "followed by a sweep-cut left, then right..."

The sound of clanging metal produced by the practice blade was now very loud, and very deliberate.

Calling out each move I was performing, I went into a complicated routine featuring a stop-cut, a dangerous spinning upwards slash, and a series of follow up lunges. The instructor, while competent enough, looked flabbergasted to find himself fencing against someone other than his pupil.

"And then, once you've driven me back and can see the fear plainly upon my 'scar-streaked face', you make your move and perform a magnificent overhand crescent-" I said, heaving the blade upward from behind my back, steel whistling as it cut the air. The instructor tried the obvious block, bracing for heavy impact.

...which never arrived. Arm high in the air and blade at an awkward angle, he looked down his nose in genuine surprise at my foil, which now had its point at his chest.

"-that you'd pull at the last possible instant, leaping forward with your point, concluding the fight. Indeed," I said, lowering the foil from the chest of the unfortunate instructor, whose face was now flushed with either exertion or suppressed embarrassment, "there's simply no way I could survive a well-executed routine like that. I'd be a goner."

I looked at Teuring with amusement, the pale youth looking anything but amused. His eyes were glassy and his jaw muscles were clenched, but his eyebrows were no longer set in an expression of anger. They lifted slightly upwards, apprehension and fear apparent.

"Sorry, did you not catch all of that?" I asked, tilting my head slightly. "Tell you what, I'll do it again with my left hand, because you're standing over there. You'll probably be able to see better that way."

"Milord Teuring," said the instructor unsteadily, "is this the man you spoke of dueling two days hence?"

"Yes," he spat, recovering his poise enough to begin glaring at me once again.

"Have you considered a duelist, Milord? I could not in good conscience allow you to-"

"Shut up!" he growled venomously, turning toward the older man, who now wore a distressed look.

No matter what his level of professional detachment, there was likely nothing comfortable about the prospect of training someone just well enough to get them humiliated or killed. I guess it would be kind of like sending a small boy out to kill a rock lion armed with nothing but courage, a dead pheasant, and sharpened wedges of fruit.

"Milord please, I-" he began again.

"You will do nothing except what you have promised to do, and that is to instru-" he paused and gritted his teeth, as if annoyed for having momentarily misspoken, "to *practice* with me so that I might sharpen my skills for my upcoming duel. You," he said, whirling and pointing a bloody finger at me, his hand still displaying evidence of his previous error in judgment, "will cease bothering me here. I wish to train uninterrupted, away from your sarcastic jibes and your disrespectful, ill-mannered temper. Fail to grant me this, and I shall take my grievance to the prince. That goes for your friends, as well!" He waved his blood-soaked digit toward the two men behind me, who had been watching the exchange in sniggering amusement.

"Fair enough," I said, stabbing the foil point-first into the wood of the fencing run and stepping away, my hands raised in mock surrender. "I'm probably not doing myself any favors being this close to a master swordsman like yourself. Doubtless I'll be up for hours, pacing nervously in my room. Gods, the sweet, mocking embrace of death...it all seems so unavoidable now."

Turning my back to him, I began walking toward the two duelists who had accompanied me, both of whom appeared to be enjoying themselves mightily. I noticed, for the first time, the presence of a long buckskin bag that lay on the floor tucked neatly against the wall, the kind with a shoulder strap that was not uncommonly used to haul equipment to and from the stables. It looked as though it contained something slender and sword-like within.

"Before I go, Teuring, I shall do you this one singular favor," I said, hopping over to his bag and crouching down before it, fingers working the drawstring. "I'll show you which end of the sword is the dangerous one. It's pointy, and it's sharp, and judging from your hand, you haven't quite figured out which-"

I stopped once the leather flap had been pulled aside, a little stunned by what I saw before me.

It was a sword hilt. No real surprise in and of itself I suppose, seeing as how these bags are designed to carry swords. However, what I could see of this particular sword practically demanded attention: leather grips well-worn with age and cunningly stretched over recessed bright, shining metal filigree, forming a pattern that would be both elegant and useful when fit into the hand.

And beautiful! The hilt had a guard crafted to look like two leafy branches snaking their way outward, the detail on the leaves so perfect that each one seemed to dare you to touch it, if only to prove to yourself that you beheld metal, and not some new form of silvery metallic plant.

The sword was older than I was, without question, and it paid mute tribute to a time when the art of crafting weapons of violence was taken so seriously that a single sword would take a craftsman months to make, sometimes years. It was gorgeous.

What was more, it was not alone. Behind the first there appeared a second sword handle, which had leaves as well, and-

Teuring was suddenly there, far more quickly than I'd thought possible, throwing the buckskin flap back over the metal blades in anger.

"Get out, I say! Leave us, now! I'll not suffer your presence a moment longer!" he shouted at me, standing protectively over the bundle. There was a different tone to his anger now, an edge that hadn't seemed to be present during our previous exchanges.

"Gracious...I only thought to help," I said, raising my hands in mock innocence and stepping away with an apologetic look. He stood there, a study of furious anger, studying me.

Giving one last sarcastic chuckle, I turned back to my fellows, who were grinning and turning back toward the main hall as I approached, the amusing spectacle having reached its conclusion.

Ismir had put one hand on my shoulder as we walked and was shaking his head sadly. "Young. Proud. Deserving of humbling. But in this...I feel sorry," he said.

He was getting much better with the language in even the relatively short time that I'd known him. I smiled over my shoulder at him.

Part of me wasn't smiling, however.

A familiar uncomfortable, nagging feeling in my shoulders was back. It had been lessening ever since I'd arrived at the stables, and had almost disappeared entirely. It was back now, even stronger, and I didn't understand why.

The swords. What did they mean? They'd carried with them a sort of feeling, something I couldn't place. Surprise, perhaps, like their presence didn't add up somehow.

He'd need a sword in order to fight a duel, though - I had assumed that there was a sword in the bag when I saw it. Opening the bag and revealing a sword, even two, should not have come as a surprise at all.

Troubled, I made my way back to the table where Ashkin waited patiently for our return. Mouser had rushed ahead and was already in the process of telling his friend what had happened, describing Teuring's ineptness in glowing detail.

I sat, only half-listening, taking the opportunity that Mouser's fine storytelling provided to consider things.

Those swords were wrong somehow. Why?

I needed answers, I realized.

As luck would have it, I was best friends with exactly the kind of person who might have the answers I was looking for.

Chapter 10

THEODORE'S KEEP IS within view of mine, the dark-stoned structure located perhaps a little more than a city block away from Tucat Keep. Despite its closeness, the fact that we publicly pretend to hate each other's guts makes it difficult to arrange a meeting with him much of the time.

Sometimes I'm forced to improvise . . .

I stifled a childish giggle as Theo entered the largest stairwell in his keep, the one that led to his library, and then walked right past where I was hiding. I was glad to see him finally descending the stairwell I'd hidden in, as the ledge I was perched on was cramped, my legs were beginning to complain vigorously, and the only company I'd had for the past half hour was a stone gargoyle.

"Theo!" I whispered, loudly.

The twitch of his shoulders as he spun around, combined with the look of alarm on his face, very nearly caused me to break into peals of laughter.

"Who-" he began, hand reaching for his sword.

"Theo, it's me! It's Vincent!" I whispered, as I stood up and away from the statue that obscured me, half to reveal myself and half because my legs demanded it. I rubbed them with a pained expression, attempting to encourage blood circulation.

"It...Vincent? You...what in the name of *Hades' hammock* are you doing here?" he said, in a whispered voice that was so loud it likely carried up and down the hall.

"I had to talk to you about something."

"Baal's bleeding bastard, Vince! I-"

"*Shhhhh!*" I hissed, making downward gestures with my open palms. "We probably don't want to attract notice from your household. I don't think either of us have an excuse prepared that would explain us conversing freely in the middle of your keep."

"Well," he said, voice dropping to an urgent, annoyed whisper, "that's true. How did you even get in here? And what in all the gods' names could be so damned important that you'd risk your own neck just to see me?"

"As to the former, if I told you how I got in here you'd just go and put some extra security there, and I couldn't very well use it the next time, could I? As to the latter, I've . . ." I trailed off, uncertain how to express my concerns.

"You're paranoid again." He didn't phrase it as a question, and he didn't quite roll his eyes as he said it.

"Theodore - we're thieves. This is a city ruled by thieves. You and I are Thief Lords, in fact, for whom paranoia is a survival instinct."

"Well, what is it then? What's got your hair all twisted now? What couldn't have waited until tomorrow evening?"

I told him in a hushed voice about my encounter with Lord Teuring in the Circles that afternoon, glossing over some of the more amusing details for the sake of brevity. He raised his eyebrows a couple of times as I described the young fellow's attempt to catch his falling blade, and subsequent injury to his hand. His expression barely changed once I got to the swords.

"Bah. He needs swords, obviously, if he thinks he's going to be fighting you himself. Did you think he'd bring a pair of sticks? Or a fork? You're making a bit of a fuss about spotting two swords inside of a building that probably houses thousands of swords, aren't you?"

"I'm not the only one who made a big deal out of these swords," I said. "I barely got a look before he came rushing over to cover them...and there was something different about how he acted right then."

"Different? How?"

"I don't know, exactly. Sometimes when he's posturing and blustering, it's like an obnoxious kind of childish pique, but this seemed to really annoy him."

"So, maybe the swords are heirlooms of some sort. Maybe he felt you were being disrespectful, just wandering over and handling them like that. It isn't exactly polite to just rummage through someone's possessions right in front of them."

"You had to see the swords though, Theo. They were magnificent. If they were heirlooms, you would hardly want them to leave your keep. What's that one sword you have, the one that you told me you'd never use sword-on-sword in case it were to get damaged? I saw it once."

"Haundeuse? The one crafted by Knothill?"

"Yeah, that one. Just seeing these blades put me in mind of the very first time you showed me that sword of yours. I'd been amazed to even consider how much work had gone into making it. Same feeling with these."

Theodore started to laugh. I started to get annoyed.

"Theo, could you please be serious?" I snapped.

"Oh, it's hard," he said, shaking his head. "Your mind works in truly unusual ways when you're all wound up before a fight, I've never seen anything quite like it. You're concerned that this kid, who cut himself right in front of you, might be carrying two priceless Knothill swords around with him, when everything we know about him suggests that not only is he poor as a mouse, but that he doesn't even know how to fence? This is good, even for you."

"What were they doing there, then? Explain how it is that a kid like him has two swords like that...in a scenario that makes sense."

"Well, they're not Knothill swords, that's for sure...probably cheap knock-offs, fancy looking trash. The fellow needs swords if he's going to fight you, Vincent. He'd been down at the Circles all day, you'd said. What if he was picking them up?"

I shook my head. "Too expensive. They could have been knock-offs, sure – I'm no expert at spotting these things, but I do know quality when I see it. So as knock-offs go, these weren't cheap. And, if he bought the swords that morning, why is he fighting the duel himself if he's got that kind of money sitting around?"

"Vincent..." he began, shaking his head sadly.

"Well? Give me some other reason, something plausible!"

"They were the instructor's, maybe?"

"Why would Teuring have gotten upset, if that were the case?"

Theo frowned slightly.

"Okay, maybe they're heirlooms, like I said. Gods, Vince, you and I both have family stuff that's been collecting dust over generations. What if this kid was going through some of the family belongings, stumbles upon the swords, figures he'll spare himself the expense of buying new ones, and get trained with the swords he has? Maybe he was down there to buy a practice foil with the same weight and balance as those swords."

"Heirlooms are for people who can afford to keep them. This kid didn't have matching tablecloths, for crying out loud. Nobody, no matter how significant the heirloom, lets a fortune in sculpted metal sit in an attic collecting dust while they live in relative poverty. Even his clothing required some serious examination by a qualified tailor, it fit him so poorly," I said, making a mental note to keep my voice down at that point, as I realized that the discussion was causing me to become forgetful of where I was. "And that's another thing. Your keepsakes, such as the sword and other things handed down to you...what makes them keepsakes exactly?"

"Errr, that kind of sums it up, doesn't it? They were handed down to me from-"

"Yes, yes, but why exactly were they handed down? They had something to do with family, didn't they? They're important. Your tablecloths, wall hangings, candleholders, they've all got something to do with wolves, your family symbol. Your sword has the family crest displayed somewhere on it, or a wolf motif if I recall."

"Both. Well, yes, obviously if we were to pay someone a small fortune to create something for our family, we'd prefer it if our crest was displayed, or the family were referred to somehow." He paused, thoughtfully. "Doesn't have to be, though. Tables, furnishings, the like. You can have a favorite chair from your childhood, one that someone special sat in whenever they played a game of *Roc'la* against you, any sort of item that you associated with good times."

"Yeah, but a sword? Even my blunted practice blades have an engraving of my family crest on them. If you've already had a seal made for yourself or your merchant, apparently getting that same relief pattern stamped into another piece of metal is simplicity itself. Why-"

"Milord Haundsing?" an unfamiliar female voice called up from just outside the stairwell entrance.

We both froze. Theodore looked stricken, and waved at me with the backs of his hands in a shooing gesture. I practically dove back behind the statue I'd first concealed myself with, and went still.

"Yes?" Theodore said, attempting to sound natural.

"Milord, is there something the matter? I heard voices."

I couldn't place the voice, and I didn't want to peek around my stone guardian in order to catch a glimpse, just in case she had entered the stairwell.

"No, no...nothing's the matter. I was just...err," he began uncomfortably.

"Talking?" said the unknown female.

"Yes."

There was a long pause.

"To...yourself?"

"To the, uh, statue...actually."

There was an even longer pause that made me a tad nervous.

"Talking. To the statue," the voice finally said.

"As it were, yes," Theo finished lamely.

There was yet another significant pause. I cursed silently as I felt a cramp begin to form once more in my legs.

"Are you feeling all right, sir?"

"Yes, of course. I'm feeling . . ." he trailed off.

"Milord?"

"Actually, no. No, I haven't been feeling good come to think of it, and I might know the reason. Judinae, could you please have a talk with your fellow knights about the burning of flitleaf while in the keep?"

"Sir?" The voice, which apparently belonged to a girl named Judinae, sounded puzzled.

"I've been getting rather lightheaded and dizzy lately, and when it's been happening, I've been noticing a pronounced haze in my study and the distinct odor of flitleaf. It must be affecting me, since I don't ordinarily touch the stuff. And I think we both know exactly where it's coming from."

"I...that is to say-" she began, sounding a little less suspicious and a little more flustered. "The other knights said you didn't mind that sort of thing."

"I don't mind, provided that at least *some* effort to ventilate the smoke is made. I mean, ye gods woman! Are they making *bonfires* out of the stuff? I'm an entire floor up from the off-duty mess hall. You'd think that would provide some measure of protection, and yet here I am talking to statues! I can't wait to see what kind of a mess I've made of this week's budget, which I was attempting to sort out in my study."

"Milord, I'm sure they had no idea. I shall talk to the other knights about this, immediately."

"See that you do. The last thing I suspect your fellow knights want would be for me to make some critical miscalculation regarding their weekly stipend, accidental or no."

"Well...yes sir."

"Oh, also," he added, seeming much more relaxed, "could you fetch me one of those heavy lemon cakes from the kitchen and bring it back to the study for me? I find myself suddenly famished for some odd reason."

There was a knowing chuckle. "Yes, Milord."

I waited in breathless silence until I heard Theo say "Okay, she's gone. You can come out again."

"Whew," I said, peeking my head out from behind the stony knee of the winged figure that scowled down at me imperiously. "That was smoothly done."

"What? The flitleaf thing? Bah, I'm pretty sure that she didn't buy it. Doubtless she suspects that I'm engaged in a clandestine meeting with a paramour, secret love or some such thing. At any rate, she's a smart one, and won't be back here anytime soon if she suspects that I'm in the middle of something."

"You made up that bit about the smoke?"

"No, I've actually been meaning to mention something about the burning of flitleaf to my knights anyway; a bunch of them have been acting twitchy and paranoid lately. Speaking of paranoia...you were saying?"

"I...right, the swords. Theo, I'm just saying it doesn't make sense. The kid has two – *two* – amazingly well-crafted swords. If they're heirlooms, why is his family symbol not present somewhere on them? Why the leaves around the guard? Why didn't he sell one so he could spruce up his place, make his announcement dinner more impressive? For that matter, why isn't he selling one in order to buy the services of a duelist?"

He shrugged at me. "Maybe they're not his to sell?"

"That doesn't strike you as odd? If they're not his, then whose are they, exactly, and what is he doing with them? If he's being supported by another lord, then which one, and why? Why would they give him swords and not offer to help in other ways?"

"I just don't think it's as big a deal as you make it out to be, Vince. They're only swords, after all. Everyone's got at least one."

"It's about questions that don't have proper answers! Look, if you were to go hunting with someone who had claimed they'd never hunted in their life, and they showed up the morning of the hunt with a bow that could easily launch an arrow farther than a man can see on a clear day, you wouldn't think something was amiss?"

"I'd figure they were rich, and had tried to impress me with an expensive bow, but yeah...I guess I would figure that was a little odd."

"That's what I'm trying to say!" I said plaintively. "It's odd, Theo, and I hate odd. There's something about this situation that doesn't make sense. Why did this kid come after me in the first place? He's never done anything noteworthy before. Why him, and why me?"

"Maybe he'd heard you were an easy target."

"Am I?"

"No."

"Correct...and I don't exactly hide that fact. So where would he have heard something like that? How would he get information to that effect, and from whom?"

"Errr." He stopped to consider that one. "Someone who didn't much care for him?"

"And that little possibility doesn't strike you as being important? What if I'm being used, Theo? Maybe Teuring is actually a victim in all of this? What if he was set up?"

Theo snorted derisively. "To what end?"

"How should I know? I've only come up with that particular notion myself. But think about it...what if someone wanted to set up Teuring but didn't want their own hands getting dirty? What if Teuring is simply a distraction to keep me occupied, for that matter?"

"Unlikely to the point of being laughable, Vincent."

"But possible, and what's more it might actually make a small measure of sense, much more so than a young lord believing that I would be a promising target for his first foray into Haraelian politics. There are other little things that seem to support something like that as well."

"Such as?"

"You received information prior to the break-in about Teuring wishing to use your territory as a staging area. You can't even be sure that it wasn't someone from Teuring's household that you were speaking to that night, can you? He wore a mask, from what you said. At the banquet I discovered that at least two others knew something of Teuring's plan as well, Lord Cleaver and Lord Marcsun, both of whom neighbor my territory."

I watched his thick eyebrows rise in surprise and then furrow, and he appeared to be uncertain for the first time in the entire conversation. "You think the information was planted? Why didn't you mention this earlier?"

"*May* have been planted, and it didn't seem like such a big deal at the time. It was just odd, that many people knowing about it...but what if I was *supposed* to have found out? Why else would so many people know about it before it happened? If I hadn't heard about it from you, chances were still good I'd have heard about it some other way."

"So what are you suggesting is going on?"

"I don't really know," I said, feeling my shoulders slump slightly, "but I need to know more. What made Teuring think it would be a good idea to rob me? Who does he know? The swords might tell us more about what's going on, and you're the most knowledgeable person I know when it comes to that stuff. Why, I know blacksmiths who wish they knew as much about swords as you."

"Heh. If I wasn't already convinced you considered this important, that bit of flattery would have given it away." He chuckled. "So, what exactly do we do?"

"Well, you were part of his original plan, right? Wouldn't it make sense if you went down to the Circles, a fellow swordsman who hates my guts, to give him some pointers? Fawn over his swords, ask him the history behind them, that sort of thing?"

"But if the information was planted as you said, he may not have even used my territory. He may not even know who I am."

"Which," I pointed out, "would tell us something. Confirm that he wasn't aware that I was being tipped off."

"I see," he said, nodding. "Get close enough to evaluate him, strike up a conversation, try to get him to talk about who gave him the swords, stuff like that. Down at the Circles you say?"

"Yeah. If you went down first thing tomorrow, I-"

"What? First thing? In the *morning?!*" Theo asked incredulously.

"Look, I know it's a lot to ask, but-"

"You'd better believe it's a lot to ask! Stones, Vincent! Do you know when the last time I had to wake up before the dueling hour was?"

"Theo, please. For me?"

He scowled at me, which I figure was only half in jest.

"Fine," he said, finally. "You owe me something considerable."

"How about I give you a detailed description of how I got into your keep?"

Theodore appeared to ponder the matter, lightly combing his short beard with his fingers.

"And dinner," he said. "Something large and steak-like. This whole thing is probably nothing, but if I'm going to spend a whole day coddling an arrogant wanna-be swordsman, in addition to an evening spent trying to cure you of your paranoia afterwards, you're going to have to have your chef make it worth my while."

Chapter 11

CERTAIN FORMS OF waiting are better than others. Personally, I believe the worst type of waiting is the kind where you fill your day with all manner of activities, as though by keeping yourself busy and your time occupied, you can somehow trick yourself into believing you're not really waiting at all.

This tactic never works for me, because I'm not an easy guy to trick. And yet whenever I find myself in a position where I do have to wait, keeping myself busy to make the time pass faster always seems to be the first thing I end up trying.

Upon waking, the first thing I opted to focus on was the acquisition of breakfast. This hardly sounds like a difficult task, but depending on what sort of mood Mosond was in, and what he'd made up his mind to cook that morning, it could become downright impossible. Don't get me wrong, more times than not I'll happily eat whatever creation he puts in front of me...but there are some mornings when you don't want a delicate filet of something-or-other drizzled with a lemon herb reduction, where what you're really after is just a bit of ham and egg, perhaps with a splash of pepper sauce. Oh, he'll eventually make whatever I tell him to, but he always seems to do so with an air of indignation, like such a thing is beneath his dignity.

This particular morning he'd chosen to make poached redfish and eggs, served with a bright green sauce that smelled of parsley and garlic. It seemed like an agreeable meal to begin the day with, so I didn't request any additions or changes, which would likely result in the kitchen being a little quieter this morning, and perhaps even make Mosond a little easier to deal with by the time lunch rolled around.

Once I'd finished breakfast, I stopped by the greeting hall briefly, checking the writing table for any new letters or reports that might have been left there by my knights during the night. Finding none, I gave a quiet grunt of approval and continued on to the staircase, heading upstairs to my study so I could address the small pile of assorted letters, petitions, and reports I had waiting for me there.

It took me less than twenty seconds to disable all the traps and alarms protecting the study, unlock and open the door, walk into the room and seat myself comfortably at my desk. If I sound a touch proud of this fact, well...perhaps I am. I won't tell you exactly how I accomplished this minor miracle, but suffice it to say that anyone else attempting to get into that particular room would likely take much, much longer than that. Even more likely is the possibility of some grievous injury being inflicted upon them during the attempt.

I take the safety of my journal collection very, very seriously.

The short stack of missives and notes on my desk turned out to be a fine example of exactly the sort of things lords such as myself have to contend with on a regular basis. For example, three tenants of mine were respectfully requesting an extension on the monthly tribute they owed me, pleading extenuating circumstances as the reason. I checked my records and granted the requests of the first two, then drafted a note asking Cyrus to arrange for the third tenant to come down to Tucat Keep and explain his circumstances in person. This was the second time in as many months this particular fellow had requested an extension, and while I'd probably end up granting it, I've found that spending some time in a room with a tenant and letting them stammer out an explanation face-to-face often times results in a noticeable decrease in the frequency of such requests.

There had also been two thefts in my territory reported these past couple of days, both which appeared to be working themselves out on their own. The stolen items had been marked with a merchant seal prior to being stolen, and had already been handed over to a local fence. Fences would never knowingly traffic an item that had been marked with a lord's seal, of course...not if they wished to keep an even number of fingers and toes. This one had notified me that I could pick the items up at my leisure, or they could return it to the proper owner on my behalf in exchange for a small fee.

Lately, I'd been requesting that any such items be brought back to me directly, so that I could then return them to the affected merchant or house owner myself. It seemed to fit my current plan regarding my reputation – a smiling, friendly Lord Tucat coming to the rescue, taking a personal interest in the wellbeing of his tenants.

The fact that I myself had a hand in stealing some of the items I'd been returning lately was a given, of course. Reputations like mine don't just make themselves.

Aside from the tenant related notifications there was also a handful of petitions from merchants requesting permission to open up shop on my territory, several polite inquiries as to what the monthly tribute would be for specific addresses, and a couple of letters from nearby lords asking permission for their knights to enter my territory, likely so they could escort a particularly valuable shipment of goods down one of my streets. For the most part these were mere formalities, but given all of the things happening around me that didn't quite make sense I made certain to scrutinize each request carefully before stamping them with the Tucat seal and putting them aside to give to Cyrus later.

Once I had finished sorting through these various requests, I locked up my study and went downstairs to do a quick check of the time. Eleven bells...not yet the dueling hour, which was the soonest Theo had said he might return from the Circles, promising that the absolute latest he'd arrive was three bells.

Lunch wouldn't be for another couple of hours, so I decided to spend some time downstairs in my exercise hall to work up an appetite. Once down there, I didn't bother lighting any of the usual vimroot oil torches, choosing instead to fire up some relaxing foxmallow and chicory candlesticks.

The velvety, soothing smells did very little to calm my nerves, and I found myself driven to distraction by even the smallest of movements and sounds. The creaking of wood as I climbed a faux parapet, the scrape of my padded gloves against the stone of my climbing wall...each noise sounded like something that might have heralded Theodore's arrival, and instantly wrenched my attention away from what I was doing and toward the secret door.

After a couple of hours of this sort of thing, I realized that attempting exercise was not relaxing me like I thought it might. I cleaned up and headed back upstairs to the main floor, opting not to have lunch sent down via the dumbwaiter as I'd originally intended. If lunch were to hold any sort of enjoyment for me, I'd have to take it in a place where I wouldn't interpret every noise as a sign that Theo may have returned.

I hadn't realized that I'd made eating down in my exercise hall such a habit. Two members of the kitchen staff were lounging around in the dining hall, looking quite startled to see me there. Several stammering attempts were made to apologize for the lack of finery being set out for me, and I brushed them away, advising that I would prefer to take lunch in the sitting room rather than put them through the trouble of setting up the dining room table just for me. The younger, lankier of the two servants, scurried off to convey that news to the kitchen with haste, presumably attempting to make up for his idle loafing with a display of blistering speed.

After receiving my plate of steaming victuals in record time, I made my way to the sitting room, where I encountered a similarly bewildered expression. Talia's flaxen curls were a blur dancing around her face as she turned her head to greet me, looking astonished.

My attractive young keepmistress was luxuriously reclining on the shallow couch against the back wall with a dinner pastry in one hand and an open book in the other, feet nearest the crackling fireplace, a combination of which made for an extremely fetching pose. The hem of her green-gray dress fell away from her upturned knees enough to reveal a shapely calf, the rest of her dress arranging itself in a manner that suggested there were many other shapely things worthy of consideration.

Talia hastily leapt to her feet in a whirl of feminine poise, despite my attempts to protest. She colored mightily, and stammered her apologies for presuming to sit in a room clearly meant for lords and ladies, informing me that it would never happen again, and had begun plaintively assuring me that she was on her break rather than shirking her duties before I finally managed to get a word in.

"Talia, it's all right. This is a 'sitting room', after all...I could hardly chastise you for sitting down while in one now, could I?" I smiled easily at her, an expression that did nothing to change the look of panic and concern she was giving me.

Her expression reminded me of the conversation I'd had with Theo...how hard I'd been driving myself. The wall I kept up between me and my staff, how others saw me. I felt a pang of melancholy.

Even the lovely Talia, whose friendly voice I often heard confidently exchanging clever lighthearted barbs with the other staff, was not immune. The Talia that I knew when speaking to her in person differed greatly from the wry and mischievous lass she became when she believed I was not around.

I fleetingly wondered if I might get to meet that other Talia someday. Judging from the look on her face and how unexpectedly flustered my presence seemed to make her, I didn't think it likely.

"Milord, I see you mean to use this room," she said, appearing to come to a decision, bobbing her head respectfully and hurriedly collecting her belongings. "I'll retire to a more appropriate place."

"Talia, by all the gods woman-" I said, allowing frustration to creep into my voice, "if I have to order you to sit back down, I will. I just came up for a spot of lunch. Please, I don't want to feel like I've driven you out of here or anything."

After some badgering, she finally relented. She sat back down upon the couch, straight and proper, and nowhere near as artistically satisfying as her previous pose had been.

Ah well.

I would have been content with her simply resuming reading, but it seemed that my presence caused her to feel obligated to attempt some sort of conversation, though the very prospect appeared to fill her with dread. She stammered her way awkwardly through a couple of social niceties as I ate, talking about the weather and such, each attempt at conversation punctuated by an awkward silence once I'd responded.

Between bites I attempted to ask a few questions of my own, all meeting with a similar kind of success...a quiet, simple answer that seemed to linger just on the cusp of full-blown conversation without actually becoming one. Then I realized I did in fact have a question of substance for her, something I'd been meaning to ask her but hadn't yet had the chance.

"Mmm, Talia," I managed to say just before nearly choking on a stray bit of half-chewed bread. I coughed a couple of times to clear my throat, somehow causing her to look even more alarmed, and she made as if to stand before I waved her a gesture that I was okay. "Sorry. A question for you, if you don't mind. It's regarding that courier from the other day. The one with the mask. Can you recall any other details about him, or anything that seemed unusual at the time?"

Talia frowned, and her eyes got a bit of a faraway look for a brief moment before she shook her head. "No, milord. The mask was the first thing I noticed, after which I attempted to glean additional information about him from what else he wore. It was all very nondescript, and he left shortly after leaving his delivery with me."

"Hmm. Voice?"

"Gentle tenor, no accent."

"Might you recognize it, if you heard it again?"

"I doubt it, milord," she said apologetically. "He spoke a mere handful of words to me."

I gave a short grunt. "Height?"

"Roughly your height, milord. Perhaps an inch shorter."

"Hmm. About as nondescript as it gets. Say, what time would you make it?"

"I would say it was just shy of...one bell?" Talia appeared to realize something and got to her feet, clutching her book to her chest, thumb marking the page she was on. "Milord, I'm afraid I may have lost track of time, and must return to my shift now."

"Well...yes, all right. Thank you, Talia." I gave her what I hoped was an appreciative nod.

She gave me a terse nod and a ghost of a smile in return, before turning and exiting the room, her skirt making the faintest of rustling noises as she did. It occurred to me as she left that her expression had contained a hint of something odd...something like embarrassment perhaps.

I sighed and looked down at my plate, realizing that I was no longer all that hungry. Perhaps the fastest lunch ever. And, to top it all off, I was also pretty sure I'd somehow ruined the rest of Talia's afternoon.

After dropping off my plate and what remained of my lunch at the kitchen, I considered my options. I'd only just come up from the exercise hall, so checking it again for some sign of Theo would be pointlessly obsessive. There was always exercise, but I'd already done more of that than I should have, especially considering I was fighting a duel on the morrow.

I briefly toyed with the notion of spending some time in the kitchen, but I could still remember the last time I'd tried that. An emotionally charged kitchen run by a chef whose only interest, aside from cooking, comes from yelling at his staff and calling them idiots in a hundred different ways...well, I wouldn't say it's the greatest place in the world to relax.

There was my study, but most of my lordly duties had already been looked at and addressed. Perhaps read a book to pass the time, much as Talia had been doing? Worth a shot.

I returned to my study and selected a journal I'd already read at least a dozen times, opened it to a random page near the front, leaned back in my chair, kicked my feet up onto my desk and began to read. Then, after reading the first few pages, I realized that I *didn't* in fact wish to read this particular journal, and got up from my chair to fetch a different one...a journal I'd read at least *two* dozen times. After sitting myself down and spending a few minutes getting comfortable, I cracked that journal open to a random page and began to read it. It only took a couple of sentences for me to know at exactly which point in the plot I was, and I allowed familiar words describing a familiar story to play themselves out in my imagination.

Quite some time later, an anxious part of my brain began to wonder what time it was, and if perhaps Theo was currently downstairs waiting for me in my exercise hall. I tried focusing on the words in front of me for a few moments, blinked, sighed, and tried again. Then I snorted in disgust, tossed my journal onto my desk and headed back down to the exercise hall.

Upon arriving, I was surprised to find Cyrus there, holding several sheafs of parchment. He looked as though he'd just arrived moments before, and had been about to leave. Looking for me, apparently.

"Milord," he said, stopping in place and straightening himself, drawing the heels of his boots together slightly as he did. "I was just about to see if you were in your study."

I smiled at him, suddenly feeling a touch frustrated. Theo could be hiding in our secret passage at this very moment, patiently waiting for Cyrus to leave before making his presence known.

"I see. I take it there's something you wished to discuss, Cyrus?"

"Indeed, Milord. As you had requested, I did some research down at the palace, going through some of the old records and comparing them to the parchment you received."

"Excellent. And you discovered evidence that it was- . . ." I gestured for him to continue, having a feeling I already knew what he was about to tell me.

Cyrus shifted uneasily in place for a moment, and licked his lips before opening his mouth to speak.

"Milord, a great many things suggest the note may be authentic."

Okay, not what I was expecting after all.

I gave him a dubious look, feeling a bit tense all of a sudden. "You're saying it's...authentic?"

"Not at all, Milord. I'm merely saying that if the note you received was not penned by Preceptor Aleksandra Cheyne over fifteen years ago, then a great deal of effort was put into making it appear so. I was able to gain access to several documents - including some of her field orders - so that I might compare. There were some differences, as always happens with handwritten documents...but there were many very curious similarities. Paper type was very similar, and even appeared to be of a similar age. Same quick flourish encircling the letter 'A' where she initialed, same slightly wavy right-to-left squiggle used in place of the letter 'L', same line thickness and letter height. I could only sneak a minute or so in the archive, but I tried to be as effective as I could with the time I had."

I considered his words. "So what you're saying is that if this note was indeed forged, then it would appear to be a very *good* forgery."

"Yes, Milord. While it is by no means conclusive, I could spot nothing that made it immediately obvious that the document was fake, and a forgery of this quality would be a costly endeavor. I'm by no means an authority on the subject, but I know of only two people who might be good enough to try their hand at forging palace archive documents, and they aren't what I'd call cheap."

"I can well imagine, considering the risk involved in forging a crown document. However, if the note is indeed a fake, it sounds like we've already narrowed down the people who could have pulled it off. And I'm pretty sure this particular job would stand out in the mind of whoever had been asked to do it. So if they had their handiwork waved in front of their face, they may react in such a way that gives them away, at which point we press them for more information about who hired them."

"That was also my thought, Milord, but I also had to ask myself...why?" Cyrus flipped through a few of the papers he held and frowned at them. "What was the point of this? If someone has money enough to pay for something that could pass as an official palace record, why not arrange for a more profitable document to be forged instead?"

"Because I suspect the whole reason it was commissioned in the first place was to keep me off-balanced and preoccupied...distracting me, making me an easier target when the time came to rob me."

Cyrus directed his frown at me. "Except that it didn't."

"No," I said, returning his frown as I considered. "No, it didn't."

I pondered that. Shelling out the gold necessary to buy a forgery good enough to pass for an official palace record penned over a decade ago, all just to make me easier to steal from? Both expensive and pointless, since the note's arrival had the opposite effect, and tipped me off to the possibility of a scheme against my interests in the first place.

And Teuring certainly wasn't rich enough to throw gold away on a costly forgery. From all appearances he was barely able to maintain his threadbare keep. So, in all likelihood, the note had to have come from someone else.

Perhaps that same someone who had furnished the young Lord Teuring with two amazingly well-crafted swords for his upcoming duel against me?

Maybe the note had accomplished what it was supposed to after all. It had tipped me off to what was happening, and in a manner that managed to piss me off. What if the whole point was to make me angry with Teuring?

And then there was the small, niggling thought in the back of my head, the one I didn't want to look at too closely.

What if the note wasn't a forgery?

What if it was real, perhaps a missive that had never actually found its way to the palace? I hadn't been distracted by its arrival because I'd been so certain it was a forgery. What if whoever sent it assumed I would believe it to be real...simply because it *was* real?

That the note was a fake was the much more likely scenario of the two, obviously. Stealing something from the palace archives just to get me wound up was disproportionately risky and nonsensical, an act akin to lighting your keep afire just to rid it of mice.

Regardless, it was looking more and more like the note hadn't actually come from Teuring. Real or fake, either would have been much too costly for some penniless young lord to arrange.

Someone had maneuvered Teuring against me. More importantly, that same someone might be maneuvering me as well, pointing me at Teuring.

It galled me that I now had something in common with the brash young lout.

"Cyrus, I would like you to drop everything else you're doing and-"

"-discover for certain if this note is a forgery or the real thing, Milord?" he asked, nodding to himself as he spoke.

"No, that's now a secondary priority. Your main one will be to get me everything you can find out about Lord Teuring. I want information on everything he's ever done, who he's friendly with, who he's quarreled with, who he's associated with in the past, everything you can find. If anything about him strikes you as odd or nonsensical, look into it. I believe someone has put a great deal of effort into ensuring that

Teuring's path has crossed mine, and I'd very much like to know why."

Cyrus nodded. "I'll gather every scrap of information I can, Milord."

"See to it. Oh . . .what time would you make it, Captain?"

He considered. "I came down here looking for you shortly after three bells I believe, Milord. Say, just shy of half past three?"

I gave him a quick nod and a gesture in return, which he correctly interpreted as a dismissal.

After he'd disappeared into the hallway and pulled the massive wooden door closed behind him, I heard the familiar cadence of his boots hitting the stone as he hopped from one safe spot to the next, deftly avoiding the many traps guarding this place. I listened long enough to ensure he was a proper distance away, then got up and practically bolted for the doorway to the secret passage, utterly convinced I'd open it and find Theo patiently waiting on the other side.

Five seconds or so later, after the sound of stone grinding against stone had ceased, I found myself staring into the empty blackness of the corridor beyond the hidden entrance.

Half past three. Where the deuce was Theo?

Something wasn't right.

Not even two minutes later, I was grabbing a hooded cloak and my sword from the cloak room, hastily securing them to my person as I strode purposefully out of my keep. My feet led me in the direction of the Circles.

Chapter 12

WALKING THROUGH THE entrance of the Circles served to remind me of the fact that I would be walking down that same path tomorrow.

The Stables appeared to be mostly empty, with maybe four pairs sparring in total, and a handful of people I didn't recognize enjoying beer near the front. I spent a few moments exploring the building and confirmed that the young Lord Teuring was not practicing in one of the runs, nor could I see any sign of Theo. I pondered where else they might be for a few moments before heading back outside onto the sandy, hard-packed ground of the arena floor.

The North Tower had a collection of liveried messengers and lackeys hanging around outside of it, so I opted to head over there. As I approached the entrance, I spied one of Theodore's knights standing outside, tight-lipped and grim. Upon seeing me, he scowled blisteringly, and then looked away, feigning disinterest in my presence. For a brief moment, I thought I saw an expression of worry flicker across his face as I was walking up to the dark copper-bound wooden doors.

Theo was here. Well, that was something, at least.

As my eyes adjusted to the dimly lit chamber, my other senses began urgently telling me things. There was uproarious, booming laughter coming from somewhere above me, and the thick, oily stench of *ha'laschi* was hanging so heavy in the air that I could taste it.

I instantly became more alert, realizing a sudden need for caution.

Though I didn't care for it myself, I didn't begrudge others the occasional enjoyment of an intoxicant like flitleaf. *Ha'laschi* is in a different category altogether, and even the most seasoned debaucher would treat the drug with the utmost caution, even when diluted in candle wax and burned in a large room. It reportedly made its users dangerous and unpredictable - they might attempt to stick a knife in your kidneys after the same amount of consideration they'd give to, say, drinking a glass of water.

From the faces I saw, once my eyes had adjusted enough for me to see them, many of the other patrons shared my anxious unease. Theo's face was not among those I inspected.

More peals of laughter came from upstairs, and I realized where I was heading next. Oh joy.

Not entirely knowing what to expect, I took my time climbing the winding stairs and allowed my eyes to fully adjust to the dim light. After a dozen or so steps the smoke caused my eyes to water, making it impossible for me to see more than ten feet in front of me. The sinister odor of *ha'laschi* was still attempting to throttle my senses, and though I am not exactly a stranger to smoke related habits I found myself coughing desperately in the presence of that much of it, eyes welling up as I attempted to blink the stinging haze away.

My coughs attracted the attention of the medium-sized group of debauchers collected around a couch on the far side of the room, some of whom let loose whooping intoxicated cries and laughed mockingly. I covered my mouth with a kerchief and continued working air in and out of my lungs, despite the fact that my throat kept closing involuntarily each time I attempted to draw breath.

"Hey! Boys, look who it is! It's the lord himself!" bellowed a drunken voice I didn't recognize.

Through the stinging tears, I could make out about a dozen figures lounging about in various positions of relaxation. A few gave all the physical signs of becoming less relaxed and more excited, half standing from their chairs or lazy crouches as I slowly became the focus of their attention. And sitting in the middle of the pack was a sleepy-eyed Lord Teuring, looking groggy and unwell despite the sickly grin plastered on his face.

Near blinded by tears and disabled with coughing fits, I simply stood there a few moments and weathered their stares.

"Lord Tucat!" Teuring's voice was slightly slurred, which was not the normal consequence of either *ha'laschi* or flitleaf. "My goodness, we were just talking about you!" He then threw his head back and laughed a silent laugh, somehow managing to knock over a nearby wine goblet in the process.

Slurring of speech. Alcohol...*and ha'laschi.* I just about turned around to leave right then and there.

"Lord Teuring," I said with a now raspy voice, trying to stave off my coughs long enough to speak the words clearly, "I would have a word." I silently congratulated myself on achieving a complete sentence without barking up a lung.

"A word? My, my, the mind boggles...what single word could be so dreadfully important that you would come all the way up here just to give it? Or, perhaps, you require a word *from* me, hmmm? That it, master thief? Have you come seeking to take one of my words?" He laughed a little too loudly at that.

"Lord Teuring. I would have...*words*...with you," I said, placing an emphasis on the 's', making it sound like 'zuh'. I gestured toward an unoccupied and less smoky niche of the room, taking a few steps in that direction. "In private, if I may."

Some of the collected assortment of ruffians made 'Ooooo' noises, one or two of them muttering juvenile, imbecilic comments intended for me to overhear. I had everyone's attention now, and the looks I was receiving that weren't openly hostile were amused and condescending. I looked around the room further.

I saw Theo, looking down from a small unobtrusive balcony located on the third floor, unhappily watching the proceedings. My vision was still blurred with tears, but I could make out Theo's left arm in a sling and pressed against his chest, his three-quarter cloak thrown back so it would be visible. We made eye contact.

He looked worried.

"-go speak with him, you just make sure I've got another drink when I get back," I heard Teuring finish unsteadily, rising to his feet as though it were an accomplishment that defied all odds. His success with that particular maneuver was short-lived, and he very nearly stumbled onto his knees, barely catching himself before hitting the floor.

He giggled, and pushed himself back to his feet with affected nonchalance, then walked an awkward, weaving sort of gait toward me. He stopped only after he'd succeeded in violating my personal space, standing near me in a manner he might have considered intimidating.

"Yes?" he said, his breath a poisonous cocktail of overindulgence. "Speak."

The abruptness of it all made me realize that I should have rehearsed what I was going to say, being the one who requested the conversation in the first place.

"I...have a few things I'd like to ask you, and I realize the awkwardness of this, so I apologize in advance," I said, frowning slightly. "It's regarding the events that, shall we say, led to the current situation that we find ourselves in."

He continued to look impassively at me, crossing his arms as he did so.

"Specifically," I continued, "I've come to the conclusion that there's a particular someone who may have given you the idea that robbing me was a fine idea."

There wasn't so much as a hint of movement from him as he stared. Several awkward, tense seconds passed.

"Was there?" I pressed, leaning forward, voice lowering to a whisper. "Did someone suggest me as a target? In truth,

Lord Teuring, I believe that we are both being set on this path for some other purpose, and I very much would like to know-"

"Why are you always doing that?" he asked abruptly.

I imagine I looked confused for a moment, and sent a question at him with my eyebrows.

"Talking all flowery like that...courtly speech. Talking out of your ass. Why don't you speak plainly? There's just us here," he waved grandly at the space around us, head bobbing unsteadily as he did so, "and *I* certainly don't require fluffy language like that. Could you try to make your point in a way that doesn't make you sound like a pompous ass who thinks he's better than the rest of us?"

Behind his bleary, unfocused stare and vicious breath (which I was quite convinced was removing the oil from my skin as we spoke), I was convinced he was enjoying this. I gritted my teeth further in an attempt to maintain a neutral expression.

"I think someone is setting you up," I said, simply. "Or me. Or both. We're being used, somehow, and I don't think you're smart enough to see it. There. Is that plain enough for you?"

His posture didn't change at all, but his facial expression altered slightly as he tilted his head.

"Really," he said, matter-of-factly. "What possible reason could you have to think that?"

"Several really, but the most compelling at the present time is the fact that several of my neighbors were tipped off about your plan to steal the goblet, including Lord Cleaver whom I'm on tolerably good terms with. And if that weren't enough, I received a delivery a few days before your attempted burglary...something designed to rile me up, which in turn made me suspicious." I watched his eyes widen in surprise, then narrow. I nodded slightly. "So I'm led to believe that someone wanted me to know of your plans, and that this particular someone wasn't you."

He stood back a little and appeared to consider for nearly a full minute, appraising a small piece of floor as he did so. I could almost see him putting it together, piece by piece.

"Why?" he asked, quietly.

I shrugged. "This is why I've come to you. I lack information, and have no idea who you've spoken to about me, or who might have reason to cause you grief and see you humiliated. I dislike being used as someone else's tool, and I'd much rather find out who's responsible and what they're after than to go along knowing that I'm dancing on the end of a puppeteer's string. Wouldn't you?"

The look on his face was a considered one, and I thought I could almost get a palpable sense of what he was feeling. Betrayal? A glimmer of hope? He had deemed his chances of winning against me so unlikely that he'd chosen to spend the day before the duel in a drunken fog. He pondered for several moments as I watched, and after a time appeared to come to a decision.

"You would like me to give you a name?" he asked.

"Yes."

"Come," he said quietly, somberly, moving towards me as if to impart some information, "I shall give you a name. Perhaps it will solidify things for you."

I turned my head slightly so that I might hear his whispered tones.

"Pestilent son of a whore!" he practically screamed in my ear, shoving me backward violently. I spilled to the floor and tumbled, legs twisting together uselessly, coming down hard on the wooden floorboards. A sharp, white pain erupted somewhere in the region of my hip, and I sensed that I had also struck my head. Dazed, I turned myself over slightly, and propped myself up to look at him where he stood, several feet away, an angry smile lighting up his face.

"There. Good name, don't you think?"

I stared at him, stunned, as he continued to speak over the appreciative guffaws behind him.

"Are you so arrogant as to believe I cannot prevail against you? Do you presume that I lack a motive to humiliate you? Hmm? Look about you, oaf!" He gestured wildly behind him as he slurred his words down at me. "We are surrounded by people who wish you humbled, noble lords who can all claim some form of injury to their honor as a result of your actions, you sniveling, cowardly toad."

I began to get my feet beneath me so that I might stand, and felt only a mild pain in my side and hip as I did so. Teuring continued, his voice raising in pitch and volume.

"You actually think I need to be *tricked* in order to despise you? To hold you in contempt? One need look no further than your blighted face, or watch your arrogant posturing and smug self-assuredness. Why, ten minutes in a room with you and total strangers could come up with a hundred or so reasons to despise your very existence!"

I was genuinely perplexed at the source of this outburst. Was it the drugs?

"Look, I-"

"No, *you* look, you pathetic, blotchy, parody of a man!" he interrupted, waggling his forefinger at me as he spoke, biting off each word sharply. "You pollute the world around me with your very existence. Tomorrow, gods willing, I shall do my part in making the world a better place and send you where you belong. Trying to weasel your way out of it just now merely confirms what I and these other lords already knew – that the mighty Vincent Tucat is nothing more than a sniveling, pock-faced *coward*."

His speech was met with roars of drunken approval behind him as well as a few cheers that were coarse in both sound and content. I was now fully upright, a little sore, and flushed with embarrassment, angry that I had bothered to show this fledgling lord any sort of respect whatsoever.

Yeah . . .

I could find out the more intricate details behind the plot later, once I'd satisfied myself with respect to this young whelp of a boy. *If* I cared to find out who was behind it at all, that is. The motivation behind someone wishing to set up this idiot child was suddenly less of a mystery than I had first supposed – how hard was it to dislike this vile, oily-haired youth?

"Well," I announced loudly, brushing myself off and smoothing my garments, "I'm ever so glad I came here and had this lovely chat. Had we not talked, I would have spent a good fortnight feeling sorry for the hollow mockery of a boy I'll be leaving behind in the arena circle tomorrow. Lord Teuring, you've taken a load off my mind, and I thank you." I nodded my head solemnly. "Please be sure to convey to your lovely wife my most sincere apologies for all of the horrible, horrible things that I shall be doing to her husband on the morrow."

I didn't even get a chuckle over that one. Tough room.

"Lord Tucat," he said in a contemptuous tone, not missing a beat, eyes half-lidded and amused. "Would you care to tell me where your family is buried?"

Silence.

"Oh...*oh!*" I said, affecting mock astonishment. "How *very* clever! 'Where is your family buried, so I can send your body there when next we meet', is that where this was going? How *very* original...do continue. I'm sure you will have scared me out of my wits once you've finished."

"Send your body-...no, you misunderstand!" Teuring laughed, oozing insincerely apologetic tones as he spoke. "That wasn't a prelude to a threat, Lord Tucat. It's just, as you may have observed," he gestured behind him to where his fellow lords were standing and sitting, all of whom watched with the silent attentiveness of starving hawks, "I've been drinking rather a lot tonight. And, since I suddenly find myself in need of relieving myself, it seemed only natural that I find an appropria-"

My sword came free of my scabbard so quickly that I wasn't fully aware I'd drawn on him until the sound of my own gently humming blade hit my ears, and I stood there in a blaze of anger that threatened to suffocate me. My upper lip was trembling, madly twitching in an effort to pull itself back into a wolf-like snarl as I fixed my eyes upon his. His eyes weren't looking at mine, but were angled downward and staring at the razor-sharp metal caressing his throat, requiring little more than a gentle nudge to seal his lips for all time.

I was dimly aware of the sounds of scraping metal around me, and in the back of my mind I wondered how this was going to end. The law said that anyone wishing to do violence upon another needed to follow the proper formalities, and yet there were notable cases where people were found behind buildings, stabbed through the chest, throat slit, or worse. I wasn't exactly being smart, drawing like this, nor was I in the right.

I didn't care.

Putting every ounce of hate into the steely look I was leveling down my blade at him, I watched as his eyes slowly followed the length of the sword to its hilt, eventually meeting my own as we locked stares.

And incredibly, he began to laugh.

"Do it!" he said, smiling so that nearly all of his teeth were visible. "Come on, show the world what kind of a man you are. Miserable coward! *Do it!*"

I sensed rather than saw the other lords moving behind him, as if to emphasize how poorly things would go for me if I actually drew blood from the drug-addled youth, who did not have a sword at his hip.

Eventually, several long moments of seething fury later, my common sense got the better of me. I lowered my sword, gaze not wavering from his, and slowly but forcibly put it back in its scabbard with a sharp 'snick'.

"You," I said to Teuring, whose expression had not changed since he'd begun looking me in the eye, "will wish to make use of a mirror. Right away. Cherish the memory of being able to look at one without wincing. Tomorrow I make it my own personal mission to ensure that every time you glimpse your reflection – every time you see your face staring back at you – you're reminded of me."

I waited briefly for some sort of response, but none appeared forthcoming. I risked a glance at the lords behind him, and quickly surveyed the rest of the room. Theo was nowhere to be seen, and the others didn't appear to be about to do anything.

Turning on my heel and giving my back to the drunken, smoke-addled young man, I walked slowly and deliberately down the stairs.

I gripped my sword handle tightly as I walked so that nobody would notice my hand, trembling from the unspent fury still roiling within me.

Halfway down the stairs I heard laughter and applause from upstairs, doubtless from some witty rejoinder that had been spoken once I was out of earshot. I didn't care at that point. Tonight was theirs, they could have it. Tomorrow's confrontation would see a far different outcome.

Very, very different.

I hardly gave my surroundings any attention as I left the Circles, kicking at stray pebbles and stones as I did so, heedless of the damage I was doing to the shine of my tooled leather boots.

This young fool was being played and was too dense to realize it, mocking me even as I attempted to be generous and share information with him. Who could possibly be so naive?

It didn't matter. I no longer cared.

The entire walk home I entertained visions of Teuring suffering violently, bleeding, his arrogant expression turning into one of shock, as though cold water had been thrown upon his face. I imagined him pleading, begging, and the circumstances upon which I would finally relent. I'd offer him mercy only after his full measure had been taken, his humiliation obvious to all who watched.

Even after walking for almost an hour, I found myself circling the streets around my keep several times, attempting to burn away the angry energy writhing around inside me. I barely even gave my guards a glance as I walked through the entrance to my keep.

Talia appeared at the front room, standing as if to greet me, a look of uncertainty and trepidation on her face.

"Milord, I wish to apologize once more for my conduct in the sitting room this afternoon. If I could- *oh!*" she said, hastily catching my cloak as I tossed it to her, my angry scowl directed at the floor.

"I wish to spend some time in the exercise hall, undisturbed. Please tell Cyrus that I wish to speak with him in approximately an hour or so. He need not come down, I shall find him," I said, barely slowing down as I walked toward the hallway that led to the back stairs.

Suddenly mute, she merely nodded at me, and appeared to retreat into herself a ways, my cloak held closely to her chest.

Briefly, I thought about apologizing to her for my abruptness, but I could do that later. I didn't wish for her to see me while I was in this sort of mood.

Practically flying down the back stairs, a slow burning anger quickening my steps, I carelessly hopped over the lethal devices and other assorted traps the short hallway offered up. I unlocked the door and placed my thumb against the small pad to the right of it, waiting for the familiar hum.

The door opened with a click-clack, and I strode through the threshold into my familiar surroundings.

I was genuinely surprised to find Theo standing there in plain view in the middle of the room, with no effort being made to hide himself as the door opened. He was looking agitated, slightly wobbly, and his arm was still hanging in front of him, carefully encased in a white cloth sling. I noticed a bright red stain mid-bicep.

Before I had a chance to confront my friend, or even open my mouth to say a single reproachful word, he lurched unsteadily toward me and began speaking in an urgent tone of voice.

"His *feet!* Tiamat's *tits*, Vincent," he practically shouted, his voice a little more exuberant than usual. "His unholy Baal-be-damned *feet!*"

Chapter 13

"UHM...WHAT?" I finally managed to say.

"His feet! Teuring's a sleeper! His *feet*, Vince!" he said a little too loudly, wobbling the tiniest bit.

This conversation was rapidly making even less sense than his first sentence had. How long had he spent directly above those assorted fellows in the tower? Had the smoke affected him?

"You spoke with Lord Teuring about his feet?" I asked, incredulous.

"No. I didn't get to talk to him at all, actually." He scowled, eyes narrowing slightly.

"Didn't get to-" I began, flabbergasted.

"No, but that hardly matters at this point. Vincent, he-"

"So you learned nothing," I said bitterly. "That's just great. Well done. Tell me, were you only down there to shut me up, or did you accidentally sleep in this morning?"

Theodore fixed me with a dark look before answering.

"Well, it's good to know that you believe I would treat our friendship so lightly. Very gratifying. Additionally, I'll thank you not to put words in my mouth. I haven't learned 'nothing', as you've so generously put it."

"You said-"

"I *said*," he interrupted, drawing himself up and squinting at me, "that I didn't speak with him. This *despite* the fact that

I was there since sunrise. This *despite* having made every effort I could think of to get within ten feet of him. *I'd* say that I learned rather a lot. Now, would you like to hear what I *did* learn, or do you want to perform a childish tantrum of some sort? I can wait."

Still looking rather unsteady, he wobbled for a few steps and made a production of drunkenly leaning against the nearby pillar, combing his fingers through his beard and looking at me with a tired, unfeigned annoyance.

"Look, can you-" I began, and then stopped. I closed my eyes and took a deep breath before opening them again.

Theo was now standing expectantly with his side to me, inspecting the fingernails of his uninjured hand speculatively, whistling softly to himself.

My shoulders were tense, I noticed. So tense that it was a miracle they hadn't started cramping. I made a conscious effort to relax them, rolling my neck a few times to loosen them up.

I took another deep, relaxing breath.

He was right. I was being an idiot.

"Theo, I'm sorry. I'm being an ass, I know. I just...I left an upsetting conversation that got me all wound up. I don't mean to take it out on you. But I was angry! That *piss-drinking*, know-nothing young son of-"

"I know," he said, a hint of sympathy creeping into his voice. "I was there, I heard it. Little wanker. Myself, I would have done more than just draw on him."

"Well, I only have to wait until tomorrow, at which point I can do more than simply draw on him," I said, feeling myself calm down as I spoke. "*Substantially* more than simply draw on him. Still, I feel terrible that I wasted your time, Theo. Say, do you want to sit down and relax a bit while I work off some of this anger...loosen up? I swear, the muscles in my shoulders feel tougher than a twenty-copper whore."

"Vincent, I need you to listen very carefully to me," he said, seriously.

I stopped in mid-stretch, then shook out my arms casually in front of me, feeling my muscles begin to loosen.

"Okay. I'm listening."

He took a breath and pursed his lips before speaking.

"Vince, I think he's better than you."

The words he spoke made no sense whatsoever, no matter what order I attempted to put them in. The only word my brain could seem to dredge up as a response was 'Huh?'

I frantically searched for a better way of phrasing my complete bafflement at what he'd just said, some more precise way of articulating my confusion.

"Huh?" I finally managed to say.

"He, Lord Teuring, may be better than you. A better swordsman, that is. I think. Gods," he said, his voice sounding both awed and excited, like he'd had too much to drink. "I scoured my memory, tried to remember it exactly, how he'd cut himself. You told me that, right? Right. Just like it. When I heard that other stuff today, I thought I was going crazy!"

I wondered if my friend was going crazy.

"Theo," I said, pressing my fingers against the bridge of my nose and closing my eyes, "could you please explain what the hell you're talking about? I'm afraid that you began this whole conversation by making no sense whatsoever, and things have gone a bit downhill since then."

He paused and took a long, thoughtful breath.

"Vince, remember when you came back from the Circles? You'd mentioned this thing that he did, catching his foil by the blade. Remember?"

"Yeah, I remember. Funny as Hades, happened when he had his back turned to us."

"I heard people talking about it," he said, nodding. "One of the lords I spoke with mentioned Teuring cutting his hand in the exact manner you described today."

"Well, it was *really* funny, so I don't doubt they're still-"

"No, Vince, *today*. This fellow said Teuring cut himself *today*."

"Uh, what? That happened yesterday, Theo."

"I know. I asked this guy - he wasn't even at the Circles yesterday, but he saw Teuring do this with his own eyes, or so he says. The exact same thing...identical. Now," he said, awkwardly attempting to remove his half-cloak with his uninjured hand, "what does that tell you?"

"That young Lord Teuring has a learning disability? Well, I'd suspected as much, but-"

"Vince, don't you get it? You practice something over and over until you're so good at it that it becomes second nature, like breathing! He didn't make a *mistake* in front of you, or this other guy. No," Theo seemed to become more animated as he spoke, "what he did was perform the same *move* a second time."

"A 'move'? What move? That? He sliced open his own hand! Tell me Theo, what exactly is a 'move' like that supposed to accomplish?"

"Exactly what it accomplished yesterday."

"Eh?"

"You don't think he's much of a swordsman. You saw him grab his foil blade, cut himself, look like a complete buffoon. You think he's terrible."

"Uh...yeah." I sent him an inquisitive look. "Seeing something like that does tend to give away the fact that you're not very good. Uhm...Theo, don't take this the wrong way, but there was a great deal of smoke in that room, and being situated where you were right above it, you-"

"I'm perfectly fine, Vincent. Watch. Big brack blugs bed brue-back...no, wait," he frowned. "Lemme try that again. Brig back...*big black* bugs br- uh . . ."

I gave him a look.

"Okay, I did take a little something for the pain. And there was a *lot* of smoke, Vince!" he said defensively, wincing and rubbing his arm under the dressing. "It was getting so I could hardly breathe in there, and at one point I thought I was going to pass out. Even so, I think I'm rather wishing I could be even less clearheaded right at this moment. Do you have anything lying around for pain? Or failing that, a drink?"

"I've been meaning to ask you, I noticed your injury back in the tower. What happened? Hang on, let me fetch you something for that," I said, gesturing for him to sit as I hopped over to the drinks cabinet. I had some sunthistle poultices treated with assorted medicinal herbs, as well as the tiniest bit of jackweed stashed back in a cabinet above the glasses, and I figured he could probably use both. After a moment's thought, I also pulled a bottle of *Teir-na-nay* from the cool reservoir of water that most of my green wines sat in, as well as two large round glasses.

Laden with various implements of first-aid and pain relief, I walked back toward where Theo was still standing, awkwardly trying to work his cloak clasp with his right hand.

"Let me help you with that, and then we'll have a bit of a sit. Maybe then, *one* of us will start making sense," I said, putting the assorted bottles and bandages down upon the dark, shiny surface of the table in front of our usual seats.

"Vince," he said urgently, slurring slightly, "you're not *listening*. He might be good, this kid, and is just pretending to be awful. We call them 'sleepers'."

"Now, before I say 'of course' and nod patronizingly at you, I should let you know that nothing you say this evening will be held against you. Those fumes were intense. I haven't seen that much smoke in one place since the palace fire that happened during Summer Solstice a few years ago."

His eyes narrowed at me while I reached up to unhook the chain clasp of his cloak, removing the heavy leather garment from his shoulders as his left arm hung uselessly.

"You don't believe me. You don't think I'm serious," he said quietly. "You think I don't have my wits about me, or – bah! You *began* this conversation assuming I was just trying to shut you up."

"Theo, I think that you and I have both had a rough day, and could use some nice fortified wine. Let's look at that cut you've got. Is it bad? That's a fair bit of blood there . . ."

"Vince," he said, voice now so quiet it was a mere grumble. "Draw."

"Pardon?"

"Draw!" he bellowed, pushing me bodily away from him with his good hand. A split second later, and in one swift movement, he had the full length of his three-foot blade shining brightly before me.

With a mighty roar, he threw himself at me, his good arm whipping his sword around in an overhand crescent that looked as though it could split a tree in two, aimed right at my head.

Heart suddenly thumping in my chest, I heard the same sound of ringing metal that had assaulted my ears a scant hour ago. My blade was before me in an instant, like the cross of a 't', thrown upward to make the obvious parry.

As soon as our blades connected, Theo pulled his stroke backwards and released his grip, allowing his sword to clatter on the cobbles behind him.

"Freeze!" he bellowed, even louder than he'd shouted only moments before. "Don't move!"

I froze awkwardly out of habit, mid-movement, my own sword almost twisting out of my grip. I held it hovering a foot over my head.

"Theo! What the f-"

"I said *freeze!"* my unarmed friend said authoritatively, sounding vaguely annoyed.

He was using the same tone as when he wished to point out a problem with my footwork, or some other small piece of potentially lethal imperfection. This was instruction, a lesson of sorts.

I remained frozen.

Theo hiccupped softly before continuing.

"Without moving anything but your head, look down and take note of where your feet are, and what they're doing," he said in a recognizably imperious tone.

I looked down at my feet, then I looked up.

"Okay, I *defy* you to find anything wrong with this. Placement is perfect, my back leg isn't 'stuck' at all, and – just *what* in the name of all that is *holy* was *that* for!? I mean-"

"You're right," he said, ignoring my last outburst, eyes focused on my boots. "Actually, I'm pretty impressed. Weight balanced primarily on your back leg, right foot placed well. A quick push on your left leg if you need to lunge. Nicely done."

"Theo!" I yelled, "Could you please tell me what in the name of *Belial's butt-crack* you are trying to prove?"

"When I drew on you, what were you thinking? Were you thinking to yourself 'My goodness, I must place my feet exactly so, and hold my sword arm thus'?"

"No, as a matter of fact I was thinking 'Oh dear gods have mercy! My drug-addled friend has finally gone completely loopy, and is trying to kill me!'"

"It was automatic. You didn't tell your body to do the things it needed to do, you simply identified a threat, and instinctively knew how you needed to deal with it. Right?"

"More or less, yeah."

"That sort of automatic reaction isn't easy to come by. It takes time, training. Years and years of training. What you did out of reflex, others have to make a conscious effort to reproduce. You've reached that point where certain actions require no thought at all, they're a part of how you approach the fight as a whole. Would you agree?"

"Yes," I said, uncertainly. I lowered my sword all the way so that the point rested on the floor, no longer wishing to expend the effort required to keep it in front of me. " Your point being what, exactly?"

"When you drew on Lord Teuring – bloody marvelous how quick you were, by the way – I watched his feet. Vince, his *feet*," he said, looking half exhausted as he spoke the words, "were *perfect*."

The confusion from the evening's madness coalesced and turned to gel, like an understanding being forcefully and quietly slapped into place. I tried to get my brain to encompass everything that he was implying, several times. I failed.

Stunned, I simply stood there, gawking, uncertain of what to do or say.

"That's what I'm trying to say," the large, bearded man said glumly as he walked unsteadily toward his chair. "This kid might actually be good. I can't really know for sure, given my limited information, but-"

"I...you . . ." I managed to croak. I tossed my sword onto a section of carpet where it came to rest with a quiet 'bong', and sat heavily on the nearby couch. "Theo, *please!* The kid reportedly *disarmed himself!* Against a wooden practice dummy! I saw him-"

"Vince, if I wanted to pretend to be awful, what would I do?"

"Just that. You'd pretend to be less skilled than you are."

"Yes, but what specific things would I need to do in order to convince a total stranger that I couldn't fence my way out of a loose-woven linen bag?"

"Wouldn't they just sort of start out by assuming that you didn't know how to fence in the first place, or were about average?"

"Did you assume that?" he asked, archly, eyebrows raised. "You got your man Cyrus to research Teuring, and even after that you were practically a basket case until you went to spy on him at the Circles. The most practical assumption is to not assume anything about the other person, slowly forming an opinion as more information becomes available. So, that being said, what would I have to do in order to convince someone I don't know that I am lousy with a sword?"

"I guess you'd have to provide them with some sort of evidence that you were as bad as you wanted them to believe," I said uncomfortably.

"More than that, because of my natural reflexes. I would have to practice, work at suppressing my instincts in order to give you a very specific impression of my skill."

"You mean like when you left your guard too low yesterday?"

"Exactly! Yes, just like that. If your guard is perfect, then seeming like you've made a genuine mistake takes practice."

"Theo, stop and listen to yourself. This kid was practically cornered into a duel, kicking and screaming. He's scared silly of me! And you think I have reason to be worried because of something he did with his *feet?* Do you know how ridiculous that sounds?"

"I've asked myself that question a hundred times. I watched as closely as I could all morning and all afternoon. He seemed to know when I was watching him, avoiding me without appearing to, slipping away without me noticing.

And when it became too difficult to avoid me, he found other ways to keep me occupied." He gestured to his injured arm meaningfully.

I felt my eyes go wide.

"Your arm...*he* did that?" I was stunned.

"What? Oh, no. No, not exactly." He rubbed his bearded chin with his good hand. "A little background. I've been on reasonable terms with Lord Leventale for several years, partly because we both have a similar interest in Cowling Street, which runs through both of our territories. I shan't get into the details of that. By the by, he doesn't like you very much, and is fairly vocal about it."

"He's got good reason to be," I said. Later, I'd have to tell Theo about the time I'd liberated Lord Leventale's clothes while he was dallying with a certain attractive, and extremely married, Countess.

"Well, he's a reasonable hand with a blade as well, quite respectable. I'd run into him at the Circles that morning, and he was just as friendly and natural as you please. Then in the early afternoon, after I've been snooping around Teuring for several hours, he comes up with a murderous look and challenges me to a duel, angry as all Hades and unwilling to explain why. When I refuse, he starts getting nasty. Doesn't draw on me, but gets physical...pushing, shoving. Ugly names, people starting to gawk, eventually I had to give in. We found seconds and a dueling circle. Good fight," he said, attempting a bit of a flex and wincing as he did.

"So, Leventale's the one who cut you, then."

"Yeah. He surprised me, cut my arm. At the time I thought he'd gotten careless - he threw everything he had into a move that left him wide open for punishment."

"And you...?"

"Punished him," he said, blandly. "Nicked him in the jaw."

"That's it?"

"Well, when I say 'nicked', I of course mean 'split his jawbone in two, right at the cleft of his chin'. I figured I would gloss over the gory details...it was pretty ugly." He shrugged, trying not to sound too impressed with himself. "Now, one of the curious bits – he was talking to one of Teuring's boys right before the whole thing started. I'd seen that same fellow of his not ten minutes before, too, talking to Lord Teuring directly. Hair worn kind of long, oiled, not quite as curly as Teuring's."

"Huh. You think the two events are related?"

"Absolutely. We were perfectly fine right up until I saw him marching up to me, hand on sword, angry as a wet ferret. Speaking of related, I do also think that Teuring and the young fellow with the long-ish hair are connected, blood-like. He looks to be playing the part of servant, but he's never too far away at any given time, and they seem to talk quietly and seriously to each other fairly regularly."

"Hmm," I mused, trying to recall anyone I'd seen at Teuring's party that may have fit that description. The youth who lit the candle, perhaps.

"So, I can't exactly figure out what he might have been told, or what exactly set him off, but I'm quite certain that Teuring is responsible, and I'm just as certain that the whole reason he was sent after me in the first place was because I was busy snooping around Teuring and trying to say hello. He knew what I was there for, Vince...he had to know."

I nodded "How would Teuring have convinced Leventale to attack you in the first place?"

"Don't know. I don't think I'm going to get an answer for that question from Leventale either, and not just because of . . ." He made a quick cutting gesture with his thumb, motioning down the front of his chin.

"Yeah, I don't imagine he feels much like talking."

"And then, once I got bandaged and went to the tower, you showed up. You drew on him, and his stance went immediately defensive, with perfect foot placement, despite being unarmed. He might actually be an accomplished swordsman, Vince. At the very least, I think *he* believes he's good enough to beat you. He wants this duel."

"Why would he pretend to be lousy, though? Why all the smoking and drinking? It's not usual the day before a duel, messes you up...why would he do it?"

"Don't know. It would be stupid, I agree, and even those *fumes* were enough to make my head swim. I just-" He exhaled blearily. "I don't know, Vince. Maybe your paranoia is rubbing off on me. It sure as Hades looked like he knew where his feet were. Did you actually *see* him drinking, or smoking anything?"

"No," I said, my eyes narrowing as I attempted to recall. "It was on his breath though, I can say that for certain. I'm just having a hard time believing what you're trying to suggest. It would make even less sense than before."

"Trust me, I know the feeling," said Theo, finally sitting down in his chair and sighing an intoxicated sigh, "and I've been trying to wrap my head around it all afternoon. No hard evidence, I could barely get near him today, but I can feel it in my gut. He's had training."

The leather of my chair groaned in protest as I leaned forward, lost in thought. It was crazy, irrational...but so were the nagging doubts that had plagued me lately. The swords, the look of anger in the stables, and everything else that hadn't felt right up until now.

Could Theo be right?

"Say, I've had a kind of exciting day, haven't I?" Theo grinned as he stretched his arms behind him, wincing slightly. "Do you think it would be possible to get your cook to rustle up that steak you promised me? I haven't had anything to eat all day."

"Of course!" I said, hopping to my feet, feeling guilty that I had not thought to arrange for food earlier. "The bandages are...on the floor, by your cloak. I guess they got knocked over when you drew your sword. There's also the herbs on the table, creams and other bandages in the skinny cabinet by the bar. Help yourself - they're all clearly marked."

I slipped out the door to the main hallway. It took maybe two minutes to get up to the main level, relay my requirements to the kitchen, and return downstairs with some wet towels. Returning, I found Theo busy chewing on something, possibly jackweed, while tending to his injured left arm.

"Careful. If that's what I think it is, that batch is pretty potent. How bad is your arm?" I asked, tossing him a towel.

"It's bad enough I won't be seeing any action for a month or so. You probably left the room just so you wouldn't have to see the painful, horrifying injury your friend suffered while trying to help you." He grinned. "You big baby."

"You know what just occurred to me?" I said, watching my friend reach for the tendril of white gauze that trailed from his arm and continue his ministrations, "I may have a real problem here. Suppose Cyrus discovers he's had training, as you suspect. What then?"

"Well, you call off the duel, obviously. If you walked into a dueling circle with someone who's deliberately hidden how good they are, I have this dangerous feeling you might get minced into burger meat."

"Can't do that," I said, simply.

"Huh?"

"It's not my duel to call off. Teuring was challenged by Greybridge, and I rather suspect that things would go poorly for me if I told him I wasn't fighting the duel for him all of a sudden. I doubt I'd still have two coppers to rub together when he was done with me. If I were still alive, that is."

I tried not to gulp at that thought. Formal duels and outsmarting someone politically were not the only means a lord could employ in order to deal with someone. Not by a long shot.

"You could always ask him to withdraw the challenge to Teuring," he suggested, now looking concerned. "The circumstances around the duel have changed."

"That probably wouldn't matter to someone like him. Actually, I just thought of something else. Doesn't it seem rather strange that he hasn't contacted me since that night at Teuring's?"

Theo nodded thoughtfully. "That is a bit odd. Even if he's convinced Teuring's a pushover, you'd think at the very least he'd have told you how badly to humiliate him. You've put yourself at his disposal, after all."

"I think I shall go and ask him," I said, sitting down across from Theo. "He may still be vexed at me for breaking into his keep and simply wishes not to talk to me. Or there might be something else."

"He might be involved?"

"I think I should make a firm effort not to assume anything about what's going on, given everything that's happened. I've already put Cyrus to work tracking down some more information about this kid, maybe he'll get lucky. In the meantime, and perhaps to kill time while we eat, we should come up with a few theories about our young Lord Teuring."

"Oh, as to that," said Theo, finishing the job of wrapping his bandage and casually inspecting his handiwork, "one obvious theory springs to mind."

"And that is?"

"He means to kill you," he said, simply.

Chapter 14

RETURNING TO THE scene of the crime.

It's a trite little saying among thieves, but like all trite and cleverly annoying sayings there's a grain of truth in it, a reason it's stuck around. Simply put - it happens.

Every now and then some dunce muddles their way through a burglary and then becomes so concerned they might have left something behind that they decide to go back. That, or they're so sure of themselves they figure they can perform the exact same trick a second time, which is just plain stupid. See, people generally don't like being robbed from. They learn.

This situation was different, of course. I hadn't *officially* stolen anything from here, and was just a lord popping by to visit another lord...nothing unusual about that. I mean, it wasn't as if I was planning on robbing him again.

Still, it *felt* amateurish. Scene of the crime, all that.

Eventually I found myself standing at the front door of Greybridge Keep, and I gave the large silk door chime ribbon a firm yank. My efforts were met with a loud 'bong', followed by several other smaller bells being struck or hit, the cascade effect producing a rather pleasant melody.

I have to get me one of those.

I'd been waiting just long enough to be considered rude, when I heard the slightest trace of movement on the other side of the door. There were several odd clicking noises, some squeaking of metal on metal, and the door was slowly pried open by a tight-lipped older gentleman.

He looked across at me and frowned, door stopping after being opened just enough to allow his head to poke out. He gave me the kind of look you might give a splatter of bird crap you'd just spotted on your shoe.

"Yes?" he said tiredly.

"Lord Tucat, here to see Lord Greybridge, if you please." I mentally started preparing myself for the encounter with Lord Greybridge, going over the opening line I'd prepared in my head.

"I'm afraid he's not seeing company at the moment. Good day," he said tersely, beginning to close the door even before he'd finished speaking.

"Uhm," I interrupted lamely, reaching out and keeping the door from closing in my rather surprised face. "Sorry, could you please tell him? *Lord Tucat*, here to see him regarding fairly urgent business. If you would? Thank you ever so much."

"I'm afraid that he's not seeing company at the moment, Lord Tucat, and that mention of your name will not do anything to change that fact. Good day." He turned his attention back to closing the door.

Once again, it didn't happen. This time, I yanked it open about half a foot, much to his sudden surprise.

"First of all," I began, "it's evening. 'Good evening', you would say. Where were you trained when it comes to manners, cretin? *A Roa'Leshi* dance school?"

He scowled. Point for me. I continued just as his mouth opened to fire off a retort.

"Second of all," I pointed at my chest, "*Lord Tucat,* who is taking care of your honored lord's duel for him tomorrow, requires a word with him about a matter very close to his honor. As it were, I've half a mind to take my concerns elsewhere, let your honorable lord suffer the consequences of hiring staff that appear to have no concept of what might be in their employer's best interests. If that is the case, sir, I will require your name. Doubtless Lord Greybridge will be suitably impressed, and wish to appropriately reward the self-important, brain-dead malingerer who turned me away."

I concluded my mini-speech with a folding of my arms, well pleased with how that had sounded.

He barely hesitated.

"My honored lord...I, *Travis,*" he said ironically, pointing to himself in a gesture that was a mirror image of the one I'd just made, "am well aware of your role in my lord's affairs, as well as my lord's wishes with respect to yourself, himself, and this lovely evening we're enjoying. I assure you that taking your 'half a mind' elsewhere will not adversely affect my employer's opinion of my performance and, what's more, I encourage you to carry out your threat as soon as possible. Indeed, the very prospect of bidding you farewell fills me with joy that cannot be described with mere words. Doubtless I shall have to attempt to express these feelings through *Roa'Lechi* interpretive dance sometime later. And so, I bid you good *evening*, most observant and perspicacious lord."

The door closed the rest of the way before I could even think to stop it.

That, I have to say, I didn't really expect. I have hopes that I didn't quite look as dumb as I felt just then, standing there at a closed door, having just been dressed down primly by the older, skinny doorman.

After taking a full second or two to compose myself, I reached out and yanked on the door chime ribbon.

Hard.

The tune from the bells rang out much more insistently this time, and a few discordant bells rang twice from the force I had used, ruining the melody completely. I scanned my memory for information regarding the interior layout of the keep, hand reaching into the hidden pocket of my tunic as I did so.

The door slowly opened in front of me for the second time, and the now-familiar aged face peeked through the opening at me in unfeigned annoyance.

"My lord, perhaps I was not clear in my *mphhb-!*" he said, his tired words ending in a muffled exclamation of surprise as I shoved the white cloth soaked with cacaothane over his mouth, holding it firmly in place with my gloved hand.

His look of annoyance, which I had assumed was a permanent fixture, was immediately replaced by a look of surprise, followed by the unfocused look of a man slipping into unconsciousness. I caught him on his way down, stepping through the threshold as he went limp, now no longer attempting to speak.

I decided that I liked him much better like that.

After dragging him further into Greybridge Keep and gently closing the door, I glanced around to confirm there were no guards posted inside the front foyer and breathed a sigh of relief.

As I propped the dozing figure up in a nearby chair just outside the cloak room, I noticed that the grey servant's cloak that he was wearing didn't seem to fit him properly, and was practically falling off his bony shoulders. The garment had been pinched in the back so that it might be worn to appear natural from the front.

I made a mental note of it, and put that note with all the other notes that belonged in the mental category of "Odd things I 'don't have a ready explanation for."

"Focus," I said to myself. I had done something that was probably one of the stupidest, most impulsive things I could have done under the circumstances. Cacaothane, which consists of distilled fermented cocoa leaves and a host of other unpleasant ingredients, not only renders those who inhale it unconscious for a while, but it usually makes them unable to remember the events of the thirty minutes or so preceding the inhalation.

'Usually'' being the operative word. About ninety percent of the time, by my reckoning. Some people were simply constructed differently than others.

It was a risk. If the doorman remembered me upon waking, I had no doubt that things would not go well for me shortly afterwards.

I brushed my hands against my tunic in an effort to keep myself from shaking. The paranoid part of my brain was sending urgent signals to the rest of me, the gist of which was "This is incredibly stupid. Let's get out of here as fast as humanly possible."

Another section of my brain, rational thought, seemed to agree, and wished to point out the fact that we'd just drugged a doorman in order to let ourselves into the keep of a very powerful lord with little or no sense of humor. It wondered openly what I was hoping to accomplish, aside from the opportunity to become some new and interesting shade of crimson, as well as much more stiff and dead-like.

I told both those parts of my brain to shut up, and spent a few long moments with my head cocked to the side listening to the complete silence that surrounded me.

One way or another, I was going to find out something from Greybridge.

Besides, the most difficult part about a break-in is managing to get in, so I'd already done the difficult bit. Might as well take a look around since I was already here.

At the end of the main foyer there was a short hallway that turned left. I poked my head around the corner swiftly three times in order to glimpse the hall and its contents, walking swiftly around the corner during my third glance and heading for the first tier of stairs twenty feet away.

My instincts told me to avoid the rug in the middle of the hallway, and I did so. Greybridge would have to be insane to set a trap in a high traffic area so close to the front doors, but all sorts of nasty traps can be armed using a timer, and I wasn't taking any chances. Ditto with the stairs, which I took great pains to avoid walking on, stepping on the trim nearest the wall while clutching the banister. The stairway had shallow steps and elegant looking fabric overtop of the middle portion, like a crimson waterfall.

Often when I've encountered a particularly nasty or lethal trap, the surrounding carpet or furnishings were red, presumably because it was easier to clean up afterwards. I'm always cautious, but if I'm in an area that happens to be displaying a large amount of red, I'm doubly so.

A few minutes later I was at the top of the stairs, having traversed the entire length of them without making a sound, without stepping on a single stair, and managing to remain in one piece. I congratulated myself for that, consulted my mental map of Greybridge Keep, and glanced around the nearby corner.

I yanked my head back quickly, heart suddenly in my throat.

Someone was walking down the hallway, about two dozen feet away.

Crap.

If they'd seen me, I was screwed, and would need to bolt. I listened carefully for a moment to try to make out footsteps, and if they were getting louder or quieter.

Nothing. There was thick carpet lining every inch of floor. Double-crap.

Cursing the fact that I hadn't brought my fingernail-sized mirror with me, I huddled up against the banister and behind the wall, out and away from the majority of the torchlight.

Sitting in perfect stillness, I waited for some sound or shadow to give away the position of the figure in the hallway.

Three minutes I stood there, waiting. Eventually, and with much trepidation, I looked around the corner a second time.

Nothing.

I threw a look down the other end of the hallway to confirm that it was similarly unoccupied, and then I stepped swiftly and silently over the thick carpet, making no sound as I-

Actually, you know what? I'm a talented thief, one who relies on stealth and cunning. It might be unnecessary to use words like 'quietly' or 'silently' again and again. Let's just assume that unless I've stated otherwise, everything I do is silent.

There was a closed door on the right, which I ignored, and an open one on the left, which I didn't. With the same sort of catch-a-glimpse gesture of my head I inspected the room through the open door. A lamp was lit, and a chambermaid appeared to be folding clothes.

I swept past the door a moment later and proceeded down the hall at a fast walk. The door was only open so much, and she probably hadn't seen me. Even if she had, a young lass all alone who sees even a hint of movement outside of her door will typically freeze, even for just a moment, and try to convince herself that she was seeing things. Just as typically, if they do pensively make their way to the doorway to investigate, it would only be after enough time had elapsed for me to have made myself scarce anyway.

Besides, I only needed about ten seconds to get to the end of the hallway, to the outside balcony overlooking the garden.

True, I was already inside, and I did mention that was the difficult part. Why go to the balcony?

Well, if you keep your valuables on the third floor, very likely you've left some rather unpleasant things lying about for those who might wish to wander upstairs and make off with them. The corridors and stairways likely harbored several of the kinds of traps that my own keep contained dozens of.

It's one of the reasons why I spend so much time practicing climbing up on ledges and scaling walls.

I went out onto the balcony and was greeted by the rapidly retreating red haze of dusk, which would be replaced by the comforting blue blanket of night before long. Looking over the ledge, I saw two guards chatting lazily near the front of the main garden. Guards hardly ever bother to look up, so if I didn't make noise I'd likely be fine.

Stepping lightly onto the stone railing lining the balcony, I crouched into a turn so that I faced the building and leapt upwards, grabbing onto the stonework of the balcony above mine, pulling myself up until my fingers were at eye level. A moment's pause later, I threw the hooked fingers of my right hand over the top of the railing above my head in a swift, sudden motion. Ridiculously dangerous thing to do, if you haven't practiced the move dozens of times every morning for years and years.

Pulling myself up the rest of the way and lifting a leg to straddle the rail, I flexed the appropriate muscles in order to roll gracefully over the railing and onto the balcony floor. At least, I presume I was graceful. I've never actually seen myself do it.

After taking the necessary precautions I threw a quick peek down a familiar cream colored hallway and inspected the corner at the faraway end of it, the one I'd spent the better part of an hour getting to know a few days ago. Something seemed different.

The spiny plant was gone. They'd taken my plant, the dastards.

Actually, it wouldn't have served as an effective hiding spot without my thoughtcloth, which I didn't think to wear this time. Then again, I'd hardly expected to be breaking into Greybridge's keep a second time.

I stood hidden just inside the hallway, remembering that this floor was patrolled by a guard, one who showed up every ten minutes or so. I waited for his appearance.

And waited.

For fully twenty minutes I stood there waiting for someone to appear before concluding that I had to do something. My time was limited, the doorman would likely be waking up soon, and even if he didn't remember me, he might become suspicious upon waking up in a chair, unable to remember how he got there. I didn't have the luxury of standing around all night.

Twenty minutes. I should have seen a guard pass at least once.

Not liking it, but realizing I had to do it anyway, I did a quick check down the length of the hallway and stepped into it. Something else had changed, though I wasn't quite able to put my finger on what.

I quickly walked forward, alert for any sort of noise.

I reminded myself how amateurish this was. No plan except for some fuzzy notion that I had to speak to Lord Greybridge, no route planned to get to where he was, no escape route once I'd done that, or if I found myself having to leave in a hurry.

What exactly did I think I was going to do if I even found him? Did I apologize for breaking into his keep – a second time – as well as for drugging his doorman, and then just casually ask "Hey, so what's up with that duel tomorrow?" Not bloody likely.

I kept walking, though. Sometimes you have to focus on what you're doing, and not allow yourself to get distracted by how stupid what you're doing actually is.

Soon I arrived where I'd hidden myself a few nights earlier, stopping with my back sidled up against the wall. I tossed a brief glance around the corner, down the hall where the vault doorway was.

Nobody. The hallway was empty.

I briefly considered what to do next.

Well, at the very least, I'd take a quick look at how many additional precautions his security staff had added to the door of the vault. Might as well, since I was already here.

With nobody in the empty hallway, I whipped around the corner and walked up to the doorway.

At first, I thought that the entire color of the door had been changed, which I thought was an odd and superstitious way of dealing with a break-in. Once I got closer, however, I realized that I was not looking at the door at all, but at the shadowy interior of the room on the other side of the door. The door was wide open, much to my enormous surprise.

Then, to my even greater surprise, I realized that I was completely wrong.

The door was gone.

Missing. Simply removed, with no trace of where it might have been moved to. In fact, there was no trace that there had even been a door there in the first place. I just stood there, staring into the empty void where I had expected smooth planed wood to be.

A ridiculously long time later, I walked through the threshold and into the formerly secure room, which I had formerly broken into for the purposes of stealing a goblet.

Empty. Not just the door. *Everything* that had been in the room was gone.

I have a hard time thinking of words to describe how puzzled I was at this development. Plinths and some other features of the room had remained unchanged, and I could see small things that assured me that I was, in fact, in the correct room. This was the very same room I had stood in days ago, but it had changed completely, dramatically. Even the stylish trim that had contained the circuit of silver had been removed, its absence not even leaving a blemish on the wall it had once been a part of.

Standing there stupidly, I wondered if stealing Greybridge's goblet had made him go completely mental.

And then it hit me, the thing that had struck me as different about the hallways I'd been wandering through. It wasn't just the plant that had been taken, wasn't just the door. The paintings, the elegant chairs positioned in the hallways I'd roamed through, the brass standalone torch lamps, the gold leaf bordered mirrors...

Everything had been removed.

My head momentarily swam, like I'd had too much to drink. Yet another thing that made very little sense. What this meant, I had no idea.

That seemed to be the norm lately.

Standing there in the still darkness, I became aware of two things more or less simultaneously.

First was the realization that standing in the middle of a room that used to house valuable items belonging to a rich and powerful lord might be a spectacularly bad idea.

The second was that there was a trace of a conversation, barely audible, coming from somewhere outside of the room.

I was torn between finding the source of the voices, and removing myself from this place as quickly as possible. I opted for the former, though I told my legs that the latter might be required at a moment's notice, and crept out of the empty room. Once in the empty hallway, I tried to get a fix on the voices.

They seemed to be coming from where my sketches indicated Greybridge's study was. I headed in that direction, listening to the two separate, distinct voices. In short order, I came to a door. It was opened a crack, spilling a fountain of light into the hallway just ahead of me. The voices appeared to be coming from within that room.

"-exaggeration at best. Your reputation is the thing, the only thing you need really. I've said it before, I'll say it again." I recognized Greybridge's voice, now that I was within earshot.

"Indeed," said a voice I didn't recognize, "you've said so a dozen times at least, if memory serves. By the way - you've had enough, I think."

"Bah," Greybridge said, in the manner of a man who's clearly had enough to drink. "I'm aware of my limits, sir. I need not be lectured by the likes of you." There was the noisy sound of someone consuming a drink, almost spitefully.

"Really, as minor as your involvement might be tomorrow, I think you could perhaps lay off the cups long enough to ensure you can actually do it. You've two days, oh most revered and noble lord," the voice mocked, "at which point you can finish moving to your new estate, and leave political affairs entirely. Why, you could then drink yourself into oblivion if you wish."

"How touching," Greybridge said bitterly.

"Lord Greybridge, I assure you that I care not a whit what you might do three days hence. Or beyond," the voice said. "I care a great deal what happens tomorrow, and the day after. And I assure you that *my* lord cares a great deal, as well. So much so, that I'm afraid I must insist that you-" the voice paused mid-sentence, as though considering how to either phrase something diplomatically, or how to make it more insulting. "That you've had enough to drink this evening. Most honored lord."

The ironic tone was not lost on Greybridge. A full minute passed before he replied.

"You...you need not be so, so-"

"Blunt?" The voice said, amused. "Come, my lord. It is played out, and you've seen the most desirable option available to you. There is no shame in that, is there? A nice country estate, away from the troubles and strife of those who dwell in the city. You're being paid handsomely, I might remind you, for your efforts."

"Yes, it's all about the money, isn't it," Greybridge half snarled.

Nothing was said for a good half minute.

"Well, yes," Greybridge said softly, the sound of a glass smashing against brick acting as punctuation for his soft words. "There, look! Done. I assure you I'll be fine for tomorrow's performance, young man."

Performance?

"And the next day?" said the unidentified man, his voice full of laughter. "You'll be able to stand upright on that day as well? We need not send a carriage full of burly lads to escort you to-"

"Damn you! I've already done it, haven't I? It's been arranged, all the details taken care of and ironed out, so you need not rub it in my face you arrogant son of-"

"Lord Greybridge, please sit back down. I fear you might injure yourself."

This time, the pause that followed was almost dangerous.

"What more do you want?" Greybridge asked, his voice plaintive and desperate. My recollection of Greybridge's legendary temper was completely at odds with the cowed, pleading voice I now heard.

"Want? My lord, I assure you that I do not desire anything from your noble self, outside of ensuring that you retire this evening in a condition that suggests that your participation in tomorrow's activities goes as planned. Did I not say that this was my intent earlier? I could have sworn that I had."

"I...indeed. Very well. I believe I shall retire then. That is, unless you have any objections to me doing *that.*"

"Retire? Why, my lord, the evening has barely begun!" Again, the voice gave a hint of mocking laughter that it seemed unable to contain. "Surely you're not that tired, so soon? If you wished to go out this evening and have a spot of something to eat, I'm sure I could loan you some coin."

Loan some coin. Greybridge, borrowing from-

Oh my.

His exclamation about money, the talk of moving estates, the quiet certainty that oozed from the voice of the unknown speaker as he smoothly handled a man who, until just moments ago, I had assumed was one of the most financially stable and powerful lords in all of Harael.

The keep was being emptied, he was moving elsewhere. Or being moved. Or-

That cussed doorman who had dressed me down earlier – the servants clothing he was wearing didn't fit him, which might suggest that he was planted there, playing a part. Possibly not a doorman at all, and probably not even Greybridge's employee. The empty hallways, the chambermaid packing clothing.

It all pointed to Greybridge selling his estate. Not because he wanted to, but because he *had* to.

Snapping out of my thoughts, I focused once again on what the voices were saying.

"-sick kind of satisfaction. Your kind makes me quite happy to be taking the path I find myself on. I've little love for politics, and-"

"Politics," the voice sneered. "Is that what you choose to call it? Watching you slick and grubby weasels in action only reinforces my contempt for the self-defeating, diseased system of government that exists today. I find no pleasure in getting my own hands dirty, rooting around in the mud as you and your fellow lords do."

"You certainly seem adept enough at it yourselves. I'm sure you and your lord will do marvelously well," Greybridge said, sounding familiarly pompous.

"Now, now," the stranger tsk'd, "just because you yourself lacked any sort of native talent when it came to managing your affairs...just because *your* life was a dismal failure doesn't mean tha-"

There was the sound of movement, like wooden legs being pushed over an expanse of carpet, followed by seconds of silence. Finally, there was a high-pitched and cruel laugh that filled the room.

"Oh, do continue what you were about to do, Lord Greybridge. Ah, see...you've stopped. Shame, that. Are you sure I can't convince you to continue? Hmmm? Perhaps if I asked nicely, or said 'please', you would-"

"I'm going to retire for the evening," Greybridge said with a note of finality. "The night is young, it's true, but I have a sudden feeling that an hour spent being dragged backwards over carpenter nails would be preferable to spending five minutes more in the presence of your...wit."

"My lord...you have but to ask, and once this is all settled I will personally ensure that you experience the former in order to satisfy your curiosity regarding how it compares to the latter."

There was more silence, and then more sounds of items being moved over carpet, which meant-

I turned and sprinted as quickly as I could down the hallway, ears only half aware of the two speakers wishing each other a pleasant evening, neither meaning it. Turning the corner as rapidly as I could safely manage, I didn't stop to observe them entering the hallway I'd just fled. I didn't worry about the possibility of guards patrolling the hallways, now that I knew they were devoid of valuables and things of interest. I simply continued on the carpeted path as quickly as I could, my only concern consisting of making it to the third floor balcony and leaving the premises as quickly as I could manage, without being seen.

What had I just heard?

Greybridge was playing along with something, and in a manner he clearly didn't like or appreciate. Country estate? He was not fond of politics – anyone with ears and half a brain knew that. What was happening to the estate that he governed, and how did it fit in with me, and what I was doing?

What was this 'performance' that was required of him?

I arrived at the balcony and stood at the shallow railing overlooking the cobbled path below me, frozen for a time, momentarily uncertain of what I should do.

Well, I should get the hell out of there. Obviously.

Grabbing onto the decorative stone pillars of the railing in a manner that might have made an acrobat gibber in terror, I vaulted over the top and pulled myself back toward the keep like a swing, depositing myself lightly on the second floor balcony below.

I wanted to drop down to the main floor, the cobbled path that led to the main garden. The two guards I had first spied with their backs turned were still there, having barely moved a single inch since I'd spotted them. The sound of my boots dropping onto the hard stone of the garden path would certainly alert them to my presence.

Easy enough to take care of, I realized.

I reached into a small pocket on my left for one of the several small marble-sized spheres I kept there. I didn't have my wrist-sling on me, but that hardly mattered – they simply needed to be thrown with enough force to break, and any hard surface would do. Once I found the one that I wished, I gave a quick glance to the two guards below, and threw the sphere onto the cobbles of the courtyard. Taking a deep breath, I vaulted over the railing and followed it down.

This particular marble hit the ground and...well, appeared to do something entirely the opposite of 'erupting', dimming the area around it. It would, for about six seconds or so, remove all of the air from an area about ten feet wide from where it had struck. Handy for putting out fires and torches, disabling certain alarms and traps, or even occasionally making people unable to breathe, causing them to panic.

Almost by accident, I discovered a dandy side effect of air being removed in this fashion – it completely negated sound of any kind.

I landed heavily within my sphere of silence and rolled, the ground forcibly clacking against the hard soles of my boots in a way that I could feel was loud, if not actually hear. I felt the cold pressure of nothingness against my skin, and my eyes and ears began to hurt slightly.

From there, I quickly moved away from the oblivious guards and toward the side yard, which would provide me with easy access to the street. My feet padded lightly across the lawn as I made my way to the edge of the clearing.

Sprinting that forty feet took an eternity.

Arriving at the outskirts of the lawn, I quickly hopped over a small fence and stepped through some bushes and onto the street, forcing myself not to pant. I nodded politely to a couple who seemed startled by my sudden appearance during their evening stroll. I didn't notice if they nodded back or not.

Safe. Maybe.

Determined not to look behind me, I forced myself to walk down the road as casually as I could, heading in the direction of my keep.

I was thinking furiously, digesting information. It was impossible for me to say if I felt I was getting closer to an explanation, or if each strange twist simply cast me further adrift in the ocean of uncertainty I'd been floating in. Was I getting anywhere at all?

This whole thing was suddenly much, much bigger than I had originally assumed. From all accounts, Greybridge was an extremely tough, cagey son of a bitch, one who was reputed to have resources at his disposal that boggled the mind.

It occurred to me that the sheer economic and political force that was required to make a powerful recluse like Greybridge bend a knee would have to be even more considerable.

It also occurred to me to wonder if I had my affairs in order.

Chapter 15

IT WAS MUCH later that evening when I finally arrived back home, the two knights guarding the main entrance of my keep greeting me with the look of someone who's just thought the words "Oh crap, it's the boss!"

Talia didn't greet me at the door, which gave me a rough estimate of the time. Even the live-in staff that I employ have lives outside of taking care of my wishes or handling my affairs. It was unreasonable to expect an employee to be at my beck and call all hours of the day and night, after all.

Except Cyrus, of course. He wasn't allowed to have a life...not while he was busy protecting mine.

He probably wouldn't be back until later in the evening, returning only once he'd finished gathering the additional information on Teuring I'd asked for. I decided that I'd wait for him downstairs, go over the original notes that he had provided me. There was nothing else to do really, save for mulling over everything I thought I knew from beginning to end, like I'd been doing for the entire walk home.

It hadn't helped. The only thing all that walking had accomplished was to make my feet sore.

Once downstairs I immediately went to the drinks cabinet and, after carefully looking over various bottles of brandy, scotch, herb infused absinthe and countless other concoctions, I sighed softly to myself and rolled up my sleeve, reaching into the frigid water of the wine cooler for the bottle of *Tull'efrit* seventeen I'd left chilling there. With all the green wine I drink, there are some days when I wonder why I bother keeping those other drinks down there.

I was towel-drying the bottle as I walked back to my usual seat, when I noticed something I didn't recognize sitting right in front of the place I ordinarily do my thinking, perched on top of the various notes I had left there.

Perplexed, I walked over to the small table. The something in question turned out to be a book, red-bound with gold threading on the outside. It was thick. Dauntingly thick.

I spied a corner of colored paper sticking out from between pages. I opened the front cover and inspected the note, which bore handwriting I recognized.

"With everything else going on, I figured I'd reconsider something you'd told me earlier as well. Do any of these look familiar? -T"

Lifting the note revealed a drawing on the first page - a colorful arrangement of rope tied in an elegant and improbable pattern, three rolling hills sitting in the background behind it, two trees perched atop the leftmost one. The crest of Knothills.

Small bits of torn colored paper lined the top of the book nearest the spine, more of them than I could conveniently count. I opened the book to the first marked page, and was greeted by an artist's rendering of a sword, hilt at the top of the page and point at the bottom, perfect in every detail.

Bless Theo's heart.

This drawing did not resemble either of the swords that I glimpsed in Teuring's possession that day at the Circles – it had a snake and a flower I didn't recognize at the center, as well as a few leaves in the guard. The page opposite it contained a wealth of information for anyone who actually cared about exactly how much birch charcoal had been used at what phase in its development, the theoretical force it could withstand, things like that. Most importantly, at the very top of that page was the name of the family that had commissioned the sword to be created – Aspyris.

It must have taken him hours, but he'd apparently gone through each sword in the book looking for any that had leaves on the guard, the only thing I'd thought to tell him about Teuring's pair of swords.

Sometimes I feel I don't deserve a friend like him.

I hastily found a piece of paper of my own to write notes on, a rough quill and some ink. Careful not to get a spot of ink on the masterpiece I had before me, I went to work.

Bottle of wine unopened and forgotten, I pored over the tome with an increasing sense of urgency. Each picture I inspected seemed to push me to the next one, and the next.

I can't be certain how much time passed, but I was about two thirds of the way through the entire book when I heard the familiar sound of boots making their way nimbly down the booby-trapped hallway toward my room. Cyrus, returning from his visit to whatever mysterious reservoir of knowledge he acquired his information from.

I had flipped a few more pages to get to the next of Theo's page markers, when Cyrus walked through the door and into the hall, every bit of him radiating breathless excitement.

"Copperthorn!" he exclaimed, holding a sheaf of papers with some loose strings aloft, like some sort of trophy animal horn brought back from a dangerous jungle expedition.

"Copperthorn," I said aloud, not recognizing the name, quickly flipping the pages in front of me back to the section which had names beginning with 'C'.

"Milord, I'm positive. It's difficult to pick out exactly how it's all connected, but it's there. The trail for some of it-"

"Bide a moment," I said, continuing to flip through the pages.

"Milord, I'm convinced he's-"

"Cyrus, I'm sure you have something very important to tell me, and I'll listen to it shortly. Bide a moment."

He opened his mouth to speak, then closed it. Then he simply stood there, bundle of papers still in hand, and looking fit to burst.

After a few minutes of scouring pages, I determined that the name 'Copperthorn' was not among those in Theo's book, and I frowned.

I did have other books I could look through for that name, however. Many other books.

"Come, we're going to the library," I said abruptly, carefully closing Theo's book and pushing it unobtrusively to the side before lurching to my feet and heading to the door.

As the two of us made our way down the booby-trapped hallway and up to the third floor I told Cyrus of my various suspicions regarding Lord Teuring, as well as informed him of my recent adventures at the Greybridge estate, giving him the gist of the conversation I'd overheard. I admit I did try to make myself look a tad more clever when relating the encounter between myself and the ill-mannered doorman.

When I was done relating the events of the evening to him, he spoke.

"Milord, the voice you heard...it was Lord Teuring, yes?"

"No, it wasn't him."

"I *knew* there was some- uh...oh," he said, frowning at me. "You're sure?"

"I've heard him speak several times, in several situations. It definitely wasn't him. Besides, when I left Teuring this afternoon he seemed capable of little more than vomiting into a bucket."

"Possibly it was Copperthorn, then?"

"I don't think it was a lord at all, actually. The speaker referred to 'his lord' several times during the conversation, so was likely a servant or knight of some sort. Although, for a servant to have the temerity to talk to a lord like that...I don't know."

Furrowing his brow even deeper than usual, Cyrus went quiet and pursed his lips in thought. For a while, the only sound filling the hallways were the clomping of our boots against the stone floor and the quiet rustling of papers that Cyrus held to his chest.

Upon arriving at the library door, I removed from my tunic a rather large multicolored key, made from four different types of metal, a piece of whalebone, and a small piece of teak wood, the combination of which would quickly disable all of my traps and grant me access to my library.

Inserting the key, I turned it a quarter-turn one way, a half turn the other, and then a half-turn back the first way. That, or I did something completely different with it. Or perhaps none of what I've described just now is real, and this is all merely a cunning ruse to confound potential burglars should they ever happen upon this description of my library's security measures. The point is that I did...something, and that something resulted in the doors slowly swinging open amid the sound of several dozen various safeguards disarming or disabling themselves.

Upon entering, I walked up to a small book that I kept on my desk. It contained the names of every author of each book that currently resided in my library, as well as any special title given to the book they'd written. I flipped it open and began to look under 'C', my index finger running down the list of names.

The name 'Copperthorn' was nowhere present. I had a gut feeling that I wasn't going to find it there, but I had to make sure.

I closed the book on my desk and walked up to the cabinet containing my collection of books written by Lord Elkgrass, a lord whose personal journals were mostly composed of bits of gossip and rumor that he'd heard. If Copperthorn had done anything notable or scandalous in the past thirty years, his name would likely make an appearance somewhere in the collection.

"So, Cyrus, tell me what you've got on Copperthorn. I'm assuming it has to do with Teuring?" I returned to my chair once I'd pulled down one of Elkgrass's books, setting it gently upon the desk and opening it to the first page, which contained a list of names and the page numbers where they could be found.

"Errr. Right . . ." Cyrus began, sifting through the papers he'd been holding as if only suddenly becoming aware of them. "Dion Copperthorn. Without an estate himself, but currently managing the estate of a Lord Eagan Redforne, Copperthorn's cousin, who owns a small country estate located to the northwest of the city."

"Redforne?" I frowned. "I think I've heard that name somewhere. Wait a second...managed *for* Redforne? How the deuce does something like that happen?"

"It's rare, but it does happen. Diplomats, dignitaries and so forth are often lords who take up temporary responsibilities and wish to return to an estate that was kept more or less the same as when they'd left it. In this case there was a medical crisis, though there's been some scandalous talk about how that came about. The property itself is unremarkable – a tiny bit of land requiring the services of about a dozen staff to maintain. However, the size of the estate Copperthorn manages is disproportionately small when compared to the estimated size of the Redforne fortune at present."

"Which is?"

He told me.

My brain was telling me that if I attempted to make it go through one more seemingly insane mental contortion or impossible leap of logic, it would simply explode with a wet, squishy 'ka-bampf' noise, and begin leaking out of my ears.

"What?!" I managed to say about a billion years later. "Cyrus, that's a hundred times more money than I have! And I'm not exactly poor."

"Milord, I'm afraid that's merely the shark's fin with respect to this whole situation. It gets quite interesting."

I closed the book in front of me, giving Cyrus my full attention and gesturing for him to continue.

Cyrus went through his papers, as if to make certain that they were in the right order, and cleared his throat.

"Okay, perhaps it would be best if I covered the items in the order I discovered them. First, we have Lord Angelo Teuring. He had a small country estate as well, also in the northwest, somewhat close to the Redforne estate. First mention of Teuring I was able to find was his bestowing ceremony, four years ago this week, where he was given the territory he currently manages, and his old estate was converted to a fiefdom. The technical requirements for establishing rule within the city were met, and he agreed to a surety imposed by Prince Tenarreau for two years because of his age." He briefly held up an official, plain looking document as proof, one that I would have given my eye teeth to find out how he'd acquired. "He was bequeathed the estate quickly and without too much fanfare or notice. More or less a typical introduction of a country lord attempting to get a foothold in the city."

I raised my eyebrow at him and gestured toward the document. "Is that...?"

"Yes Milord." He flushed slightly, putting it back on the top of the pile. "It must be back by dawn tomorrow or...uh, bad things happen."

"I can believe that," I said with no small amount of admiration. "How in Hades did you manage that, exactly?"

Cyrus coughed apologetically. "I'm sort of, uh...seeing someone who works in the palace records. She's fairly convinced that her life is rather boring, in need of excitement and intrigue, and . . ." He shrugged.

"I thought you were courting Talia. Didn't you and I have a conversation to that effect at some point?"

"Yes Milord," he said, eyes searching mine just the tiniest bit, "I asked your permission to pursue her, as we were both in your employ. I thought it inappropriate to consider it without consulting you first."

"Didn't work out?"

"I...that is, it seems she...is rather taken with someone else, Milord," he said, uncomfortably.

Poor guy. Talia was achingly beautiful, and you couldn't really blame the man for trying. Still, if my Captain's chiseled features weren't enough to win Talia over, what chance did any man have?

Cyrus continued to look oddly uncomfortable, so I opted to change the topic.

"Right. Okay, so you were able to confirm the time that he was awarded his estate. Four years ago, you said?"

"Correct. The Teuring family wasn't all that well known at the time, but the territory they were given in the city wasn't particularly large, nor did it pose any threat to neighboring estates. Documents appear to be in order, although," he gave me a brief look, "they're pretty sparse, and there's something rather odd about them."

"Inconsistencies?"

"Not really, just odd. The oldest documents that exist on the family suggest that their fortunes were not exactly positive, and they appeared to hit rock bottom about fifty years ago or so. A case of several generations of bad or indifferent luck when it came to politics, and a sudden desire to cut their losses. They appeared to sell their property and run, become country lords, and live on what money remained. Still on the books, still paying tithes to the prince, but just below the point of notice, not involved in the normal hustle and bustle."

"Right. How is this odd exactly?"

"Well, those details aren't. It's just that the family kept extremely poor records, almost criminally so. Teuring ended up having to establish his lineage through written oath and patents drawn up by other members of the Teuring family, as well as a dozen or so other lords."

"No records before that?"

"Nothing for what would appear to be two generations. It appeared as though they wished nothing to do with Harael once they'd left, though that's not entirely uncommon either. A quick check indicated that fully half of the Teuring family on record have since died, and there were a good fifteen or so I could find that never got entered into the palace records in the first place."

"I see. So, Angelo decides to be the one to move the Teuring estate back to the city, only he can't do that if he's not listed in the palace records."

"Right. So, he gets the necessary documents in order, which had to have taken him a devilishly long time, and submits them about five years ago. The patents were approved by the prince, and it's been written into the records and made official that Angelo Teuring, son of Mannas, son of Arturro . . ." He briefly squinted at the new piece of paper he'd been reading from. "Arturro Teuring? Who would name their son something so-"

"Cyrus."

"Right. So in the end, he's given an estate and has basically done nothing with it. Records suggest he makes next to nothing, presently."

"That's a bit daft. If collecting tithes for providing protection is your sole source of income, you kind of want to help it however you can, right away. Kind of defeats the whole point of him moving to the city. Why wouldn't he seek to improve his situation?"

"No idea, but it struck me as being strange enough that I should keep looking into the history of the territory, which led to," he shuffled a few more papers out of his way, "an interesting little skirmish that happened just over a year ago. Do you remember that flare-up between Whiteleaf and Harpin?"

I raised my eyebrows at that. "I'd hardly call that a skirmish. The whole town was talking about that one. It's related?"

"Whiteleaf borders Teuring to the East, and had made a few unfriendly overtures suggesting that he'd like some or all of Teuring's puny estate. There were a few pokes at his businesses, one confirmed theft, and then suddenly Harpin comes at Whiteleaf from the other side, out of nowhere. Whiteleaf retired to the country later that same year as a result - Harpin was quite thorough."

"Hmmm," I mused, sitting further back into my chair and considering. "Okay, so the timing is rather fortunate for Teuring. How is this relevant?"

"Copperthorn reportedly visited Harpin just prior to him initiating the territory war."

"So you're suggesting that Copperthorn may have financed this little flare-up?"

"It appears that way, and 'there are a few records that support the idea." Cyrus shuffled through yet another sheaf of papers. "It took quite a lot of digging, and great pains had been taken to cover it up. I had it double-checked once I'd found out. Really, Copperthorn didn't have a particularly good reason to be involved at all, so I made a note of the name."

"And Copperthorn's managing the Redforne estate, you said?"

"Correct. Learning that the Redforne estate was located near the old Teuring estate made me a little suspicious."

"It doesn't really make sense though, does it? If Copperthorn was involved, as you've said, that whole mess with Harpin and Whiteleaf would have cost a pretty copper. Why would Copperthorn be simply managing another lord's estate if he had that kind of money sitting around?"

"He didn't. I dug a little deeper into some courier and treasury records. Turns out the entire thing was funded through Redforne's estate."

"Wow. And won't Lord Redforne be a little pissed when he finds out?"

"*If* he finds out," said Cyrus, reaching for another sheet of paper from within his pile and peering at it closely. He cleared his throat. "Lord Eagan Redforne, sole heir to the Redforne family fortune, collapsed during a visit with various family members several years ago. A short while later some healers conclude that he's suffering from a blood related brain ailment, citing sudden paralysis on the right side of his body and loss of comprehension as indicators."

"Ah. We call them 'strokes' down at the Circles. I don't really know why they're called that, but . . ." I shrugged.

"Thus Eagan Redforne is whisked out of the way to recover, waited on by family and private healers, and management of his estate fell to his cousin, Copperthorn, as per his explicit written instructions. A few of the notes I found regarding Redforne's initial health suggests memory loss, lack of speech, inability to walk...and it's just been getting worse."

"I swear I've seen the name Redforne before. Or heard it. Maybe because he was rich – that sort of money always turns a few heads and gets people talking. So, Copperthorn's more or less got access to the whole fortune?"

"Although he can't simply take it for himself, if he can justify the money he wishes to spend by offering up a reason why it benefits the Redforne estate, apparently he can do pretty much whatever he wishes. Even if it doesn't really benefit the estate at all. There were very few safeguards left in place to prevent abuse."

"Why finance Harpin, though? Why not simply give Lord Teuring enough money to fight back against Whiteleaf?"

"I don't know, Milord. Perhaps Copperthorn doesn't want Teuring to know he's looking out for him."

Maybe. Perhaps this was a country squabble that had stretched its way into the city. Perhaps young Teuring was a friend of Copperthorn's. Or perhaps even a hostage, kept in the city where he could easily be put into danger, a threat to keep his parents in line? Maybe. That sort of made sense, kind of.

Not really.

I sighed, rubbing my temples.

"So Teuring wouldn't appear to be involved in politics at all, with the exception of the move against me, which Copperthorn may or may not have any connection to, because he's using Redforne's estate to prop up Teuring, but only enough so that he doesn't starve to death, and even though he doesn't really appear to have any reason to."

"Right."

"Cyrus, I have an idea," I said, fingers pressing against my tightly shut eyes. "Why don't you fetch me a large mallet from the kitchen so I can dash my brains out and bid farewell to this whole sordid mess . . ."

"Heh," Cyrus chuckled.

I furrowed my brow in thought. It made no sense. If Copperthorn was helping Teuring and didn't want his help to be noticed, how would Teuring come into possession of two fabulously expensive swords in the first place? Were they an anonymous gift?

Could Copperthorn have given him the swords and some other things, like paying for that fencing instructor, as a way of convincing Teuring to go through with the duel?

Of course, on top of everything else that didn't make sense, there was Theo's belief that Teuring actually knew his way around a sword, and was hiding it from me deliberately.

He was either a victim, or a tool. In either case, however, it appeared that my true enemy was actually Copperthorn.

Maybe I was getting somewhere after all.

"Seriously Cyrus, what is going on? If Copperthorn was responsible for financing Harpin, there had to be a solid reason. What do you have on Copperthorn, or Redforne?"

"Not much to the Copperthorn family other than what I've already told you. They'd done nothing remarkable prior to Dion Copperthorn becoming custodian of the Redforne estate. The Redforne family," Cyrus said, pulling out a few leaflets from his substantial pile and inspecting them, "was one of the 'new rich' that sprung into being a couple of generations ago, much like your rather abrupt neighbor, Lord Haundsing. It had become fashionable to hire duelists at the time, so much so that laws were created specifically to prevent nonsensical duels from happening over contrived insults or similar fictions. The current Lord Redforne inherited the estate twenty years ago when his father, an exceptional duelist by the name of Salvatori Redforne, was found dead at the bottom of a rather tall set of stairs."

Click. I had it.

"Salvatori. That's it. A moment," I said, standing up suddenly. I stood briefly in front of the collection of my father's books, pausing thoughtfully before grabbing the third one on the left. Cyrus stood mute as I flipped quickly through the pages near the front, finger tracing over the handwritten words as my eyes scanned the page for the name I sought. After less than half a dozen pages, I found it.

"Salvatori Redforne," I said with a hint of triumph, turning the book and placing it open on the desk, my finger pointing to one of the pages. Cyrus came closer and leaned down to inspect it.

It wasn't long before his eyes widened.

"Killed? Here?"

"Accidental," I shrugged, "or perhaps 'unintended' would be a better word. From what my father wrote, there was an array of pressure-sensitive concussive traps lining the tops of the walls of the keep at some point in time, which aren't exactly lethal per say, but . . ."

"Enough to kill someone attempting to climb over the walls and engage in a bit of high-altitude burgling," Cyrus said.

"For someone who wasn't looking for it, yes. Father felt horrible about it, based on what he wrote about the incident. He figured that the late Lord Redforne wished to shed his reputation as a 'newly titled' lord who bought his way into an estate, perhaps gain a little prestige through some high-profile robberies or clever thieving. A very skilled swordsman, from what I understand."

"Fearsome reputation, and I couldn't find record of a single duel he'd lost," he agreed. "His dueling fees were quite substantial at times, borderline absurd at others. And of course, if the current state of the Redforne fortune is any indication . . ."

"Right. That's a lot of money. So I'm guessing it happens like this; a talented swordsman finds himself with whopping loads of cash as a result of being really, really good. He decides to grab the brass ring and retire from dueling, buys himself a title, lordship, but then encounters a brand new problem . . ."

"He's not respected among the other lords?" Cyrus ventured.

"Right. He's suddenly gone from commanding huge respect, to receiving very little." I sat back down in my chair and parked my boots on a corner of the desk, leaning back with my hands behind my neck. "And so, he attempts to garner the respect he's used to, through the traditional means by which Haraelian lords acquire respect from each other."

"Cunning, subtlety," Cyrus nodded.

"Thieving," I agreed. "There were many of them about that time - a bunch of inexperienced would-be burglars with lots of money, hunting for prestige. Most were unaware of what they were up against and ended up either looking very silly, or very dead. Or both."

"This was common?" he asked, looking interested.

"Common enough that some lords jokingly made a sport of it...catching would-be thieves in non-lethal traps and hosting a banquet or impromptu luncheon while the inept burglar hung upside-down from their rafters, humiliated. Or worse, if the lord's tastes ran that way." I pointed at the book. "Father wrote that the trap that got Lord Redforne was not exactly lethal per say, and could be survived by anyone who knew how to fall properly. Redforne apparently did not, and had not."

"And now, he *is* not."

I nodded. "Broke his neck. Dad felt pretty terrible, like I said. He didn't even try to claim responsibility for thwarting the attempted theft, saying something about it being beneath his honor. He simply moved him elsewhere and staged it to look like an accident, which is precisely what it was. And thus, I believe you mentioned a tall flight of stairs?"

"Indeed. Well, your father managed to successfully keep his name out of it. There was no mention of your family at all, when I was researching it."

"Father was good at covering his tracks, this I know for certain." I nodded for him to continue.

"Right. Well, that left Eagan as sole heir to the Redforne estate, Lady Redforne having died giving birth to him. Salvatori died when the lad was six years old. He was left in the care of the Copperthorn family, Redforne's brother-in-law, who took him to the countryside and forfeited the city estate."

"Just like that? They simply left?"

"Well, there are indications that they'd been encouraged," Cyrus amended.

"Ah. Yes I see. Taken to a country estate, out of harm's way." I waved for him to continue.

"With his uncle, yes. He grows up amid considerable wealth and takes possession of the country estate and inheritance upon turning eighteen years old, country lords not being required to wait until twenty-three. He does an okay job of managing things, but that wouldn't be hard given the enormity of his family fortune. He was fairly well regarded prior to his collapse."

"How bad was this stroke exactly? Maybe it was Copperthorn that I overheard, mentioning his 'lord'. Could Redforne still be calling the shots, maybe coordinating things from his bedside or something?"

"Not according to my notes. Barely responsive, doesn't talk. Confined to bed, no visitors whatsoever, except for healers and family. Miserable luck for someone so young."

"Pretty miserable luck for an entire fledgling family, when you stop and think about it. First the mother, then the father, then the son," I said. "A stroke is a serious thing, and can happen from a head injury, from bleeding out...even just from being too uptight. In my experience, nobody comes back from a stroke the same as they were, and for duelists they're pretty much a career ender. If that kid wanted to follow in his father's footsteps, or had any measure of talent with swords whatsoever, he-"

Click. I had it.

Oh . . .

Holy crap.

"Milord?"

It was right then that I saw it, the whole thing in its entirety. All the pieces fit suddenly, and perfectly.

Even the bit with Greybridge made sense now. The whole thing - it was gorgeous. It had everything a cleverly wrought scheme could have asked for. The subtlety of it, the patience, the sheer *audacity* that was required...

"Milord!" Cyrus was looking alarmed.

"Gods above and below!" I said, breathlessly. The beauty of it! Awe and admiration bubbled up inside me. The conversation I'd overheard, the swords, this new information, everything that he'd-

"Milord, are you all right?"

"Cyrus, I think I've figured it out, but...*gods*," I marveled, unable to keep from smiling and shaking my head as I looked at the ceiling, eyes not really focused on anything, "I've never heard of anyone doing anything quite like this before. It's brilliant, and I don't even...hang on a second, I just thought of something. We need to go back down to the exercise hall."

I got up and walked briskly out of the library. Cyrus had to practically run to keep up with me, arms clutching his various papers to his chest.

He was looking somewhat alarmed, and I realized that he had a good reason to be. I'd just figured it out - understood why things were happening the way they had been...

I had no idea what I was going to do to stop it.

It only took a couple of minutes for us to make our way to the solid wooden door of the exercise hall, Cyrus waiting patiently for me to finish hopping over the assortment of traps guarding the hallway before attempting the feat himself.

"Cyrus, in your notes there, do you have information on where the Redforne estate used to be?" I asked, disarming the last of the locking mechanisms and swinging the door open. "Unless I've missed my guess entirely, I'm positive that we'll find that information very interesting."

He was already flipping through documents as he walked into the hall, his fingers finding and tracing over the details of a crudely hand-drawn scrap of a map on yellowing paper, following the lines marking streets and other landmarks within the city, reading whatever names had been listed there. His finger stopped under a particular word, and his eyes got the tiniest bit wider.

"North of Silhouette? But...but that's . . ."

"Our friend Lord Greybridge's territory, I'm sure you were about to say," I said, shaking my head. "The other thing that you're going to be confirming for me in a few moments is precisely when Lord Redforne suffered his stroke. No doubt the actual dates haven't been recorded, or may be a little off, but I'm certain that you'll find that his unfortunate and sudden debilitating event happened just over four years ago.

"You'll also find that he hasn't been seen or heard of by anyone other than close family, and that other well-wishers, friends, and acquaintances have all been turned away. There's probably some talk of conspiracy of some sort, his cousin attempting to usurp Redforne's estate from under him, keeping Redforne isolated like a prisoner, doesn't matter. What does matter is that nobody's seen him...nobody who isn't extended family or trusted servants, anyway."

"Milord? I'm afraid I still don't understand how a detail like that can-"

"Don't you see?" I interrupted excitedly, "This was never about an inept young lord trying to make a name for himself, or even someone wanting to set him up. This was about revenge, the most simple and basic motive there is.

"My father was thorough, and although he probably erased every trace of his name from the accident involving Salvatori, he missed an important detail. Father wrote stories detailing his own activities and escapades in his journals, usually after the fact. Not all lords do it that way. Some simply record what they've done on a given day, or document what they plan on doing. Salvatori's son, just a boy, grows up with the knowledge that his invincible swordsman father was found dead at the bottom of a set of stairs. Later, he reads in his father's journal that the very night of his death he'd been planning to steal something from Tucat Keep. It doesn't take a genius to figure out what must have happened.

"And so, as soon as he's of age he becomes the dutiful, prodigal son. He concocts a plan to strike back at those he considers responsible for his father's death. He somehow manages to bankrupt Greybridge, who would appear to be the lord responsible for squeezing what remained of the Redforne family out of Harael and into the country, given that he currently controls the old Redforne territory. Ironic, poetic justice...he regains possession of the family estate in addition to all of the property that Greybridge had worked a lifetime to acquire. All this he has to do covertly, without notice, because he's not done there.

"And that's because there's me, the last surviving member of the Tucat family, the very family he believes responsible for his father's death. He wants me to suffer, wants it to be personal, and with the most fitting form of revenge possible. And so the proud son of one of the best swordsmen who has ever lived decides to fake a medical crisis, hires an expert forger to draft the proper patents of nobility, and re-invents himself as a naive, young backwoods country lord of no great significance or intellect . . ."

Cyrus gaped at me.

"You're saying-" said Cyrus, his voice a hoarse whisper.

"...that Lord Teuring is Lord Redforne," I finished, quietly.

There were several moments of silence.

"Just look at what he gets to accomplish by doing so," I continued, walking over to the table which still had Theo's book resting on it. "He bankrupts the lord responsible for driving him out of the city, going so far as to use him as an unwilling accomplice. He learns all he can about me and how I'll react, hires whoever forged his nobility patents for yet another job, and attempts to incense and upset me with a counterfeit note regarding the death of my family...which works *despite* the fact I'd suspected it was counterfeit, just because it pissed me off that someone would try something like that in the first place! All of it done to narrow all of the options available to me down to one, which is to accept a duel against an opponent that I'm utterly convinced I'm better than."

I was flipping through the pages of the Knothill book hurriedly as I spoke, sorting through the bookmarked pages with names beginning with the letter 'R'.

"But why?" asked Cyrus, mystified. "Why not just arrange to have you killed? He certainly has enough money for it."

"Because in the end he gets to *personally* kill me, the son of the very man he believes killed his father. And he gets to do so in a public duel, the very hallmark of the Redforne fortunes. The distasteful act of murder is overshadowed by the subtlety required to pull it off, doing more for his reputation than a hundred small and clever token thefts could have. He gets revenge for his father's death, reacquires his family's estate from Greybridge through financial brute force, and restores the prominence of his family name, all in one fell swoop."

At that point, I found the page I'd been looking for. The drawings of the swords they contained practically leapt off the page at me. There was no question – I was looking at the same swords I'd glimpsed in Teuring's bag that one day at the Circles.

The name 'Redforne' had been penned very carefully at the top of the page.

"And look," I said quietly, pointing to them and looking over at Cyrus. "He even gets to use his father's swords."

The silence continued unbroken for half a minute as I watched Cyrus staring at the pages of the open book, putting it all together much like I had moments before. He began to nod.

"Oh crap!" he said, breathlessly.

Chapter 16

THE CIRCLES BECOME a completely different place when you're there for some sort of potentially fatal activity like crossing swords with someone. Certain details stick out more, like the presence of old, dried blood that had somehow managed to survive the rains.

I was noticing a great deal of blood around me as I stood in the center of the magnificent open air marble structure, ten feet or so away from the main dueling circle, a simple shallow metal ring that had been set into the well packed earth. There was more blood on the side of the ring nearest me than elsewhere, I noticed.

I don't believe in omens.

The very air seemed charged with the undercurrents of potential violence, like a suspended moment of time between seeing lightning in the distance, and hearing the thunder that you instinctively know is coming. The throngs of people that had shown up were not beyond my notice, either. The stands were positively crowded today.

I suspected that many had been invited, or encouraged, to come. Redforne's doing, obviously – you didn't go to all the trouble he did, without wanting to share your success with as many people as possible.

Staring at the many faces in the crowd, I idly wondered what kind of headache I was about to create amongst the gamblers and bookies. It wasn't hard to get them all riled up, and with what I had planned I could almost picture some of them staring aghast or gnashing their teeth in frustration.

"Milord?" asked Cyrus.

"Hmm?"

"You're smiling. Is there something new you've noticed or thought of?"

"Ah, no. Sorry, I was just thinking of something funny and useless. How are you holding up?"

"Well enough, Milord," he said, his voice making him sound like someone who might commit murder in exchange for the promise of eight hours of unbroken sleep. Small wonder, given how shamelessly I'd overworked him the last twelve hours.

"Cyrus, I can arrange for things to be delayed long enough for you to fetch a replacement, if you feel it necessary."

"I'll be fine," he said, coming as close as I've ever heard to actually snarling at me. "I'm just – uh ..."

"You'd kill someone for a good eight hours of sleep?"

He blinked, and then smiled ruefully.

"Close. I'll be fine Milord, honest. I...say, do you happen to have any more of that tea handy?"

"No, fresh out. The only thing I thought to bring with us, aside from the healing reagents, was some vimroot oil, if that'll do."

"That would do fine."

I handed it over after reaching into my satchel to retrieve it, and continued to inspect the crowd as he applied the sharp smelling stimulant to his forearms and neck. Yes, there were many, many people here today. I briefly wondered how many had come to be entertained, and how many had come to watch me die.

"Vincent?" A much different, heavily accented voice ventured apologetically.

"Yes, Ismir?" I responded, turning to my left. I also frowned slightly. "Uh, actually Ismir, we're on the clock right now. Perhaps you should use the honorific 'Milord' or 'Lord Tucat'."

The tall, swarthy man looked down at me, wearing an expression that made it clear he didn't quite comprehend.

"We, uh . . ." he said, looking down at his own feet for a moment, "on time? A clock?"

I sighed. "Never mind. What is it, Ismir?"

"Ah, okay. Vincent...money I do have. This thing you do is not necessary for me."

"Ismir, I've already told you," I said, patiently, "this isn't charity. Trust me, I'm not that nice a guy. I need someone who knows what they're doing."

He frowned at me, a tiny amount of suspicion apparent in his eyes. Then, shrugging a little, he went back to scanning the crowd.

"And me, Lord Tucat?" came another voice. "I'm still not certain what I'm doing here exactly."

"Tanin, you're being paid twenty gold marks to simply stand with our party, as we discussed, and give an opinion regarding your area of expertise when and if the time presents itself. The less I tell you, the better off you'll be – I need you to be impartial, in case your motives are questioned."

Tanin, one of the most accomplished and respected instructors the Circles had to offer, leaned forward and frowned in disapproval at me from behind Ismir.

"I suppose that is what I agreed to. I just don't want to be on the receiving end of an unpleasant surprise is all. You have a certain reputation."

"It's nothing like that – I anticipate your involvement to be fairly minor. You have my word on it."

"Fair enough," he sniffed, turning away and inspecting the crowd.

I opted to study the crowd as well. We were the only ones currently on the floor of the arena, and there wasn't much to do *besides* look at the crowd while standing about awkwardly. I stifled a yawn, hoping that I looked more bored than tired as I did so.

"Milord," said Cyrus, stepping closer and speaking softly. "Greybridge, behind us and to the right."

I nodded my understanding without looking behind me, then took a moment to shake off the last bits of tiredness while simultaneously forcing myself to relax.

Deep breath. Time to begin.

I idly turned around as if to survey the state of the audience behind me, allowing my eyes to widen slightly and acting as if pleasantly surprised to see Greybridge plodding toward me with four rather large men in gray uniforms serving as escort. Given what I knew of his affairs, I suspected the men with him weren't actually an escort, but rather were there to ensure he didn't run off somewhere.

They walked up as a single unit. I smiled at the dour-faced lord, and he frowned back at me, possibly because it was the easiest thing for his face to do.

"Honorable Lord Greybridge! Delightful to see you again," I said cheerfully.

"Lord Tucat," he scowled, sizing me up and down and then peering at my face. "You don't look like you've quite gotten enough rest."

"Lordly duties keeping me up all hours, you know the drill. It never ends. Ah, but *you* Lord Greybridge - you look marvelously relaxed and well rested! What's your secret?" I asked even more cheerfully.

"My secret? Healthy living, not having to perpetually worry about ruffians at my gates, or the prospect of various treasures getting stolen from me. Which, of course, brings us to today's little affair."

"Ah, right you are," I said, throwing the front flap of my cloak over my shoulder and twisting from side to side, making a production of loosening up muscles. "I'm assuming that you have some sort of special instructions regarding what you would like done to young Teuring? Dance around him, make him look silly, that sort of thing? I know of this one particular move – dreadfully embarrassing, but unfortunately it relies on him wearing a certain type of belt, and rather baggy pantaloons, or-"

"Yes, well," he said, waving his hand as if it were capable of negligently brushing my words aside. "I'm sure that whatever you think is best will do. From what I've heard of your skill and of his, this little event will hardly even qualify as exercise for you."

I laughed at that, and then laughed a little louder...just long enough to perhaps cause him to wonder if he was being mocked.

Which he was, of course.

"Indeed Lord Greybridge! Ha! Why, just the other day a few of my men saw him attempt to practice lunging on a sack that had been stuffed with straw. Bookies in attendance were taking bets on the sack to win," I chuckled. "Why, a man would have to be a complete and utter buffoon to be bested by the likes of him."

His cheek twitched a little at that.

"Well, that's-"

"I mean, the very notion of being undone by a low-rent, blubbering *fop* like him, why, a man would have to have half his brain missing!" I smiled a ridiculously large smile at him, projecting innocent good cheer with all of my being.

He looked the tiniest bit flustered, then the tiniest bit angry. He had, of course, been outwitted by the very man we were talking about.

And then he smiled at me.

It was an ugly kind of smile, smug and secure...the kind that seemed to take great delight in the fact that there was no way I could possibly know what was in store for me. Obviously I was going to find myself tremendously surprised shortly, and Greybridge knew it.

I smiled back, because...well, obviously. How could I know?

We spent a few moments smiling at each other, for drastically different reasons.

"Yes, well...I shall be watching, of course. I expect I should be here for at least an hour before I tire of this, so feel free to take your time. Good fortune today Tucat. Gentlemen," he said, nodding to the rest of my assembled party. They nodded back to him.

"Enjoy the performance, Lord Greybridge," I said, waving at his back as he turned and plodded toward the stands. "You've certainly paid enough for it."

He stopped dead in his tracks.

Turning slowly, he gave me a piggy little stare, his brow furrowing.

"What?" he said in what he probably presumed was a dangerously quiet voice.

"Errr...sorry, bit of a joke there!" I said, spreading my hands palm-up before me apologetically. "A small attempt at humor – I was being ironic. This whole arrangement has, of course, cost you nothing."

It was an unkind remark - his empire lay in ruins, after all. I watched him fume in silence at that, with my innocent smile fixed firmly in place, counting the several different emotions crossing his face. A moment later, he stiffly turned and continued his walk into the stands, followed closely by his four burly, gray-clad escorts. There had been a small trace of uncertainty in his eyes just before he'd turned away.

I chuckled.

Well? He was helping to set me up. It's not exactly like I felt *bad* for the guy...

Once Greybridge had departed, I didn't have to wait long before spying Redforne entering the grounds. He entered with a look of bleary-eyed desperation, once again wearing that ill-fitting tunic he'd been wearing at his banquet. His dueling party appeared to consist of a shabby curly-haired youth who bore a grim expression, and a young light-haired lad, who was expending considerable effort to keep a large deerskin bag from touching the ground as he walked.

Redforne didn't meet my eye as he approached the main dueling circle, and was projecting the kind of despair that one has when one knows they are as good as defeated, even before a contest begins. It was masterful.

I briefly wondered what Theo, who was keeping watch from somewhere in the crowd, thought of the performance. I'd managed to meet with him the night before, and explained to him both what I'd discovered about Redforne, and what I intended to do about it.

He'd called me a sneaky bugger.

Redforne and I didn't look at one another as we stood at opposite sides of the circle, thirty-five feet away from each other. He presumably wished to give as little away as possible, as did I. After a few moments of standing around, the 'Teuring' party began to converse amongst themselves.

I spied the herald on duty stepping through the crowd at the edge of the stands, about a hundred feet away from us, walking toward the ring, two smaller robed men trailing in his wake. After a glimpse at me and a familiar nod, he altered his course and made his way to my group.

"Lord Tucat," he said, nodding.

"Herald Cartwren," I nodded back, respectfully.

"In regards to the duel being fought on this day, four-hundred and first day of year twenty-and-two Tenarreau, the matter of Greybridge versus Teuring - have there been any changes, or negotiation for extension?"

"None."

"Is there any hope of reconciliation?"

I stifled a chuckle. "None whatsoever."

"Very well. Is there anything that you, the party representing Lord Greybridge, requires from the Crown?"

"No – all standing with me are familiar with the dueling laws and swear to abide by them. The party undertaking to resolve matters on behalf of the Lord Greybridge stands ready."

"The Crown hereby recognizes that the party representing Lord Greybridge stands ready. Good fortune, and may the gods smile upon this contest," he said solemnly. Then, formalities done with, his face split into a wicked grin and his eyes twinkled merrily. "May the gods also have mercy on that poor, poor bastard."

I've always liked Cartwren.

"Actually, you'll probably want to stay fairly sharp...things could go sideways for anyone acting in an official capacity today. Can I quickly check the list to confirm something?" I gestured to one of the smaller robed men standing behind him.

"Eh? Well, certainly. Varnie," he said, catching the attention of one of the young men accompanying him and indicating that he should step forward. "Please show Lord Tucat what he requires."

Startled by the odd request, the clerk stepped forward and turned his tablet toward me so that I might be able to read its contents. I began to do so rapidly.

"So," said Cartwren, seemingly intrigued by my lack of usual wit-laced and smarmy bravado, "I should perhaps hedge my bet a little? I've currently got something in the neighborhood of four-hundred and fifty gold wagered on you."

"What?" I practically choked. For a Herald, even one working for the prince, that had to be a small fortune.

"Too much? This was pretty much the closest I've seen to a sure thing in the past year - the odds are dismal, and I'll only make about a twenty or so if I win, but I figured I'd capitalize on it if there was a bookie stupid enough to take the bet. Twenty marks is twenty marks, after all." He looked at me shrewdly, considering. "There some reason I shouldn't have my money riding on you? You know, if you mess with the odds or get caught throwing a duel, especially one the prince is required to attend-"

"No," I said, rubbing my neck thoughtfully. "Nothing like that. I like my neck as it is – unadorned by noose or garrote wire."

"Hmmm. But you're not telling me not to worry, either. And, you're not going to tell me what's happening . . ." he said, not making it a question.

I shook my head. "Too many knives in the air right now. Sorry."

He nodded thoughtfully. "Think I still have time to get my money back?"

"May as well ask, beat the rush," I said. "At the very least, I believe that we'll be surrounded by hundreds of extremely pissed off people in very short order."

It was then that I realized an aspect of Redforne's plan that had eluded me completely – wagering. What sort of profit did he expect to walk away with from this match? Odds were twenty to one, if Cartwren's wager was any indication. A man with enough cash could bankrupt several bookmakers in a single day!

Redforne had a *lot* of cash.

Cartwren gave me an odd look before nodding to me in a vaguely thankful manner. I nodded back, quickly continuing to scan the document before me. It appeared to be in order, and my dueling party was being announced first. Perfect.

"Thank you. Yes, everything looks fine, I apologize for troubling you, Varnie," I said, waving the clerk away. "And thank you, Herald. Wish me luck."

"If you believe you require luck today, Lord Tucat, then I'm suddenly very anxious to talk to a certain bookie I know," he said, making a face. Then, motioning to the two clerks standing dutifully behind him, he turned and made his way over to the party standing opposite us.

I really shouldn't have told him anything...not that there was much chance of things falling apart at this stage. Still, I watched the herald's interaction with Redforne very closely.

There seemed to be nothing to their conversation, covering the formalities and nothing more. Soon Herald Cartwren was making his way back toward the stands.

He'd made it halfway when some small murmur ran through the crowd. Squinting against the sun that hung high in the sky, I could make out the royal booth in the distance, a handful of knights swathed in purple parting the crowd gently, yet insistently.

Trumpets sounded. The prince was taking his seat.

Everyone stood and craned their necks to try and catch a glimpse of the royal figure. They always did, like it was borne out of habit, but they needn't have bothered trying. Warren Tenarreau, Prince of Thieves and Thief-Lord of all Harael, master of intrigue and cunning, the single most powerful man in the city...stands three-foot-eight inches tall.

It's actually an amazing advantage, and one of the many reasons for his extraordinary good fortune. Some people don't realize just how useful something like that can be for a thief.

The hairs on the back of my neck and arms started bothering me. I had a few minutes before things would begin. The familiar nervous energy of pre-duel anxiety crept up my back, and my head began swimming a little in that unreal 'have I forgotten something?' sort of way.

"All right, here we go. Everyone clear on what they're supposed to do?" I asked.

"No," said Tanin, a bit of an edge in his voice.

"Uhm," said Ismir uncertainly.

Cyrus appeared to be half asleep, and was staring into the crowd with a distracted look on his face, possibly not having heard me at all.

Fantastic. Just the sort of pick-me-up I needed right then.

The trumpet playing ended abruptly, indicating that the prince had taken his seat. Five or so minutes passed as everyone else in attendance milled around and found their seats. I glanced over at Redforne out of the corner of my eye.

He was doing his best to look nervous, scanning the crowd, occasionally saying something out of the corner of his mouth to the older of his companions, who was listening and nodding in a tight-lipped fashion. The other, younger lad was busy scanning the crowd with wide eyes, looking thoroughly awestruck.

Even with the phony nervousness Redforne was projecting, I could sense excitement in how he held himself. Anticipation.

Herald Cartwren appeared at the Prince's booth, looking slightly flushed and out of breath. After a few words were exchanged, he began making his way toward the main arena. By the time Cartwren had made it to the bottom of the steps and across the arena floor to where we stood, the chatter from the crowd had died down to hushed whispers.

He paused to compose himself, turning toward the main seating area.

"Lords, ladies, honored Haraelians," he boomed, "you are here to bear witness to resolution of a matter of honor between the families Greybridge and Teuring, whereby it has been asserted via petition that the Lord Teuring did assault the reputation of the Lord Greybridge, and whereby the Lord Greybridge does demand satisfaction of the honorable Lord Teuring as a consequence. The honorable Lord Teuring has accepted the judgment of Prince Tenarreau, who has decreed that the matter be settled by contest of arms to be carried out this day, four-hundred and one of the year Twenty-and-two Tenarreau. So says his highness, Prince Tenarreau - so say these men here, the party for the accused, and the party for the injured. Good fortune to you both."

He turned toward the circle and looked to his right, meeting my eye, and in that same loud booming voice said "The party for Lord Greybridge – do you have a duelist?"

"We have," I shouted, trying to speak as loudly as Cartwren and failing

"Please announce the names of both your duelist and your second for this contest."

"Thank you, Herald," I practically shouted, hoping my voice carried far enough to reach the stands. Gods, there were a lot of people here. "If it pleases you all, before I announce the duelist for this event, I would like to first take a second and announce our second...first."

That wordplay produced a couple of chuckles, and a muted clap. Grinning, I continued.

"Sadly, due to his rather solitary nature brought on by a tragic series of unfortunate events that left him brutally disfigured as a boy, the other lords and ladies in attendance may not have had an opportunity to meet this fellow. Indeed, the very sight of this poor wretch is enough to cause babes to cry, women to flee to their houses, and milk to spontaneously curdle. And yet despite all of his handicaps, both physical and mental, he has risen above his circumstance and into prominence. Without further ado, I would request that second for the party of the Lord Greybridge...be-"

I paused and enjoyed the pregnant silence, looking directly across the dueling circle at the faces on the other side. I didn't want to miss a moment of their reaction.

"Lord Eagan Redforne, son of Salvatori Redforne, Earl of Fen-Arryl!"

The reaction that provoked from the audience was negligible - doubtless throwing out the name of a lord nobody had ever heard of wasn't going to result in gasps of astonishment or anything like that.

Ah, but the reaction from Redforne, on the other hand...

The mask of despair he'd been carefully maintaining had fallen away at the very first mention of his name, and he stood like a man frozen in the act of moving. He simply stared at me, eyes wide and looking astonished, and then looking as though he were attempting to murder me through sheer act of will. Even at that distance, I could see the muscles lining his jaw standing out, his face now taking on a slightly ruddy complexion.

Oh, was he angry!

I looked at him smugly for a while, and then began to cast my eyes about the arena as if confused. I looked behind me, making of a small production of measuring both Ismir and Cyrus up, a perplexed look on my face.

"Lord Redforne?" I called out forlornly, looking around as though expecting someone to leap out from behind a small rock or speck of dirt on the arena floor. "Funny, I could have sworn I saw him here not two seconds ago! Where could he have gone?"

Redforne's complexion was fast becoming a vibrant shade of crimson.

Ignoring the murmurs of disquiet in the crowd, I cupped my hands to my mouth and began yelling, *"Yoo-hoo! Lord Reddddd-Foorrrrrrne!"* at the top of my lungs toward those in attendance, shading my eyes with one hand as if attempting to pick him out from the ocean of faces in the distance, ending my small production by putting my fists on my hips and looking perplexed. There was a smattering of chuckles, as well as a dull roar of mutters as spectators looked questioningly at one another, as if to ask each other if perhaps they knew what was going on.

The taller youth beside Redforne was very urgently whispering something into his ear, probably telling him what I already knew.

He was screwed. You did not have to accept the mantle of second for a duel...you didn't even need to state your reason for refusing it, but protocol demanded that if you were named as second in a duel that the prince himself was required to attend, you formally acknowledged the request. Period.

Redforne had probably even thought that he was being extra clever, arranging things so that he could announce his name – his *true* name – just before the duel was scheduled to begin. I would have been taken by surprise, slowly realizing that things were not at all what they appeared. He could no longer do that.

He was trapped. He could remain mute and simply make as if the name meant nothing to him, but he couldn't very well lay claim to the name Redforne after the match without people being scandalized over the gross violation of protocol.

I watched him grind his teeth in impotent frustration, hardly even blinking as he stared, paying no attention whatsoever to the advice being urgently whispered in his ear.

Herald Cartwren looked as though he wondered whether he should step in, and what sort of unpleasant smelling thing he might be stepping into as a result.

"I say, this is dreadfully embarrassing! I don't know what could have happened to him," I bellowed theatrically, deciding it was time to force the issue a little. "Terribly, terribly unfortunate. Ah well, if Lord Redforne *isn't* present, then I shall have to-"

"I, Lord Redforne, *reject* Lord Tucat's request to serve as dueling second for the party of Lord Greybridge!" Redforne spat the words as though they tasted bad, his lips curling into an angry snarl.

That provoked some muted reaction from the crowd, and even caused Cartwren to raise an eyebrow. The murmurs of confusion surrounding us increased, and I made a tight little moue of surprise with my lips, as though taken aback by this sudden revelation.

"But...Lord Teuring! I don't understand! Are you saying that *you* are Lord Redforne?" I said, filling my voice with disingenuous astonishment. "Why, I can't ask a member of the other dueling team to perform as second for Greybridge! Dear me, how dreadfully awkward! Oh, if only I had *known in advance!*"

Really, under the circumstances, nobody could blame me for some smart-alecky comments, could they?

Redforne continued his campaign in search of new and interesting shades of red to adorn his face with, standing there mute, glaring at me. I was content with simply grinning back at him. It would have gone on for longer had Cartwren not chosen that moment to assert his Heraldic authority.

"Err. Lord Tucat! Your request to have Lord . . ." he paused for the barest instant, "Redforne...act as your second has been denied. Please announce another. If that request is likewise rejected, a second will be appointed and provided for by the Crown for the sake of expediency."

"No need, no need," I said, waving my hand dismissively. "So sorry about that. As luck would have it, I know a fellow whom I am utterly confident will fulfill the duties of second for the party of Lord Greybridge here today. A gentleman of unquestionable character, and unassailable integrity. A marvelously handsome and striking fellow, whose reputation for cunning is dwarfed only by his reputation as a superb dancer, and snappy dresser. A veritable demigod of a man, who-"

"Get on with it!" Redforne shouted, unable to contain his fury any longer.

I shrugged, and sent him a half-smirk.

"I would request that second for the party of Lord Greybridge be . . ." I said, one hand behind my waist and standing in a manner that I hoped would be perceived as annoyingly melodramatic, "Lord Vincent Tucat, son of Giles

Tucat, Viscount of E'ren-Dell." I bowed as theatrically as I was able. "I accept, of course."

The reaction that prompted was immediate, and drew gasps of astonishment as well as a good deal of angry muttering and other chatter from the crowd. The face of Lord Redforne and his two retainers were comical in their bewildered confusion.

I imagined bookies in the crowd were looking at each other, asking themselves if they'd heard that right. For several moments I simply stood there and enjoyed the reaction, the noise from the stands pouring over me in waves of disapproval and surprise.

A rather small portion of the crowd had made its way through the throngs of people lining the seats at ground level, and was urgently pushing its way toward us, the figure in the center positively blazing in anger.

"No!" Lord Greybridge bellowed. *"This will not do!"*

Chapter 17

YEAH, I WAS expecting that.

I made as if perplexed to see the rotund form of Lord Greybridge pushing his way past the indignant spectators in an effort to get to the arena floor and stalk to the center. His face was nearly as red as Redforne's had been, and he was spluttering with rage as he stomped his way to the main dueling circle, stopping a few feet away from me.

"Lord Greybridge," I began. "Are you all right? What could possibly be the-"

"You, Tucat," he said accusingly, pointing a chubby finger directly at my nose, "told me – *assured* me – that you would be dueling on my behalf this day. I will not accept anything less! You came within a hairs breadth of insulting my honor yourself, and fighting this duel for me is compensation for that! We *agreed* on that!"

"Did we?" I asked, a sardonic eyebrow raised.

"Yes!" he spat, "We did!"

I tried again.

"Is that exactly what we had agreed to, Lord Greybridge?" I raised my eyebrow again and gave him a dubious 'I think not' sort of look.

"Why," he asked through clenched teeth, "do you insist on asking the same question over and over? Yes, that's precisely what we agreed to!"

Okay, maybe he missed the whole point with the eyebrow thing. Perhaps I'd been giving him entirely too much credit over the years.

"What I recall of our conversation, Lord Greybridge, is that I agreed to take over all *responsibility* for the duel on your behalf. Surely one can do that without fighting the duel themselves, wouldn't you agree?"

"I-" Greybridge paused, nonplussed.

"I mean, what if I had suffered some sort of injury? Surely you would not expect me to shuffle lamely into the arena to fight for your honor when not at my absolute best. And, of all the cursed bad luck, I've got this terribly wicked pain in my shoulder. Damnably difficult to hold a sword at the moment, or do artful things such as whisk it back and forth in a terrifying manner. No," I shook my head, "I'm afraid that I could not in good conscience fight this duel myself. Your very reputation *demands* that I sit this one out!"

There were a few moments of stunned silence, during which it was very hard not to chuckle.

"Your reputation as a swordsman," he said, still attempting to maintain a certain level of outrage, "was the very thing that caused me to accept your proposal in the first place! You were to fight the duel, personally guaranteeing that my reputation was...was-"

"And I agree!" I interjected, not allowing him time to pick out his next word, though I may have in fact been saving him from an awkwardly long pause. "However, knowing that an illustrious lord such as yourself would settle for nothing less than the best, I opted it would be best to let someone more qualified than I, in my feeble and injured state, fight in my stead."

I motioned to Ismir, who took that as his cue to step forward and nod at Lord Greybridge, who looked terribly uncertain and frustrated.

"The duelist for this contest shall be Ismir Hantaan, a swordsman of renown from Vereet. No estate, or title," I said, waving toward him and bowing my head after finishing my formal introduction.

Ismir bowed his own head toward Lord Greybridge, who was at a loss regarding how to object to this newest development.

Redforne pulled the eldest of his dueling party closer to him, and was angrily whispering something in his ear. After a couple of nods, the young man trotted away from Redforne and stood before Lord Greybridge, who cocked an uncomfortable ear to the lad's urgent whisper and listened carefully.

Everyone in attendance would probably be wondering what *that* meant. Why was one of Redforne's dueling party speaking privately with Greybridge?

Slowly but surely, it was becoming apparent to all who watched that things weren't as they seemed.

I stole a glance at the prince's booth, and saw that he was both standing and leaning forward, as if greatly interested in what was transpiring on the grounds below.

"Lord Tucat," Greybridge said loudly once the youth had scurried back to Redforne's side, "I accept that you find yourself...that, uh, you are unable to participate in this duel because of injury. Because of this, I've negotiated an extension so that the duel may be fought at another time, one that sees you at the height of health and readiness. I have no doubt that-"

"There is no need, Lord Greybridge! I've already made provisions for Ismir to act as champion for your honor, paid him for his trouble in full, and he stands ready and able. I, for one, would not think of dragging our beloved prince out to the Circles to act as witness today, as is his duty, only to have the whole thing cancelled and rescheduled for another time. No," I said, shaking my head sadly, "as much as it grieves me to do so, I must allow Ismir to stand in my place. This matter between you and...this Redforne person must be resolved immediately."

"This Ismir fellow," Greybridge said, as though suddenly struck with an idea, "I've never heard of him. You pull this last minute sort of substitution, some cock-and-bull story about your shoulder giving you a bit of trouble, toss in this virtual nobody of dubious skill and declare that he's my 'champion'? How could I possibly find this an acceptable replacement?"

"Perhaps I may be of some help on that score, Lord Greybridge," Tanin said, stepping forward.

I grinned inwardly.

"Oh? And just who in Hades are you?" Greybridge asked.

"Tanin Hauklim, my lord," he said, sketching a stiff bow from the neck, not from the hip as was customary. "I have the honor to be an instructor for swordsmen down here at the Circles, and am familiar with the prowess of both Lord Tucat and Ismir. Of the two, Lord Tucat is the inferior swordsman. I say this without any doubts or reservations whatsoever."

Okay, he didn't have to say it *exactly* like that.

"Oh? I find that hard to believe. Most of us here are very familiar with the reputation of Lord Tucat," Greybridge snorted.

"My lord," Tanin said patiently, "I would stake my very reputation on it. In a practice bout between these two, you would be lucky to see the honorable Lord Tucat score two touches in a best-of-ten match. I've seen both of them fence various opponents, and I've seen them fence against each other. Ismir is the more talented of the two, without question."

I coughed. Tanin glanced over at me, then looked as though he'd just realized something.

"Of course, I mean no offense with respect to your level of skill, Lord Tucat." He bowed his head in acknowledgement. "You are in fact a quite capable swordsman, all things considered."

"Oh, no offense taken," I said, sending him a quick, wry nod back. "But still...*two?* I mean, come on."

"Outrageous!" sputtered Greybridge, who looked as though he could feel the momentum of his righteous indignation slipping away. "I find this unacceptable!"

"I cannot possibly see how you could. I mean, I've spent a thousand gold marks of my own money on Ismir here, just to make sure you'd be adequately represented today. You've heard that not only is he a fitting replacement, but that he's much," I gave Tanin a meaningful look, "*much* better than I am. What possible reason could you have to be dissatisfied?"

He didn't answer me, but instead looked to Redforne, who continued to stare in my direction while remaining perfectly still. Doubtless he'd worked out what Greybridge had not - I'd outmaneuvered them. I wasn't about to fall blindly into their trap, or set foot inside that circle with Redforne today.

Just to be an ass, I looked to Redforne and winked.

"Lord Greybridge, though it would be considered unusual, you can ask that Lord Tucat no longer represent your interests with respect to this duel, which would then have to be rescheduled. Do you wish to do so at this time?" Herald Cartwren asked.

"I-" he began.

"Lord Greybridge, please relax and take your seat in the stands. This duel is on me," I laughed. "Enjoy yourself! If you wish some wine, or perhaps a spot of something to eat, I'm sure I could *loan you some coin.*"

He looked at me, baffled. Then, seeming to comprehend the meaning of my words he took a sharp breath and looked to Redforne in shock. I also noticed that the curly-haired youth standing to Redforne's left had become noticeably paler upon hearing my last comment. He whispered something under his breath while looking at me.

Redforne looked to Greybridge, then looked to me again, the hate-filled expression softening into a resigned look of disgust. Then he looked back to Greybridge and gave the slightest shake of his head.

"N-no, that won't be necessary," Greybridge said uncertainly.

"To be clear - you find the current duelist and second to be satisfactory?"

Greybridge could only nod, a bleary look on his face.

I cheered inside.

"The party for Lord Red- uh, Teuring - please announce the names of both your duelist and your second for this contest."

"Thank you, Herald," the youth to the left of Redforne said through clenched teeth, his voice identifying him as the speaker Lord Greybridge had been arguing with the night before. "The duelist for this contest representing the Teuring estate, currently managed via proxy by the Redforne family, will be Eagan Redforne, son of Salvatori Redforne, Earl of Fen-Arryl. Acting as his second will be myself, Dion Copperthorn, current custodian of Fen-Arryl."

"So let it be recorded. Gentlemen, please take your places. The duel will commence once both duelists have entered the circle and have signaled their readiness to me, beginning and ending on my word," Cartwren said, looking positively relieved that the ad lib stuff was over and done with.

The crowd went to muttering, and likely there were many who were suddenly wondering about the status of their own wagers, if they'd placed one. Cyrus said something softly to Tanin, who nodded, and they both retreated several steps away from the dueling circle.

"Okay, Ismir, like we discussed. I have reason to believe that this guy is good, pretending to be bad. If you see an opportunity to beat him, take it, but I want you to stay protected even when you do. Got that?"

"Vincent," Ismir said, sounding dubious, "you worry, should not. Good, bad, pretend...no matter." His face lit up in a wicked grin. "He fights *me*."

"Ismir, I'm serious. Protect yourself out there. If you get cut, I'll offer up a draw right away. I figure they might accept a draw, given the level of confusion around here. If they don't accept, and if things start to look bad, we yield."

"Yield," he snorted derisively, shaking his head.

"Do not take this kid lightly!" I lifted my chin across the ring at Redforne, who had moved so little in the past ten minutes that he resembled a statue. "He's probably extremely angry right now, and-"

Ismir just chuckled and patted me on the cheek before shifting his shoulders slightly and removing his tunic.

He was wearing a simple foreign-looking sleeveless shirt that emphasized his substantial sandy-brown arms, not that they needed emphasizing. They bulged impressively as he opened the thick cloth wrap covering his dangerous looking and elaborately curved sword. It was a large, thick piece of metal, and he lifted it almost effortlessly.

From a raw power perspective, he could easily compete with Theodore, who was no slouch in the muscle department himself. There were a couple of appreciative murmurs from the crowd.

Hopping over to the circle edge nearest us, Ismir stepped into the ring and twirled his sword a couple of times, blade slicing the air expertly. Then, after making a small production of cracking his neck, he grinned across the ring at Redforne, and made an inviting gesture with his hands.

Muscles began to tighten in my back, and I began to feel tense. This was it. Once Redforne entered that ring not even the prince himself could step foot inside it, on pain of death.

I walked over to my spot as second for Ismir, just outside of the top of the ring, and a few feet away from Herald Cartwren. I gave him a nod.

"You couldn't have given me more of a heads up?" he asked out of the side of his mouth.

"Didn't know exactly how it would happen. What you saw was the best case scenario, actually. There was an outside chance that he might have just drawn steel and attacked me right in front of everyone."

He snorted. "Now he'd have to get in line. Some folks in the crowd seem awfully angry with you, taking yourself out of the match and playing havoc with their wagers."

"Wait until they see the match. I suspect that a lot of them will suddenly find themselves wanting to thank me."

Which was true, unless I missed my guess. Now that Redforne had owned up to his true name, if he had any degree of skill with a sword whatsoever he would apply it here and now, for the sake of his family honor.

I watched Ismir caper about and perform a couple of crowd pleasing warm-up moves, prompting some appreciative applause and the occasional cheer. He seemed to be enjoying himself - a crowd like this didn't come along every day, after all. Occasionally, he'd glance at Redforne and make inviting gestures with his hands.

Lord Redforne was dividing his attention between Ismir and myself, hardly paying any attention to the young man known as Dion, who was urgently speaking into his ear. Then, quite suddenly, Redforne snarled something out of the side of his mouth at him, and gestured with his head toward the herald.

Dion stopped speaking mid-phrase, closing his mouth slowly. Nodding, he turned and also took his place a few feet from Cartwren, studiously ignoring me as he did so.

Scowling, Redforne turned to the other of the youths who had accompanied him and held out his hands expectantly. The boy hurriedly unwrapped the bundle he was carrying, allowing his lord to draw the two magnificent swords I had glimpsed what seemed like an eternity ago.

Task finished, the youth retreated hurriedly to his designated area under the watchful eyes of Cyrus.

Redforne held these marvels of weaponsmithing before him and negligently thrust both swords point first into the hard packed earth just outside the dueling circle. Hands reaching to his neck, he pulled open and removed the lumpy, ill-fitting garment he wore, practically tearing it off his body and discarding it behind him.

The sound of a thousand jaws dropping at once is a strange thing to experience.

I'm very fit. I can run for hours at a stretch, perform acrobatic routines, all manner of athletic endeavors. I keep myself trim, and would go so far as to say that there are those who believe me attractively built.

I don't go out of my way to avoid mirrors, despite my multitude of scars, is what I'm saying.

But this kid, well...ye gods!

His resemblance to a statue now no longer limited itself to how still he'd been standing. If he were turned to marble in that instant, I would have assumed that he was an elaborately exaggerated monument that was being dedicated to some new exercise-conscious deity at the city cathedral.

I mean, it was *ridiculous* how this kid was put together. His muscles stood out appallingly. Even his little muscles, the ones that had no business even being there, cast shadows in the afternoon sun.

The outfit was an act, much like his show of poor swordsmanship...he'd wished to give absolutely nothing away.

Like the fact he was built as though he could tear a rock lion in two. After beating it in a foot-race.

Giving me one last look of utter hatred and contempt, he prowled into the circle as he yanked his two equal-length swords out of the ground, one in each hand. Then, casually, almost negligently, he whipped the swords around his body in a manner I'd never seen before, all half turns and slight bows that turned his movements into a complex dance of whirling steel and death. It appeared as though its sole function was to impress and intimidate.

It did a really, really good job.

The routine only lasted a few seconds, ending very deliberately with an idle one-handed twirl of each sword, him crouching in an elaborate-looking guard position, the points of both swords leveling themselves toward his opponent's chest at two different heights. He stared across the ring at Ismir.

All good cheer and high spirits now utterly removed from Ismir's face, the Vereetian stood in the classic guard position he favored, crouched and presenting his left side forward with his sword arm raised and slightly behind him, blade running level with his cheek, and dagger in his left hand held with the point down. He licked his lips nervously, suddenly having eyes only for his opponent. Redforne was wielding two longswords, which was unusual among swordsmen, and what was more he clearly knew how to use them.

I suddenly got a very bad feeling.

"Duelists...begin!" Cartwren called out, his voice containing the barest trace of a squeak.

Ismir didn't move, opting to stay in his modestly defensible pose and see what this surprising young lord did. He didn't have to wait long.

Redforne moved quickly and decisively forward two steps before leaping into the air. His torso twisted as if to deliver a savage overhand blow powerful enough to shatter stone.

Ismir pivoted on his back foot and brought his sword around to counter.

Somehow, in a blur of motion that defied all logic and reason, Redforne twisted in midair and spun in the opposite direction, his sword becoming a silver arc that whipped around his body at a speed that shouldn't even have been possible.

There was a sharp clack of metal on metal, followed by the sound of a sword skipping along the ground. The audience was mute, amazed. I stood there in wide-eyed shock.

Redforne had batted the sword out of his opponent's grasp as though he were a child.

Ismir stared dumbly at his empty right hand, and then to the edge of the circle where his sword had somehow ended up. Then, finally, he looked at Redforne with an expression of disbelief.

The young lord had turned his back to Ismir and wasn't paying his fellow duelist any attention whatsoever, walking toward me with an air of supreme confidence, fixing me with a hateful, steely-eyed glare. He tilted his head to the side and gestured meaningfully at Ismir, who was scrambling to retrieve his sword.

Then, raising his eyebrows and chuckling smoothly, Redforne walked back to the portion of the circle he had started from. Languidly stretching as though he did not possess a care in the world, he moved into the exact same guard position he'd begun with.

Ismir, sword recovered and now holding himself with a great deal of uncertainty, moved back to his original spot and took his guard position. His eyes seemed much larger, and a little wild.

Seconds passed, neither of them moving.

I watched as Redforne nodded to Ismir, a gesture that I assumed was an invitation to attack him. Ismir frowned and licked his lips, seeming extremely wary of his young counterpart.

Then, with no warning whatsoever, Ismir lurched forward with a mighty battle cry...then pulled back and into guard position almost instantly. I'd experienced a couple of those feints of his first hand - they were unnerving.

Redforne hadn't even flinched. He stood impassively, a bored look on his face.

Ismir attacked in earnest not two seconds later. He charged forward, sweeping his sword from the side in a downward arc with one arm, flipping his dagger around and stabbing with the other, two attacks being launched simultaneously.

Redforne met them solidly, two sharp clangs announcing to all that each blow had been deflected with considerable force. During this, he nimbly stepped sideways to riposte, as well as avoid a second thrust from Ismir's dagger.

Ismir parried the slicing cut coming at his neck, feinted again with his off-hand blade to draw a block, and then kicked himself forward to deliver a strange, downward lunge with his curved blade.

Rather than meet it or simply backing up, Redforne twisted bodily around Ismir somehow, seeming to spin sideways and through his larger opponent. For a brief moment, it was as if they occupied the same space.

Ismir fell heavily to the ground with a surprised 'oomph', having tripped over one of Redforne's bright silver blades, which had unexpectedly snaked its way between his legs.

Momentarily stunned, the burly swordsman could do nothing as Redforne, still managing to look bored, twisted in place and brought his sword sharply toward Ismir's exposed back.

There was a loud 'slap' as the flat of Redforne's blade smacked Ismir between the shoulder blades, a move that a mere turn of the wrist would have made fatal.

For a second time, Redforne walked straight up to me and gave me an intensely meaningful look before returning to his original starting position, still looking relaxed and unconcerned.

Ismir, coughing, made his way back to his feet only to see Redforne standing exactly as they'd started, patiently waiting for his quarry to recover so that they might begin anew.

Redforne was toying with him.

"Draw?" I ventured, my head peering around Herald Cartwren, addressing the offer to Redforne's second.

Dion simply continued staring forward as though I hadn't spoken, not acknowledging me in any way.

I looked back to the dueling circle, and saw that Ismir had mostly recovered, and was now crouched in an Eastern-style guard position, but of a type that I'd never seen before. He stood there, eyes on his opponent, waiting.

Redforne crooked his head at Ismir inquisitively and chuckled sadly. Then, he bolted toward his foe and...

He lobbed one of his swords skyward.

Everyone held their breath at once, it seemed, watching the off-hand sword sail through the air in a slow arc toward the astonished Ismir.

Still rushing forward, Redforne hopped and spun, swinging his remaining sword at Ismir's head.

There was another ring of metal on metal that hurt the ears, followed by a second. The young lord danced out of the path of Ismir's questing dagger, snatched his own airborne blade mid-arc and, with a contemptuous downward thrust, pierced Ismir's boot, pinning the large man's foot to the dirt of the arena floor.

Ismir let out a howl of pain and fell to one knee, dagger falling to the ground. His left hand reflexively reached for his injured foot, his right hand still clutching his strangely curved blade.

Redforne sneered and yanked his blade upward, freeing it from the flesh of Ismir's foot. Once more giving his back to the dark skinned swordsman, he gave me a mocking smirk, as if daring me to say something.

It was quite obvious who the better swordsman was, despite Ismir's unusual style.

"The party representing Lord Greybridge yields to Lord Redforne," I announced, quickly.

Herald Cartwren, who was standing there rather wide-eyed himself, looked quickly to me and then back to Ismir, then letting his breath out explosively. Drawing himself up, he cleared his throat.

"The party for Lord Greybridge yields the matter of honor to the party for Lord Redforne. Would the party for Lord Redforne please indicate their acceptance?" he said, sounding slightly out of breath.

There were a few moments of silence, the only sound being the agonizing, hissing intake of breath through Ismir's clenched teeth. Redforne was walking slowly back to his original starting position. I stared at his back for a few moments, then looked over at the man who was acting as his second for the match.

Dion wasn't looking at me or making any sort of indication that he'd heard the offer, but was instead staring off into the distance, his jaw firmly set.

Redforne's eyes met mine, briefly, and his face took on a devilish grin that was more than half sneer.

And he winked at me.

Oh gods!

It seemed he now wanted to send *me* a message.

"Redforne!" I cried, an icy feeling of dread enveloping me. "We yield! There's nothing more to prove. You've won!"

If he heard me he didn't acknowledge it, turning back to Ismir and resuming his deadly looking guard position. He watched as the larger man lurched to his feet, muscles in his shoulders knotted, every inch of him radiating pain and shock.

Ismir looked for his fallen dagger, slowly bending down to retrieve the small, wicked looking blade...

The tip of Redforne's sword flicked at the guard of the dagger, causing it to skitter out of Ismir's grasp, and sending it flying out of the dueling circle completely.

Ismir turned to raise his sword in a clumsy defensive parry. It was struck soundly by one blade just as Redforne's second blade came out of nowhere and struck the left side of Ismir's exposed head.

Once again, the flat of Redforne's sword connected rather than the edge, turning what would have been a fatal blow into a ringing, shocking crack to his temple. Ismir's eyes became unfocused...

And then they focused very abruptly.

Specifically, they focused on the blade being held by Lord Redforne, the very point of which had been thrust between Ismir's teeth.

Not bothering to look at his wide-eyed opponent, Redforne gave me a look that seemed to be equal parts anger and boredom.

"Redforne, this isn't necessary! You-" I began.

Sneering, he flicked his wrist with idle contempt.

The point of the blade sliced easily through Ismir's entire cheek, a horrific cut now extending from the corner of his mouth to the underside of his cheekbone in a grotesque half-grin.

Ismir shrieked with pain and fell to his knees, sword clanging to the ground, forgotten. Blood began to trickle through his fingers, which were pressed rigidly against the side of his face.

"Redforne!" I screamed at the young lord's back as he nonchalantly made his way back to his starting position. "We yield! This man has done *nothing* to you!"

Redforne once more took up his dangerous looking guard position, a sleepy sort of half-smile on his lips.

I began to tremble noticeably, and seemed no longer in control of the muscles of my face.

It had never occurred to me that Redforne might use Ismir as a way of venting his frustration as he watched years of careful planning fall apart around him. With his family name to consider, and all the political ramifications of his actions here, this wasn't rational.

Perhaps he'd gone a little crazy at seeing all of his hard work unravel in the span of a few heartbeats. Whatever the reason, it was becoming clear that he had no intention of letting Ismir leave the dueling circle under his own power, if at all.

"Dion!" I called out to my left, unfeigned urgency in my voice. "He's not thinking straight! You've won! Accept the yield, if only for the sake of your family's reputation!"

I may as well have been talking to stone. Redforne's second continued to stare into the distance, affecting not to notice what was going on around him.

Several horrifying minutes stretched themselves into an eternity. Ismir, still clutching his cheek, seemed unable to do more than uncertainly raise his blade as a token gesture of defense, as the insatiable Lord Redforne swooped in again and again. Whirling arcs of steel caught the sun's rays as he danced around his injured opponent, drawing blood at will. Ribbons of sweat-streaked blood began to decorate Ismir's torso and arms.

Once, after tripping Ismir and sending him tumbling embarrassingly, Redforne crouched into a spin, his main sword arm stretched out dramatically, razor sharp steel singing its way past a spot just over Ismir's head.

A small tuft of black hair leapt upwards with a twitch, containing the tiniest suggestion of bloodied scalp.

"Stop!" I cried, desperately. "We yield, dammit!"

He snarled at me, turning his back.

"Eagan! What would your father think?" I shouted.

He froze.

The last of my words seemed to finally get through to him, though the effect they had was not at all what I had hoped ...

He slowly turned back toward me, radiating anger. His eyes contained a fury that seemed to steal air from my lungs.

Those same eyes darted back to Ismir, and narrowed.

In a flash he was on him once more - a backhanded sweep with his sword producing a deep cut high on Ismir's wrist, a sharp downward cut opening the flesh of his shoulder.

Ismir twitched feebly with each cut, his attempts at parrying becoming more erratic, likely going into shock.

Redforne was no longer even pretending that there was anything artful to what he was doing any more. The masterful style he had displayed fell away and was replaced by straightforward, savage moves that spoke of a bestial kind of cruelty, a desire to inflict pain.

Again and again he dove at his foe, his sword flashing mercilessly. Patches of blood decorated Ismir's arms, his tunic, his face, everywhere. Large droplets of the stuff darkened the earth beneath him.

"This is your fault, you know," Redforne shouted, turning his glare upon me briefly after yet another cut to Ismir's shoulder.

"Eagan!"

"See?" he swept his blade frighteningly close to Ismir's face, producing yet another trickle of blood, this time from the bridge of his nose. "Just look at what you've done."

I pleaded, threatened, tried anything I felt had a chance at ending this travesty. Ismir's eyes had become glassy and unfocused, filled with pain and confusion and fear. Redforne's had not lost any of the fire that had burned in them upon mentioning his father.

My ears picked up a close-mouthed scream of frustration, and I realized it was coming from me.

And then, not content with simply cutting Ismir, Redforne lifted his swords and spun in place to deliver a savage mule kick, leg connecting solidly with the Vereetian's head. Ismir fell over to his side awkwardly in a tangle of pain-contorted limbs, his head thudding against the ground.

The blood from his cheek and other wounds too numerous to count had mixed with the earth, producing a sinister black mud that clung to his hair and forehead as he began to rise.

Redforne's eyes locked on mine as he kicked Ismir again, more violently. There was the sickly crunch of cartilage.

Again he struck, even harder this time, an expression of unholy glee lighting up his face. Ismir tried lifting his head upright, receiving a clanging blow from the pommel of Redforne's sword for his trouble. As he cried out in pain, the young lord sneered and leapt backward a step and whittled a gesture at Ismir, cutting his ear nearly in half.

I opened my mouth for the hundredth time to protest uselessly, desperately, feeling as though I would have a more productive time negotiating with an enraged bear.

"Why hullo, Lord Tucat," a familiar voice said from somewhere behind me. "I must say, this is a frightfully bizarre sort of situation, neh?"

I didn't look behind me at first. However, when I saw the new expression adorning Redforne's face, I quickly turned to see who the unidentified speaker was.

After momentary confusion, I realized that I should be looking down.

Prince Tenarreau, Lord of all Harael, was surveying the scene with one eyebrow raised.

"Highness," I said, looking down at the young-seeming grey haired figure and bowing slightly from the waist. I couldn't think of anything to say beyond that.

Some astonished muttering was beginning to make itself heard. Maybe the crowd hadn't noticed him as he'd made his way down to the arena floor. None of his guards were standing nearby – maybe *they* hadn't noticed either.

He's sneaky that way.

"Please, don't pay me any mind. I just thought I'd come down here and observe from a better vantage point. It's part of my job, after all, attending these things." He gestured toward the ring. "Did I hear correctly? Redforne?"

I looked at Redforne, who had stepped back from his bleeding quarry and was looking at Prince Tenarreau uncertainly. I turned back to the Prince.

"Yes. Eagan Redforne. I believe he is the son of Salvatori Redforne, Highness."

"Really? Salvatori? Well, how unusual. You know," he said, his voice suddenly carrying much further, "I recall watching Salvatori fight when I was a boy. Remarkable swordsman. Ridiculously good, really. Don't recall him ever losing. A true gentleman, too. Always conducted himself honorably, inside the Circles and out."

There was an awkward silence, as nobody seemed to move. I once again looked to Ismir, who was on his knees with half a blood-streaked arm wrapped around his head, rocking back and forth in agony. Redforne was still staring at the prince.

"Oh, please, continue what you were doing. I didn't mean to interrupt," Tenarreau said, face unreadable. It was unclear exactly who he was speaking to, and he wasn't looking at anyone in particular as he said it.

Redforne licked his lips nervously, still looking at Tenarreau. He stepped back a few paces, looking down at his helpless opponent as if considering something. Then he twirled both swords familiarly, looking to once more take up his devastating guard position.

"I say," the prince interjected once again, his voice arresting Redforne's movements, "who is that fellow on the ground there? Is that Ismir Hantaan?"

"It is," I said, simply.

"Oh dear. Damnably inconvenient...he's my current favorite for this year's tournament. I believe he's scheduled to compete in a few days time, though I don't suppose he'll be in any shape to make that engagement. Pity, that. Did you know that he is actually Vereetian royalty?"

I didn't know that.

"No. I had no idea, Highness."

"It's true, though he doesn't like others knowing. Cousin to the current reigning monarch there, fellow named Teresh, if memory serves." He peered curiously at the semi-prone figure huddled in the dueling circle. "I do hope nothing unfortunate happens to him – I imagine I'd have to put together some sort of formal apology, make an official visit or some such thing. Inconvenient, those. Have you ever been to Vereet, Lord Tucat?"

"I can't say I have, Highness."

"Dreadful. Hot. Can't say I care for it," he sniffed, turning his head toward Ismir.

I looked to Redforne to see his reaction, as it was clear the words were intended for him to overhear. A prince did not take sides, officially, and could not bring about an end to a duel, even one that he himself had granted.

Tenarreau was, however, making it perfectly clear to Redforne how he felt about the current situation.

The angry young lord's attention went from the prince, to me, back to the helpless dark-skinned figure who sat half-curled in the ring, blood still flowing from his cheek, his foot, and countless small, sadistic wounds.

The crowd's murmurs grew louder. Redforne's lip was twitching slightly, and he wore the expression of a man who's just been smashed in the groin with a brick.

All of us were still for a long, tense minute.

Redforne's sword tips lowered, and his head drooped slightly.

He turned away from the injured combatant, walking toward his second. I could hear him speaking quietly, under his breath. Dion looked surprised as he nodded at the swordsman, who was already turning away from us, and cleared his throat.

"The party for Lord Redforne does accept the-"

Redforne let out an incredible shriek of frustration and fury that seemed to be directed at the gods themselves. With the same unbelievable speed and athleticism he'd shown during his duel he spun in place, savagely hurling his main-hand sword clear across the dueling area to the very edge of the arena. Its flight seemed to defy gravity, and the pommel hit the marble retaining wall with a force that was certain to have damaged wall and sword both.

Ringing madly, the small fortune in forged steel fell to the ground and was still.

Ashen-faced, the young lad holding the deerskin pouch raced quickly to pick up the fallen sword.

Redforne, planting the other sword point first into the ground, head bowed, began walking out of the circle.

"-does accept the yield offered by the party for Lord Greybridge," Dion finished morosely.

"The matter has been ceded to Lord Redforne by the party for Lord Greybridge, by way of a yield being offered and accepted. So it shall be recorded," Herald Cartwren announced, his voice wavering slightly. "This duel is ended, the victor is Lord Eagan Redforne."

It was over.

"Well, wasn't that exciting?" Prince Tenarreau remarked dryly.

"Healer!" I yelled, rushing forward into the ring to help my fallen friend. Both Cyrus and Tanin were running toward us as well, and I saw that Cyrus clutched the bag we'd brought tightly in his hand. Several healers were also running toward us.

As I eased Ismir into a reclining position, I saw his eyes darting back and forth, confused, like a boy who has been spun around too often and is dizzily attempting to get his bearings. The blood was still weeping from his multitude of cuts, but not nearly as profusely as I'd expected.

Cyrus came up, hurriedly kneeling and already pulling out bandages and braces.

At some point I felt myself being lifted up and away from Ismir, several hands entering my field of vision, voices assuring me that they'd do what they could. Nodding, I stood back dumbly. The air smelled of copper after a rainfall.

Eventually, I realized that Redforne was standing beside me.

"Know this," he said darkly, his hushed voice deep and confident, utterly unlike the one I'd heard him using as part of his Teuring persona. "The time you have left on this earth would cause a fruit fly to despair. I will see you dead by week's end, I swear it. No matter how tightly you bottle yourself up in your keep, how cleverly you hide from me, I shall find you."

"This man is my friend," I whispered back through clenched teeth, tearing my own eyes away from the macabre scene in order to meet his. "If he dies this day, I promise you won't have to look very hard."

We locked stares for a good, long while.

"Redforne, is it?" Tenarreau said, still sounding as if nothing going on around him were out of the ordinary.

Reluctantly, Redforne tore his murderous gaze from mine.

"Highness," he said, bowing slightly.

"Expect me to be calling on you later this day. I'm very interested in some of your more recent activities, and how you came to be known as Lord Teuring," he said, giving Redforne a look that was completely at odds with his calm, reasonable tone.

"Yes, highness," he replied, bowing in acknowledgement.

"I take the integrity of our city's family and property records very seriously, and dislike it when such records are altered. Or borrowed," he said. Then, peering at the scene inside the dueling circle, he added "Cyrus Crowfoot, I would make a note of that as well. For future reference."

Cyrus turned and gave a small gulp of surprise. "Yes, Highness."

"Well then, good," he said, drawing up his shoulders slightly and giving a small sigh of satisfaction. "Lord Tucat, if you would please attend me, I shall require a moment's conversation with you as well. Sort of now-ish, in fact."

"Highness, might I be allowed a few moments to ensure that Ismir is taken care of?"

He pursed his lips, considering, and then nodded his assent.

"Capital idea. Yes, be sure to let me know how he's faring. I shall let my knights know that I'm expecting you within the hour."

I nodded.

Tenarreau turned and signaled to his knights, most of whom had just arrived on the arena floor with panicked expressions on their faces. They quickly fell into step behind him.

Once the prince had his back to us, Redforne spun on his heel and walked speedily away, with Dion and the other youth trailing awkwardly behind him.

The chatter of the crowd became a dull roar of astonishment and disapproval. Doubtless they'd be talking about this one for years.

It was over. I had won, for the moment. The attempt to trick me into a duel that would have meant my death had been thwarted. I had outsmarted my foe, proved myself more clever than him.

I watched as the healers ordered a cart for Ismir, debating with each other on what the safest way to move him might be. Face no longer a twisted mask of agony, Ismir lay quite still in the blood-soaked dirt.

There was entirely too much of it.

I suppressed a sudden urge to vomit.

Victory.

"Oh yes," I said, bitterly. "I'm just so damned clever."

Chapter 18

"INTERESTING," PRINCE TENARREAU said, finally, his voice jolting me out of my exhaustion-induced half-sleep. The only sound of the previous half-hour had been that of shifting paper as he pored over some of the records marked 'Teuring'.

"Yes, interesting. Quite," I said, sitting upright in my chair, doing my level best to clench my teeth together and hide the yawn that I suddenly found myself unable to avoid.

I hoped he wouldn't notice. Yawning while in the company of the prince? Inexcusable!

It would almost be as bad as giggling madly upon seeing him sitting at his desk, diminutive form propped up on the seat of a chair that was noticeably higher than mine. Given the size of the furniture in the room, he left you with the impression of a child seated at his father's desk.

This 'child', of course, was presently the most powerful man in Harael, one who could probably have me killed on a whim. I'd reminded myself many times of this fact, whenever I'd been tempted to chuckle.

Although I'd sworn his attention were elsewhere, he gave me the tiniest smirk once I'd finished stifling my yawn.

"Sorry, am I boring you?"

"No, not at all," I said, admitting to myself even as I spoke that a private audience with the prince wasn't nearly as exciting as it sounded. "Sorry, long day, full of thwarted attempts on my life, acts of butchery, all sorts of exciting mayhem. I'll live."

"Ah, of course. Speaking of which, how is Ismir faring?"

"Well enough," I said, attempting to quell the sick, guilt-ridden feeling re-emerging in my belly, "and the healers expect him to make a full recovery. The majority of his wounds looked a lot worse than they were. He did take several blows to the head, though, so they're watching him for any signs of erratic behavior. And, of course, there's the scars..."

"Yes, he got marked up rather badly, didn't he? Dangerous sport, neh? Still, these things happen. I suppose you're not entirely comfortable with what transpired out there this afternoon, given your intimate familiarity with scars and all."

I didn't answer, not really trusting myself to speak. I could still see Ismir in my mind's eye, fingers reaching to clutch at his face as razor-sharp steel sliced through his cheek from the inside, a hideous flap of skin folding outward along his jaw, hanging there like an improperly applied wall treatment.

My fault, I reminded myself, cursing silently.

"Well, there's no point in agonizing over it, I suppose," he continued smoothly. "From what I know of Ismir, a display like the one he was subjected to this afternoon will just drive him to work harder to understand Western style fencing. He was getting just a wee bit too proud of himself, by my reckoning."

"Highness, is he actually royalty, like you said out there at the Circles?" I asked.

He fixed me with an amused look. "You don't know much about Vereet, or some of the other countries East of us, do you?"

"Not at all, I'm afraid."

"Yes, he's royalty. Of course, approximately nine people out of ten who are born in Vereet can claim ties to royal blood. From what I understand of the place, entire families, even distant blood relations, routinely go to war with each other and attempt to exterminate entire branches of various other families for no other reason than that they simply believe such a thing to be overdue. Barbaric and unproductive, obviously, but one of the more interesting consequences is that you end up with the majority of your ruling class being related to one another. Fascinating, to an extent."

"I see. I do appreciate you coming down and pointing out that particular fact today."

He shrugged. "Someone had to save poor Ismir. And you, of course."

Err...

"Me?" I asked. "I wasn't aware I required saving."

"You had taken several steps toward the dueling circle, and had made several motions that suggested you were on the verge of leaping in there yourself in order to stop what was happening. You'd moved up a full four feet, and were practically leaning into the ring by the time it was over." He sniffed disdainfully. "I dislike executions if they can be avoided."

"I, uh - I hadn't noticed," I said, bewildered at this revelation. Was he serious?

"You are aware that it was the whole point to Redforne doing what he did out there, aren't you?" he asked, tenting his fingers in front of him, considering me. "Brutalizing Ismir, wounding him in a manner that would leave an obvious scar...all done to enrage you. He wanted you to break the circle while attempting to prevent your duelist from getting butchered. If the entire point of this was to kill you, as you've said, then no doubt he would have stopped working on Ismir at that point and gotten to work on you. Armed or no, it would be his right according to dueling codes. It was a fairly crude and desperate gambit on his part but, to be fair, it looked as though it was working. He's frightfully smart, that one."

"Frightful I get, but smart?" I attempted to keep most of the outrage I was feeling from my voice. "He tortured and brutalized Ismir out there in a display that nauseated all but the most sadistic, depraved individuals watching, and you call what he did 'smart'?"

"That's right. Smart. Intelligent. It's the act of divorcing your thoughts from your emotions, and doing something for the express purpose of achieving a result. You've done it from time to time I'm sure, unless of course you feel absolutely dreadful for each of the highly entertaining robberies and other escapades you've managed to pull off over the years. Some of them caused quite a lot of embarrassment, I recall."

I crossed my arms and frowned over the desk at him. "Hardly the same thing."

"If you wish to believe your actions do not fall into the same category, by all means do so. The fact of the matter is that young Redforne knows what he's doing, as I think he's proven just recently."

I gave a reluctant grunt of assent. "His plan was very elaborate, I admit, and did seem somewhat insightful."

"Somewhat," Tenarreau scoffed, sitting back in his oversized chair. "The boy understood you so well that he even knew the manner of counter-trap you were likely to snare him with. From what you've told me, the planning for this goes back years – he has patience as well as a devious mind. Your original plan to flush out your unknown enemy was rather unique and clever. Knowing that that's precisely the sort of thing you'd likely do well enough in advance to set you up to do it in the manner of his choosing...well, I dare say that's even more clever. How did he manage to set you up with just one of the Copperfen goblets? Was it pure chance and opportunity, or did he manufacture a situation where you would wish to borrow one?"

"I truly don't know," I said, uncomfortably. *That* bothered me. If I'd been set up with the goblet I'd not been aware of the fact. A lord needs to be aware of everything going on around him at all times, and if not for a bit of luck and a healthy dollop of paranoia, I'd have missed this completely.

The prince read my expression and smiled.

"Oh come now. You were outsmarted, or at least you had been until you managed to pull your own fat out of the fire. It happens to us all at some point or another." He swiveled in his chair and hopped lightly to the ground, desk momentarily hiding all but his head from view. Walking unhurriedly to the counter nearest the wall he looked over at me, hands sorting through various items. "Would you care for some tea? A candle perhaps?"

"I really shouldn't, I've been burning candles all morning long," I said, scratching at the sparse growth on my stubbled chin. I'd forgotten to shave these past couple of days, I realized. "As it is I'll probably sleep well into tomorrow morning, and will still look like death on toast for the ceremony tomorrow."

"Very well, though I hope you don't mind if I help myself to some tea in front of you. I've got a busy evening lined up. Busier than I had thought, now that today's events have worked themselves out, what with tomorrow and all. It seems that every year about this time I end up burning the midnight wax." He took a few moments to pour himself some steaming liquid from a small carafe before walking back to his chair. He sat down (sat up) and, after a moment spent getting comfortable, casually lifted his cup to his lips for a sip before fixing me with a considering look. "I find that I've got a bit of a problem, Tucat."

"I'll say," I snorted. "Young psychotic country lordling wheels into town intent on murder and mayhem, determined to carve a nice chunk of city territory for himself, wielding a couple of priceless swords with more skill than anyone has a right to have. There are days I don't envy you."

"Ah. See, that's not exactly my problem," he said, setting his cup back upon the saucer on the dark wooden desk and once again tenting his fingers while looking over them at me. "It's you."

"Me?" I asked, startled.

"You're a clever fellow. What am I about to tell you?"

I furrowed my brow at him, perplexed, and pondered. After a few moments of contemplation I understood, and anger began to burn hotly in me.

"You can't be serious!"

He lifted an eyebrow and tilted his head slightly, as if to say 'Well...'

"You're granting him territory. *Lordship* in Harael," I practically choked. "He's a psychotic, conniving, bloodthirsty, unstable little boy, highness! What possible use could you have of someone like that, if you wish to maintain some semblance of order in our city?"

"I dare say, that's quite amusing coming from you," he said, mirthlessly. "One might think that you thought yourself completely guilt-free when it came to such things – that you yourself were behaving in a manner consistent with the principles of order and balance. Why, that delightfully droll incident regarding Lord Leventale leaps to mind. Oh, and let us not forget what happened to poor Lord Twigg."

"That was-" I began defensively.

"Lord Tucat, I know exactly what that was. That was the act of someone who believes themselves as terribly funny as they are clever, and wishes to prove that fact to the whole world. It was the sort of act that builds a very specific kind of reputation; one that serves as a warning to others that you are not the sort of fellow to be trifled with. It was effective, and actually quite entertaining to hear about at the time - livens things up, and gets people emotionally involved in the day to day politics of the city. It was not, however, the act of someone who is particularly concerned with balance and order."

I closed my mouth, perhaps scowling slightly.

"Don't get me wrong. It's what I expect of you, and you do a remarkably good job of it. You see, Tucat...balance and order, that's *my* responsibility. Everyone serves a purpose, and it's my job to ensure that I know what that purpose is, and the manner in which it can be best applied. Yours is to do what you do best - annoy other lords. That, and you find spectacularly interesting new ways to embarrass them or harm their reputation. From my vantage point, you're like the highest tree in the forest during a lightning storm. Bullies, brutes, cruel-minded people who might laugh at something unfortunate such as disfigurement, all of them seem to take exception to your antics, and flock to you. Some of the more sensible lords tend to avoid you for exactly the same reason.

"You yourself are not a cruel man, despite your many antics. From what I can tell, anything you yourself have initiated against another lord has been tentative and quiet, respectful almost. On the other hand, if someone attempts to make a move that threatens your own reputation or things of value, or if they are simply tactless and obnoxious when it comes to sensitive things like your appearance, you're merciless. I hear about these attempts against you, and their outcome tells me as much about the person you've thwarted as it does about you. All these assorted things factor into my decisions...who gains territory, who loses it. Whose petition for a duel I grant, whose I don't."

I maintained my silence, pondering his words carefully.

"The same thing is true with everyone who governs in Harael," he continued. "Your friend Lord Haundsing to the North of you, for instance, is an incredibly accomplished swordsman. He serves to remind other lords of their own mortality, and that the straight-forward threat of violence can be an effective type of protection in and of itself, when managed properly. Other lords situated near him have come to realize this over the years."

"I believe you're mistaken regarding one small detail, highness - Lord Haundsing and I are not friends," I said, trying not to sound alarmed.

There was a long pause, followed by the sound of the prince coughing politely into his hand.

"Yes, of course. The two of you are bitter enemies who squabble constantly in the streets, after all. Whatever was I thinking?" he asked mildly, peering up at the ceiling with sudden interest, as if lost in thought.

Ye gods, was there anything this man *didn't* know?

"Now, we've established that there's a certain amount of good that can come from just about any individual who governs territory. Do you know what the most dangerous threat to order is?"

"No, your Highness."

"Unpredictability," he said, voice becoming grave and serious. "Something new. An unknown, or a factor outside of your direct control. Now, we have a situation where a young country lord wishes to acquire territory in Harael in addition to...other things."

Like killing me. I nodded my understanding.

"So, we know one aspect of what he wants. Doubtless with the resources at his disposal he could think up some rather clever, unpredictable ways to get what he wants, but . . ." he picked up his cup and took a brief, satisfied sounding sip, "we happen to know what he's been up to this past while. I could thwart him easily enough - quash some of the more subtle claim agreements and title exchanges happening between him and Greybridge that some of the more dense and untrustworthy clerks in my records department don't think I'm aware of. Or, I could allow certain aspects of his plan to come to fruition, gradually introduce him into Haraelian society in a controlled, useful manner."

"And how exactly does one make use of a bloodthirsty young psychopath?" I asked, snidely.

"Simple. You give him a fledgling estate, something considerably smaller than what he's attempting to acquire stealthily, and you tell him to prove himself. His introduction into society serves two purposes. First of all, once news of this elaborate attempt on your life comes out into the open, the presence of this subtle and unpredictable young lord will do much to create an air of uncertainty among certain other lords in town-"

"I thought you said unpredictability was a bad thing," I muttered without thinking.

The library is a very quiet place. He stared at me in absolute silence, long enough to make me vow to myself never, ever to interrupt him again.

"-which will cause the smarter, more cautious lords to focus on maintaining their estate, becoming more security minded," he continued, sniffing slightly while idly whisking away an invisible speck of dirt from his desk. "There has been a rash of thefts as of late - last-minute attempts to curry my favor, the sheer quantity of which has been disturbing. I'd like to see things tightened up. Redforne - a new lord desperate to prove himself – arrives in the thick of things, his very presence changing the mood amongst the nobility quite nicely. The second, equally important thing he provides me with is the opportunity to prune some dead wood that has been problematic as of late."

Dead wood? Was he talking about me?

"Uhm," I said uncertainly, looking a question at him while pointing a finger to my own chest.

It took him a moment to piece together what I was asking, at which point his face split into a grin, and he laughed.

"No, not you Tucat. Dear me, no. Things would become dreadfully boring around here without you tweaking someone's nose every now and again. No, I'm referring to Greybridge. He was quite good at managing things when he was younger, but as of late he appears to have no desires that extend beyond a few bottles of wine and a nice comfortable chair. He's old, weak, and owns far too much territory to be allowed that sort of complacency."

"So in the end you're allowing a lord to retire to the country, in addition to introducing a new lord to replace him, only he's not really replacing him . . ." I said, nodding with understanding.

"Redforne acquiring the bulk of Greybridge's estate would be a catastrophe, I think you would agree. He has to be managed, started off small. An inexperienced lord, even one with the substantial resources young Redforne appears to have, would cause havoc if given that much territory at once. So, I give him a portion of what he wants, a parcel of city land that includes the old Redforne Keep, and I put the remainder of the Greybridge estate into surety."

We sat in silence for a while, the only sounds being the occasional click of cup and saucer as he took small sips of tea. As much as it galled me to admit it, I was beginning to see where he was coming from.

"Okay," I said, uncrossing my arms and trying to look less defensive than I had been for most of the conversation. "I can see the necessity for that. In what way am I a problem?"

"Well," he said, swirling his tea cup idly, "like I said, I know what young Redforne is after. I can tell him that one of the conditions upon which he gets his father's estate is that he make no move against you, subtle or no, for a period of one year. Even with him wishing you dead, he would be something of a fool to turn down that opportunity. One way or another, I can get him to agree not to move against you for a time, promising dire consequences if he should breech any agreement made with me. You, on the other hand, are a different story entirely."

"Moving against him, you mean?"

"That, as well as the fact that I'm not entirely certain what it is that *you* want. My hope is to allow Redforne to acclimatize himself to life in Harael, get a feel for how things are done here, keep his options open. He can't do that if he continues to focus on you. I presently have no real influence over you, Tucat, and cannot ensure that you won't act against young Redforne to preserve your own safety."

"Truthfully, I'm more than a little uncomfortable with the notion of a 'truce' of sorts," I replied after a few moments thought. "You say you can keep him from plotting against me, at least for the first little while, but how can I know he's not? His original plan to kill me was subtle enough, who's to say he's not subtle enough to arrange something similar that doesn't appear to involve him whatsoever?"

"And thus your problem becomes my problem. You see, I need to ask this of you despite knowing all of the perfectly reasonable objections you might have to such a plan. Incredibly unfair of me to do so, but necessary if my plans for Redforne have any chance of succeeding."

Neither of us spoke for a good long while, and I sat there pondering what life would be like knowing Redforne was out there, a fellow lord in my city. Even with my vague impressions of such a thing, imagining situations in which I might find myself, I saw that all my instincts were pointing at removing the threat that Redforne posed – to get him before he got me.

Even if he wasn't granted lordship, I realized that was the direction I'd been headed anyway. A ruthless and intelligent country lord wanted me dead, and had enough cash on hand to ensure that such a thing could happen. How long would I have been able to sit by and simply allow the situation to continue?

Not long at all.

I looked back to the prince who was looking into his teacup distractedly, respectfully waiting for me to sort out my thoughts. My eyes narrowed as a new thought occurred to me.

"You're trying to offer me a bribe," I said. "You want me to name some sort of price for leaving Redforne alone, strike some sort of compromise with you so that I can perceive myself as being bound by this arrangement."

He smiled, still looking at the contents of his cup.

"See? Clever fellow." He drained the last of the cup's contents and put it down upon the saucer with a clink before drawing himself up in his chair and looking at me seriously. "At the end of our talk, you would most likely grudgingly agree not to go after Redforne. While I do not doubt your word, you would probably begin rationalizing all manner of actions against him that would not truly violate your promise to me...all in the interests of self-preservation. If, on the other hand, you were to accept something of value, I have confidence that your agreement would be kept, both in letter and spirit."

"And so...a bribe."

"Think of it more as a proposal to secure your goodwill for the benefit of the Crown."

"Yes, I see," I said, frowning in thought.

Too much had happened recently for me to treat any decision lightly. There were enough things going on that I couldn't afford to stumble around blindly, even when it came to once-in-a-lifetime bargains that were being offered by the prince. He was presumably hinting that expansion of my territory, within reason, was for the taking – I could increase the size of Tucat estate more in one day than with twenty years of careful planning and calculated risk. A mere week ago I'd never have dreamt that an opportunity like this were even possible.

A week ago, I would never have considered rejecting it. Did I wish to put myself under his thumb like that?

"Could I be forgiven the need for a little time to consider this proposal? This is rather a lot to digest at the moment, and I want to think on it carefully," I said.

His expression was unreadable as he studied me, and he waited several long moments before giving me a tight-lipped and patient smile.

"Yes, of course. Take some time to consider. Busy, busy day, after all. Come, I'll show you out," he said, rising (hopping down) from his chair and gesturing toward the door. I stood up to bow, and began walking behind him as we made our way out of the small library. We traversed several hallways in silence, eventually coming to the rear palace entrance that led back out to the Circles.

"I shall attempt to have an answer for you shortly, highness," I said, noting that the sky was several shades darker than I'd been expecting. "I appreciate being allowed to think on the matter."

"Quite. Do not dawdle, Tucat." His tone was reproving. "While I'm sure that you have much to think about, tomorrow sees Harael's territorial lines being redrawn. A prudent person would take that into account."

"I understand, highness."

He sniffed, looking into the distance as he stood beside me on the topmost steps overlooking the arena, suddenly seeming hesitant. "Very well then. There is one other thing that I would like you to at least consider while making up your mind."

"Oh?"

"It seems like a very hard thing to do, but try to consider in what ways you and young Redforne are similar – the things you have in common."

"I don't care to believe that I'm anything like him at all," I said, waving a dismissive gesture.

"I know you don't, and that's because you're focused on the differences. Try looking at what you have in common. Both of you are devilishly smart, for one. You're both young, comparatively speaking, as well as ambitious...capable of great things. He is an extremely talented lord driven by a desire to prove himself, as are you. His father died as a result of choosing to better himself, not completely aware of or prepared for what he was getting involved in. Your family . . ."

He trailed off and looked skyward. I frowned down at him.

"My family's death was an act of the gods, highness," I said, furrowing my brow. "Rose blight, if you recall. Redforne's father chose the path that led him to his unfortunate death. My family didn't. A chance outbreak of a fatal disease like rose blight doesn't offer up much in the way of choices."

The silence that greeted me stretched on for far longer than it ought to have.

Prince Tenarreau coughed politely into his hand.

"Yes, of course," he said finally, turning to look at me. "Chance. Fortunate timing, I suppose, that all of your household's servants had been given leave to attend the Harvest Moon festival the very eve you and your family contracted the disease. Almost like it was planned, really. Odd that we haven't had any outbreaks since then.

"Oh, speaking of which, it was brought to my attention that you may have come into possession of an official field order from the palace archives. I'm not going to ask how such a secure and potentially sensitive document could have possibly found its way into your hands, but I should like it returned to the palace at your earliest convenience. I *would* ask you to disregard anything that may have been written on it, but it would appear as though you already have."

He broke eye contact, turning toward the palace entrance to return the way we had come. With the swirling vortex of thought in my head, I barely had time to register the last of his soft-spoken words as he was walking away.

"Indeed, a whimsical act of the ever capricious gods. Whatever was I thinking?" he murmured.

His diminutive footsteps on the marble palace floor were the only sound, as he slowly disappeared into the shadowy recesses of the main hall.

Chapter 19

IT WAS ONE of those times when 'off balanced' wasn't nearly a strong enough description.

Murdered.

That's what the prince had just told me, wasn't it? He was insightful as hell, and knew exactly how his words would be interpreted. Tenarreau had all but told me the note I'd received was authentic, and not a forgery. He was perhaps the most talented politician in all of Harael, and you don't get to a position like his by speaking carelessly, or dropping something by accident.

Murdered.

The whole carriage ride back to Tucat Keep went by in an instant, so wrapped up was I in my thoughts. Everything had changed. The world tasted differently. My fatigue had burned away and evaporated in the face of this new revelation, leaving me feeling as though I were on the verge of tears, but also brimming with a unending supply of raw, angry energy. If I were to hop out of the carriage and run alongside of it for an hour, it felt as though I'd scarcely make a dent in the reservoir that burned within me, like my very soul was suddenly trapped in an unending primal scream that could never run out of breath to power it.

I could picture my family clearly in my head, much more clearly than I'd ever been capable of before. Often in the past

I would imagine them as they had been, smiling and laughing, small hazy flashes of remembered conversations, or other moments that indelibly burned themselves into my memory.

Now I could see every single detail of their faces in my mind's eye, like they were right there with me. Jillian, my mother, my father...all three of them were looking at me, the laughing and joyous faces from my memories replaced by somber, serious expressions, the warm vibrant colors of my recollections replaced with a cold grey. I could see them, standing there. Staring at me, waiting expectantly.

My family. Murdered.

Who, though? Had it been Redforne?

While I found myself desperately wanting to believe it was so, the notion didn't make sense. He'd been all but a babe back then, quite younger than I'd been at the time. I also found it highly unlikely that Tenarreau would hint at something like this if Redforne was the one responsible...not while simultaneously attempting to solicit my agreement to keep from moving against the young lord.

Who then?

Was there perhaps some sort of clue in the last of my father's books? Or somewhere deep in the palace archives?

"Milord?" a deep, familiar voice said tentatively.

"Hmmm?" I managed to croak, looking up from the floor of the carriage that I'd been staring through with my unfocused gaze.

"Lord Tucat, we have arrived," said my coachman, eying me with a wary concern.

"I...Tarryl, thank you. Sorry, distracted there. Say," I said, getting up from my seat and stepping lightly out of the door he'd been holding open for me, "do you know where Cyrus is?"

"Brought him back here as instructed, Milord, before returning to the palace to wait for you," Tarryl said, shrugging. "Best guess would put him in bed, judging from how he looked. Did you need me to summon him for you?"

"No, no...not at all, Tarryl," I said, waving dismissively. "He's probably extremely tired and deserves a long, uninterrupted sleep. I suspect I'll be rather envious of him in a few hours..."

"Very good Milord," he said, standing at attention and giving me a terse nod. His expression softened a little, and a flash of concern crossed his face. "Lord Tucat, is everything all right?"

I paused, closing my eyes and taking a deep breath.

"It will be, Tarryl. Soon, I hope," I nodded. "Thank you."

He returned the nod before turning his attention to the whickering horses harnessed to the front of the carriage. I left him to the remainder of his duties, the heels of my boots clacking against the cobbles leading up to the front of the keep. I gave my knights at the front entrance a distracted nod as I went inside.

Upon entering, I seemed to do things more or less automatically, dropping my cloak and gloves on a chair near the closet. Leaving my outside garments where they lay, I made my way to the dining hall.

As usual, delicious aromas lingered from behind the double doors leading to the kitchen, despite the fact that dinner had likely been served hours ago. I didn't find myself hungry at that moment, so I didn't risk a look into the kitchen to see who was around, or what remained of the evening's feast. I'd missed every single meal Mosond had cooked that day, so doubtless he was in his back room, sulking. I would have to remember to eat later, despite my lack of hunger.

A drink, on the other hand, sounded like a fantastic idea.

I made my way around the back to the garden entrance and strode down the stairway, lost in thought. I hadn't done the sort of thinking that I'd wanted during the trip home – considering the prince's offer and determining how I might take advantage of it. I would need to decide quickly, if I wished to reap the benefits at the ceremony tomorrow.

Every time I tried thinking of how I might use this opportunity, my thoughts drifted to the last words he'd spoken, and all thoughts concerning territorial expansion were swept from my mind. Occasionally I would picture myself striding into the palace, finding the prince and naming my price – any and all information he had regarding what happened to my family.

What if he didn't know anything definitive? What if he couldn't give me a name? What then?

As I walked past the wines stored in the cellar, I grabbed a bottle of *Feirtu-ett,* a nicely dry green wine, to replace the one that was waiting in my exercise room. Holding it close to my chest with my left hand, I carefully hopped over the hallway traps in my familiar, elaborate dance. Pulling my key from my tunic, I unlocked the door and pressed my thumb lightly against the grey square near the hinges, which buzzed and verified that I was allowed to enter by way of a series of loud clicking noises.

Once inside, I gave the door a negligent shove and headed toward the drinks cabinet, still pondering furiously. What if I could find out more about my family on my own? It hadn't been more than an hour since I'd been introduced to the notion that someone had actually intentionally unleashed a fearsome disease upon my family, killing all but me. I had an opportunity to secure my fortunes, a once in a lifetime sort of thing. Did I want to use it to find out something that I hadn't even tried to look for myself?

Some of the torches lighting my exercise room had gone out, I noticed.

I made a note to fetch a lighting stick as I pulled the dark bottle of green wine from the chill water of the cooler to make room for its replacement, which I cradled in my other arm. I idly listened to the last of the secure sounding 'clunks' coming from the door as it finished closing, bolts ramming into place, and various other security measures arming themselves.

And then I heard a very loud and unexpected *'tang!'*

The door erupted in a shower of sparks so bright that I had to shield my eyes. White smoke began spewing into the room from the area around the door, occasional explosive popping sounds being drowned out by a noise like the loudest rainstorm ever heard. The air became reminiscent of fire and forges, the smell of hot metal assaulting my nose and throat.

Coughing, I stood there with my eyes wide, unable to fathom what was going on.

Within seconds, the noise subsided and the smoke turned a darker grey, snaking lazily upwards rather than billowing violently outward. I took a few uncertain steps toward the door, mystified.

The thick, sturdy door remained closed. Actually, at first glance it looked as though it would remain closed for a long, long time.

A glowing trail of rapidly cooling red-hot metal zig-zagged its way from the top of the door all the way to the bottom, all along the side opposite the hinges. The hinges themselves had been reduced to an ugly, glowing slag, as had the door handle and keyhole. Any part of the door that was not metal continued to smoke and sizzle from the heat that I could still feel on my face, even standing several feet away from it.

"Well now," chuckled a voice from the darkness. "I bet you thought I was joking earlier, hey Tucat?"

I quickly spun around, the twisted wreckage of a door all but forgotten.

There in the shadows, sitting cross legged and straight-backed in the middle of my dueling circle, his two priceless swords laying on the hardwood floor, was Eagan Redforne.

Chapter 20

YEAH. OF FREAKING course.

The unreality of the situation hit me nearly as quickly as my own anger over having overlooked yet another crucial fact, a detail that did not seem quite important enough to notice until this very minute.

Someone had had to break into Tucat Keep to steal the goblet...and one does not do that without detailed planning, information, and skill. Perhaps I'd figured Redforne had simply hired someone to get the job done, but it was now quite obvious who had broken into my keep, and avoided my carefully laden traps and security devices.

I was looking at him.

Well, crap.

He was now garbed in a much more stylish outfit of almost entirely black save for some red piping and embroidery here and there, clothing that was obviously much more suited for his trim physique than his previous tunic had been. He was exuding the same sleepy confidence he'd displayed during his match at the Circles.

I looked from him back to the smoldering door, which was still popping merrily and giving off a smoky odor that fell just shy of being pleasant. It was quite ruined, and would be impossible for me to open on this side - the hinges had been fused together and no longer moved. It was a big, heavy door, specifically designed to keep very determined people out of my exercise hall.

Now it appeared to be keeping people in, rather than out.

And Redforne was enjoying this moment, I could tell. He hadn't even risen from his cross-legged position on the floor. The torches he'd doused made it dim enough that I wouldn't notice him upon entering the room...not that I'd stood any chance of noticing him with everything going on in my head.

My stomach dropped for what seemed like the twentieth time that day. I cursed my oversight, fate, everything I could think of. I'd assumed he had no backup plan, that all of his hopes had been pinned on one shining moment of glory at the Circles.

This development had been so obvious that it was a wonder Theo hadn't spotted it. No subtle elegance, not a spot of complexity or single trace of intricate planning. Straight-forward and to the point – trap me in a room and kill me. Simple, effective...

I turned away from the door a final time while keeping my features as placid as the circumstances allowed, facing the smiling young lord who was watching my every expression with smirking glee. Doubtless he would expect me to plead with him, knowing I was by far the inferior swordsman. Doubtless he'd been imagining my reactions ever since he'd arrived in my keep, thoughts full of revenge for his thwarted attempt at achieving glory.

I wouldn't give the bastard the satisfaction, I decided. Even as the complete desperation of my circumstances became apparent, I knew...I wouldn't beg for mercy, wouldn't plead for my life.

Screw that.

I'd do what the most powerful man in Harael said I was best at.

I'd annoy him.

And there's probably nothing quite as annoying as being completely and utterly out-cooled when you're the one holding all the cards.

"I say," I sniffed, affecting a look of slight dismay, "that door does look to be in terrible shape all of a sudden. Damnably inconvenient, and I suppose I must apologize for the smell. Terribly sorry. Would you care for some wine?"

His smile lost a great deal of intensity, and I saw his head tilt slightly to the side. Whatever reaction he'd been expecting, that certainly wasn't it.

"That door," I continued, nodding behind me as I walked over to the drinks cabinet, "was made from four different types of wood. At least that's what I was told when I had it made...what do I know about wood, hey? Still, I was charged an arm and a leg for it, and I'm not even certain the craftsman who made it is still around. Tish and tosh, such a bother. Sorry, I didn't hear - did you want wine or no? Don't get up, I'll fetch it for you. There's a quite nice aquavit I've got back here, if caraway seed is more your thing . . ."

My back was to him as I retrieved my gold and copper goblets, so I couldn't see the expression on his face.

Perhaps he was wondering if he truly knew everything about our situation, or if I knew something that he didn't. Had I foreseen this eventuality? Was there a counter-trap I'd left here that he'd been oblivious to?

Of course, there was none. I was damn near helpless.

Yes, okay...*completely* helpless.

"Wine," he finally said from the center of the room, voice filled with cocky amusement. "Yes, I do believe I'll have a glass of red, if you please. It seems so gauche though, drinking red at an execution, don't you think?"

"Well honestly, I don't much care for red regardless of the circumstances. Would you rather a glass of green if you don't feel that red would go with our current, shall we say, ambiance?" I reached for the bottle I'd been fishing out of the chill water of the cooler. "It's a *Tifii* thirty-six, quite light with just a hint of almond to it."

"Actually, you might want to give that green a miss, stick with the red," he said, his voice suggesting that he had fully recovered from his surprise at my reaction and had now switched back to 'arrogantly amused'. He understood this game, and wasn't about to let me out-cool him in this, his backup moment of glory. "I suspect that green you've got there might be a little bit off."

As I was in the process of pouring a glass of the green wine, I noticed the ring on my right hand light up. It was emitting a very bright glow...just from me holding the bottle.

Poison. Extremely strong.

Momentarily unsettled but determined not to show it, I stopped pouring and set the bottle down on the counter carefully, dumping the contents of the glass I'd been pouring onto the floor near the wall. Then I turned to the center of the room and gave Redforne an arch smile.

"Really, Lord Redforne. First you ruin my door, and then you go and spoil an entire bottle of a premier vintage like *Tifii* thirty-six. You know, it's things like this that will get you uninvited from my keep in future, if you're not careful."

He laughed at that in a manner that appeared quite genuine, and unfolded himself from his seated position so that he might stretch his legs as he sat on the floor.

"Well," he smiled, "I simply couldn't make up my mind whether or not I wanted to kill you with a blade, or if I should watch from the shadows as you drank poison and choked to death in front of me. And honestly, as good as the thirty-six was, thirty-nine was a much better year, even when considering the comparatively low grape harvest."

"Really? I can't say I've had the pleasure."

"Truly? Well, you'll forgive my terribly poor manners in not bringing a bottle with me. Pity you won't have an opportunity to sample it, it's quite lovely. As for the door, I do offer my most sincere apologies, of course. I had to ensure that we were not disturbed while we," he paused long enough to give me a predatory grin, "discussed your future. As it were, I'm afraid I must also offer my most sincere apologies in advance for the actions I will be visiting upon you, which will no doubt ruin that fine shirt and vest you have on."

Damn it, he wasn't getting flustered. Flustered people make mistakes. I'd lost the element of surprise, and now we were running about even when it came to overall cool - me with my relaxed lack of concern for my dire situation, him with his smarmy graciousness and banter. He still knew he had the upper hand, and had doubtless had time to check my exercise room thoroughly. He'd poisoned my wine, which made me wonder what other little surprises he'd left about the place. No doubt I'd have to scour my keep for them all later.

I almost laughed aloud at *that* little piece of unbridled optimism, given my current chances of survival.

Finishing pouring two glasses of red, I took a goblet in each hand and walked slowly out to the dueling circle where he remained sitting, bright eyes wide and alert for any hint of treachery on my part, even as a relaxed, self-assured expression lit up his face.

I held out a glass that he took with a nod and a grin, not getting up from his relaxed pose. Much to my dismay, I noticed that my hands were trembling.

He noticed as well.

"I say, Tucat, do I make you nervous? Dreadfully sorry, old boy. I'd attempt to calm you somewhat and say that I'll make your death quick and painless, but I don't think I'd be able to pull off such a bald-faced lie with any amount of conviction whatsoever. Honest face - it's something of a curse."

"Nervous? Me? Not really, no," I lied, affecting disdain as I swirled the contents of my wine glass. "I just returned from a meeting with the prince, learned a few things of interest. Got rather excited is all, hasn't quite worn off yet. *Sal-vachi.*" I lifted my glass out to him.

He did the same, briefly waving his own ring-adorned hand over his own cup, proving that he wasn't a complete moron. Seeing no flash of color from it, he smiled an amused sort of smile and took a long sip before speaking again.

"So, how was your little meeting with the prince? I suspect things went rather well for you, once you'd explained everything. Got to tell him the tale of how you thwarted the evil young hellion's sinister plans, made yourself out to be quite the hero. Doubtless the crown knights will be coming down to humble Teuring Keep in short order, if they're not there already, intent on hauling me in for a taste of the prince's tender mercy. Such is the price of high-stakes politics, hey?"

"Hardly," I said, noting the small hint of distaste that had crept into his voice during his last sentence. "In fact, while I understand the reasoning behind what he proposes, I can't say I much care for it. He is going to offer you lordship. Well, 'was' would be a better word, I suppose, given what you're likely here to accomplish."

That he didn't seem to expect. He dropped the act for a brief moment and lowered his glass to about chest level, looking at me with wary disbelief. I pretended not to notice, continuing to focus on swirling my wine goblet, tasting the contents periodically. A long moment passed.

"You're lying," he said cheerfully. "No prince in his right mind would grant me lordship after all that I'd managed to arrange, in secret, right under his nose. He'd be daft to agree to that."

"That's pretty much exactly what I told him, actually. It's surprising the uses he can find for people, even those as clearly deranged as yourself, given the right situation. He has his reasons. Still, I suppose it doesn't much matter now. By the by, he did know most of what you had been planning. I mean, he's a very smart fellow, and even *I* managed to figure that bit out."

"Ah, as to that," he said, putting his wine goblet down on the floor and looking at me inquisitively, "how exactly did you figure things out? What gave it all away, if you don't mind me asking? I mean, don't get me wrong," he grinned in a manner that would give a shark pause, "I'm still killing you, obviously. Nevertheless, I wouldn't mind knowing."

A part of me simply wanted to tell him that I'd been on to him the entire time, and start picking away at him one insult after another until he became tired of the facade of polite civility, and simply attacked me.

I told that part of me that it was no longer allowed to contribute ideas. However, I did find it interesting that he didn't believe me when I told him what Prince Tenarreau had suggested.

Maybe there was a way out of this, after all.

"It started when I learned that several of the lords around me had happened upon knowledge of the theft prior to it happening."

"Ah yes. Well, I did have to make sure that you were informed of the plan to rob you. Multiple lords knowing about it was necessary, alerting whatever informants you might have had, in territories neighboring yours."

I nodded. "And then there was the parchment that showed up at my doorstep, presumably to further tip me off, or distract me. I believed it a forgery at first, but its authenticity would appear to have been confirmed for me just this afternoon by the prince himself. Very impressive."

Redforne looked momentarily puzzled.

"You mentioned that before, a...parchment?" He knit his brow and gave an annoyed frown. "What information did it contain, exactly?"

"Information about my family...like you don't already know."

He shrugged lightly. "I sent you nothing."

"Oh please. The timing, the masked courier? It was way too coincidental."

"Believe what you will, Tucat. I've hardly got a reason to lie." Redforne indicated the swords on the floor before him, then gave a quick nod to the still-smoking remains of my ruined hall door.

Hmm...he did have a point.

"Well, if not you, then who sent it?"

"I'm rather curious myself now, actually. I may need to investigate later. It was instrumental in revealing my plans, I take it?"

"Not quite as much as seeing your swords at the stables was."

He grimaced. "I was getting too excited, I admit. I wanted my swords with me just in case you challenged me prematurely, and I hadn't counted on your lack of manners.

Merely handling another duelist's weapons is enough to get you executed in some places. Terribly bad form."

I bowed my head apologetically before continuing.

"And then, lastly, there were your feet."

He raised his eyebrows. "My feet?"

"You were a good swordsman pretending to be bad – your foot movements gave you away. In the tower, when I drew on you. Speaking of which, if you wouldn't mind answering one of my questions in return...was that mistake due to the drinking and smoking you were doing that night? I must say, your breath was something from the very depths of Hades itself."

"You liked that?" he grinned. Then, without any warning at all he leapt up from his crouched position and onto his feet, a move that I would have thought impossible given how he'd been sitting. I found myself taking a half-step back, and cursed my involuntary reaction.

He chuckled at my sudden distress, stepped away from his swords a few paces, and assumed an unsteady and bleary-looking expression, very much like how I had seen him in the tower the day before. For all the world, he now looked like a man who was lost in the throes of epic debauchery. The transformation was impressive.

"Step forward, adjust the belt," he said, walking toward me slowly with exaggerated movements so that I'd see what he was talking about, "palm a small pill that you've tucked in there, pretend to stumble."

He fell awkwardly, catching himself with his hands just before coming into contact with the ground.

"Then, put the pill in your mouth as you stand, pretending to wipe your cheek with a lost sort of expression, simultaneously shaking your foot as though you may have injured it, distracting the viewer." He stood up and finished the demonstration before me with a small bow. "A combination of aromatic herbs mixed with a very unpleasant gel, guaranteed to leave anyone with the impression that you've had far too much of just about everything. I made a point to breathe on you, all part of my 'oafish lout' routine. I'd actually been nursing the same glass of wine all evening, prior to your arrival. Aside from that, I hadn't had a thing."

"Quite clever," I admitted. Even that had been staged. And right in front of other lords, no less, all without anyone suspecting a thing.

"I was fairly proud of it, and frankly I was dying to tell someone. Truly, the hard part about coming up with something clever like this is not being able to talk about it, or otherwise let it be known by those who would appreciate the effort that went into it." He fixed me with a slightly perturbed look. "These last several years have been very trying for me in that regard."

"Understandable," I said, walking slowly to my drinks cabinet and setting my wine glass upon a nearby table. "Eagan, can I be frank with you?"

"By all means."

"I don't care for you. Even now, knowing what I do about how clever you are and the reasons behind your actions, I don't care for how you've put things together, or the things you've done. I agree that you are smart. Dangerously so, I might add. You have a masterful understanding of intrigue, perception...and are perhaps the most subtle individual I've ever come across. You have talents that other lords could only dream of, not the least of which is your expertise with a sword. In many ways I might consider myself envious of you, but...I don't like you."

"Lord Tucat," he smiled, bowing extravagantly, "If you could only know the joy that your words have brought me just now."

"The prince," I continued, "is not a man who concerns himself with things such as like or dislike. Perhaps 'outraged' is too strong a word, but I do confess that I was quite alarmed when he first broached his plan to me, with regards to yourself. He plans to offer you lordship."

"You're lying," he repeated in a cheerful, singsong voice while shaking his head sadly. "You wish to deceive me with this notion so that I might become plagued with self-doubt, because you're backed into a corner and can see no other way out. Really, Tucat. I mean, even *begging* would be more seemly than this last-ditch hopeless effort you're attempting here."

"You are to be offered a small parcel of city land, which includes the old Redforne Keep, and the title of lord here in Harael."

"Seriously, Tucat...you-"

"Eagan, I swear on my father's grave," I said, evenly and seriously. "It is the truth."

That gave him pause. Mid-word, he found himself slowly closing his mouth and giving me a very new and uncertain sort of look.

He knew enough about me to understand what an oath like that meant.

I nodded. "It's true and, as I believe I may have mentioned, I'm not terribly happy with it, though I do understand the rationale. The biggest problem Tenarreau sees in all of this, he says, is me. He's concerned that I shall come after you because I fear what you'll do, wishing me dead and all. I do admit, it's certainly a likely scenario, despite the fact that I hadn't even known you existed until mere days ago. Given how dangerous you are, I wouldn't feel safe knowing that you were out there, somewhere...

"I think he suspects that in the end, we will end up as nothing more than two cats warily circling each other in the street, hissing and spitting, constantly on guard for the slightest movement made by the other. In that sort of situation, you aren't free to do the things he predicts you might, and neither am I – we become so focused on each other that we stop behaving like ourselves and, in so doing, we both perhaps end up getting run over by a cart. The very thought of it wearies me - nobody wins. Unless . . ."

"Unless?"

"We come to an agreement, you and I," I said, earnestly. "An understanding. Some situation where we both win, or at least have a chance to win."

"And so, being the only one of us two able to see reason, you come forward and say 'Hey now, let's stop fighting, shall we? Perhaps have a spot of lunch, talk things over,' and everyone gets to go on with their lives. How lovely," he laughed, bitterly. "I trust it's very easy to become champion for such a plan when confronted with the knowledge that you won't live to see another dawn."

"It's an option, Redforne...and it's one you didn't even know you had, a minute ago. Tell me, if you're so damned clever, what becomes of you after I'm killed here? Hmmm? How fares your fine actress of a wife once you-"

"Shut up," he said, quickly.

Something about how he said that came off as terribly anxious and distressed.

I looked at him quizzically, and then my eyes widened as a very new realization dawned.

"Oh, gods! She doesn't know, does she? You haven't told *anyone!* Your wife, she hasn't been playing along at all – she really thinks she's Lady Teuring! You haven't told her who you are, or what-"

"Shut up!"

"And you care for her, obviously! Eagan, this is madness! Think about what you're leaving-"

"You shut your filthy mouth!" he bellowed, lurching forward as he spoke. His face had suddenly become flushed and dark, and his eyes looked daggers at me.

(The highly abstract part of my brain noticed that he completely lost his cool just then – point for me!)

"Okay, okay," I said, raising my hands disarmingly. "The issue remains, however. There are limited options once you've committed to something like what you intend here, extremely limited, and none of the options are good. The alternative to killing me provides far more possibilities. Legitimate possibilities no less, opportunities to earn the kind of respect that your father dreamed of. Land in the city, Redforne Keep. Tell me, how is that not everything you could possibly want?"

"Well for one," he replied, recovering his former poise smoothly, "it is missing the rather significant element of your gruesome and untimely death. I'm afraid that particular point is a bit of a deal-breaker, when it comes right down to it."

"But why?" I asked, plaintively. "Why must you kill me? How does my death improve your own situation?"

"Ah. Now we get to the part I was expecting. Next you plead, and then you beg, and it all goes rather rapidly downhill from there. No," he said, walking back to where he'd left his swords sitting, bending over to scoop one up with one hand and picking his wine goblet up with the other. "It's been a lovely chat, and I thank you for your hospitality, but I'm afraid that it's time we got down to settling matters between you and I."

"*What* matters?" I practically shouted. "What could you possibly pretend exists between us that you need to give up everything just for the sake of killing me."

"It's about family, Tucat. It's about being raised fatherless and motherless, your family reputation in shreds, all the while knowing that there's someone out there responsible for your pain, your suffering. It's living each day with the understanding that someday you'll do something about it. These things you speak of – lordship, property, money...it means nothing! Material possessions fit only for the soulless wretches that crawl gleefully among this diseased wreckage of a society. No," he shook his head, quickly draining the last of his wine and tossing the metal goblet aside to the cobbles with a clang. "I've bested this travesty of a city at its own game. I've found fitting retribution for one enemy of my family already, and I shall move on to what's fitting for the second. Time for the last son of the Tucat family to experience first-hand the kind of suffering that his family inflicted upon others...upon me. I care not a single copper mark what might happen after that."

"Eagan," I practically croaked, sensing opportunity slip through my fingers, "the whole thing with your father was an accident, not intentional whatsoever! If it's proof you require, I can get it. All I require is a minute to go upstairs and-"

I looked over at the blistered, smoldering door guarding the exit to the main basement hallway.

"Well, okay," I said, scratching my jaw a little. "I'll probably need a little more than a minute, and maybe a little help getting this door open as well. Still, I know exactly where it is, and once I show you-"

"Your father's journal? Yes, I've read it," he said, casually.

We stood in silence for a while.

I recall making an oath right about that moment. Briefly, it went like this; if I managed to survive this ordeal, I vowed to travel to the single most boring place I could think of, pull up a chair and sit there for an entire week just to enjoy how it felt to not be surprised at the drop of a hat.

"You've . . ." I couldn't even think of the words.

"Yes. I mean, obviously I needed to find out everything I could about my father, and that meant cracking open a few of your books. So sorry, forgot to mention it. This was years ago, of course but, yes...I've read them."

"You've read them. You've seen my father's journal - know your father's death was an accident. What reason could you have to want me dead, if you know how your father died?"

"I'm sorry, was that a *joke?*" he spat, bending over to pick up his second priceless and razor-sharp instrument of death. "Did I hear you ask *why*, just now?"

He was working himself into a rage, I saw. I nodded, not trusting any of the words I might use to explain my situation. Remaining mute might not be the best course of action, but I could do little else. The sword at my hip may as well have been an arrangement of flowers for all the good it would do me at the moment.

"My father was the greatest swordsman ever to live," he continued. "Undefeated in his lifetime...he'd never lost a single duel, ever. To hire him as a duelist meant that your honor was secure and you were victorious in whatever petty, sordid squabble you were involved in - it was as simple as that."

He looked to me for any sort of reaction. I warily nodded for him to continue.

"So successful was he in his endeavors that he was able to arrange for lordship, buy an estate outright. And he became an active lord, engaging in what could loosely be referred to as the 'politics' of the realm – the backwards, idiotic contests of no consequence that you and other lords seem to take such great delight in. Despite his inexperience, he began building a reputation for keen intellect that could have easily matched or exceeded his reputation for sword play. And then . . ."

The pause was my cue to interject. Hesitantly I spoke.

"A terrible accident," I said. "Nobody's fault."

"And then," he continued, as if my words held no meaning for him, "he was found. At the bottom of a tall set of stairs behind Two Oaks Street, where it meets Tanners. Lying there where the prostitutes and less savory herb merchants would gather back then, and gather still to this day. It was morning when they found him. It had been raining all night, else he might have been found earlier."

"Eagan, I know how-" I began.

"By the time they'd found him, it was impossible to tell who it was that lay dead there in the alley. You see, the rats had come during the night as he lay there, and there were not many present who had the stomach to look at him for very long. Half of his face had gone missing, as had both his eyes."

I closed my mouth and swallowed uncomfortably.

"It took most of the morning to figure out who it was. I may have played a small part in that, waking my uncle and informing him that father hadn't shown up for my morning fencing lesson. Later that afternoon, my uncle gently told me the terrible news. I wasn't allowed to see him as they'd brought him in, nor was I permitted to see him as he was being consigned to his crypt. I found out that there was good reason for it later, once I'd snuck away from the grief-ravaged eyes of my uncle's family, intent on seeing for myself what had become of my father, my idol. Oh, some effort had been made to be respectful and tactful," he said, waving dismissively. "The visor on his head masked his face and most of the damage done to it. Of course, I couldn't have known that myself, back then when I'd lifted it to see if it really was him that was laying upon the marble slab.

"I remember staring, and thinking it odd that I didn't scream at the time, looking upon this eyeless, macabre horror of a face and realizing I was looking at the face of my beloved father. You can't even imagine."

I could do better than simply imagine. Unsettling memories of my own experiences were called up in vivid detail just then, and I had to suppress a shudder.

"And then there were the gloves, yet another thing that didn't make sense to me. Father never wore dueling gloves, considered them an abomination. And I thought...did anyone around me understand him at all? Did *nobody* care?

"I couldn't stand the sight of it, and I went to remove them, knowing that he would have wanted it that way. I remember being distinctly confused when I pulled the first glove away, encountering no resistance.

"Someone had taken his hands, you see. Trophies, I would assume. Once it became known who it was that had been laying in that alley, well, it isn't hard to imagine society's dregs picking away at him like sub-human vultures. And his hands were legendary, were they not? Why, an exotic trophy like that might fetch ten, maybe fifteen gold marks!"

"My father...he didn't-"

"Your father," he interrupted, quiet voice filled with seething, righteous anger, "was a thoughtless, sniveling coward. For years growing up, ever since spying the name 'Tucat' in dad's journal, I thought him responsible for my father's death. Later, upon coming of age and gaining more information, I realized he was responsible for much, much more than that. Chance and misfortune took my father from me, it's true...but your family, Tucat, destroyed who he was. His reputation, his legacy, his memory, everything my family was or could have been. Destroyed utterly and completely," he said, lip curling slightly. "It seems only fitting that I return the favor."

"Now, hold on just a moment!" I said hotly. "I mean, that's a bit of a stretch, isn't it? You can't think that it was intentional, what happened to your father! And even if you did, how could you possibly see fit to blame *me* for it?"

"Bah. Enough talking. You've already remained alive a hundred times longer than I'd planned since walking through that door." He rolled his shoulders and stretched his neck, sword at the ready in each hand.

I backed away from him.

"Look Redforne, this is pointless! Think about this for a second, dammit!"

"A second? Lord Tucat, I've thought about this all of my life," he smiled. His swords were idly twirling on either side of him, humming softly as they parted the air.

I licked my lips nervously.

"Any last words?" he asked.

If an opportunity had existed to reason with him and possibly deflect him from his murderous course of action, that opportunity had passed. Damn it, this wasn't good. This was the opposite of good.

This, unless I missed my guess, was what might be considered 'bad'.

And yet, my anger was back with a vengeance now, rekindled by his use of 'coward' as he'd referred to my father. I wanted to wipe the too-confident look from his face, wash it in some mud for a while. He was facing a Tucat, after all, and it was bloody well time he came face to face with that realization.

I had to do something. And what did I, Vincent Tucat, do best?

I took a long, hard look at him.

Well, okay...he looked plenty annoyed already. Scratch that. What else could I do exceptionally well, possibly better than anyone living?

I blinked.

And where was I, exactly?

A smile crept upon my face, and I continued backing up a few more paces, away from Redforne.

"Last words? Yes, I think I've happened upon the perfect last words. Are you ready?" I put my hand on the pommel of my sword, attempting to appear dangerous. "Trust me, they're really good . . ."

He cocked his head, looking at me expectantly. I grinned at him.

"More wine?" I asked.

Reaching to the drinks cabinet behind me, I grabbed the open bottle of *Tifii* thirty-six and sent it spinning haphazardly in his general direction.

Realizing the nature of the missile speeding sloppily at him, he very quickly leapt sideways out of its way, a distressed look on his face. Just holding the bottle had lit up my ring like a small emerald sun - doubtless that much poison would cause him significant difficulty if it even came into contact with the skin.

He recovered quickly, sweeping both blades toward me, his grunt of effort punctuated by the sound of breaking glass. I heard his swords connect sharply with the empty patch of stone floor I'd heroically vacated, sprinting as fast as my legs could carry me. I heard a muffled curse of surprise behind me.

Seconds later, I was at my climbing wall.

I leapt mid-stride, jumping up to one of the large wooden blocks that had been set up to simulate the lip of a balcony on the side of Greybridge Keep, throwing my outstretched hands in front of me in desperation. I'd made that particular leap hundreds of times before, but had always had the benefit of stretching and warming up beforehand, and had never been quite so rushed before.

My hours and hours of practicing didn't fail me.

With a quick pull, I flipped myself up and onto the ledge. Without taking the time to think about it, I leapt straight up, reaching for the rope that I knew was dangling above me, next to the wall. The moment my fingers found the rough braided rope, I began to climb. I heard another clang of metal on stone behind me.

I continued scuttling up the swinging rope as quickly as I could, heading toward the faux parapet that loomed above, thirty feet or so from the floor. Temporary safety at best, but considering that the alternative was certain death, I'd take what I could.

I heard a grunt of effort below me, and decided to risk a quick look. Then, gasping, I curled into a tight ball, lifting my legs up and gripping the rope with every ounce of strength I possessed.

There was another sharp tang of metal on stone as he completed his swing, and a muffled curse came from below me. He'd probably missed my feet by mere inches.

I looked down again. Redforne had opted to keep his main-hand weapon, leaving the other on the floor so he could pursue me up the wall one-handed. The white knuckles of his left hand stood out as he gripped an outcropping of stone, recovering from his swing, twisting precariously below me. I had an evil thought.

Ah, what the hell...

I relaxed my legs and loosened my grip on the rope simultaneously. A moment later I straightened my entire body, stomping downward with both feet as hard as I could.

The heel of my right boot connected with the top of Redforne's left hand very satisfyingly.

Letting out a sharp bark of pain and outrage, he released his hold on the rocky surface. He retained enough presence of mind to send his sword swinging upwards toward me as he fell, but I'd pulled myself out of harm's way by the time he did.

Instead of hitting the stone floor solidly, he managed to roll out of it at the last possible second, reminiscent of the athleticism he'd displayed against Ismir in the Circles. Leaping back onto his feet, he threw himself at the wall. Somehow, he'd managed to sheath his sword during all this, and was now employing both hands to climb up after me.

Rapidly.

I turned my attention back to climbing as fast as I possibly could.

Scaling the uneven, rocky upper wall was like greeting an old friend, and we reacquainted ourselves in record time. I quickly found myself within arms length of the ceiling, stepped onto the stony ledge of the parapet and went into a crouch, looking down.

Redforne was clawing his way upwards very quickly, hand over fist, glaring up at me balefully. I gave it about fifteen seconds before he was about level to where I was.

Frantically, I reviewed my options. He had a sword, and seemed adept at swinging it even while climbing a wall. I had swords as well, though I had a feeling that keeping them at my hip was probably about as useful as anything else I could do with them at this point. What else did I have at my disposal?

I almost wasted precious moments slapping my forehead with my palm. Quickly, my hand flew to an inside vest pocket, and I pulled out a small, nondescript spherical object.

You never knew when something like wrist-sling ammo was going to come in handy.

I inspected the spherical object to ensure that it was a type that I recognized. Once I had confirmed the type, I gave a small smirk and leaned over the lip of the precipice, looking down at the furious young Redforne as he climbed upwards, about a dozen or so feet below me.

"Uh-oh . . ." I said, carefully letting go of the sphere right above his head, a few inches from the wall.

He paused briefly to determine the nature of this new threat, and pulled himself slightly closer to the wall so that the bauble would bounce past him.

The small orb struck a jagged bit of wall directly above him, though it did not bounce away as a small marble of its size should have. Upon smacking into the irregularly shaped rock it exploded into a large ball of white, goopy, tar-like foam...

...which continued its way down until it encountered the extremely surprised looking face of Lord Redforne.

"Glaaff!" was all he managed to say before his arms jutted out to either side of him, releasing their hold on the grey rock. Marshmallowy globs of white fluffy tar muffled any further exclamations of surprise he might have been attempting to send my way as he fell.

If a word exists to describe the sound he made upon hitting the floor, it has several amusing consonants, no vowels whatsoever, and sounds really, really wet.

I sent an amused grin down at the white, sputtering, sopping mess that was Lord Redforne. Coughing, he got to his feet amid mounds of the pale, sticky foam, taking a brief moment to spread his hands palm-up and stare at them.

And he began to laugh.

"Oh, Tucat," he said, holding his arms up in mock surrender, "that was truly well done. Ha! I swear, it's been ages since I've been so surprised."

He coughed slightly as he chuckled, clutching his ribs, proving that he was perhaps just a little bit human, and that falling ten feet onto a stone floor might have caused him *some* difficulty at least.

"Glad you liked that. I've got a few dozen more surprises up here for you," I said, holding another marble up for him to see. "Feel free to try climbing up here again, see what happens. Oh, here's a fun one! I wonder what it does . . ."

Redforne smiled up at me, his white, foam-streaked face looking sinister even as it projected amused good humor.

"Oh come now, Tucat. Come and face your death like a man, and not as a pathetic, weeping weakling. Seriously, how long do you think you can stay up there, hiding from your fate?"

"You'd be surprised," I called down, grabbing a rope tethered to the ceiling and leaning forward over the lip of the precipice so I could peer down at him. "I packed a lunch."

He shook his head with a sad chuckle.

"Tucat, you know you're beaten," he said, once again wiping a portion of the sticky white substance from his face in a tiredly amused fashion. "You seek to delay the inevitable. Come, I shall give you a sporting chance. Choose whatever manner of fencing weapons you wish, in any combination, and I will face them with but a single blade. We can finish this matter honorably, you and I."

The man offering these terms had made Ismir look like a bumbling fool. The warning bells simply don't get any louder than that.

"Sorry, rather comfy at the moment," I said, assuming a relaxed pose, hand still on the rope and one leg hanging over the corner of the ledge. "Can't really see myself coming down there anytime soon."

He frowned.

"Name your terms, Tucat. Craft whatever dueling scenario you wish, and I swear upon my father's honor that I'll abide by it."

To be honest, I doubted my ability to survive a contest that saw Redforne armed with nothing but a sliced pickle. If he agreed to anything, it had the potential to be lethal.

Before I could yell something frightfully witty to that effect, a third voice made itself heard.

"Vincent," it called out in a manner that suggested it was tsking, if that's even a word to begin with. "I mean, I know I've told you that you need to expand your circle of friends, become more social. But, really...him? Do try to discriminate, please. You can't just let *anyone* into your keep, after all."

Lord Theodore Haundsing stood a few yards from the secret entrance, hands on hips, looking evenly at the much-abused figure of Lord Redforne.

Chapter 21

IT WAS THEO!

And, gods love him, he was *bristling!*

"Hey there, Theodore," I waved, not quite able to keep the relief I felt from my voice. "This is a pleasant surprise. How are things?"

"They're well," he said, tearing his eyes away from Redforne and looking up at me for the first time. He squinted slightly, as if surprised. "Goodness! What are you doing up there? And don't say 'just hanging around', or I shall have to climb up there and beat you."

Damn. So much for my first answer.

"Nothing much, really. Relaxing, enjoying the view. I really *should* be cleaning, though," I said, making a small production of whisking dust and small pebbles off the ledge. "With all the torches I burn in here, the stonework can get pretty sooty, and-"

"Lord Theodore Haundsing," Redforne smiled, his voice full of good cheer. "Oh, I had hoped that it was you. Of all the lords I suspected to be working with this walking dead man, you were the one I wished it to be most of all. Of all the many surprises that have happened this day, I do have to say that this is one of the more pleasant."

"Really? How special," drawled Theo.

"Indeed. If I may say, it is quite an honor you're about to do me. Unless you're about to suggest we do something ridiculously boring, like talk things over," said Redforne, still grinning.

"Wouldn't think of it," said Theo, rolling his neck. "Not the talky sort."

"Rules?"

"Let's not bother – you don't strike me as the type to adhere to gentlemanly agreements."

"Ah," said Redforne sarcastically, briefly placing his palm on his chest. "You wound me, sir."

"Yeah, that's sort of the plan, actually." Theo drew his sword with a distinct lack of flourish and inspected its length, still standing a good twelve feet away from the young lord. "I'll give you a moment to wipe some of that white goop off of yourself, perhaps look a little less like someone who's just been intimate with a street clown."

I noticed that while Theo was speaking, his left arm remained at his side, perfectly still. He wasn't drawing attention to it, but he wasn't using it either, thumb hooked casually at the top of his sword belt. I had forgotten that his arm had been cut badly in the Circles just yesterday...and hadn't he said he wouldn't be doing anything with it for a month or so?

Maybe I had no right to be relieved, him showing up like this. Who was the better swordsman, after all? I had no clue.

"Theo," I called down, realizing I should actually be doing something. "Be careful of the puddle on the floor there. Poison, extremely strong."

"Noted," he called back, eyes briefly darting to the puddle I'd referred to.

"Also," I called out, "I stomped on his left hand a while ago – it's probably still really sore."

Theo frowned, and appeared about to say something.

"Oh, and another thing," I said, scooting over to the side of the precipice, preparing to slide forward and lower myself, "he seemed to favor the ribs on his right as he got up just now. Rather nasty fall...he's probably a little tender on his whole-"

"Vincent," Theo said, in his best I'm-being-patient voice, "I know you're trying to help, but please let me handle this. Details like that are just as likely to put me at a disadvantage when discussed openly. I'll explain exactly why in about five years or so, once you've reached a certain level of expertise. Also, stay up there where you are, I don't want you coming down here just yet."

I stopped lowering myself before committing to anything particularly acrobatic, pulling myself once more atop the stony ledge. I looked down at my friend, puzzled.

"Okay, why not exactly? It's not like this kid's gone out of his way to be fair, what with breaking into my own keep to ambush me."

"Pffft, to hell with fair," Theo said, twirling his longsword a couple of times. "We've just never practiced two-on-one before, and it's actually quite hard to coordinate moves in a useful way. Plus, he might do something drastic, even with me here, just to get you."

"Well," Redforne tsked, shaking his head in mock disappointment as he finished wiping the worst of the mess from his tunic, "It appears that you're not the brainless, bloodthirsty barbarian type I'd figured you for."

"Oh, don't you worry about that." Theo's face lit up in a frightfully wicked grin. "I've been known to enjoy a cup of blood or two. By the by, how's Lord Leventale faring?"

"He's in pain, obviously," Redforne shrugged, as if such matters were of no consequence. He slowly drew the blade at his hip while reaching down to recover his other sword from the floor. "I don't think his smile is ever going to be the same though, not after the job you did on his chin. Still, I suppose we'll see what kind of smile he's capable of later this evening, once he learns of your rather violent death."

"Gee, I've never been *threatened* before. Now I'm all worried," Theo said, blandly. Finishing one last mighty stretch, he turned to his left and presented Redforne his right side, sword angled down slightly with his palm toward the floor, left arm held slightly behind him for balance.

Theo hadn't so much as drawn his off-hand blade yet, I noted uneasily.

"Shall we?" Redforne asked, taking up his now-familiar guard position.

"Lets," Theo said, looking unconcerned as ever.

They both stood motionless for several seconds. My breath caught in my chest as I watched them, afraid to move for fear of disturbing the silent contest of wills, or triggering some premature violent explosion between them.

Redforne was first to break the stillness. Nearly silently, he leapt forward with his two swords raised above his head, his entire body suggesting sudden violent mayhem...and then just as quickly he leapt back to where he'd begun.

I don't think Theo so much as blinked.

Chuckling lightly to himself, Redforne assumed a much less dramatic pose and began to side-step, circling to his left while keeping both swords before him, watching Theo carefully. His eyes were bright, and his excitement was unmistakable.

Theo began to circle as well, simply having to step forward while turning slowly, presenting only his side.

And then it began in earnest.

I wasn't even sure I caught everything happening between them, even as I watched. I mean, I know what I think I saw, but I'm sure that some moves were so outside of my comprehension that I can only describe how it looked from my vantage point, perhaps doing the sheer artistry of the deadly contest a gross injustice.

Redforne struck quickly, bounding toward Theo and bringing one sword around in a wide arc while simultaneously beginning a second tremendous swing with the other, vaguely reminiscent to how I'd seen him attack Ismir in the Circles.

Theo, rather than bothering to parry the swords fully, simply shifted his own massive one-handed blade to deflect Redforne's savage downward-angled blows ever so slightly, allowing them to miss him entirely. He repeated this time and time again, barely modifying his stance, effortlessly allowing the ribbons of deadly steel to slide off his blade or simply whoosh by him.

Pressing forward like a wildcat, Redforne continued to turn and leap and slash at his opponent, constantly whirling and spinning, silver arcs of light dancing dangerously before him. Both swords moved far faster than my eye was capable of registering. He was perpetually in motion, dark curls bouncing around his face as he spun and leapt from one position to the next, always attacking or otherwise sending his deadly blades forward one after the other, relentlessly.

Each attack was expertly deflected, and it looked like Theo was barely even working. Every time I expected the clang of metal on metal to assault my ears, I instead heard the *'wshhhing!'* of one blade sliding down another, barely seeming to touch at all.

Redforne's attacks got wilder and heavier, becoming more desperate looking, his mighty overhand swings streaking toward his opponent again and again. The young lord began to look the slightest bit clumsy, as if desperate to break through Theo's simple and effective defense with a display of brute force.

And then Theo broke from his calm defensive stance, half-spinning into a turn to face Redforne mid-swing. His left hand drew the shortsword from his belt, and he shifted as if about to leap forward.

I'm not entirely sure how, given Theo's foot position and momentum at the time, but instead of leaping toward Redforne, he leapt backwards and away from him.

I didn't even have time to question the wisdom of his strange move. Even as my brain was trying to make sense of it, I saw Redforne's off-hand blade scythe purposefully through the space Theo's head had occupied a split second before. Even with how far he'd leapt, the point missed Theo's face by mere inches.

Gulp.

"Cute," Theodore sniffed, sounding unimpressed. He casually walked back to where he'd been standing mere moments before, sword lowered back in place, once again presenting only his side.

Redforne gave an amused half-shrug in reply, face still radiating cocky amusement.

"You gonna do more than throw cute tricks at me all night, or do you want to maybe give up now before you get hurt?"

The look of amusement fell from Redforne's face, and was replaced by an ugly sneer.

"Yeah, I'll just use the best move I know on the first pass," Redforne said, snidely. "What a novel idea."

"Just trying to talk you out of forcing me to commit infanticide is all. You catch your breath a bit, junior...I'll wait."

Redforne glared at him, and attacked anew a fraction of a second later.

The next several passes were slight variations of the first, if breathtaking skill wrapped in a dance of death could be so lightly dismissed by such a description.

Both would step away from each other and pause after expending about half a minute's worth of effort, testing each other out. Theo was still calmly deflecting everything that Redforne was throwing at him, but Redforne didn't appear to be getting frustrated or upset. Each studied the other warily between flurries of activity, as if lost in peaceful contemplation.

During one pass, Theo became very animated after Redforne's third swing, parrying the blows fully instead of gently deflecting them. He advanced one step, and then another, launching several powerfully vicious attacks of his own. Redforne was forced to retreat about a half dozen steps before they disengaged. Theo calmly took a few steps back as well, chuckling loudly enough to be heard.

Redforne scowled, assumed his guard position once more, and just as quickly they were back at it.

Just as it was starting to look like the two swordsmen would fight each other to a standstill, Redforne shifted his body slightly, took two tentative steps backwards and froze for the briefest moment.

And then, in a manner nearly identical to how he'd done it in the Circles that afternoon, his left hand sent his sword sailing high into the air. An instant later he rushed Theo, armed with a single sword.

Theo whipped his sword above his head sharply, knocking the flying blade out of the air and sending it to a nearby corner of the room where it landed with a clatter. His off-hand sword moved swiftly, to fend off the attack being mounted by Redforne with the blade he still possessed.

Redforne all but ignored his knocked-down weapon. With both hands on the grip of the gleaming sword he still held, the curly-haired youth gave a small battle-cry as he brought it down sharply, striking Theo's defensively positioned shortsword with such force that it made my teeth ache just to hear it.

Theo gave an exclamation of pain.

Instantly, his strike finished, Redforne dove to the floor rolling toward his fallen sword, narrowly avoiding a devastating follow-up swing from Theo. A few tumbling, acrobatic leaps later and Redforne was on his feet, crouching in the corner of the room. Carefully watching the other swordsman, the young lord's empty hand quested along the stone floor for the sword that Theo had batted out of the air.

The attack hadn't made it past Theo's defenses, but it hadn't been intended to. It was an attack that was directed at the sword itself, and the arm holding it.

Redforne probably saw the same thing I did – Theo had the clenched jaw and pallor of someone in extreme pain. Small beads of sweat were beginning to form on his forehead and upper lip. He'd been forced to block a two-handed swing entirely with his injured left, and even though he tried not to acknowledge the injury, it was obvious to anyone who knew what to look for that he was hurt.

As if for added emphasis, a thin line of blood began to trickle down to his elbow from underneath the high sleeve of his shirt.

"Yeah," Redforne laughed, giving Theo an arch little smirk from across the room. "Thought so."

He all but flew at Theo, both swords flashing before him.

Theo attempted to continue presenting only his side, but Redforne's new strategy made that all but impossible now. The black-garbed lord constantly shifted and turned, moving around the larger swordsman to change the position of his attack.

Gone were the fancy spinning moves, the large forceful arcs that Theo had been deflecting up to that point. These were precise strokes, lunges, and some sword movements that I didn't even recognize...all of which seemed designed to force Theo's arms to work much harder than they had up to that point.

Maybe I was the only person in all of Harael who could have detected the subtle changes in my friend's expression and poise, but I knew. Even as Theo projected the same stoic calm he'd shown at the beginning of the fight, I knew...

Theo was worried.

He was not even attempting to mount any sort of offense, and had a look of intense concentration as he parried or deflected these new attacks from Redforne. The sweat from effort and pain was clearly standing out on his face now, and I could see the slightest hint of a wince every time I saw him use his left arm.

I sat there high up on the wall, watching helplessly and cursing my impotence.

And then, once again, Redforne made a calculated retreat backwards before sending his off-hand blade up into the air, rushing at Theo a moment later.

Gods, but I was getting tired of seeing him do that.

As he had the time before, Theo made as if to bat it out of the air and away from him. This time, Redforne's approach was much different than before. Both of Redforne's hands were gripping his remaining sword, but with the blade point extending before him like a lance.

There was a clang as Theo sent the airborne sword sailing away once more, twisting sideways as he did so to avoid the oncoming spear-like attack. Then, after a quick cut at Redforne's knees, he practically threw himself atop the young lord in an effort to tie him up. If even partially successful, he could maneuver Redforne away from his fallen sword, which meant that Theo would suddenly possess a distinct advantage, injury or no.

Redforne moved to embrace the oncoming attack, and once more slid around the space Theo occupied, in that serpentine manner of his, somehow ending up behind him. I watched as the point of Redforne's remaining sword snaked around Theo's shoulder, gleaming at his throat a mere eye-blink later.

Theo's longsword slid upwards from his chest and purposefully wedged itself into the nearly non-existent space between his neck and Redforne's own razor-sharp steel. An instant later, Theo's biceps were straining to push the gleaming sword edge away from his neck, a feat that it appeared he was more than capable of performing, despite his injured left arm. Redforne's blade slowly yielded to Theo's superior strength.

And then it yielded far too quickly.

Practically letting go of his blade, Redforne allowed Theo's own muscles to propel his arms and longsword forward due to the unexpected lack of resistance. Redforne's left hand had snuck to Theo's back in order to assist my friend's sudden momentum, and he shifted his own stance in a confident, practiced manner.

Theo's legs connected solidly with the younger swordsman's outstretched limbs, causing Theo to lurch forward unsteadily, his feet parting company with the ground below them.

And as Theo was in the air, falling, I saw Redforne leap up, positioning his own body directly over the falling form of my friend, his knees protruding below him.

Theo slammed into the floor, already in the process of rolling away so he might put some distance between them.

Redforne's knees, driven by the weight of the rest of his body, connected with Theo's head. There was a sharp crack.

The two individuals collapsed in a tangle, and it was Redforne who recovered first. He hopped back up just high enough to allow himself to fall, extending his elbow in the same way he'd done with his knees. His back obscured my view of Theo's upper body, but I could hear the dull thud of impact as Redforne's elbow connected with its target.

A second time he raised himself up high enough to bring his elbow down upon Theo's head with a sickening thud. And again.

"Theo!" I cried.

Barely hesitating and not sparing me a glance, Redforne took his single sword and raised it over his head, still sprawled atop Theo's struggling form, further obscuring him from view.

He brought the pommel of the sword down swiftly, like a steel battering ram. I heard rather than saw the solid, gleaming metal smack against Theo's temple.

Theodore's right hand released its grip, and his sword clattered apologetically as it fell a half-inch onto the floor.

Chapter 22

REDFORNE STOOD, REVEALING the prone figure of my friend. Theo's eyes were closed, and there was blood marring his forehead and most of his right ear.

"Pity. A brilliant, brilliant swordsman," he said, sounding out of breath but still grinning mightily, "with appallingly bad taste in friends."

"No!" I shouted, fingers attempting to dig themselves into the stone ledge that supported me, "Theo!"

"Oh come now. He's not dead. See?" Redforne said, savagely kicking Theo in his exposed side with the toe of his boot.

Theo didn't make a sound or even twitch, despite the horribly loud sound of Redforne's foot connecting with his torso.

"Well, okay...I suppose you'll just have to take my word for it. I must say, that was quite fun...he almost nicked me on that third pass there," he chuckled, his face unwilling to part with the grin he'd fixed upon it.

"Eagan, look...let's-"

"And even though he is still alive, I'm afraid that he probably can't hear you right now. Still, I suppose you'd like to say something, hey?"

I looked at him, uncomprehending.

"Don't want to say goodbye to your friend? For shame. Ah well, I guess you're not the sentimental type," he said, adjusting his grip on the sword he hadn't sent sailing through the air during the fight. He stood straight-backed, and put a single foot on top of Theo's chest, extending his arm so that his sword point touched the ground about six inches away from the big man's exposed neck.

"Redforne! Stop!"

"One…" he said simply, looking upwards at me.

Gods! I crouched there, frozen, not knowing what to do.

"Please, Eagan!"

"Are you sure you don't want to say goodbye?" he asked, bowing his head slightly to get a better view of his sword and the helpless swordsman underfoot. "Two . . ."

I have utterly no idea how I was able to get down to the floor so quickly.

Hands scraping against rock, the sudden pain in my knees and hips, drawing my saber and shortsword, running over the hard stone cobbles, screeching a furious sort of battle cry…I'm sure these things happened, but I can't really remember them at all.

The only thing I remember was this overwhelming sense of hatred, an impossibly strong need to succumb to insane berserk rage.

And so, before the word 'three' had escaped Redforne's lips, he found himself having to defend against a red-hazed onslaught of viciousness I hadn't even known I was capable of. His sword removed itself from the vicinity of Theo's neck in order to parry the multitude of savage swings that I began throwing at him.

Snarling, I lashed out again and again, spinning and turning, left and right, utterly lost in my own zeal to destroy this man who had threatened the life of my friend.

I swung countless times, putting everything I had into each swing. Dozens of blows rained down on the object of my hatred from every possible angle, each strike bringing with it a sharp ringing sound. Not a moment passed that didn't see me swinging, turning, exploding with anger at my foe.

Hours seemed to pass as I swung at him hundreds, perhaps thousands of times.

Though oblivious at first, the part of me that was 'me' began to emerge from my scarlet fog of rage, noticing a few things. Important things.

I noticed stitches in my side, and the sweat cascading from my forehead. Rage requires energy to feed it, and even the most athletic of individuals would be hard pressed to maintain that level of aggression for more than a minute or so. Judging from how I now felt, I'd had more than my fair share of minutes already.

The other thing I noticed was that the savage, primal, berserker part of me needn't have bothered getting all worked up. Redforne was unmarked, having blocked each of the dozens of blows calmly and expertly with his single sword, one right after the other.

My main-hand saber felt exceedingly heavy just then, and I let it linger upon the edge of Redforne's blade as he gently parried the latest of my flagging offensive. We stared over our crossed blades at each other, the only sound being my ragged, gasping breaths, my chest pumping like furnace bellows. A delighted grin lit up Redforne's face.

"Yeah!" he cried, exultant. "*That's* the spirit!"

And it occurred to me that I was about to die.

He calmly stepped to the side a few paces with his eyes still on me, his single sword still crossing mine defensively, moving away from where Theo lay. It was almost as though Redforne did not wish to risk accidentally stepping on him or involving him further, though whether out of respect or simply so there would be more room for footwork, I couldn't tell. I noticed, as well, that he happened to be moving in the direction of his discarded second sword.

I leapt at him, moving swiftly toward the patch of floor where his sword lay, hoping that I might get close enough to kick it away, denying him a second blade to fight me with. It was already a hopeless fight, I knew, but two swords versus one was an advantage that I couldn't ignore at this point, now that I was thinking again. Maybe I would be able to last longer by going completely defensive against his single blade.

The point was moot. He slipped under my attack with a roll and scooped the sword up from where it lay before I could even get halfway to it. I stopped my advance abruptly, watching him return to his feet and spin about into a flamboyant and cocky guard position, a variation of his usual one.

"There," he said, taking a deep breath in through his nose as if savoring some delicious aroma, slowly exhaling with exaggerated calm and contentment. "Isn't this nice? Doesn't this feel better, us here like this? Both of us armed, we finish this like men of honor, uninterrupted...just you and I."

There was a sharp series of thuds that came from my ruined door, like someone urgently pounding on it with a closed fist. I heard a deep, muffled voice call out what I believed to be my name.

Raptor-like, Redforne's head snapped toward the door.

"Damn it," he said, sounding more annoyed by the timing than actually concerned.

"Cyrus!" I yelled as loudly as I could manage. "Help!"

"Of course. With everything else having gone awry, why would this be any different?" Redforne shook his head almost imperceptibly, and gave me a look of disgust before taking a step forward, attacking with a simple lunge.

I parried while leaping sideways, avoiding his fairly obvious thrust.

He stepped back, and so did I.

It was lazy, and wasn't the sort of attack that was meant to get through at all. He just wanted to make sure I was ready, and that he had my attention.

Then, he began.

As with anything I take pride in, I like to think that I know how to fence reasonably well. I'd fought in several duels, which takes a certain amount of grit and determination, given the possibility of injury or death. I know what I'm doing, I guess you could say.

I've never been more baffled, though, than that moment when the fight with Redforne became serious.

Redforne's attacks seemed almost unconcerned, lackadaisical. And *alien!* I mean, you spend years of your life learning certain moves – how to block them, how to employ them. What certain moves are good for, in what manner they're weak, things like that.

I wasn't seeing anything I recognized.

Whenever I saw something that *did* seem familiar it would either be coming from some angle that was clearly impossible for a move like that, or it turned out to be a completely different move than I'd thought.

Sometimes I had to scramble clumsily to one side or another in a panic, because both of my swords had somehow gotten tied up at the exact same moment. Other times I would move to block a sinister looking strike angled at my head, my sword encountering nothing but empty air. I'd find myself reacting to one movement being made by Redforne, only to see it turn into something else completely, forcing me to correct my movements in a manner that was likely to make me stumble or turn awkwardly. He'd make gentle swipes that were insultingly casual, yet that were well placed enough that I had to take them seriously or risk being cut.

Once, as I moved my off-hand shortsword to block one of these unexpected thrusts, I accidentally cut a shallow scratch on my left leg with my own sword tip.

Between passes he would give me a mere second's respite, during which the only sounds that could be heard were my ragged breathing as well as the urgent thumping coming from the door. Both were getting louder.

Through it all, Redforne managed to maintain a look of joyous glee, giggling mirthfully despite the racket coming from the door, laughing occasionally at the sight of me stumbling over my own feet or otherwise being made to look foolish.

As he had with Ismir, he was simply toying with me.

He hadn't marked me with a single wound yet, though the opportunity had existed a dozen or more times. This was what he'd been waiting for his entire life - he wanted to draw it out for as long as possible.

More than that, he wanted me to know it.

Emotionally, I began to fall apart. I knew the hopelessness of trying to beat him, even as I knew I'd refuse to simply lay down and die without so much as a whimper. Cyrus was beating against the door, attempting to get into the room I was trapped in. Would he fare any better against Redforne, or be able to prevent him from killing me?

Not likely, and Redforne knew it as well. He appeared unconcerned that the steady pounding at the door was becoming louder. He was taking his time, looking as though he were savoring every moment. This was retribution he'd been waiting his whole life for, after all...revenge for the death of his family.

That last thought caused an unexpected stir in my own emotions, familiar energy from the coach ride home welling up inside me.

My family. Murdered.

I stopped my defensive posturing abruptly and flung myself at him, snarling, catching him mid-movement and a little surprised. I belted out a cross-body backhand cut that he had to leap backwards to avoid, his swords held high in the air, and I followed it up with a lunge that attempted to see the point of my sword split through his backbone.

Redforne deflected my thrust wide, but I didn't care at that point. Spinning like a dancer while sending my off-hand blade out point-first, I forced him to parry while my heavier sword arced toward his unprotected side. I shouted with effort this time, putting as much force into the blow as I could, as if pinning all of my hopes on this single attack.

He didn't parry. I don't really know what he did - I missed him entirely, with both blades, and the force of my spin caused me to stumble sideways a half-step.

As I attempted to recover myself, I saw Redforne flick his sword toward my exposed head. Unlike his fight with Ismir, he didn't bother to use the flat of his blade.

I felt the sharp metal edge slam into the side of my temple with an impact that seemed to rattle the teeth inside my head, and everything flickered dark for a brief moment.

Pain blossomed above my left ear, and a good quantity of blood began to trickle down the side of my head and along my jaw. A lock of blonde hair that had been decorated with a hint of the dark red fluid fell gently to the ground beside me.

In a frighteningly short span of time, I realized I could feel the blood begin to drip from my jaw to my chest. The left side of my face felt different, and I was dizzy.

Cursing, I lurched upright and took two bounding steps toward Redforne, who had taken up his deadly guard position and was awaiting me intently. All but ignoring the silvery blades pointed directly at me, I leapt into the air while bringing my sword arm tightly into my body, holding my left out behind me for balance. Upon touching the floor I sprang forward in a full extension, the point of my sword traveling at a speed that surprised even me. It was a desperate kind of jumping lunge, which I may have actually made up right there on the spot. Whatever it was, it felt violent, it felt solid...it felt right.

It missed completely.

Redforne managed to slide around the sword thrust and brushed past me, to my right, just as I stretched out in my full extension. My flank suddenly exposed, I moved to stand up from my elongated crouch so that I might turn to face him.

The room lurched unexpectedly, which I attributed to dizziness at first. Then, I realized I was still locked in a rather exaggerated and dramatic crouch. I looked down at my right leg, which I couldn't seem to unbend-

Because it now had a sword sticking through it.

About a foot of Redforne's magnificent blade remained visible to me, the rest of it either hidden underneath my leg, or inside of it. The sword had gone completely through, in at the top and out the bottom. This probably meant that it had missed the bone, or simply nicked it. I didn't really care which at the time – I mean, there was a *sword* in my damned *leg!*

The pain didn't even register until I saw it sticking out of me, almost perfectly vertical, making my still bent leg appear as though it were some macabre sword holder. I saw my left hand reach to clutch at it, which made me realize that I'd dropped my own blade upon the floor.

The air around my face was thick with the smell of blood. I could only stare at the column of steel that protruded from my leg. The insistent thumping at the door seemed to grow louder, become more solid.

"Well, as much as I've enjoyed this time we've spent together, Tucat, I'm afraid that this is probably where we say our goodbyes," Redforne said, his voice filled with mock sadness. "You're getting rather sloppy with your attacks now, and that wound you forced me to give you will probably take all of the fun out of things, what with you limping around pathetically. Also, the pounding on the door is starting to concern me...I should probably try to have this all wrapped up by the time your men break the door down, hey?"

"You've got nowhere to go, Redforne," I said through clenched teeth, trying to keep from falling to my side as I maintained the awkward crouch I found myself in. Blazes, did my leg hurt! "You're trapped in here too - only one way out."

"Why, you're right. Or rather, you were. Coming in here, I thought there was but a single entrance and exit, with the exception of the dumb-waiter leading to the kitchen, which I also took pains to disable. However, Lord Haundsing here has shown me a delightful and surprising *new* way out that I hadn't counted on! If it leads outside to – no, wait. It probably leads directly to his keep. Does it? I'll bet it does."

I grimaced, both at the unexpected revelation and at the pain I felt as I pulled experimentally on the hilt of the sword embedded in my thigh. Even that gentle touch sent waves of rippling agony downward.

"Everyone will still know it was you, Redforne, the moment anyone sees you. Hope ambushing me was worth it, you spineless cretin, because the Redforne name will mean less than nothing after this. You're finished."

"Oh, I think not. If even a fraction of what you've said is true, I think there's some wiggle room when it comes to getting into the prince's good graces. And, as far as someone seeing me is concerned, I wonder what would happen if I ran down Lord Haundsing's passage and into his keep, grabbed the first knight I could find, and told them that their master was in dire need of help after being ambushed by the infamous Lord Tucat," he said, grinning slyly. "They rush down here, your fellows break down the door, both you and Lord Haundsing lying there, dead...why, there'll be all kinds of opportunity for entertaining confusion, won't there?"

Theo, as if on cue, began to stir.

Glancing over at my best friend, Redforne appeared about to say something when a staggeringly loud *'boom'* shook the door, small bits of metal and burned wood falling off of the enormous obstacle, which now stood slightly askew.

"Oh yes," laughed Redforne easily, peering over at the door as if fascinated. "I definitely think it's time to finish up here."

I gritted my teeth and yanked on the handle of the sword, which pulled the blade up out of my leg about two inches. White-fringed pain like I'd never known existed shot through me, and I feared I might pass out, even as I braced myself for another pull.

"I do have to hand it to you though, Tucat," he said, pausing for a moment to wipe the blade of his other sword, "I'd had years to put all of this together, plan everything down to the last detail, and still you almost managed to get out of it alive. I must say, even though the outcome was never in doubt, what you managed to pull off at the Circles today was really quite unpredictable."

He sniffed unconcernedly as he inspected his blade and tested its edge with a thumb, presumably in a manner that he'd imagined himself doing for many years. Doubtless, he'd have some sort of clever prepared line to deliver when the time was right, killing me in one of the many dozens of ways he'd visualized since hatching this plan as a young boy. I could almost see him trembling with anticipation and joy.

I wasn't trembling. I was no longer thinking of how terrifying my situation was, how afraid I was, or praying to any of a dozen deities whose sudden thunderous manifestation might prove helpful. I found myself focused on the last words Redforne had spoken aloud. The Circles.

Unpredictable.

A feeling of hope rose up from the center of my chest, followed by a strangled scream of purest agony as I threw every ounce of will into the act of pulling the sword upward and out of my leg. I could feel every inch of the cool steel scraping along the muscles of my thigh. Slight shifts in how I was holding the handle sliced the cut open further on either side of my wound as the blade came upwards and out. Then, about halfway along its length, the blade got thinner and began to glide out, slick with the blood coming out of the newly aggravated wound. The pain caused me to clench my jaw so violently that I feared I might crack a tooth.

I saw the tip of the blade come free, and awkwardly lobbed the bloodied masterpiece away from me, toward the wall. It fell with an ignoble clatter, which caught Redforne's attention. He looked to it, then to me...

And then he smiled cruelly.

"Come now. Let's get about this – your father is waiting," he said, hefting the gleaming blade with exaggerated menace, "as is mine."

Overly dramatic asshole.

He stepped toward me as I glared up at him from my crouch. Then, depending mostly on the muscles of my left leg, I rose and flung my sword arm behind me, putting every scrap of energy I had into an overhand crescent, aimed at Redforne's torso at the point where his neck met his shoulder.

He made the obvious parry with his single longsword, and then countered with his own version of the same thing, blade singing through the air.

I made an awkward leap toward him and to my right, my plan being to avoid the blow entirely. As Redforne's edge came swinging down toward me, I curled forward and tucked my entire lurching, pain-wracked body into a shoulder roll.

A really, really bad one.

It was the sort of shoulder roll that you'd fumble through if you didn't know where to put your sword as you were doing it, the sort of bumbling, inept move that would cause a fencing instructor to wring his hands in frustration.

It was the kind of awkward, clumsy roll that someone like Mouser might do.

I rolled over onto my knees in order to spin back around behind me, still gripping my sword, the position of my arm causing the sword blade to scythe sideways as I turned, quickly.

A quarter-turn in, my arm was nearly wrenched from its socket as my sword edge buried itself deep into the back of Redforne's calf muscle.

"Glaa-" he cried, collapsing mid-spin and falling awkwardly to the ground. The very tip of Redforne's sword altered its course slightly, slicing my vest open near the shoulder before connecting with the floor with a mighty ringing sound.

Still mostly on my back, I pushed with my legs so that I could put some distance between us, ignoring the pain the simple move produced. Though the newest cut had not broken the skin, the front of my shirt clung to me like hot sticky tar as a result of the blood from my head wound. I could still feel it trickling down the side of my cheek, drips falling from the point of my chin with the regularity of a heartbeat.

The pounding at the door was now accompanied by the sound of splintering wood, and I could hear Cyrus urgently calling to me through an opening he'd made in the entrance.

With agonizing slowness, I began to crawl backwards with my arms as well, heading toward the front of the room where my couches and other assorted items of leisure were located. I no longer had my sword, which I'd left buried in Redforne's leg once it had been forcibly wrenched out of my grasp.

I was still struggling to move away when I saw Redforne rise unsteadily, hunched over with his weight on one leg, his face a mixture of confusion and anger. He gingerly moved his damaged leg so that he might inspect it, see what had caused his fall.

I'm pretty certain he didn't expect to see my saber sticking out of him like that, almost perfectly horizontal, no part of it touching the ground. It had struck incredibly deep into the glossy leather of Redforne's thick high-topped boots, which appeared to be holding my blade in place.

From my angle, I was all but certain I'd connected with bone.

Redforne, perhaps seeing things differently from his angle, sneered as he looked at the sword, a fine layer of perspiration covering his face. He raised the leg with my sword in it, hopped uncertainly once or twice, and then sharply brought his own blade down to swat the sword free from his calf.

It was entirely the wrong thing to do.

My sword clattered on the stones behind him, free of its fleshy prison. Myself, I don't know if removing it like that was what caused the damage, or if the damage was there the entire time just waiting for the sword to be removed, but damage there was. And it was substantial.

The simple act of Redforne putting weight on that foot resulted in his leg sheering sideways fractionally, boot buckling at the back. An urgent, closed mouth scream erupted from just below his violently clenched jaw.

A pool of blood appeared on the floor beneath his foot, and began expanding rapidly.

I resumed scrambling away from him, realizing that I'd stopped. Pushing myself up a little with my arms, I tried a similar experiment with my own leg, putting a small amount of weight on it. I was likely in shock, so I probably wasn't even feeling the full extent of the damage to my thigh, but the pain I could feel told me using my leg was a bad idea.

I collapsed back to the floor, and continued to pull myself away from him. Redforne simply stood there staring at me, as if considering.

"Tucat!" He tightened his grip on the sword and hopped once toward me, face twisted with pain. The black, glossy pool of liquid beneath his foot was growing bigger.

"Redforne, you're bleeding! Lie down, you idiot!"

"You think so?" he said, words growing ever uncertain and distant. "You think a little blood loss is gonna stop me? Here? After all I've done? Is *that* what you think?"

He all but slurred his last words. The next hop forward, his foot made the tiniest splashing sound.

Emptied of all of my rage, and horrified at what I was seeing, I felt something akin to guilt very suddenly. Pity.

"Eagan, stop! Your leg-"

"My leg, your leg...irony...*cute!* You're not going to-" he said, hopping once more and then abruptly stopping, as if surprised. His head shot up alertly, as though hearing something, and his eyes began looking around frantically. They had an unfocused quality about them.

He crouched awkwardly with his hands out in front of him, eyes still casting about, face a deathly shade of white. He fell, not by accident, but the kind of controlled fall that you might do in the dark...arms stretched before you to sense where the ground is. The sword, still clutched in his right hand, clinked softly as it touched the ground.

Redforne was fading impossibly fast. As if suddenly finding himself in total blackness, he tilted his head to the side as if about to listen to something.

"Tucat?" he rasped.

"Eagan. Roll onto your back. Get your legs in the air, we need to staunch-"

A sloppy swing from his sword clattered off the stones a foot away from my legs, and he turned his ear toward the sound with a look of expectation.

"Get him? Did...father?"

He didn't sound good at all. My heart squeezed uncomfortably in my chest.

With a tremendous, creaking roar, the bulk of the door finally splintered and gave way, falling to the ground with an earth-shattering thud.

"Milord!" Cyrus cried out, clearly. I saw my captain rush into the darkened room, stepping over the door, his sword drawn. Three small, dart-like arrows were protruding from his shoulder, pinning his half-cloak to his arm, great beads of sweat rolling off of his forehead.

Theo groaned, pushing himself up into a slow roll onto his side. His movement was spotted by Cyrus immediately.

"Haundsing! Son of a *bitch!*" he cried, striding forward with his hand on his sword.

"No!" I gasped from the floor.

I didn't sound so hot either.

"Milord!"

I held my arm up so that he might see where my voice was coming from. "Not him! Haundsing...he's a friend. Cyrus, over here."

An instant later he was kneeling beside me, telling me not to move, warily regarding the figure of Redforne that was stretched out a few feet distant. Redforne's skin was an unholy color, eyes wide, his head rolling gently against the floor in an effort to raise it.

"Bandages! Tourniquet! Cut off the blood he's losing from his leg! Quickly!"

"Lord Tucat, you're bleeding!"

"Get a bloody tourniquet for Redforne!" I shrieked, pulling myself up so that I could crawl on all fours toward the young lord, whose grip on his sword had relaxed completely. *"Now!"*

Cyrus jumped up and bolted to the cupboard where I stashed my various balms and poultices. I finished making my way over to Redforne, pulling the remaining sword from his unresisting hand and tossing it away. It would be a miracle if he had even one swing left in him, but I'd been on the receiving end of a few dozen miracles in the past couple of days, and wasn't interested in taking chances.

I inspected his boot, which had been split open awkwardly, part of the boot actually curling into the deep red wound. Blood was thick, and everywhere.

"Father . . ." I heard Redforne mumble, weakly.

"Relax, Eagan. Save your strength," I said in a hushed tone. Then, angling my face away from him, I called out behind me. "I need a knife to cut this boot! Hurry!"

"Father, I'm-" he began, impossibly quietly, just as Cyrus came skidding along the floor beside me on his knees, bearing bundles of bandages and rope. He looked at the wound, the blood surrounding us, and his eyes went wide.

"I'm sorry," I heard Redforne whisper.

Chapter 23

I REALIZED THAT hot, pungent tea was being pushed into my hands, and I looked up from the section of floor I'd been staring at in order to acknowledge the gift.

"Thanks," I said, wrapping both hands around the sides of the mug, concluding from how pleasant the warmth was that my fingers had somehow become cold during the time I'd been sitting there in my chair. Odd, I thought, since my sitting room had a fireplace that was burning away merrily.

Talia gave me a slow nod, looking concerned. I suppose I looked a wreck, still garbed in my blood-soaked clothing. The chair I was sitting on would never be the same after this night.

Nor would I, I suspected.

I stared into my tea for a moment. I was in the middle of debating whether or not to take a sip, how much of a sip to take, if throwing the cup I held across the room might make me feel any better, and whether any thoughts concerning tea even mattered at all...when I felt a gentle touch on my still bloodied left shoulder.

Looking, I could see Talia's hand squeezing a message of unspoken sympathy, a gesture that was oddly comforting. I put my hand over hers and gave her a wan smile and grateful look, which she returned before turning and quietly heading back in the direction of the dining hall, the room where she had herded the dozen or so of my knights and other staff members. Once she'd learned what had happened she instantly took over, rounding up everyone with a polite but firm hand and escorting them there. Not just that, either - from what I gathered she was also calming everyone down, easing their concerns, and answering their questions.

Which left me alone in the sitting room, with nothing but my thoughts.

I sighed softly.

Dead. Redforne had tried to kill me even as he lay dying - even as I tried to stop his life's blood from spilling onto my stone floor. Unable to see, barely conscious near the end, he'd still tried to lash out with his bare hands in an attempt to do me in. He had hated me that much.

I couldn't hate him, though. Mere hours ago, I might have been capable of such a thing...possibly even going so far as to be celebrating news of Redforne's death. It was staggering just how wildly your perceptions could shift in the span of a few hours.

As I'd watched Redforne standing there, bleeding from a mortal wound I'd inflicted, I had a flash of insight...saw very clearly how his own situation seemed to mirror my own. Watching him, I thought of my own pain, my own sudden burning need for revenge and retribution. I imagined what it might be like to feel yourself fading away, your sword hand unfinished inches away from the objective you'd molded your whole life around.

Having only had the span of a couple of hours to come to terms with what the Prince had told me, I could likely only understand the barest fraction of what had been going through his head. It was enough.

Additionally, with Redforne's death I knew that any potential to negotiate with the Prince for information about my family's murder had slipped through my fingers. That was almost as bad as everything else.

I attempted to run my fingers through my hair, only to rediscover the bandage there, preventing me from doing so. It was wrapped tight enough that I shouldn't have been able to ignore it.

The cut to my head had made Cyrus nervous enough to have his fellow house knights go into the streets at a truly ungodly hour, offering a hundred gold marks for any healer who might be persuaded to come into my keep to treat me. They found one rather quickly, too...one who seemed to share Cyrus's sense of urgency upon seeing me. Never before had I heard 'thick-headed' used in such complimentary terms, or accompanied by such a look of frank astonishment.

Generally speaking, if someone has cause to look at any part of your head and comment on the condition of the bone they're able to *see,* you've been hurt rather badly.

"Lord Tucat?" an unsympathetic voice I didn't recognize called out from the hall.

I looked to the doorway and saw yet another crown knight I didn't recognize standing there, regarding me.

"Yes, sir knight?" I responded, tiredly.

"I'm looking for Cyrus Crowfoot, and any of my fellow knights that may be with him."

"They're downstairs in the basement hall," I said, turning back to my tea and my dismal, depressing thoughts. Then, grunting quietly to myself I added, "Follow the hallway you're in until you get to the back of the keep, turn right and keep going until you get to the wine bottles, left, then right and down the stairs."

"My lord," he said, nodding perfunctorily before turning and disappearing from view, presumably to walk the path I had described to him. There were already four knights down there with Cyrus, I thought bitterly. How many more were needed to ask him the same five questions, over and over again?

Then again, Cyrus hadn't wanted to bring the crown knights into the picture at all – I'd been the one to insist on that. It was necessary, I reasoned, given the circumstances of the past twelve hours or so. Considering the duel earlier that day, for Redforne to simply show up dead somewhere, well, you would have to be some sort of idiot not to make the connection.

No, I needed the crown knights there right away, I reasoned. Once it was obvious that there was nothing that could be done to revive Redforne, it was the first thing I had told Cyrus to do.

And then, realizing in a panic that my best friend was still groaning softly a dozen feet away from me and attempting to rise, I made it his second priority.

Theo seemed pretty much okay, though he'd suffered several hits to the head in his encounter with Redforne. They'd been serious enough to knock him unconscious a while, but Theo didn't regard them as being serious enough to prevent him from standing up. Cyrus and I both helped him to his feet and walked him over to the still open passageway connecting his keep to mine.

Quite the sight we must have made – me practically soaked with blood, Cyrus with several painful-looking darts still sticking out of his shoulder, both of us on either side of the burly swordsman who was sporting an unfocused look on his bruised and bleeding face.

The confusion I'd seen in his eyes and the occasional look of puzzlement made it clear that he considered it a miracle we both still lived. I couldn't have agreed more.

I hadn't felt there was time to brief Cyrus thoroughly, so once we'd seen Theo through the passageway and seen the false wall close itself behind him I stressed the importance of not mentioning the presence of Lord Haundsing to anyone.

He'd agreed instantly, and while I didn't notice it quite as strongly as I had in the days previous, I could still detect a small amount of hurt in his expression and his body language.

Cyrus has always been lousy at hiding his feelings, one of the reasons that I was becoming more and more concerned the longer he remained in my basement, being questioned by the crown knights. His part in this entire affair had been minimal, and yet he'd been down there with them for nearly twice as long as I'd been.

They'd come, they'd asked me their questions. They'd removed the body, or the victim, or whatever they'd taken to calling the remains of-

The boy I had killed.

In all that had gone on in my life up to this point it was something of a miracle that it hadn't happened before, and yet there it was. I was now a killer.

I was no stranger to death. Given my circumstances, I'd had more than a passing familiarity with the concept. And yet this was different. This was something that I had done, not merely something that I'd been witness to. As with before, it felt that I was a completely changed person, but this was so utterly unlike my previous encounters with death as to have nothing in common with them whatsoever.

I used to think that I knew how I'd feel if something like that were to happen to me. I'd say to myself 'Well, it was either him or me. I did what I had to do.' and I'd accept my words at face value. Life would go on. I wouldn't blame myself, or let it bother me.

Yeah, right.

It was too new to make any sense of, even now, this impossible feeling that had been thrust upon me. I wanted to scream, to cry, to run out into the streets, demand an explanation of the gods, all at once. I wanted to reduce the walls of my keep to a fine powder with nothing but my fists, to dash my head to pieces against the cold stone floor. I wished to become invisible, to simply lie down in some neglected corner of the world and wither away into nothingness. It was like being so tired that you can't even find the energy to fall asleep.

Feeling this way, it had been tough to maintain my composure in the face of the questions posed by the knights once they'd arrived. They'd been officious, rude, and I'd quickly found myself resenting their suspicious looks as they asked me what had happened, or reviewed with me the order they happened in. Poor Cyrus hadn't had so much as a wink of sleep these past two days. I wondered how he was holding up in the face of questioning by a group of inquisitive crown knights.

As if summoned by my thoughts, Cyrus appeared in the doorway at that moment, flanked by two of the knights I'd allowed into my keep earlier. He had an apologetic look on his face.

"Cyrus," I nodded.

"Milord," he said, attempting an awkward bow from the door. "I fear I must leave you for some time. In my absence, might I recommend that Kavi take my place? I've kept her well informed of my responsibilities-"

"What?" I asked, standing up suddenly from my chair, or at least attempting to. My leg buckled under the stress I had put on it, and I gripped the armrests of my chair in order to avoid falling. The effort had suddenly made me dizzy.

Cyrus seemed torn between leaping forward to assist me and remaining where he was.

"We're taking this man to the palace, Lord Tucat."

I looked to the mustached knight who had spoken, easing myself back down into my chair.

"For what purpose, exactly?"

"This is a grave matter, and there are some additional questions that we need him to answer for us," said the other knight.

"Questions you've left at the palace and forgot to bring with you?" I asked.

"There were inconsistencies in the information he gave us," the first said, simply. "We'd like to go over some of the details with him."

"Inconsistencies? Why drag him all the way back to the palace?"

The first knight gave his surroundings a meaningful look, followed by a meaningful look at me, as if that alone might answer the question.

Of course...they wanted home turf advantage, so they could be even *more* rude and officious...possibly even use some *new* interrogation techniques they'd been dying to try out.

I closed my eyes so that I could safely press my fingers against them, suddenly exasperated beyond all reason.

"Cyrus?"

"Milord."

"You told them everything, right? The burning smell, you coming down to check on me...having to use an explosive charge to break down my door. All that?"

"Yes Milord. Several times."

"You mentioned that you didn't even see the fight, that Redforne was bleeding as you came through the door?"

"Yes Milord."

I nodded, turning back to the first knight who had spoken.

"I'm afraid that I require Cyrus here with me, gentlemen. Terribly sorry, but if there are further questions you have of my captain, they'll have to be asked here. I myself cannot think of a single question that might somehow be answered more *correctly* simply because it was asked at the palace instead of here in my keep."

The knight's mustached lip twitched, and his face showed the beginnings of an arrogant sneer.

"Your captain's whereabouts were unaccounted for during a significant amount of time after the duel, and being your captain he may be in possession of information that he doesn't wish to share within these walls. I'm afraid I must insist that he come with us. My lord," he said, his voice containing the barest trace of an accusation.

The 'my lord' he tacked on to the end had also contained just enough of a pause to be mildly offensive.

Clearly, this one thought he had something. That, or he wished to flex some of his authoritative muscle at the expense of someone who appeared to be in an awkward situation.

Crown knights report directly to one of four preceptors, who in turn report directly to the prince. In terms of the hierarchy within the city, preceptors were the only individuals who outranked lords aside from the prince, since it was their job to enforce certain laws and precepts set forth by the prince in whichever of the four quadrants of the city they'd been assigned

Reporting directly to someone who outranks a lord can have an effect on someone's perception of their importance within the grand scheme of things after a while. To put it succinctly - crown knights can be real pricks sometimes.

Clearly, this was one of those cases.

Crown knights *were* representatives of the prince, true, and as a result lords tended to extend every courtesy to them, mostly because it was just better for everyone that way.

It was not, however, mandatory.

Clearly, this man had no idea what kind of day I'd just had.

"Cyrus, you were right. Fetching crown knights was a horrible idea," I said, leaning forward in my seat and attempting to stand much more carefully than I had before.

"Kind of you to say so, Milord," he said tiredly and with just a hint of amusement, the two knights on either side of him suddenly affecting looks of surly indignation. The remaining three knights appeared just then as well, emerging from the basement that had served as their interrogation room and remaining in the hallway behind Cyrus and the other two knights.

"Right, well I shall pay close attention to such suggestions in future. Could you perhaps ask Talia to fetch me a cane or some such thing? Oh wait, I still have my sword...that's handy. I don't think I'd be able to make it to the carriage by myself with this injured leg."

Standing awkwardly, I grimaced as I began hobbling over to where they stood at the doorway.

"Lord Tucat!" said the mustached knight, perplexed. "What are you doing?"

"I'm coming to the palace with you, obviously," I snorted, reaching out to Cyrus for support. He stepped forward to help me stay upright, looking concerned.

"Y-you're not under arrest, my lord," a third knight managed to stammer. "We don't require your presence at this time. If we need you at the palace, we can summon you."

"Oh, I know that. However, I believe I mentioned that I can't be without my captain at this time. Besides, I'm not coming along to answer questions...I'm going to see the prince." I unbuckled my belt and removed my sword from my hip, keeping it sheathed in order that I might lean on it. The pain in my leg caused me to grit my teeth. "Come on, let's get about it."

"Prince Tenarreau is terribly busy at the moment, Lord Tucat, preparing for tomorrow's ceremony and all," the mustached knight said, smirking. "Doubtless you'd forgotten. Perhaps if you wished to come down in a few days ..."

"He'll see me tonight," I said, shrugging slightly and motioning to Cyrus that I was okay to stand on my own. "Of this I have no doubt. Well? Shall we go?"

"My lord," one of the other three knights at the back called over the heads of his fellows. "If you insist on accompanying us, we shall wait outside. Doubtless you'll want to change into some more suitable attire."

"No need, no need," I waved irritatedly, limping with my makeshift cane through them and toward the door.

"But," he said, perplexed, "you've been wounded! You're covered in blood!"

"Quite right. Very astute observation, keen eye...I can see why they chose you."

"You can't just show up at the palace covered in blood!"

"Really? You going to stop me?"

"But, the prince-" he ventured awkwardly, not really knowing what to say.

"He'll notice? Why, by the gods, I suppose you're correct! He'll see me in the very same clothing he saw me wearing a few hours ago, and he'll say 'Good gracious, what happened?' And you know what I'll tell him?"

Several knights shook their heads 'No', now looking quite uncertain of themselves.

"Why, I'll tell him exactly what I've told you," I half-shouted, allowing annoyance to creep into my voice. "Word for word in some cases, I'm sure. And when I'm done describing how I was set upon in my own keep, how I was thrust into this harrowing ordeal, how I barely managed to stay alive...I'll mention sending Cyrus out to fetch some crown knights once it was all over, as a good citizen of Harael should.

"I'll also be sure to mention how, once you arrived at my keep, you insisted that my captain, who has not slept a wink in two days and who nevertheless managed to save my life, accompany you back to the palace for questioning, all apparently because some statements from a sleep deprived man didn't make sense to you. This, of course, despite my protests over his wellbeing, and the fact that he'd done *nothing* wrong.

"I'll mention that you were obviously suspicious of some diabolical plot involving Cyrus kidnapping Lord Redforne as he left the Circles today, snatching the *master swordsman* off the street in broad daylight. I'll mention how reasonable such concerns are, given that you noticed Cyrus was somehow able to weld the *inside* of my door shut from *outside* the room, presumably doing so in order that I might not be interrupted as I sliced my head open and stuck a sword clear through my leg in front of Lord Redforne, nearly *dying* from what are obviously self-inflicted injuries.

"Then, once I've mentioned all of those things, I plan on throwing myself at the prince's feet and begging for tender mercy, for I can see now how suspicious and damning this all looks, and how *reasonable* people like yourself might conclude that carting my captain away for questioning is a perfectly logical thing to do."

The silence was deafening. The only sound was the occasional pop of burning wood coming from the fireplace. No one spoke or moved, and the knights all wore the same kind of uncomfortable, wary look.

"Come on, then," I said, once it was obvious that none of the knights wished to be the first to contribute to our conversation. "We can all take my carriage, I've got one that should have enough room for all of us. What say you? Let's see what the prince has to say about this comical series of events that a few overzealous knights have forced me to bring to his attention."

Looks were exchanged, and a few of the knights shifted their feet uncomfortably.

"I suppose that there would be no harm in allowing him to stay here," the mustached knight said in a distinctly surly tone, "provided that we can come back to ask further questions later."

"I'm afraid that his duties will make setting up an appointment impossible - I work him shamelessly," I said, hobbling over to the pompous knight so that I could stand before him. He appeared to be the one in charge, having spoken the most. "So I'm afraid that if you have questions that need answering, you'd better ask them in the next ten minutes or so. I'll be ordering him to bed soon." I looked from face to face inquisitively. "Anything else?"

Tight-lipped and furious, Mustache shook his head. He was quite obviously not used to having his authority challenged.

"Well if that's all then, sir knights, I'm afraid that I must ask you all to leave. I do thank you for coming by and taking care of the body, as well as your sensitivity during this terribly awkward ordeal, which-"

"When Preceptor Borshank finds out we've-" began Mustache.

"Do not presume to interrupt me ever again!" I shouted fiercely, drawing myself up and thrusting my face into his, the tiniest bit of spittle flying from my lips onto his cheek. "I don't care who you *think* you are, you *shut your mouth* when I'm talking! You come into *my* keep, look down your nose at me as if I were some drunk in the street, imply that I'm either lying or a simpleton by asking me the same questions five different times, and all but insult me by *instructing* me what I may or may not do with my own staff! Were I in better health, sir knight, I would be inclined to *beat you to death!"*

Maybe he didn't really deserve it, but I'd had enough of just about everything at that point. His eyes were wide as he stared at me, mouth hanging open. The other knights were looking about the same.

So was Cyrus, actually.

"Leave! Get out!" I bellowed. "*Goodbye* already! Tell your preceptor that, if he wishes either myself or my captain to answer the same question again and again, he can bloody well come down himself to ask it!"

A few awkward moments later, they shuffled down the hallways and out of sight, swords and armored uniforms clanking noisily. There was the sound of some brief muttering just as the front door was closing behind them.

"Wow," Cyrus gulped, sounding impressed.

"Rough day. They pissed me off," I said, wincing as I once again sat down in my chair.

"I've just never seen you upset like that, or seen *anyone* talk that way to crown knights before," he said, grinning. "Is it okay if I make you my own personal hero from this point forward?"

"Cyrus, after all you've managed to do for me this week, you have my permission to do whatever you like. I suggest you begin by confining yourself to quarters and seeing how long you can sleep in one sitting. Say, I didn't get a chance to ask...how is it that you're still awake at all? For that matter, how is it you thought to check in on me in the basement?"

In answer, he held out his arms to me. They were trembling noticeably.

"Vimroot oil," he said ruefully. "It didn't occur to me at the Circles that the oil you'd brought with you would be so pure – the stuff I usually encounter is thinned out a great deal. I was cursing my oversight as I lay in bed, exhausted and unable to sleep. Then later, I smelled smoke and decided to investigate."

Pure dumb luck is triumphant once more.

"A substantial bit of good fortune. Damn it," I said, shifting forward and leaning on my sword once more, "I shouldn't have sat back down again."

"Agreed," Cyrus said, helping me up with his right arm. "We should get you upstairs and off your leg. You could probably use a healthy dose of sleep yourself."

"Can't. No time," I said simply, leaning forward in order to stand. "Could you go get Kavi for me, please? Aside from yourself, she's about the best hand with a sword around here from what I recall."

"Milord? What do you need her for?"

"I wasn't bluffing about going to see the prince, Cyrus." I grimaced slightly as I gingerly walked forward. "Call me paranoid, but I'd rather not go anywhere alone right now. I need to get down to the palace. Tenarreau let me know some of his plans, and I'm sure he was half expecting me to contact him this evening...but given what's happened I most certainly need to talk to him before tomorrow. Actually, it was stupid to bring crown knights into this, considering I could have gone directly to the prince and explained things."

"I'll fetch Kavi, and get her to arrange a carriage for you," he nodded.

"Tell her to take her time. Now that there's no need for dramatic threats involving bloodstained garments, I think I shall change clothes quickly first."

"Right away Milord," he said, walking toward the hallway.

"Cyrus?"

He stopped mid-stride and turned to look at me.

"Thank you," I said, hoping my voice was capable of carrying some hint of the gratitude I felt.

Cyrus seemed a little startled by that, then gave me a quick grin and a nod before turning and continuing on his way, disappearing from view.

Well, really...the guy accidentally trips a trap in my hallway while trying to rescue me, and doesn't even think to stop long enough to pull the painful wooden darts from his shoulder, so great was his concern for me. If that doesn't deserve a 'thank you', I don't know what does.

I began what promised to be a slow, painful trip up to my bedroom in order to find some loose-fitting clothing and to redress my bandages. As I walked, I wondered exactly what the prince's reaction would be when I told him what had happened.

I no longer had a strong bargaining position with respect to the offer he'd made earlier that evening – Redforne was dead, and obviously any agreement that involved me staying away from him was null and void.

Would Tenarreau still be willing to share information? Would he even believe my side of the story?

How understanding would he be regarding this rather large hiccup in his plans? Would he become annoyed, perhaps suspicious of the timing, and seek to punish me somehow?

One way or another, I was sure I'd be finding out soon.

Chapter 24

THE PALACE RECEPTION room had been lovingly and breathtakingly transformed, as it was every year, into a display of such opulent perfection that only the most hardened and jaded soul would fail to be impressed by the sheer beauty of it all. Lords and ladies were everywhere, all wearing their very best in pretentious ornamental finery. Everyone moved smoothly and eloquently, as if attempting to be worthy of where they stood at any given moment, mingling amongst each other like bejeweled butterflies.

Puke.

It's rather difficult to be sarcastic and miserable when surrounded by something like that, but I managed. If you're ever interested in learning the trick, a good portion of the secret involves making certain that you've had a sword shoved through your leg the night before, or possibly slammed into the side of your head. Both, if you can arrange it.

Finding out your entire family had been murdered instead of dying from natural causes like you'd originally thought, and then being unable to find out anything further from the one fellow who might have more information...that also helps.

I watched the other lords and ladies below me from the balcony, my limited mobility and dark mood preventing me from doing likewise. Very few people came over to visit me or say hello, given the out of the way location I'd chosen. Or perhaps the vibe I was projecting. Those who did come by merely stayed long enough to nod, inquire about my health, make their excuses and leave. Undoubtedly several dozen versions of what transpired between Redforne and myself were already circulating mercilessly, and I could only guess as to their contents.

Perhaps I was still numb with shock, but I found myself not really caring what anyone thought. I sat alone, having told Tarryl to wait for me with the carriage, preferring to limp to my seat without the benefit of any assistance. In truth, I wanted nothing more than to be alone.

Surrounded by glittering beauty and starry-eyed lords and ladies bursting with excitement and eager anticipation, I felt very alone indeed.

My mind went in circles as I sat there waiting, wisps of thought again and again returning to Redforne and all that had occurred the previous evening. It seemed like I could not go five minutes without experiencing the pang of realization anew, this feeling of overwhelming remorse, sadness, and anger. At times, my thoughts would wander - seeing some lord I recognized, or wondering idly what sort of delectable food item a servant was in the process of bringing out...and the very absence of that feeling would suddenly hit me like cold water, reminding me once again of Redforne, and pulling me back into the familiar, frustrated despair.

Hours passed as I sat there, unmoving, my chin resting on the banister of the balcony overlooking the hundreds of people below. I barely even moved when the trumpet fanfare finally announced the arrival of the prince, the man who would be meting out both fortune and misery this day, news both good and bad.

With the diminutive prince's arrival there was an immediate cessation of mingling as everyone focused on finding a seat, or returning to a seat they'd claimed earlier. Though there were hundreds of seats available on the main

324

floor, a few dozen unhappy lords and ladies would doubtless be forced up to the balcony area where I had parked myself.

Tenarreau didn't simply show up from behind the far curtain and sit down on his throne...there was far too much pomp and ceremony involved for something as simple as that. He and his entourage walked into the grand hall slowly, his feet moving to a regular and steady cadence that was being belted out by invisible trumpeters, his every move somber and serious. It took him three full minutes to traverse a distance it would have taken me fifteen seconds to cover at a comfortable walk, a fact that had nothing to do with the length of Tenarreau's legs.

Just seeing him was enough for me to recall my last meeting with him the night before.

I'd been escorted to him in record time once I'd identified myself at the palace, and when I entered his study I found him appearing distracted and preoccupied. He'd looked at me, said my name, and waited for me to speak.

I wished I'd been in possession of news he'd wanted to hear.

Everything had spilled out of me in a tumble. I'm not even certain how much sense I made, trying to describe what happened.

All the while Prince Tenarreau stood there with an open book held before him, face devoid of expression, listening impassively as I recounted the details of the incident at my keep, my attempt to convince Redforne to reconsider his brash act, the very real effort I'd made to avoid bloodshed.

In the end, he'd simply stood there for a couple of minutes staring blankly at the floor, as if pondering, book still open in his hands. Then he looked at me once more. Expressionless, he'd simply said "Thank you, Tucat. You may go."

Asking about my family, or how this sudden turn of events might impact the offer he'd made...well, it didn't exactly strike me as a wise course of action. The prince had some very sudden changes to try to accommodate, and he looked like he'd been hitting the tea a little hard, the fumes in his study suggesting that he'd been burning the candle at both ends. Not the most opportune time, I figured.

I left, having heard a mere handful of words from him, went back home and tried to sleep.

When that failed, I opted to simply lie on my back all evening long, staring at the ceiling and thinking bleak thoughts, trying to ignore the ache in my leg.

I spent most of the night haunted by images of Redforne, plagued by feelings of guilt, and kept awake with thoughts of my murdered family. When I wasn't torturing myself, I was wondering what changes the ceremony would bring about. I'd done nothing overly spectacular that year in terms of creative thievery, having concerned myself more with maintaining the healthy equilibrium of the territory I currently managed.

Despite the prince's offer, I found that gaining property wasn't what I really wanted, anyway. What I craved was information.

I needed to know. Title, estate, wealth...none of it meant anything compared to finding out about my family. Finding out, and then putting things right.

A situation almost identical to that of the boy I'd killed.

Irony, see? Life's full of irony.

Howling in frustration felt like a good idea. It was maddening, knowing just enough to whet the desire for retribution, your only source of information someone you couldn't pressure, couldn't force the knowledge out of.

A sudden silence fell, jolting me from my thoughts. The ceremony was beginning. Tenarreau was at the lectern and about to speak.

He stood in front of his throne, looking nothing like the creature I had encountered in his study last night. He'd looked bedraggled and tired then, his bleary red-rimmed eyes evoking my sympathy despite the dangerous glitter of coldly calculated intelligence that I saw lurking beneath them.

Now he stood before the collected lords looking refreshed and energetic and spry, even seeming a little bit taller than usual. He looked pleased, and his smile was relaxed and easy.

Some herbs were capable of amazing things, I mused. No doubt Tenarreau would pay some harsh price for it later, but for now he looked confident and in control...just as a prince should.

The first fifteen minutes or so involved a small announcement regarding the condition of the city of Harael, a carefully prepared and fairly well-crafted speech, one that used some impressively descriptive words throughout. There was a smattering of applause after, which he accepted with a small bow.

Once that had been taken care of, he listed off the names of lords who were being struck from the civil list, having pocketed their fortunes and moved elsewhere in the country, or died suddenly, or transferred ownership by mutual agreement, or one of a dozen or so other reasons. I won't attempt to recite the list, since I was only half-listening anyway.

The mention of Greybridge's name provoked quite a stir, however. Several faces turned to one another in astonishment, and one or two turned to focus on me. I had, after all, undertaken to represent Greybridge in a duel a mere day ago. Was I somehow responsible? Those who had heard about the duel were likely wondering exactly that.

Let 'em wonder. I simply stared down at the assembly below, chin resting on my forearms, which were in turn laying upon the banister on the very edge of the balcony.

The news concerning Greybridge also caused ripples of excitement amongst those in attendance, which was not surprising. That much territory up for grabs meant that your chances of an unexpected windfall increased dramatically.

And then, preliminaries done with, Tenarreau got to the portion of the speech everyone was there for.

There were no maps on display or any sort of means to illustrate the area the prince was talking about...he simply recited your name, waited for you to stand, and then described your new territory in terms of the streets that formed its borders. Sometimes your territory grew a little, sometimes it shrank.

Nobody applauds during the delivery of this portion of the speech, since it is a nearly impossible feat of memory to remember specific territorial details that are not your own. I mean, imagine if you'd heard the prince recite the boundaries of a formidably sized territory, and you became so impressed that you clapped heartily...only to discover that the lord in question had formerly occupied nearly twice that amount. Awkward...

Sitting quietly eliminated the possibility of misunderstanding. Usually, you could tell by a lord's tone of voice as they phrased the traditional reply of thanks whether or not they viewed the new territorial boundaries in a positive light, or a negative one. I'd heard lords practically sputtering with rage as they recited the politely worded thanks, and heard others who sounded so bewildered and baffled by their own good fortune that they gave the impression of forgetting how to speak entirely.

I'd been to a total of seven of these events since turning twenty-three and laying formal claim to my estate. I'd gained territory three times, and remained unchanged for four. I'd never actually lost territory, which was a common enough occurrence amongst lords that its absence was a point of personal pride for me.

A very small part of me wondered just how upset the prince was with how things had turned out, and if I'd be subjected to my first territorial loss as a result. It was a small, silly thought – Tenarreau was a politician, someone who didn't care a whit about personal feelings or grudges, so long as a person could perform in the capacity he required of them. I'd served my purpose, he'd told me as much in his study.

Still, that fact might also be the only thing keeping me out of the palace prison.

I half-listened to the list of names and the prince's subsequent description of their territory, the responses to which seemed mostly positive. There were a few disappointed voices here and there – in some areas of town it was not possible for someone to gain territory without it being at the expense of another.

Overall, it seemed that most people were fairly happy with the news, and were gratified to learn that Tenarreau's perception of their performance nearly matched their own.

Theo's name was called, and his holdings had changed not at all, yet again. His territory had not gained a single yard since he'd taken possession of it, something that he claimed was precisely what he wanted. Given his holdings were twice as large as my own, this could hardly be disappointing for him. While it may lack ambition, there is a certain satisfaction that comes from knowing that you have what you would consider to be enough, and that the prince believes you capable of maintaining it well. I'd be sure to congratulate Theo later, once everything had returned to normal.

I'm usually mentioned right after Theo, or just before. This time, however, the prince went from Theo to Lord Marcsun (who lost some territory, I noted with some small measure of glee), followed by Cleaver, seeming to bypass my territory entirely. I tried not to read too much into it.

Dozens of names trickled by, one after another, the street names and description of territories blending together and becoming indistinguishable to my ear.

And then I heard another name I recognized.

"Redforne," Tenarreau said, glancing down at the assorted jumble of cards he held just below the specially designed lectern he stood behind. "Vita Redforne."

Near the back of the main floor, I saw the serene and lovely woman who had introduced herself to me as Lady Teuring rise slowly to her feet. She was garbed in black, and wore a solemn expression.

I remained absolutely still as I watched her rise, emotions too numerous to count suddenly churning within the confines of my chest. Sorrow, pity, remorse...I'd taken her husband from her. Regardless of the circumstances, the various twists and turns that had been offered up by fate, it was something that I could not deny. No matter how hard I wished to.

Tenarreau continued his address after receiving a respectful nod from the black-clad figure.

"It is with a heavy heart that I acknowledge learning, even as I prepared to bestow upon Eagan Redforne the rights and privileges of lordship in Harael, that tragedy had befallen the Redforne Family in the form of a terrible, terrible accident, one that cost young Eagan Redforne, only son of Salvatori Redforne, his life."

Accident?

"It pains me to learn of the passing of such a talented man, one who held so much promise," he continued. "I would like to take this moment to extend to Lady Redforne the Crown's most heartfelt condolences. All of Harael suffers with you – what this fair city could have become with the benefit of your husband's guidance, the infusion of his spirit, has been lost to us forever."

...Accident?

What in the name of all the gods was he doing? One would have to be stone deaf not to have heard at least a dozen different rumors concerning myself and the late Eagan Redforne. For Tenarreau to actually use the word 'accident' to describe his death was tantamount to him declaring the matter settled, for all intents and purposes.

I decided to start paying very close attention to what the prince was saying.

"Thank you, your highness," was all Vita was able to say. Her voice gave the strong impression of someone in extreme emotional distress.

I felt another razor-sharp dagger of guilt thrust itself into my chest, needling my soul.

"As tribute to his skill, and the solid promise that he showed as a lord of Harael, I bequeath the following. Four Stones and Saxon North to Tippany Road, Tippany East to Forecastle, Forecastle to Silhouette, West along Silhouette to Banes Bridge, North up Chelsea to Two Stones, back to Four Stones and Saxon. The building that was once known as

Redforne Keep is contained within that spot, I believe," Tenarreau said, nodding his head toward Lady Redforne.

Well. Surprising, but not an unpleasant thing to happen. I'd never heard of a widow being honored in this way before, but I suppose there is a first time for everything. Still, she had all but confessed to me her naivety when it came to politics, and being given territory was much, much different than being able to hold it. I felt a touch of worry over that. From what I was able to recall, it wasn't an easy neighborhood she'd just been given, part of Greybridge's old estate, with-

"This property will be held in surety by the Crown until such time as it can be claimed by his son, Faene Redforne," the Prince continued. "Upon his twenty-third birthday he may negotiate with the Crown the terms by which he will take possession of this property."

...Son?

I experienced another spiritual kick to the crotch, yet another unexpected twisting of the invisible knife that had buried itself deep within me.

History repeats itself. Another Redforne whose father had been stolen from him by a Tucat. Yet another vendetta, another blood feud pitting this family against what remained of mine. Another child raised amid the anger of loss, allowed to soak up the poisonous and heady fumes of revenge and murder. A boy brought up to hate me, just as Eagan Redforne had.

My eyes closed, my heart feeling heavy in my chest, a sick feeling in my gut. I almost missed Tenarreau calling my name a minute or so later.

"Tucat. Lord Vincent Tucat," he said, looking out to the crowd as if he had no idea where I was, though I'd caught him looking upwards and in my direction at least a half dozen times over the course of the ceremony.

I stood, slowly. A great many faces turned to look up at me as I did so.

I resisted the urge to snarl at them all.

Suddenly, none of it mattered. I didn't care. I *wanted* to be punished, to have territory taken away from me. Just leave

me my keep, I thought to myself. They could take everything else, for all I cared.

I was tired, I decided. Tired of nothing being what it seemed, tired of the suspicious glances being leveled at me, or murderous ones. I had been working far too hard on my reputation, and had reached the point where I wanted nothing to do with the activity at all any more. I was done. Let someone else pull off bold, daring thefts designed to humiliate and impress. Look where being clever and sneaky had gotten me, after all.

Screw it.

Drawing myself up, ignoring the pain, I looked down at the assembled lords and ladies below me. Then I set my jaw, pressed my lips together tightly and looked to the prince, bowing my head slightly.

Do your worst, I thought.

"Tournay and Robe Street West to Finnay, North to Pike . . ."

Familiar roads being recited in a familiar order. A part of me seemed to feel a sense of profound disappointment that was surprising, like it had almost been looking forward to the idea of being stripped of land and title, like it would have come as something of a relief.

"Pike to Flaine, West to Chimney Rock, North to Yellow Shoal . . ."

Yellow Shoal was new, and...hey! I was being given some of Marcsun's territory, the area that he'd lost! The thought of what kind of apoplectic fit that was likely to inspire from him cheered me somewhat. It was a healthy chunk of land, large enough that it would probably sting his pride a little bit, as well as hurt his income. I risked a small smile at that, just in case he was watching.

Asses like Marcsun got what they deserved from time to time. The news buoyed me, somewhat.

Perhaps some small measure of justice still existed in the world. I tried to focus on the positive side of the situation. Maybe I didn't need something quite as drastic as having my territory stripped away from me.

"-to Crab Tree Lane, to Painter's Lane, North to Corby Street, to Speakswell . . ."

Wait a minute...

" -West to Herod, North to Redbrick, to Hastings, to . . ."

What the hell was this?!

I didn't recognize any of the street names Tenarreau was rattling off, one right after the other. I was being given brand new territory.

A *lot* of new territory.

"-Richford, North to Fowl Alley, West to Fortress Hill, to Jade, South to Fallow's End, to Grape Leaf Trail, to . . ."

Those streets had a familiar ring – the very streets I'd traveled during my recent exploits, the roads and paths near the keep of a certain lord I had stolen from.

I was being handed Greybridge Keep!

By now there were looks of astonishment on the faces of those assembled, even those who were not overly familiar with my old territorial boundaries. These were streets and neighborhoods that people were familiar with, lords especially. Several extravagant, well-to-do shops were run there.

The list of street names went on and on, distinctly longer than anyone else's had. Dozens more. At one point he had to actually flip over the card he was holding, as well as take a breath.

"-South to Smithy, to Hutchins, to Tournay, back to the corner of Tournay and Robe Street," he finally finished.

Everyone was stunned. Hell, *I* was stunned...

And I began to suspect that I knew why the prince had done what he'd done.

Even the largest of territories could usually be described with a half-dozen or so street names, the vast majority of the designated land conforming to the shape of rectangles. Even if a street did wind or meander, the border it described would meander with it. A single city block or a few miles, the description of the length of the border was about the same size, verbally.

My own territory was square, or had been, more or less. Now, near the north end, it extended up along a tiny corridor that had been opened up through Marcsun's territory in order that it might tie most of Greybridge's old territory to my own, like two boxes tied together with a thin piece of string.

And this was not a reward...

A target had been painted on my head, though likely it was only the prince and myself who knew it. I didn't know the exact size of the portion of Greybridge's territory I'd been given, but it sounded substantial. Quite substantial, and oddly-shaped enough so that the lengthy description of it would catch the attention of everyone assembled. Very likely it also bordered several territories of lords whose behavior had become problematic as of late.

I would be fulfilling the role the prince had told me Redforne was going to play, in keeping some of the other lords in line. The only difference was that, instead of a young lord desiring to prove himself, I was a lord who was being thrown into the wolf-pit, given an impressive amount of new territory and put in a situation where I would have to fight tooth and nail just to keep it.

A fortune in well-developed territory in the right hands, with some hefty strings attached.

Strings I didn't want.

All this flicked through my mind in the barest instant as the last dying echoes of the prince's words faded away amid the astonished silence.

I cleared my throat, coughing lightly into my hand.

"Highness, the honor you do me is too great. Modesty and humility aside, I fear I am unworthy of such a substantial offering, of such prominence within our fair city. I assure you that the only reward I require is a few kind words from your most noble self, words that I would treasure more than any amount of gold."

Roughly translated - Screw all that other stuff. Just tell me about my family.

It wasn't the traditional reply, but any scandalized murmuring went unnoticed by me. I was too busy looking Tenarreau in the eye, staring down at him from the balcony where I stood.

His expression barely changed, still radiating calm confidence and good cheer. He cocked his head at me, acting as though there was nothing unusual about my breech of protocol, my utterance of this message, the significance of which only he and I understood. He knew what I was saying, and my tone couldn't really be misinterpreted either.

The smile he wore got a touch wider, and he responded.

"Lord Tucat, this is not a gift with which I give to you, but is simply a token of the honor that you are due – a measure of what you have demonstrated you so richly deserve. I have no doubt that a year from now, when you have fulfilled my expectations and your territory has flourished, the words of gratitude you shall receive from me for the service you have done for all of Harael will render all other words pale and trite in comparison."

Roughly translated – Tough beans. I know that's what you want, and you'll have to work for it. You helped create this problem, I want your help fixing it. Survive for a whole year, do as I wish, and then we shall discuss your family.

I couldn't really tell if he was able to notice the look I was giving him, given the distance between the two of us. I stood there unmoving, as countless lords and ladies watched us with unfeigned curiosity, blind to the nature of the words that had just been exchanged between us.

I cleared my throat.

"I know the land of which you speak – I thank you, and do accept responsibility on behalf of the Crown. I pray to be worthy of the honor that has been done me this day, and swear to protect the lives of the citizens you've entrusted to me as if they were my own," I said, reciting the traditional, time-honored words...

Very sarcastically.

I sat down, my leg sending me searing reminders that I shouldn't be attempting to use it. There wasn't going to be anything more to announce - my news was the obvious finishing note that he wished to leave fresh in the collective minds of the lords and ladies present. I stared at my feet, avoiding any looks being sent my way, blocking out what I could.

There was the gentle sound of trumpets a minute later. I felt my lip curl, and continued scowling at the floor.

Almost everyone rose to their feet as the prince departed. I chose to remain sitting because I was exhausted, and standing made me dizzy, and my leg hurt, and I didn't feel like going downstairs to socialize...

And I wasn't thinking very happy thoughts about my prince at the moment.

He didn't need to do what he'd just done - there had been time to talk beforehand. I'd attempted to see him that morning, in fact, only to be turned away by the very same tired-looking guards who had all but whisked me off my feet in their efforts to bring me to the prince's study the night before.

He'd wanted me unbalanced and astonished in front of everyone, perhaps so I wouldn't find some way to weasel out of what he'd just arranged. As it were, I admit that I was shocked at my own temerity, responding to him the way I had. It was hard to know which people would be talking about more – my scandalous lack of respect for tradition, or my bewilderingly sarcastic acceptance of what most lords would view as a priceless and undeserved gift.

I shouldn't have sounded quite so sarcastic, I know. He'd surprised me, and I hate being surprised.

"Lord Tucat?" a quiet, feminine voice said from nearby, jolting me from my thoughts.

Oh, son of a bitch...

"Lady Redforne," I said bleakly, recognizing her voice. I didn't look up, not wishing to look at her at that moment. Then I considered how rude such a thing was, and began to look up...and paused, conflicted. I tensed as if to rise, and stopped. Clearing my throat quietly, I opened my mouth to speak, wondering what it was I'd say.

A strangled sounding 'I-' was all that came out.

Damn it.

"It feels so strange to be called that, I keep forgetting people are referring to me," she said, sounding as though she were giving me a sad sort of smile. I don't know if she was – I still couldn't look at her.

"Lady Redforne, I...words can't express-" I stammered, shaking my head. "If I could have, I...I tried to-"

"Please, Lord Tucat," she said softly, sitting down on the chair beside me. "I know. Prince Tenarreau, he told me everything this morning, explained it all. I'm so terribly sorry."

I very quickly turned my head to look at her. Her red-rimmed eyes were fixed on mine, filled with a mixture of sorrow and compassion.

"Lady," I croaked hoarsely, "of all people, you are the last who should have reason to be sorry for anything, and if you feel you do then I fear that what the prince has told you may not be-"

"He told me that my husband broke into your keep after the duel, and that he died attempting to murder you," she said, quietly. "He told me that you tried to stop him, talk him out of it – that you even tried to save him when he...when-" she broke off, perhaps stifling a sob.

I stifled one of my own. She'd become the slightest bit blurry all of a sudden.

"I'm so sorry, Vita. It...I tried, and we couldn't, but...but it was still me who ended . . ." I took a shuddering breath. "Gods, how you must hate me."

"I don't hate you, Lord Tucat," she said gently, sadly, putting a tentative hand on my arm a moment later. "I...I became aware of certain things. There was something different about him lately – something wrong. I had thought that it was something to do with his plans, the dinner that you'd attended...I'd been so terribly anxious about that whole thing. But things somehow went even more wrong after that. He didn't act the same, he looked at me differently, treated people differently. It scared me a little...made me nervous.

"It was as if he were a different person – ironic, I know. Perhaps he sensed my unease, for two nights ago when he came back from the Circles smelling of evil substances, he bid me come to our library once I'd put Faene to bed for the evening. When I did, he sat me down and told me everything, and when it became clear to him that I didn't believe his words he provided me with proof. It was...quite convincing."

Redforne's fortune made mine look like the contents of a beggar's hat. When you're that rich, it isn't exactly hard to convince someone you're rich. I nodded attentively.

"But it made me angry, so *very* angry! The man I knew and loved seemed not to exist at all. It was funny – he had thought I would be overjoyed when I learned that my husband was, in fact, a man of considerable wealth and power, that we needn't live in a keep with boards lining exposed holes to ward off drafts...like it mattered not at all that he'd lied about everything, right down to who he was. And yet he professed to love me, this person I almost didn't know at all."

"I believe he did, Vita," I said, feeling like I should contribute something. The wounds to her heart were still fresh, after all, and yet she had come to me at the first opportunity, attempting to balm my soul. "He...we talked, and I tried to dissuade him, point out everything he might lose through his actions. Your name was mentioned, and he became emotional. Nothing else caused his resolve to flicker, but mentioning you . . ." I let the words hang there, uncertain of how to continue.

A minute passed in silence. I looked away because, contrary to what some people might think of me, I don't derive any pleasure from watching a fellow human being in pain.

"I tried talking him out of it as well," she said, her words quiet and heavy. "He said I didn't understand, couldn't understand, what he needed to do. And he was right, because it made no sense! I begged, pleaded with him to give up this notion that you were somehow responsible for what happened to his father, that you deserved to die. I tried...so hard. *So* hard," she sniffed, the back of her hand quickly wiping her cheekbone.

I had taken to staring at the ceiling by this time, having swallowed the lump in my throat at least a half dozen times.

"I cannot hate you, Lord Tucat. You wished for none of this, nor did I. And though my heart-" I heard her voice catch suddenly as she sobbed and broke off mid-sentence, eyes closing tightly.

The two of us simply sat and stared at nothing for a while, neither of us saying a word. Minutes went by.

"I'm so sorry," I said, finally, making an effort to breathe normally, turning to look at her while trying to loosen the tight grip of sorrow that was squeezing my chest.

"As am I," she replied, sounding as if she were experiencing something similar.

We both pretended not to notice how much of a wreck the other was. She was the first to stand, smoothing out some of the wrinkles that had appeared in her skirt, and sniffling as she did so. She waved a gesture toward a woman who was waiting patiently out of earshot, and who was holding the hand of a small boy who was looking at me with biggest green eyes I'd ever seen.

"I should go. Faene needs his nap soon," she said quietly. "So much to do suddenly, and...apparently, I need to plan a move to a new keep."

She attempted a brave smile, her eyes still glassy and her lower lip trembling.

"If you should need help with anything at all, please...call on me," I said, feeling my own face following her trembling lead. "And please, tell Faene when he's old enough to understand, tell him I'm-"

My voice went hoarse and I slowly shook my head, as if to express my inability to articulate what my heart was attempting to say.

She looked at me, and after a few moments she nodded.

"Faene will know of his father, Lord Tucat. He will know that it was his father's own anger that stole him from us," she said, raising her chin slightly. "I don't understand what drove my husband to do what he did – I will not allow the seed of that same anger to blossom in my son. I do not blame you for this, and neither will he. I wished for you to know this."

Tears began rolling down my cheek silently, and the entire room decided to become a blur of golden reflected light for a while. I didn't notice when she silently departed, no further words being exchanged or needed. Perhaps she sensed that there was truly no good way of ending a conversation like ours.

I sat there for a good, long time. Long enough for the throngs of mingling lords who had crowded the large hall below me, to dissipate into a few hundred, and then to a mere dozen or so.

Long enough that my thoughts began to drift to things other than profound sadness mingled with regret.

Like the fact that Tarryl was probably still anxiously waiting for me outside.

I sighed and rose to my feet carefully, picking my black walking stick from against the wall where I'd left it, and somehow managing to make it all the way to the stairs without leaning on anything. I wasn't silly enough to attempt the same feat on the stairs, and chose to hobble down the several flights leading to the main entrance area with a firm grip on the bannister.

With so many of the other nobles having already left, my own carriage was easy to locate, being one of the only ones remaining. Mine was also the only one that had a pensive-looking Tarryl standing beside it. Upon recognizing me, he quickly set about preparing the horses and opening the door in anticipation of my arrival.

"Sorry Tarryl," I said, limping to within earshot and gratefully accepting his offer of assistance for the last few yards. "I didn't mean to make you wait quite this long. Some things came up."

"No need to apologize, Milord," he said, sounding more concerned for my wellbeing than annoyed at the lateness of my return. I'd have to give him a raise, I thought.

...I'd have to give *everyone* a raise!

Oh gods, I'd have to hire new staff, just to handle the new responsibilities that had been thrust upon me. I'd have to introduce myself to new shopkeepers, win them over...I'd have to-

I pressed my fingers against my closed eyes firmly, idly wondering if the headache I could feel coming on would distract me from the pain I felt in my leg.

"Home please, Tarryl," I said as I gingerly lowered myself into the carriage seat. "Straight home, if you please."

"Aye Milord," he called back.

Yes, home was where I needed to be. I had large amounts of wine there.

And a towel I could scream into.

I looked out the window, bleakly, and then spoke up once more before he was out of earshot.

"If we should pass by a temple on the way, would you be so kind as to stop and let me know?" I asked, bitterly. "There's a few gods I'd like to give a piece of my mind."

Chapter 25

"NOW THIS IS the life, is it not?" Theo gestured expansively at the contents of the table in front of him with a hearty grin, the stub of what remained of his lightly oiled cigar leaving cobwebs of smoke in the air as he did so. "Just kicking back in a chair, relaxing, and reaping the rewards that your hard work has earned you. Almost makes up for life's little annoyances, like getting the living tar soundly beaten out of you. A truly spectacular meal, followed by brandy and wine of equal, uh...spectacularity," he said, frowning slightly at the last word he'd spoken. "And, to top things off, we have these amazing cigars smuggled in all the way from Alledesh - purest tobacco and tana leaf, rolled and dried to perfection before being lovingly dipped in something very, very unhealthy for us." He puffed gently on the aforementioned cigar, producing clouds of smoke around his satisfied looking face. "Yep...as moments go, this one doesn't suck. The only thing I can think of that could possibly make this evening any better-"

He stopped talking mid-sentence as I leaned forward over the table, reaching out to pluck the card second on the left from the collection of similar cards in his hand. I saw a ghost of a wince come from him as I did, and felt the faintest phantom tug of resistance as I purposefully lifted that particular card from his grip. Turning it toward me, I smiled.

"Three ladies, two of them natural, ten chaser," I said, placing the four card hand I'd announced onto the table before discarding my remaining four, face-up.

"...would be if I could actually win a hand or two, you ash-snorting little cheese-weasel!" he said disgustedly, shaking his head as he allowed his remaining cards to drop face-down before him. "That's three times you've had three knights or better in a row! I don't understand it...I mean, logic dictates that I can't lose *every* hand, right?"

"What I don't understand Lord Tucat, if you play cards every week as you'd mentioned earlier," said Cyrus, who had carefully put down his own cigar and was leaning forward to inspect the four cards I'd just discarded, "is how you do not own half of Lord Haundsing's territory by now."

"Is he always such a smart-ass?" said Theo, thumbing a gesture at Cyrus.

Cyrus chuckled lightly, and once he'd finished inspecting my discarded cards, he pulled a single face-down card from the deck. He glanced at it briefly, then sighed a lightly intoxicated sigh as he lay his hand face-down on the table.

"Fold," he said to me before turning his head slightly and raising an inquisitive eyebrow at Theo. "And perhaps I'm just being a smart-ass to make up for having been called a 'timid, simpering, door-mouse of a lackey' in public two weeks ago by a certain large, bearded lord I could mention."

I looked to the large, bearded lord in question, who was busy inspecting the ceiling innocently.

"Theo," I admonished.

"What?" he asked, defensively, "I was merely keeping up the fictional Tucat-Haundsing bickering for appearances sake. And besides, you should have heard the comment *he* made about the tunic I was wearing that day!"

"You should have seen it!" Cyrus said in a voice that was a little more exuberant and relaxed than usual, shaking his head in mock sorrow. "It was orange. Errr, well...orange-*ish* at least, with-"

"Oh, *that* tunic. Yes, I'm familiar with it," I said, looking back to Theo expectantly.

"He'd asked if he might offer me a towel," scowled Theo darkly, "in order to hide the fact I'd been assaulted by a Vereet kebab wielding scoundrel, who also appeared to be armed with various mustards."

The gods know I tried, but I just couldn't keep it in.

My laughter was sudden and explosive. I shook in my seat as I laughed, high-pitched and loud. Soon all three of us were laughing hard enough that it seemed nearly an impossible task to remain balanced upright in our chairs, sitting around the card table. It was the kind of laugh that you wonder why you don't do more often, even as you're laughing.

Within a minute or so I managed to recover, hand wiping the moisture from my eyes.

It felt good. I'd needed that.

"That was great. Ow," I said, adding the last word with a rueful grimace, still chuckling softly as my hand went to the bandage wrapped around my injured left temple.

"Milord!" Cyrus said, seeming to sober instantly. "Do you require some additional herbs for that? The ones in the poultice might be wearing off, and the healer said-"

"Cyrus, please. You're off duty! I'm not 'Milord', I'm 'Vincent'. If I need anything, you can tell me to get it myself. Tell me to go to Hades first, in fact! You've earned some off-duty time, in addition to the rather substantial raise in your monthly stipend we discussed...and by all the gods, you're going to relax even if I have to beat you unconscious to get you to do so!"

"Unconscious people are very relaxed," Theo said, nodding sagaciously.

"You would know," Cyrus said, attempting to sound innocent.

"Ouch!" Theo said, throwing Cyrus a quick grin. He drew two cards from the top of the deck and glanced at them briefly before tossing them, and the rest of his hand, face down on the table. "I fold too. I think I'm gonna like this guy, Vince." He gestured at Cyrus. "You know, once we've loosened him up enough to throw in the odd jab at you, of course."

I smiled at that, also making a note of the sheepish grin that Cyrus was unsuccessfully attempting to hide.

"Cyrus," I said, repositioning my injured leg that lay extended on a chair beside the table, rubbing the bandaged thigh area gently to assist with the circulation there. "In addition to giving you the raise we discussed, I think that some sort of bonus may be in order. Behind my wine cellar in the cold rack, there's an unopened bottle of *Tifii* thirty-six that is worth about twenty gold marks or so. I'd like you to have it, on the condition that you open it this very evening and share the contents with myself and Lord Haundsing here."

There was a moment's hesitation, followed by a greatly amused chuckle from Cyrus. His chair squawked in protest as he stood, his right hand pressed against the bandages of his injured left shoulder as he did so.

"Certainly, and I must say that I'm most honored. I mean, if you were ordering me to *fetch* another bottle of *Tifii* thirty-six I'd tell you to go to Hades and get it yourself, but since it's a *bonus* we're talking about..."

The three of us laughed, and a grinning Cyrus walked toward the ruined door of my exercise hall and disappeared from sight a few moments later.

"Vincent," Theo said seriously, "I'm glad you're finally paying him what he's worth. The guy is an unholy terror when it comes to protecting your reputation, if you aren't already aware. I've seen him do it first-hand, and not just when I've been intentionally needling him. You can't buy that kind of loyalty, you know."

"I know," I said, retrieving my cigar and awakening the angry red embers within it with a few short puffs, watching the fragrant smoke swirl around my face. "I imagine that I'm going to be giving him another raise soon, too, once all of the property I've been assigned has been catalogued, and collection dates have been coordinated. A minimal staff was okay before...I could get by with a half-dozen domestic staff and ten knights or so for security, doing most of the dirty work myself," I sighed. "Of course, those days are behind me now, what with my new acquisition and all. Everything's changed - it's a whole new game all of a sudden. I can't even duel for a little extra cash anymore."

"Uh...and why is that?"

"Think about it, Theo. What duelist wouldn't seek to advance their own reputation by killing me? I'm the man who is rumored to have bested the only son of Salvatori Redforne, after all."

"True," Theo said, nodding thoughtfully. "Of course, you're not getting out of your weekly practice sessions with me...don't even think that you can get out of those."

"Oh, not at all. If anything I may have to spend more time practicing, just in case someone gets it in their head that they should try to push me around. So, that being said," I puffed theatrically on my cigar as I swirled my remaining wine in its glass, "I suppose all that's left is for me to find a new fencing instructor."

"Uhm, what?" said Theo, looking bewildered.

"Well," I said, as if broaching a delicate subject, "it seems that my current instructor was defeated by an opponent I was able to best in a contest of arms. By my reckoning, that-"

Theo scooped up a few petite food items from a nearby tray of snacks and began pelting me with them.

"You utter horse's ass!" he laughed, firing a small cocktail sausage across the table, hitting me in the shoulder.

"Well, it's true!" I said, holding up both arms defensively.

"Yeah, and I'm sure that if you`d had most of your left arm muscles severed, you would have done as well!" His eyes casted about for some other stray morsel of food to throw. "As it is, you're crazy if you think you could have pulled that off without me softening him up for-"

A small piece of frosted tea cake interrupted him mid-sentence, hitting his cheek with a moist sounding slap.

As if on cue, we both began hurling handfuls of food at one another. After a few moments we both simultaneously picked up our dinner knives and held them out at one another other threateningly.

Both of our blades fell to the table with a clatter a second later, and we burst into peals of laughter.

Cyrus returned with a perplexed expression and bottle of wine cradled against his forearm, looking at the two of us as though we'd gone mad. His expression did nothing to dull our laughter. If anything, it doubled it.

I don't know how long our second round of laughter lasted, but I wished it could have been longer still, despite the pain.

"Ow," I said once again, chuckling as I rubbed my throbbing temple.

"Lord Tucat, a question if I may," said Cyrus, putting the wine bottle on the table and reaching for the corking lever. "I noticed in the cold rack that there was a bottle that had been marked with a red kerchief. I looked a bit closer and saw it was a *Tifii* thirty-nine. Now, I don't claim to be an authority on the vintage, but-"

"Ah yes, please make certain that the bottle you're speaking of is not disturbed, Cyrus. I'm saving it for a special occasion."

"Earlier this morning you were given an increase in territory the likes of which no lord in the history of Harael has ever been given all at once." He raised an inquisitive eyebrow at me. "If that's not considered special enough, I'm afraid that your standards may be just a tad high. By the way, you have a little-" he trailed off, pointing at a spot on his face while looking to a similar spot on mine.

I hastily wiped the unidentified remnants of Theo's food assault from my cheek.

"Well, as much as this new territory is going to add new income and new opportunities, it's not precisely a cause to celebrate," I said, my tone becoming serious. "In fact, this might even be considered punishment. I'm going to be stretched very thin, and this next year is likely going to be a memorable one for anyone who works for me. No, that bottle of wine is special...I intend it to be opened when I've discovered who was behind my family's murder, and have dealt with them accordingly."

We all sat in silence for a little while, the atmosphere becoming a little less jovial. Theo swirled the remaining wine in his glass and looked introspective, while Cyrus continued his efforts to uncork the bottle of green wine he'd retrieved.

Ah well, the laughter had been good while it lasted.

"I'm not sure I entirely agree about the territory being punishment," Cyrus said, once he'd uncorked the bottle and refilled the contents of my glass. "If it is, I'd have to say it's damned short-sighted of Tenarreau. Does he even realize what kind of turmoil there would have been had you fallen in the Circles? With the odds being what they were, the fortune Redforne would have made would have caused chaos!"

"I suspect that the chaos would have been intentional, possibly so that he would have the leverage necessary to influence the prince's decision when the time came for him to approve property arrangements and redraw territorial lines." I gave a sidelong shrug and took a sip of wine. "Tenarreau might have known about that as well, though...all of it. I wouldn't put it past him. The guy seems to know everything going on in this city."

Cyrus grunted his assent as he finished pouring wine into Theo's glass and then his own, sitting down once more at the table. We sat in silence for a few moments.

"Oh, before I forget," I said, remembering something, "if you're not busy tomorrow Cyrus, I'd like you to draw five hundred gold from the treasury. Find out how Ismir fares, and make certain that all of his healer fees are paid for. Two hundred and fifty...that should cover his expenses, and anything extra can be considered a little bonus on top of what I already paid him for the duel."

"I can do that," Cyrus said, nodding. His brow furrowed. "And the remaining two-fifty?"

"I would like you to see that Mouser gets it," I said, receiving nearly identical puzzled looks from both Cyrus and Theo.

"Mouser?" Theo asked.

"Yeah. He'd stumbled upon a clever little trick with a sword completely by accident, and remembering it precisely when I did was the only thing that saved my life."

"Two hundred and fifty gold, all because you borrowed a move of his?" Cyrus asked, looking at me dubiously.

"Well, I suppose it's more for me - I feel indebted to him, and I always pay my debts. If he asks, you can tell him that it's a retainer for future services."

Cyrus shrugged. "I can do that, certainly. Doubtless with your new income from the new territory, five hundred gold will be a proverbial drop in the bucket."

"I can't even be sure about that, actually," I said, tenting my fingers before me as I sat back in my chair. "We eventually figured out that Greybridge's was damn near broke. I don't know enough about the territory he was managing, or how Redforne was able to bankrupt him. It might not be that profitable at all, in its present state."

Well," Theo said, scratching his chin as though considering something, "my own territory is running smoothly right now, so if you need some help behind the scenes, or maybe some extra cash to get things rolling in the right direction, let me know."

"Thank you Theo, but I'm actually in pretty good shape on the financial side of things. As for the management of my new territory, I'll simply do what I always do when things get difficult."

"Which is?"

"Why, I'll square my shoulders, strengthen my resolve, and then make it the job of my remarkable captain Cyrus here." I gestured toward Cyrus with a winning grin. "A man with a towering intellect and nerves of iron. The pillar of strength that holds the roof up over our heads. A man I trust implicitly, who-"

Cyrus snorted derisively, making a *'pffft'* sound.

I raised an eyebrow at him. "You don't agree?"

"Oh, I'm fine with most of it. Towering intellect, pillar...all that stuff. But 'trust implicitly'?" Cyrus snorted. "Please..."

"Come now, I trust you enough to have let you in on my and Lord Haundsing's secret, haven't I? None of his knights or other staff can claim this privilege."

"You didn't exactly 'let me in', as it were. You were discovered, and now you're simply making the best of it. That's not exactly trust as I see it."

"He's got a point, Vince," said Theo, casually taking a sip of wine as he stubbed out the remains of his cigar in the dark glass bowl that had been fetched for that purpose. "Accepting new circumstances with grace isn't the same thing as trust."

I frowned. "I suppose that's fair. Well then, what if I shared something with you, some piece of information that was so sensitive and potentially damning that the mere mention of it could undo everything I've accomplished as a lord. Something I haven't even told Theo here. Would you take that as a sign of trust?"

Cyrus folded his arms and raised a speculative eyebrow, waiting for me to continue. Theo regarded me as well, listening intently.

"My family was murdered. Prince Tenarreau has all but admitted the fact to me, and hinted that he might share more of what he knows by next year's ceremony," I said.

"Right. We've established that," nodded Cyrus.

"Now," I continued gravely, "I've decided to give the prince one year. He appears to have a plan, and I will do what I can to help it along for the sake of maintaining order and stability in Harael. Once a year is up, if I am not given the information I crave from the prince?" I pursed my lips and tented my fingers. "I intend to take it from him."

I watched the somber expressions on the two men's faces as they took that in, considered the implications.

"I do not know the manner in which I shall do this, as much will depend on the circumstances. I may exert pressures equal to the pressure he seeks to exert on me. I may trick the information from him, or steal it, or perhaps engage in activities considered treasonous. If I must, I'll dangle him by his feet from the highest window of the palace and wring it from him that way. It may cost me everything I have, getting this information, but get it I shall."

Theo was nodding to himself, lost in thought. Wide-eyed, Cyrus gave the slightest gulp before grinning at me.

"Yeah. I suppose you do trust me. Hades," he said, shaking his head slightly, "the more I'm finding out, the more I'm beginning to suspect I should be asking for a bigger raise."

"Bah. What could you possibly want another raise for, considering all these bonuses I've been handing out today? Speaking of which," I sat back in my chair in a thoroughly satisfied manner, "Cyrus, I think you deserve another bonus. Beside my drinks cabinet, there is a box of frighteningly expensive and lightly oiled Alledesh cigars. For all that you've done for me lately and as a tribute to your much valued service, I'd like you to have three of them, provided that you-"

"Lord Tucat," Cyrus smiled, standing up from the table slowly. "Would you and Lord Haundsing like another cigar?"

"Why, what a fine idea! Grab one for yourself while you're at it." I said with a chuckle.

Cyrus went to retrieve a few more cigars from the box as I watched Theo collect the playing cards laying on the table, turning them all face-down and gathering them together in a pile so that he might shuffle.

Remembering I'd won the last hand, I gathered up the rectangular playing chips from the center of the table, and had sorted a third of them into orderly stacks by the time Cyrus appeared at my side, offering me a cigar. I took it from him with a nod of thanks, and as I lit the tip I happened to glimpse the scar on the back of my hand.

I wondered idly what kind of a scar I would end up getting from the wound on my temple. Likely it wouldn't be too visible - once my hair grew out, it might not be that noticeable at all.

Besides, what was one more scar for people to look at, more or less?

As I watched cobwebs of smoke rise from my cigar, I was reminded of the times I`d watched my father write, the drying sand mixing with the oily ink and burning his thoughts into place.

I wondered what he would have thought about these recent developments – more territory thrust into my hands than had ever been managed by any member of the Tucat family before.

He'd probably have smiled, and asked me what the heck I was going to do with it all. I grinned at the thought.

I knew exactly what I was going to do with it, too. I'd do some familiar things, force myself to try new things, and occasionally attempt impossible things, learning as I went along. I would throw out all the old rules and make up new ones as I went. I'd kick a little ass.

I was a Tucat, after all.

And this was a whole new game all of a sudden.

"Gentlemen," I said, setting the cigar between my teeth, feeling my lips draw back in an easy smile. "Let's play."

About the Author

Aaron Kite is a writer/artist who likes putting slashes between occupations and who very rarely refers to himself in the third person. He was born on the exact same day that São Paulo Metro was inaugurated in Brazil, which the authorities claim is pure coincidence.

He has been interviewed by Science Magazine, the Calgary Herald, National Geographic, and this shady fellow named 'Jimmy' who kept pointedly asking him about his success as a writer with questions like "Got any spare change?" and "C'mon, really, do ya? I gotta catch a bus."

Aaron was one of the founding members of the amateur writing group "Starting Write Now", as well as countless side-projects which he'd mention by name if the government would finally get around to granting him immunity. He lives in Calgary, Alberta, Canada, which really ought to have another sub-section to it, because another comma there would look really slick.

At present he has four finished novels - "Two Cats", the sequel "Jade Mouse", the third novel "Ten Arrows", as well as the standalone (but with sequels percolating in his brain) novel "A Touch of Poison". He's currently in the middle of writing the novel "Revenant", and a collaborative work titled "Shiftless", as well as about eleven or so other books that are all in varying states of doneness. When writing, he likes to disable his spell-checker and make up words, as is illustrated by the use of 'doneness' above.

He's allergic to cats, and thus he tries to arrange it so he's living with one whenever possible, probably just to prove a point of some sort.

Other Evil Alter Ego Press Books

The Fountain Series
By Suzy Vadori

The Fountain
The West Woods

Mik Murdoch: Boy Superhero Series
By Michell Plested

Mik Murdoch, Boy Superhero
Mik Murdoch: The Power Within
Mik Murdoch: Crisis of Conscience
Mik Murdoch: Haunted Happenings (coming July 2019)

Finding Atlantis Series
By JM Dover

Finding Atlantis
Return to Atlantis (coming October 2019)

Scouts of the Apocalypse Trilogy
By Michell Plested

Scouts of the Apocalypse: Zombie Plague
Scouts of the Apocalypse: Zombie War
Scouts of the Apocalypse: Zombie Masters

Anthologies

Dimensional Abscesses
(edited by Jeffrey Hite & Michell Plested)